# The Conquest of Liberty

## Book Two
## Honor, Heretics, & Highwaymen

## Kent Merrell

# The Conquest of Liberty

## Book Two: Honor, Heretics, & Highwaymen

Copyright © 2026 Kent Merrell
All rights reserved.
J Remington Press
jremingtonpress.com
kentmerrellauthor.com

My purpose in writing The Conquest of Liberty series is to present history with fidelity while telling it with life and meaning—so that we might more deeply appreciate the rare and precious gift of self-governance.

I hold a profound reverence for the United States Constitution and the freedoms it secures. Its principles have not only preserved liberty for Americans but have also stood as a bulwark against tyranny throughout the world. Again and again, those ideals—individual agency, moral accountability, and the inherent worth of every soul—have checked the advance of oppression and offered hope to those who yearn to be free. History testifies that when these principles weaken, civilization itself trembles.

For more than four decades, my professional life required me to see the world through the experiences, needs, and motivations of others. That discipline has shaped how I tell stories. It compels me to enter the hearts and minds of both historical and fictional characters, to portray history not as distant facts, but as lived struggle.

In this second volume, Honor, Heretics, and Highwaymen, I continue to trace the collision between the quest for liberty and the hunger for domination and control. Within these pages dwell characters—real and imagined—who labor, suffer, hope, and endure within that eternal conflict. They have become dear to me. My hope is that they will become dear to you as well.

ISBN: 979-8-9903523-3-9 (Paperback)
ISBN: 979-8-9903523-4-6 (Hardback)
ISBN: 979-8-9903523-5-3 (ebook)

# Acknowledgment

To my extraordinary wife, whose unwavering love and support breathe life into every page of *The Conquest of Liberty: Book Two.* You are my cheerleader, coach, and referee, guiding me through the intricate dance of crafting historical fiction. Your passion for history illuminates my research, pushing me to delve deeper, clarify, and enrich the tapestry of these stories.

With patience and love, you've endured the creation of my third historical novel, insisting I get it right while offering encouragement like no other could. This book is as much a testament to your strength and inspiration as it is to the stories we've woven together. Thank you, from the depths of my heart.

# Prologue

Stand with me in the year 1528—the world is being torn apart and remade before our eyes. This is the second book in my series, The Conquest of Liberty, and though the battles, kings, and empires here may seem far removed from the hard-won liberty we seek to preserve, know this: the struggle begins here. It will span oceans and generations before man is truly free to govern himself.

In Europe, the unity of Christendom has shattered. Eleven years have passed since Martin Luther nailed his Ninety-Five Theses to the church door in Wittenberg. The Reformation now shakes thrones as well as pulpits. Princes choose sides, mobs burn cities, and truth itself has become a dangerous possession. In this fractured world walks a young orphan named Martín—quiet, observant, gifted in languages beyond his years—drawn by providence into the presence of men whose words will change history. He will hear Luther thunder against corruption. He will witness William Tyndale risk everything to place the scriptures into the hands of common souls. And for this proximity to forbidden truth, he will one day be branded a heretic and cast from the Old World toward an uncertain fate across the sea.

The Holy Roman Emperor, Charles V—who also rules Spain—faces a near-impossible task: defend the Catholic faith, hold his empire together, and keep France, England, and the restless German princes from tearing it apart. Treaties are signed in one season and broken in the next. War waits just beneath the surface, and suspicion stalks every scholar, every preacher, every gifted child who listens too closely.

Across the Atlantic, the Spanish have unleashed a conquest unlike any the world has seen. In 1521, Hernán Cortés brought the Aztec Empire to its knees, raising New Spain from the ashes of Tenochtitlán. Galleons heavy with gold and silver now cross the Ocean Sea, feeding Spain's hunger for more.

And now the talk is of Peru—a land richer still, ruled by a Sapa Inca whose armies are countless and whose golden cities are built from stone so perfect a knife blade cannot slip between the seams. Francisco Pizarro has chased this empire for decades and failed every time. Yet he is not a man to yield. In this very year, he stands in Spain, petitioning the crown for ships, men, and royal blessing to make one final attempt.

But far to the south, in the high Andes, his prey is already bleeding. Huayna Capac, the mighty Sapa Inca, lies dead—claimed, they say, by a strange pestilence from the north. His sons, Atahualpa and Huascar, have turned on one another, and the empire trembles beneath the weight of civil war. Amid this unraveling walks Sarpay, First Priestess of the empire, daughter of the Sapa Inca, charged with a sacred and terrible duty: to traverse a fractured realm and offer her own blood in sacrifice, believing her death may yet appease the gods and preserve the world she loves.

This is the world into which we step—Christendom divided by faith and fear, the New World aflame with conquest and prophecy, and two souls born on opposite sides of the earth, each set upon a path they did not choose. One will be driven from his homeland in chains. The other will walk willingly toward death. Their journeys will cross oceans, empires will fall, and in the ashes of both, the first fragile sparks of liberty will begin to glow.

## Meet the historical characters in The Conquest of Liberty.

The thrill of meeting true historical characters and inviting them into a fictional story creates an exciting and challenging opportunity. It demands maintaining enough plausible reality in both time and space so as not to suspend all credibility. Each of these many historical characters are represented as accurately as possible. Please consider the sources of information are five hundred years old, and they are written by humans with personal insights and motives. Many times, respected sources disagree with each other. In those cases an author gets to choose how a character is presented. Forgiveness in these cases is appreciated. But the historical events are as accurate in time and place as possible. With one caveat— sometimes the years needed to be squeezed or expanded a touch.

---

**Ann Bolin** – Future Queen of England to Henry VIII - Friend to Marguerite

**Atahualpa** – Last sovereign emperor of the Inca Empire

**Bartolomé de las Casas** – Dominican friar & outspoken defender of native peoples

**Beelzebub** – Humphrey Kynaston's powerful, temperamental black warhorse

**Cacica (Careta)** – Indigenous princess of Darién and wife of Balboa

**Charles V** – Holy Roman Emperor ruling Spain and vast global territories

**Coya Cusirimay** – Inca noblewoman of royal blood and political importance

**Coya Rawa Ocllo** – Queen consort of the Inca and revered royal mother

**Cusimi** – Young Inca noblewoman shaped by courtly intrigue, Sarpay's friend

**Diego de Deza** – Archbishop of Seville, Torquemada's successor as Grand Inquisitor

**Francisco Pizarro** – Ambitious conquistador destined to overthrow the Inca Empire

**Frederick the Wise** – Elector of Saxony who shielded Martin Luther from arrest

**Gerard Calvin** – Strict father whose discipline shaped the young John Calvin

**Gonzalo Pizarro** – Brother of the Francisco Pizarro

**Governor Dávila** – Ruthless Spanish governor. His greed fueled colonial conflict

**Governor Ríos** – Corrupt governor of Panama entangled in political schemes

**Henry d'Albret** – King of Navarre navigating survival between rival European powers

**Hernán Cortés** – Cunning conquistador who dismantled the Aztec Empire

**Hernando Pizarro** – Brother of Francisco and ruthless political enforcer

**Hernando Talavera** – Compassionate cleric and trusted confessor to Queen Isabella

**Huáscar** – Inca emperor whose rivalry ignited devastating civil war

**Huayna Capac** – Great emperor who expanded the empire to its height

**Humphrey Kynaston** – English outlaw turned mercenary

**Johann Tetzel** – German Dominican friar and papal indulgence preacher

**Joan of Arc** – Inspired peasant girl who led France against English domination

**John Calvin** – Theologian. His doctrines reshaped Protestant belief and governance

**John the Steadfast** – Saxon prince who advanced Lutheran reform after Frederick

**Juan Pizarro** – Fierce conquistador brother who died during brutal campaigns

**Ferdinand II** – King of Spain who funded exploration and enforced Catholic unity

**Francis I** – Renaissance King of France and rival to Emperor Charles

**Francisco Jiménez de Cisneros** – Powerful cardinal and inquisitorial authority under Ferdinand and Isabella

**Mama Ocllo** – Mythic Inca mother who taught women civilization and virtue

**Manco Capac** – Lesser half brother to Sarpay, Huáscar & Atahualpa

**Marguerite of Angoulême** – Learned queen who protected reformers and patronized scholars

**Martin Luther** – Reformer whose defiance fractured Christendom and altered history

**Ninan Cuyochi** – Promising heir to the Inca throne, claimed by illness

**Pachacuti** – Visionary ruler who transformed a kingdom into an empire

**Pope Martin V** – Pontiff who restored stability after the Western Schism

**Quizquiz** – Loyal Inca general who resisted Spanish invasion with fierce resolve

**Rumiñawi** – Brilliant Inca commander who served Atahualpa's armies

**Sarpay** – Inca Priestess shaped by tradition, loyalty, and inner resilience

**Sir Thomas More** – Scholar-statesman executed for refusing the king's supremacy

**Tomás de Torquemada** – First Grand Inquisitor. architect of the Inquisition

**Vasco Núñez de Balboa** – Explorer who discovered the Pacific Ocean and established the first permanent settlement in the new world

**Viracocha** – Supreme creator god worshipped throughout the Andean world

**William Tyndale** – Scholar executed translating Scripture into the English tongue

# Introducing the Inca Empire

Few civilizations organized territory as intelligently and symbolically as the Incas.

At the height of their power, they ruled the largest empire in pre-Columbian America, stretching across modern-day Peru, Ecuador, Bolivia, northern Chile, and parts of Argentina and Colombia .

What made this empire so effective wasn't just conquest—but how it was divided, governed, and connected.

The Inca Empire, known as Tawantinsuyu, was divided into four regions—or suyus—radiating from Cusco, the sacred capital.

Each suyu had distinct landscapes, cultures, responsibilities, and strategic importance, yet all were united by a shared ideology, language (Quechua), and an extraordinary road system.

# The Four Suyus of Tawantinsuyu

**Antisuyu** – Amazonian frontier region east of Cusco

**Chinchaysuyu** – Northern region, most populous and powerful

**Collasuyu** – Southern highland region toward Lake Titicaca

**Contisuyu** – Western coastal and sacred region

# Some Inca Definitions

**Aclla** – Chosen women trained for weaving, ritual, and elite service

**Acllahuasi** – House where the chosen women lived and were trained

**Ayllu** – Kin-based community forming the foundation of Inca society

**Capacocha (Capacochas)** – Sacred state ritual of child sacrifice to the gods

**Chasqui** – Relay runner who carried messages across the empire

**Coricancha** – Sacred golden Temple of the Sun in Cusco

**Coya (Qoya)** – Queen, principal wife of the Sapa Inca

**Inti** – Divine sun god central to Inca religion and kingship

**Intihuatana** – Sacred carved stone used for solar observation and ritual

**Inti Raymi** – Great annual Festival of the Sun

**Mallki** – Mummified ancestor preserved and honored by descendants

**Mama Quilla** – Moon goddess, wife of Inti

**Mit'a** – Mandatory public labor service owed to the state

**Pachamama** – Earth mother goddess of fertility and agriculture

**Pukara** – Fortress or fortified hilltop settlement

**Qhapaq Ñan** – Vast imperial road system connecting the empire

**Qhapaq Raymi** – Major festival honoring the sun and royal initiation

**Qollqa (Qullqa)** – State warehouse storing food, textiles, weapons, and supplies

**Quipu (Khipu)** – Knotted cord system for recordkeeping and accounting

**Sapa Inca** – Divine emperor, "The Only Inca"

**Sara** – Sacred maize (corn), staple food and symbol of abundance

**Suntur Paucar** – Royal staff symbolizing imperial authority

**Tambo (Tampu)** – Waystation along roads for travelers and messengers

**Tawantinsuyu** – Official name of the Inca Empire, "Land of the Four Quarters"

**Ushnu** – Ceremonial stone platform used for offerings and ritual sacrifices

**Waka (Huaca)** – Sacred object or place: shrine, rock, spring, or temple

**Yanacona** – Servant class bound to nobles or the state

# Chapter One

## 1528 Quito, Northern Capital City
## Tawantinsuyu - Inca Empire

Afternoon sun reflected off the intricately molded golden medallion shaped like the sun. It was suspended on a silver chain hanging around the neck of Huayna Capac, the Sapa Inca, son of the Sun God Inti. Along with the golden medallion, other gold ornaments draped around his neck and bouncing on his shoulders should have sounded jubilation for his recent victory over the Cañari people. Their tinkling felt out of place.

Seated on an ornately carved chair upon a litter carried by eighteen lords, Huayna Capac entered the plaza. The carriers halted in front of the royal palace. Only Sarpay, First Priestess of the Empire, dared look the Inca emperor in the eyes. He returned her smile. As his daughter and the only child of the emperor's first wife, Coya Cusirimay, Sarpay was one of the few in the empire with direct access to the emperor's heart. Sarpay was but a young child when her mother died of illness.

A finely woven vicuña dress dyed a deep red hung over her right shoulder, tufted and held with golden rings matching the long golden loops hanging from her ears. As the fine shimmering fabric draped loosely over her smooth bronze body, a golden rope gathered it at her waist. Thin strands of gold woven into her long, black hair cascaded loosely over her bare shoulder.

Her regal visage commanded awe from onlookers who stole moments to gape. Yet, it was her kindness that endeared her to nearly all who fell under her watchful eye. As her emperor father Huayna waited for the porters to lower the litter, Sarpay recognized the concern in his somber face. The smile now gone, he stepped down and strode past her, entering the palace. His soft leather sandals barely made a sound on the marble entryway.

Huayna quietly entered the huaca, the sacred resting place of his mummified mother, Mama Ocllo Coya, upon whose spirit he relied for inspiration.

Days of fasting passed before he reemerged from the huaca, looking more concerned than when he prepared for battle. Sarpay and Huayna's new wife, Coya Rawa Ocllo, who he took as a principal wife when Sarpay's mother died, waited quietly outside his private chamber for his command. Huayna invited them both to enter.

"A great plague has come," he told them. "A plague with no concern for who it kills. The gods will take both lord and vassal. Our people are being punished."

How could the mighty Sapa Inca fear something so invisible? Sarpay wondered. All she had ever seen was courage from him. To her, he was God. Never had he shrunk.

"The gods demand a great blood sacrifice. Only a sacrifice of the firstborn will redeem this people." Huayna sat, legs crossed on a vicuña fur covering a golden platform supported on twelve short silver inlaid posts. "Inti, my father the sun god, and Quilla, my mother goddess of the moon, require this ultimate sacrifice." He took Sarpay's delicate hands in his, forcing himself to look her in the eyes. "My firstborn, the First Princess of the Empire, daughter of my first wife, only through your blood will our people be saved."

Great tears flowed down his bronze cheeks. He pulled her close and buried his head in her neck. Never before had Sarpay seen her father weep. Inca emperors never wept.

His strong, once solid frame shook. She kissed his cheek and pulled back, lifted his chin to look the mighty Inca in the eyes, and repeated, "I will do this for you, for my people, for the gods. For this, I was sent from the gods. For them, I will give my life." She pulled him tight and whispered, "I will go prepare myself."

"If there was any other way, I would not require this. But the very heavens demand that without the purest, most innocent blood of the firstborn, mercy cannot have claim upon the people," Huayna said, shrinking again into her arms. For a long moment Sarpay held her father as if absorbing his strength, letting it fill her with courage.

But she did not need his courage. Her mighty father had conquered armies much stronger than his own. He had brought peace throughout the mighty Tawantinsuyu empire, uniting the people more than had any of his ancestors, the previous Sapa Incas. Yet, here now, he wept for the sacrifice the gods demanded of his firstborn daughter. Sarpay realized she must fulfill this responsibility alone, and her father was trying to strengthen her with his love. She could not take his strength. She loved him too much to be so selfish. She released her embrace and stood.

She bowed her head toward her father's new principal wife, Coya Rawa Ocllo, who quickly took her place and now held the mighty Inca. It would never cross Sarpay's mind to do anything but obey her father and sacrifice herself. Though Sarpay had many brothers and sisters from her father's other wives and concubines, she and she only carried the purity of blood that could satisfy the requirements of Inti, God of the Sun.

Sarpay was the only living offspring of the Inca Emperor Huayna Capac and his first principal wife, his sister Coya Cusirimay, who was also of pure blood. Both Huayna and Cusirimay were born of parents of pure Inca blood, making them literal pure children of Inti, god of the sun and Mama Quilla, goddess of the moon. Though this expectation had never been spoken, Sarpay recognized that only her blood could save the people. She wondered if this was the very reason she and only she had thus been purified and ordained as the high priestess of Tawantinsuyu, the great Inca Empire.

She slipped off the platform and summoned the priests and priestesses to help her prepare for and make the journey to the Temple of the Sun for this ultimate sacrifice.

For the perfect youth sacrificially offered to the gods, it was a lifelong preparation. Tribes from throughout the empire selected a perfect boy or girl to be dedicated to the gods of the empire. These children, sent to the sacred Coricancha in the capital city Cusco, grew up separated from the major population. They spent lives in service to the gods. Undefiled, they grew up to serve. In times of famine, war, or celebration, the most perfect were chosen by the priests and anointed for the honor of giving their life for the empire.

For these children, tradition required a procession to Cusco from the home of the sacrificial child, then a trek to the chosen Andean peak to be buried alive. She now wondered if these children felt the same resolve as she was now feeling. Could they?

It was now time for the most perfect of them all to seek the divine blessings of the gods.

Sarpay's virtuous life had also been a lifelong preparation. She recognized that now. Where others of her sisters had already been given in marriage to one of her many brothers or other nobles, she had been preserved for this very time, she thought.

Sarpay knew that unlike child sacrifice, this would be an offering of blood—her blood, on the sacred altar in the Temple of the Sun in the empire's capital Cusco. Though other sacred temples were dedicated to Inti, god of the sun, only the Temple of the Sun in her father's own citadel Picchu and the sacred ancient Temple of the Sun on Lake Titicaca matched Cusco's temple for importance for this sacrifice.

This would not be a personal sacrifice for her. It would be an honor to give her life for her father and for the empire. Soon she would join the gods looking over the people.

Huayna dried his tears, regained his composure, and motioned for his chasquis to enter. These native runners arrived breathlessly at court. In a sophisticated system of relays, young runners carried messages across thousands of miles of roads. These two arrived with messages from the coastal town of Tumbes. Kneeling, and with bowed heads, they confirmed the reports that a sickness had appeared in the north. This terrible sickness was devastating the inhabitants. It wiped out complete villages. In their limited courage to describe the disease to the very Sapa Inca, they told how the plague inflicted its victims with horrific disfiguring of the skin, accompanied by the pain of mind and body. The chasquis claimed to have remained apart from the inflicted but reported the sickness was now spreading toward Quito.

Hoping to protect himself from the invisible invader, Huayna Capac, the mighty Inca, retreated into seclusion. Following three more days of fasting, food was carefully prepared and provided to prevent any contact with the outside world, as he struggled to keep himself away from the sickness' lethal reach.

Days turned into weeks, and when a month ended, he realized it was too late. Shadows danced on the walls of his secluded palace bed chamber. The air was thick with a mixture of despair and the pungent scent of sickness. The mighty emperor's once-powerful form was becoming a fragile shell. The memory of his strength and spirit seemed like a distant dream. It began innocuously, with a fever and a dull ache that settled in his bones. His forehead burned and his muscles screamed with every movement. At first he brushed it off, then tried to pray it away, but as the days passed, the illness tightened its grip. Fatigue gave way to an agonizing headache and an unrelenting backache that left him bedridden. He realized he was suffering just as his people were suffering.

His skin, once smooth and bronzed in the sun, now bore the cruel marks of the disease. It started as a rash, small red spots that dotted his face and forearms, then spread with a malevolent persistence to his chest and legs. The spots swelled into blisters, filled with cloudy, thick fluid. Each pustule was a testament to his suffering, bulging and angry against his skin.

Huayna regretted that he hadn't commanded his daughter to give her life there in Quito. Though the temple in Quito was not as the great Temples of the Sun in Cusco, Picchu and Tiwanaku, he now realized the months it would take for Sarpay to prepare and travel to those most sacred temples may have cost the empire its hope of redemption. He knew it would cost him his.

As days passed, Huayna realized he would likely die, and he called for his nobles. "I command you to seek the sign of the llama to confirm my choice for my son Ninan Cuyochi to inherit the empire. If he is not the gods' will, then I anoint my son Huascar."

Huayna laid motionless, drifting in and out of delirium when new chasquis arrived from the coast. Huayna rose to his elbow, mustering what strength he had to receive a report.

"Great Inca, a strange floating craft arrived from the north and moored before your conquered Tumpis city of Tumbes. Its people have white skin and hair on their faces. And one is black like the night. They carry with them curious tools which make smoke and speak like thunder. These strange men stole two of the Tumpis boys and used the wind to carry their craft across the great waters. Two of this enemy, one black and one white, were captured by the Tumpis. They remain as prisoners. The Tumpis await your will."

After a long silence, the emperor drew a laborious breath. He was teetering on the edge of consciousness. Huayna said nothing.

"We await your will," the second chasqui said, never raising his head. Silence, except for the struggle to breathe, filled the air. The two young runners backed away from the emperor, leaving him alone with two attending priests.

Huayna lowered his weary head back down upon the royal pillow, whispering to himself, "Will the gods not wait for the sacrifice of my beloved firstborn daughter? Will I be in the heavens with my Creator God Viracocha, waiting to receive my daughter Sarpay?"

The priests slaughtered a llama, opened it up and removed its lungs. They looked carefully at the animal's veins for an omen. The pattern of the veins unfortunately foretold a bleak future for the Sapa Inca's two sons Ninan Cuyochi and Huascar.

When the priests returned to the palace with news of the omen, the great Huayna Capac, ninth ruler of the vast empire of the Inca, laid motionless on his great royal bed. When they were told by Coya Rawa Ocllo that the gods had taken the great Inca, the priests dutifully went in search of the new young emperor, Ninan Cuyochi.

After nearly three weeks following one of the great Inca highways, the small entourage of priests arrived at the secondary northern capital Tumi-pampa only to find the local priests preparing the body of the young emperor Ninan Cuyochi who was already dead of the pestilence.

Huayna's priest told Sarpay of her father's death as she continued preparing for the trek from the northern capital of Quito to the central capital in Cusco. Soon she would see her father in the next life. Would he be pleased that she fulfilled her royal duty, or disappointed she did not proceed more quickly? Could she have proceeded more quickly? Was the royal procession to the Temples of the Sun not an important part of the sacrifice? It did not matter now. Her father was dead. Tears flowed down her smooth bronze cheeks and disappeared into a rich, deep red royal cloak covering her shoulders, which shook as she wept.

It was time to begin her own pilgrimage to the Temple of the Sun. Could she make it move faster? How quickly could her entourage of hundreds of priests and nobles travel on foot? There were more than a thousand miles between her and Cusco. With the network of tambos, the way stations, the chasquis could cover that distance in less than a month. For her caravan, it would require several times that.

She climbed up onto the golden seat padded with alpaca fur pillows under a finely woven wool canopy dyed a royal red with golden fringe and tassels. Her own select porters raised the litter, and her procession left the palace. She pulled the silken curtains closed so the people could not see her collapse in grief.

# Chapter Two

## 1528 - Trujillo Spain

The squeak echoed through the empty courtyard. Martín wondered if he would ever hear it again. In ten years, why had the gate never been greased? His preparation for postulancy to begin sharing the work of the novitiate was now over. At eighteen, he was eager to finally enter the monastery as a postulant and eventually become a novice monk. Monastic life promised him peace, fulfillment, and purpose.

The few remnants of his solitary life lay still in the empty manor house. After his mother's murder those many years ago, it still felt as hollow as his heart. He hoped life in the monastery serving Christ would fill that void. Martín pulled the gate closed and turned his back on the past.

The silence that seemed to haunt the abandoned cobblestone street was suddenly shattered by panicked screams. He knew those screams. They were loud and frantic. Martín quickened his pace. One more solitary day was all he wanted. Then he would be safely beyond their reach, inside the monastery.

He rounded the corner to find exactly what he feared. Two of Trujillo's worst bullies, the Pizarro brothers, trying to subdue the one young girl they failed to conquer even after multiple attempts. Martín carried many a scar from his entanglements with these two. He couldn't permit this. He just could not. But why now? Why today? He dropped the satchel containing his only earthly possessions worth keeping and readied to earn a few more scars.

But he froze. Martín stood paralyzed, unable to will his feet to intervene as Juanita fought back, arms flailing as the brutes pushed her against a wall.

Señora Lopez and her two hundred pounds of fury rounded another corner at the sound of Jaunita's screaming. Before she could levy her first blow, the brothers backed off laughing, claiming only to be having a little fun. "No harm was done," they claimed. They both scowled as they passed the frozen Martín. Juan stepped closer and slammed Martín against a wall. Martín said nothing.

Señora Lopez, with an arm around Juanita, accompanied her on her way past where Martín stood. Neither of them acknowledged him. Did they see him as the coward he felt he was?

Slowly, he worked his way through the labyrinth of squalid homes and headed toward the chapel, then to the monastery. Inside the holy walls, everything would be better. After his mother's violent death, when Martín had barely reached his ninth birthday, it was the new Friar Tomás who became his guardian angel. He was the first and only friend in this inhospitable land.

These months later, since Friar Tomás was given the new assignment in Toledo, Martín stood alone, once again, without family or friend. Though it would not be Friar Tomás, he wanted a blessing from the new friar before entering the monastery.

For the third time in three days, he crossed the portico and climbed the stone steps. He stepped into the chapel. It smelled of incense, the same that burned during the services held before each of his lessons. No candles burned. The only light was provided by tall windows cut high in the stone walls. The first image that met visitors to the chapel was that of the Savior Jesus Christ hanging lifeless on the large cross. Martín genuflected and continued across the empty room, each step echoing against the cold stones. He passed the altar and knocked on the recently arrived friar's door. With no answer, he pushed it aside. Empty as well. His heart and stomach ached.

"He is not here. He is not coming back. It is time you grow up. The church is not here to care for lazy boys. Be gone!" Pablo, the large caretaker, pulled the large wooden door closed so hard its echo reverberated throughout the chapel, putting an end to Martín's hope of a blessing before entering the monastery.

"I am not lazy," he muttered, leaving the chapel. He wondered if the new friar was never coming back. Was he also called to Toledo? Or was he just not coming back today?

As Martín entered the small market, he wondered if they all knew he shrunk when Juanita needed him. Would he shrink when Christ needed him? He felt the imagined disdain.

At the other end of the market, a commotion gathered a crowd. It was near where the only merchant Martín felt was a true Christian sold melons. Martín, just as curious as any youth would be, worked his way into the crowd to see the disturbance.

"Away from here, Gitano!" The Pizarro brothers had just transferred their earlier failed assault on Juanita to a young man Martín did not recognize. But when he heard the word Gitano, his skin bristled. His mother spoke kindly of the Romani groups that often passed through his own homeland up north. He remembered when his mother anxiously took him to one of their camps when he was very young. All he remembered was her disappointment when the Gitanos did not know some friends of hers from before he was born.

Martín felt repulsed at the voice contending with the Gitano. It was like recognizing the squeal of a familiar swine. "Gonzalo," Martín whispered to himself in disgust. Gonzalo had his hands on the tufts of the young man's shirt, pushing him away from the stand of melons. With a jerking push from Gonzalo, the young man hit the dirt, puffs of dust accentuating the fall.

Who Martín only guessed was the young man's girlfriend or sister struggled to free herself from the grasp of Gonzalo's brother Juan.

With fire in his eyes, the young man on the ground surprised Gonzalo, lurching at his legs, bringing him down hard on his back. The young man was on Gonzalo so quickly, Martín caught his breath and found himself imitating the rapid blows of the young man pounding on Gonzalo's face and chest.

Juan released the struggling girl and dove onto the young man, freeing Gonzalo from the shock and surprise. Martín wondered if that may have been the first time anyone ever had the better of Gonzalo. Now the two Pizarro brothers, against one boy, delivered blow after blow. The young Gitano received the worst of the battle.

Once again, Martín stood frozen as injustice took place before him.

Then, as if out of nowhere, a wild cat joined the fight. The young girl, not even dusting herself off, rose from the ground and ripped into Juan with a fury of claws and screams that shocked the crowd as much as it did the Pizarro brothers. With only Gonzalo on the young man, he now reengaged and threw Gonzalo onto his back and leveled a powerful blow to the side of his head, stunning him. The young man pulled his arm back before leveling a final blow to end the fight. Just as he did, Juan caught the young woman in the face with his powerful fist. The blow sent her flying onto her companion. The young man caught her and knelt, holding the unconscious young woman.

Gonzalo, still somewhat dazed, struggled to his feet and readied to finish the fight when he found himself facing Señora Lopez again, who seemed to be the only person on earth with power to control these bullies.

"Bastante!" Señora Lopez gave no room for Gonzalo to object. She also gave him the ability to retreat. Now, in his mind, the crowd could perceive him as victor, though for the first time, he had been bested by another man, and worse, a Gitano.

Taking the posture of victors, the two men spit at the Gitanos and marched off triumphantly. The crowd cleared as the Pizarro boys stomped away. Nobody dared show their pleasure that the Pizarros had been bested, or the disappointment that the Gitano hadn't finished them off for good.

As the Pizarro brothers strutted away, Martín noticed Juanita was helping the young woman.

"Martín!" Juanita woke Martín from his frozen stupor. The quick motion of her hand commanded Martín's help. He quickly knelt and helped lift the young woman to her feet. Señora Lopez took Martín's place, and she and Juanita helped her into the shade of a large umbrella, protecting several carts of vegetables from the sun. Martín turned to the young man and offered a hand to help him up.

"Thank you," he said. Blood from the large cut on his forehead ran past his swollen eye. It met with a small stream of blood pouring from his nose, only to collect with the blood oozing from his lips. When he opened his mouth to utter the thank you, Martín saw more blood filling the cavity once held by a proud tooth now lying in the dirt.

Martín knew himself well enough to recognize the tensing of hate in his muscles was not aimed at the loathsome Pizarros, but at his own failure to live up to the hero-like image of his father carved by his mother. With great pride she told him the stories of how Martín's father gave his life to protect the rights of Muslims who rejected being forced to become Christians, and himself being a devout follower of Christ. His mother told how she was named after the woman called Maria Magdalena who was cured by the Christ. She taught Martín there was a responsibility to live worthy so he too could be blessed by His grace.

Now, as a young man, all he became was a weak, frightened sheep. He hated himself for it. Could he be a sheep in the monastery? One of Christ's lost ones, anyway?

"I am Faustino. Faustino Moreno," the young man said, looking into

Martín's sad eyes.

"Martín de Bolibar," Martín repeated back.

"I thank you, my friend Martín," Faustino said, working to form a smile between the blood running down his face.

How could he call me a friend? I stood afraid, like all the other sheep as a wolf tore into an innocent lamb, he thought to himself.

When they reached the spot where Juanita and Señora Lopez attended to the bruises, cuts, and torn dress on the young woman, Faustino said, "Martín, my friend, this, my valiant protector, is my baby sister Carmelita. As you may have noticed, it is not wise to cross her. Carmelita, this is my new friend Martín."

Señora Lopez stood and turned her attention to Faustino's face. He winced at her not-so-gentle grasp of his chin, turning it side to side to reveal the damage inflicted on both cheeks.

"Sientese!" she commanded, and pulled him down into the reach of her wet cloth, where she immediately revealed the true damage done to his smooth, sun-baked face.

"And to my liberator, whom do I owe the honor?"

How could a man battered and beaten, bloody and bruised be so hearty? Martín never knew anyone like this. Was his father like this?

Señora Lopez took her attention away from the cut above his eye, which was supplying the bulk of the blood, and looked into his eyes, now mostly free of the red river. "You will not be so fortunate next time you tangle with those devils. I would advise you and young Carmelita here to scoot on. Those two will not settle until their hunger for blood is satisfied." She returned her attention to his forehead.

"Is that a welcome, Señora Protectora?" he asked.

"Lopez. Señora Lopez," Juanita said. "She may be the only person on earth who can keep those two from killing all who get in their way."

"We are pleased to make your acquaintance," Carmelita said. Martín turned his head sharply toward her in disbelief. The sweet voice surprised all three of them. It was not at all what he expected coming from the jungle cat that sprung to her brother's aid.

"Are they always like that?" Carmelita asked. "We did and said nothing. They pounced on us like dogs after raw meat."

Señora Lopez did not look up. "You are different, thus inferior, thus deserving mistreatment. They prey upon the weak. You stood up to them. You defended yourself. Therefore, in their sick and twisted minds, you must pay. Here with me right now, you are safe. We will get you fed, get you what you came to the market for, and get you as far from here as possible." Señora Lopez could not be more firm or honest.

"We have faced worse than those two," Faustino said, wincing as Señora Lopez dug dirt from the cut above his eye then wrapped a cloth around his brow and pulled his hat over it to hold it tight.

Señora Lopez led them through the cobblestone roads to a small hacienda. She sent Juanita back to gather the supplies they needed from the market.

"Are you traveling alone?" Martín asked, finally joining the conversation.

Faustino turned to Martín, peering at him as if he were reading something into the question. The pause was awkward for Martín, like he was opening himself up to be hurt.

"No, my friend, our people are working their way toward Toledo. We are enough. We do not fear bandits. My sister and I volunteered to stop here at your market for fresh produce and will catch up later."

"Toledo?" Señora Lopez asked, "Why Toledo? They will not welcome your kind."

Faustino's grin wiped away any offense, if any were intended. "Señora, you are a rare exception in the world. Nobody welcomes our kind."

She shrugged off the comment and placed plates of corn wrapped in their husks, large chunks of bread, and cheese blended with peppers in front of the two visitors. After she filled stone cups with wine, she went back to the kitchen and returned with another plate for Martín. More than once had she saved Martín from starvation, yet Martín's pride kept him from becoming a beggar. He mouthed a silent gracias to her.

"Martín, you will do me a great favor if you accompany these two as far as Madroñera by way of Don Diego's Colonia."

"Through the mountains?" Martín asked.

"You have been that far before. If Carmelita and her brother travel past the vineyards, they will never meet up with their friends. The Pizarros will be waiting for them by the vineyards."

Martín knew that was true. He looked from Faustino to Carmelita. Both sets of eyes welcomed Martín's company.

He knew Señora Lopez was aware the abbot expected Martín at the monastery. He hesitated at her suggestion. How long he had waited and prepared for this very day. Today, he would make his sacred vows and escape the world and dedicate his life to God. How could Señora Lopez ask this of him?

"I will tell the abbot you are serving Christ in another way for a few days. He and God can wait," Señora Lopez said.

Is she reading my mind? Does God wait? He looked back at the two Gitanos. Bandages and bruises softened Martín's resistance. The slight tip of his head accepted the request.

Juanita returned from the market, and Señora Lopez busied herself packing bundles. She put Juanita and Martín to work gathering not only the produce Juanita brought from the market but added items from her treasure of baked breads. As the foodstuffs grew, Martín wondered if Señora Lopez was sending him not for safety but as a pack mule. She disappeared with Juanita and Carmelita for what seemed like an hour gathering supplies, though it was only minutes.

"You are kind, my new friend, to leave home and escort two strangers into the wilderness," Faustino said.

Kindness? Martín thought. No, hate for the Pizarros. A strange feeling of delight trickled through him as he thought of the brothers' disappointment when they realized the Gitanos got away. A tiny grin pulled at the edge of his mouth. He said nothing. He did not know what to say. He was just called a friend. Martín did not have friends. He did not know how to have friends. Could he be a friend?

The three women returned, and Señora Lopez gave Martín an additional bundle she claimed would sustain him on his return voyage. He wanted to look inside. It was heavy. She ushered them on their way.

The three said their goodbyes and, with Martín leading the way, slipped through the cobblestone streets and empty alley and headed toward the hills, leaving Trujillo behind them.

# Chapter Three

## Trujillo - On the Road to Toledo

"Your señora, is she family?" Faustino said.

When Martín turned to respond to Faustino's innocent question, his eyes halted abruptly when they met Carmelita's dark ones. Accompanied by a broad smile and long black hair cascading past her shoulders, she captivated him.

The folk tales of how the Gitano women with their exotic beauty could lure even the sturdiest men jousted in his head against the scene of this young exotic beauty plunging into an attack and drawing blood against the Pizarros.

Where did the flowers come from? The thought broke the lock on her beautiful face. He quickly glanced down, realizing she picked several wild Rockrose flowers and tucked them in her hair. Their rich white petals, with striking crimson spots at their base, were in contrast against her black hair and stunned him.

"Is Juanita your girl?" Carmelita added.

Family? My girl? Martín just shook his head.

"You disapprove of the Pizarros," Faustino said, breaking Carmelita's trance holding Martín captive. "Do you fear what they might do when they learn you thwarted their plan?"

Martín had said but a few words since he met these two. Was his face doing all the talking? Time to use words. "Nobody likes them. Everyone in Trujillo wanted you to finish them. I prayed that you would," Martín finally said.

Martín wanted to return his full attention to Carmelita, but he found that Faustino in his own right had a strongly masculine and interesting face.

Had Faustino captured Juanita's eye as Carmelita caught his?

A small trickle of dried blood peeked below the bandage Señora Lopez used to patch Faustino's brow. When it caught Martín's attention, he could not resist asking, "Does that hurt?"

Faustino raised his eyebrows as his eyes motioned upwards toward the brow. "No, I have had much worse. The girls from our camp can do more damage than those two." Faustino's eyes shot toward Carmelita, reminding Martín of the fury he just witnessed hours before.

Martín's eyes followed Faustino's back toward Carmelita who just picked and held more Rockrose blooms in her hand. She pulled them to her face, her eyes closed as her lungs expanded, drawing the warm earthy fragrance in. If his struggle to keep from staring at Carmelita continued, this was going to be a long journey, he thought. Only then did he realize how the same scent, slight, balsamic, blended with herbs, often filled Señora Lopez's kitchen. It clung to his memory, wild and sweet, almost reverent, and broke Carmelita's lock on Martín's mind.

"Señora Lopez asked why your people head to Toledo. Did I miss your answer?" Martín asked.

"No, my friend. Strangely, our people are both loved and hated, but mostly misunderstood," Faustino said. "The king is in Toledo and he is who we seek."

"King Charles?" Martín asked.

"The very one. You see, since Alfonso V of Aragon first issued us safe conduct through his kingdom ages ago, the kings have permitted our freedom," Faustino said. "We maintain that freedom with gifts and appreciation."

Martín listened with rapt attention. Their climb through the fields of wildflowers, which he made countless times as a young boy, had never been as interesting as it was this time. It was as if his senses were awakened for the first time, from the Rockrose in Carmelita's hair to the scent of the fields of wildflowers to the unique accent in Faustino's words.

Martín, only a few feet ahead of Faustino, turned and asked, "Are you offended if I ask many questions? Friar Tomás says it is rude when it is personal." Martín was too curious not to ask. He turned back to concentrate on the path which now left the fields of wildflowers and began the rocky trek into the foothills.

"An open conversation is always welcome," Faustino said.

"My questions will all be personal," Carmelita said. Martín's heart skipped a beat.

"What is the accent I hear? It is one I do not recognize."

"We Gitanos speak Calo. It is much like Latin, with various other languages mixed in. You could learn it easily. Señora Lopez slipped a Latin book into your bundle. You must know how to read."

Martín stopped immediately, dropped both bundles, and opened the sack she'd given him for his return journey. Stunned, he looked inside, back to Faustino, and back into the bag. Slowly, he reached in and reverently retrieved a leather-bound collection of scripture. "Paginae de Epistolae y Evangelio de la Biblia de Gutenberg," he whispered to himself, the rest of his breath escaping his open and stunned mouth. He could do no more than stare at the treasure in his hands.

He looked up to a smiling Faustino and curious Carmelita. "Where did she get these?"

"She told me to tell you, they are a gift from Friar Tomás. He wanted you to have them when she thought you were ready. You must be ready."

"You know what these are?" Martín asked, the words barely making it out of his still shocked mouth.

Faustino nodded his head. "I too know Latin. They are our holy scriptures too."

Several minutes later—or maybe it was only seconds—the shock wore thin. Martín returned the volume to his bag, turned, and walked on in silence for the next few hours as his mind struggled to comprehend what Friar Tomás, Señora Lopez, and now Faustino and Carmelita expected from him.

Now off the plains and with the sun behind them, the trio kept a steady pace hoping to reach the small valley whose shallow lake was fed by a river Friar Tomás referred to as the River of Hope, a name he gave it when he and fellow men of the church were forced to spend a day recovering from a devastating fever as they traveled from Madrid.

By nightfall, they reached a small shallow river and followed it for a few hours in the moonlight. Too tired to cook or even build a fire, the three settled down for the night. With too little light to read, Martín simply held the precious gift in his hands as he silently praised his God somewhere above in the star-filled sky. Even the chill of the night could not disturb the warmth of his love for Friar Tomás. "Why did he have to leave me?" he muttered as he put his head down to sleep. A newfound love and appreciation for Señora Lopez found its way into his sleepy mind. He began to reflect on the countless small things she had done for him. He thought back to her love of his mother and her support when they first arrived in Trujillo. He regretted his shortsightedness, his lack of appreciation, his lack of recognition of her constant quiet care. He drifted off with a heart full of love for people who supported him, and self-loathing for his ingratitude.

Martín woke to the smell of citrus wafting off a small fire tended by Carmelita. He blinked his eyes clear as she poured a cup of steaming horchata. He sat up as she stooped to hand it to him. The steam rose from the cup, accompanied by the sweet smell of cinnamon and lemon.

The look on his face when the first taste reached his mouth rewarded her anticipation.

"You have never had horchata this way, have you?" she asked.

His head barely moved as he took a second sip.

"You know the Gitanos originate in ancient Egypt. Depending on the legend you believe, we not only invented horchata, we brought it to Spain," she said as she stood and walked back to the small fire.

"The Indians try to take credit for our beautiful race. They say the Persian king was concerned his people worked too hard and looked for a way to help them enjoy their lives more. He brought thousands of our people to live and dance and sing and teach his people how life can be lived. That is what we do, you know." She paused to take a drink from her newly filled cup. "We live."

Faustino returned from the river, drying his face with his shirt, "Of course, the king expected our people to work the land for his people. That is not what we do. As you also know."

These two were a refreshing change to his lonely, self-pitied life in Trujillo. He stood and refreshed his cup. "If you care for me like this, I may not return to Trujillo. Thank you." Now is as good a time as any to be grateful, he thought to himself. It felt good.

They quickly packed their bundles and were on their way. By late morning, they were well past Madroñera. He so enjoyed their company, he never thought to leave them and return to Trujillo. "How far are your people?" Martín asked, realizing they were beyond where the Pizarros might catch up to them.

"We expect to meet them in Guadalupe," Faustino said.

Martín's eyes widened. He'd never been to Guadalupe, but Friar Tomás told him about its sacred monastery on the bank of the Guadalupe River where a statue of the Blessed Virgin was found, apparently hidden by local inhabitants from the Moorish invaders hundreds of years ago.

A chapel was built there, and later under the command of King Alfonso XI, following his invocation of Santa Maria de Guadalupe in the Battle of Rio Salado and thus gaining victory, he declared the church at Guadalupe a royal sanctuary because of the Madonna's intercession in his battle. Following the king's declaration, massive rebuilding took place. There was no way Martín could return to Trujillo now! He might never get this close again. He had to continue with Faustino and Carmelita at least as far as the Royal Monastery of Santa Maria of Guadalupe.

He reached inside his bundle and pushed the book aside to look at the provisions Señora Lopez provided. They wouldn't last the two days to Guadalupe and four days back to Trujillo. He decided as foolish as Señora Lopez or Friar Tomás might think it to be, Martín decided to continue with these two new friends.

They continued up out of the valley. Faustino and Carmelita told stories about the Gitanos, the Romanis of Spain.

The various legends about the origins of the Gitanos that Faustino and Carmelita shared with Martín both intrigued and amused him. One tale claimed that the Gitanos were originally Egyptians who had refused shelter to Joseph and Mary when they fled to Egypt with the infant Jesus to escape King Herod's massacre. As punishment for their refusal, they were forced to leave their homes and wander for seven years. Eventually, they were given special papers by the pope that allowed them to enter other lands and cities.

Martín had learned enough history from Friar Tomás over the recent years to see that such a legend couldn't hold up under any serious scrutiny. How simple the people must be to believe such stories.

The second story confirmed to Martín these legends were created to help establish the Gitanos as Christians, which, depending on where they were wandering, would help or hinder their access to the cities and towns they entered. He wondered if they had an equal library of stories establishing the Gitanos as Muslims when they were with the Moors.

The second Christian story told of the Gitanos making four nails to be used when crucifying the Christ. Since they wanted to save Christ from so much suffering, they stole one of the nails. Because of this act of mercy, some groups of Gitanos claimed it gave them permission to steal from non-

Gitanos. But because of the other three nails, they were forbidden to ever cease wandering.

Martín wondered why they couldn't create legends far more complimentary to their state as eternal wanderers. As proclaimed Christians, he thought he could come up with tales and myths that would endear the Gitanos to the people better than those telling stories of their mistreatment of the very Christ.

Finally he couldn't help but say, "Faustino, I must ask. Could you not create more favorable stories as to your origin?"

Faustino laughed out loud, obviously having wondered that question himself. "My friend, you Christians frequently do pilgrimages to expiate your own sins. If people believe that if our constant traveling to fulfill a vow is like their pilgrimages, people will give charity to us as pilgrims and feel they gain spiritual merit.

"Perceived as pilgrims, the great oak gates of walled cities open to us, we are welcomed in. Our flowing costumes and our talented dancers bring crowds. And wait until you see how Carmelita here can seduce even the most pious men to empty coins from their pockets when she dances."

Martín believed every word. As Faustino bragged of Carmelita's skill, it was as if Martín was given permission to stare at her, which he did. He perceived a slight glint of pride in her beguiling face and wondered, *Am I risking my safe return to Trujillo with these two because of the Royal Monastery of Santa Maria of Guadalupe? Or for the royal seduction of the alluring Carmelita?*

They reached the summit of a small hill covered only by shrubs and an occasional woody tree. Martín hadn't ventured this far from Trujillo before, and with each new species of vegetation, he recognized how little he knew about the world. He wondered how much of what Friar Tomás tried to teach him was lost on a boy with so narrow an interest of the world. That interest was growing.

Far below them and barely visible in the valley was a small encampment. "There," Faustino said, pointing to the valley floor, "are our people."

Rough canvas tents and colorful wagons circled in loose clusters formed a patchwork that spoke of shelter and stubborn identity. The wagons were brightly painted with geometric patterns and animal motifs—bearing traces of journeys across centuries and kingdoms. Near the center of the camp stood a large canopy fashioned from crimson cloth stretched over tall wooden poles. Smoke curled lazily from small fires, where copper kettles steamed with something Martín wished he were near enough to smell. It wasn't to be long.

Faustino didn't hesitate to take in the scene. He and Carmelita increased their pace almost to a run, leaving Martín behind. Martín struggled to catch up.

"Carmelita and Faustino, my lost children, you return from the city!" The deep voice echoed through the camp. The man stood a few inches shorter than Faustino's six feet. His bushy black beard was accented by silver, matching the silver strands reaching out from beneath a ragged brown hat and down to the black collar peeking above a leather jacket. Sparkling brown eyes shined above his rich brown face. Martín immediately saw the man's strong features had been generously passed on to Faustino. Martín looked to the woman standing to the man's side hugging Carmelita. Faustino's sister definitely got her beauty from her mother. Just as striking and shapely, Martín could easily mistake her for Carmelita's sister.

"Martín!" Faustino said. "My father, Vano! Father, my new friend Martín." Faustino put his arm over Martín's shoulder and pulled him close. "Martín generously led us back to you."

Vano's head shook slightly. His eyes slowly assessed Martín's presence as if he were absorbing his essence. Martín felt awkward, almost naked, as Vano stared. He then nodded slightly, and a smile became solid. It was as if Martín had just passed a test.

"You are welcome here with us." Vano took Martín's hand, shaking it vigorously, then pulled him into his arms. How long had it been since he was embraced like this? Ever? Martín knew Friar Tomás cared for him, and his mother certainly loved him, for she worked her life away caring for him, but in these many years alone, he'd never known this feeling. There was no hurry to leave this man's arms.

"You must thank your father for me, for sending you to serve my children," Vano said, releasing Martín and looking into his eyes.

Vano's eyes seemed again to look into his soul. There was love and understanding behind them.

"I've never known my father," Martín said. "He was murdered before I was born."

"And your mother?" Vano asked.

"She died many years ago."

Vano stared as if remembering something important. "Later, I would like to know about your mother. Will you tell me about her?" Vano's deep voice never wavered. It was firm, but kind.

Martín shrugged and nodded.

"Do you have brothers or sisters?" Faustino's mother asked.

"None."

"Then you are my new son!" Vano proclaimed it to the small group gathered in welcoming Faustino and Carmelita back.

Vano put his arms over Faustino's and Martín's shoulders and turned to usher them into the gathering crowd. However, they all paused, noticing a pair of riders breaking over the horizon.

 Clouds of dust followed two riders as they charged toward the camp. All eyes watched as the two men arrived and hopped from their mounts. Faustino took the reins. The two riders approached Vano.

"Diego de Deza's inquisitors are stirring up trouble with Archbishop Alanzo. It won't be safe for us in Toledo," the horseman said.

Vano's smile never faded. "And what kind of dangerous heretic are they hunting now?"

The horseman's earnest attitude didn't waver at Vano's poke at the inquisitors. "Your kind. Holy Scriptures in the hands of non-clergy. Independent heretics. You know the Church cannot permit common people to have the word of God."

Martín's hand slowly reached into his bag, confirming the pages Señora Lopez stowed away were still there. He couldn't help but wonder if he was a heretic.

"We are not the objects of their terror," Vano said confidently. "Charles is in Toledo; I seek only the renewal of our charter to travel freely."

The horseman spoke confidently, "Vano, the king is no more than a pawn in the pope's game. Pedro, the pretend Bishop of Toledo, wants so much to impress the pope he has lost all sense of right."

Vano laughed out loud, his shoulders shaking. He placed his hand on the horseman's arm to keep the horseman's passion at bay. "Lucio, Lucio, Lucio, Clement is nothing, Charles is as much pope as he is king. Holy Roman Emperor, he calls himself. No, with Charles's writ of passage, we will stay clear of Deza's inquisitors."

Faustino handed the reins of one of the horses to Martín and together they walked the panting horses to a makeshift corral created by stringing ropes from small trees through the small shrubs. "Do you ride?" Faustino asked as he removed the saddle and noticed Martín easily removing the other. "You seem to know horses."

Martín shook his head no. "But for a time I worked helping care for such horses owned by the priory. Friar Tomás let me ride from time to time. Not enough to be comfortable."

"If you stay with me, you shall."

May I stay? Martín silently begged in his heart. Please, may I stay?

The two young men joined the others as Carmelita and her mother served a hot stew with chunks of meat and vegetables. The clay bowl, filled to the brim, was too hot for Martín's bare hands. He sat and rested it on his leg, the heat quickly passing through the thin fabric. He shifted it from leg to leg, noticing Faustino doing the same.

"Carmelita here says you read," Vano said between mouths full of stew.

Martín finished a bite. "Friar Tomás insisted I learn."

"Our Friar Tomás? In Toledo?"

Martín nodded his head, his mouth full again trying to chew without burning his tongue.

Vano continued, aware of Martín's burning tongue, "One of the only few worthy of the title. If you are willing to join with us a few more days before returning to your home in Trujillo, you may see him again."

Martín's heart leaped. An invitation to travel with this group and an opportunity to see Friar Tomás again? He couldn't ask for more. The question of how to get back to Trujillo didn't enter his mind. Nor would it have been entertained if it had.

Martín's smile, behind which was a mouthful of steaming carrots and a grateful heart, nodded and accepted Vano's invitation.

Contrary to what Martín anticipated, the men worked alongside the women cleaning up after this very welcome meal. Vano then took Martín by the arm and led him to the bundles he, Martín, and Carmelita carried and then set aside upon arrival. Vano picked up Martín's bag. "My friend, let's see what Friar Tomás so generously shared with you."

Martín found it curious the man first asked about his literacy and then wanted to see the collection of scripture Señora Lopez slipped into his bag.

Apparently, Faustino shared that tidbit of information with his father. Martín opened the bag and removed the pages. Vano, almost reverently, took them from Martín. With no words, but his mouth moving as he read, he shuffled from page to page.

"Have you read these?" Vano asked.

"Yes, but not since they came into my keeping. I hoped to read them again when we got settled."

Vano continued shuffling pages. Martín recognized them as being from the New Testament. Pages he, as a peasant, was not legally able to possess. What was Friar Tomás thinking entrusting them to me?

Then Vano paused, holding up a section of pages unlike the others. He smiled and slowly looked up into Martín's face. "And these? Have you read these?" Vano turned them toward Martín. Martín shook his head. They were not written in Latin.

"My dear, dear friend Martín. Come with me." Vano led Martín and Faustino to the door of the largest wagon. Martín hadn't yet paid attention to the detail of the collection of wagons positioned in a large circle. Each unique wagon now took turns capturing his attention. The fine woodworking and painting of Vano's wagon finally got its turn, capturing Martín's eye.

His attention to detail started with the four stairs that led up to the intricately carved divided door. The top of the door was already open. Vano marched up the stairs, opening the lower section of the door, and ushered Martín and Faustino inside. Martín was amazed how much light streamed in through the curtained windows on each side.

Vano turned and motioned for Martín to step back a few inches. He lifted a panel on the floor, which Martín hadn't noticed nor would he have seen even if he were looking for it.

From inside the false floor, Vano pulled two large books. He closed the floor panel and set the books on a small table that hung from a hook on the wall below the window. Martín's eyes darted from the books to Vano's face. The drama on Vano's face was as entertaining to Martín as was his curiosity about the books. Vano opened the first book and the answer to the question about what this was all about became crystal clear.

Vano set the pages written in the unfamiliar language taken from Martín's bag alongside the open page of the large book. They were written in the same language.

"You, my friend Martín, are now a heretic. These are German." Vano again laughed. "Welcome to my family of heretics!"

Martín was stunned, both at the laughter and at the discovery. Friar Tomás' smuggled pages of the New Testament printed in German and tucked them in with the Latin pages he left for Señora Lopez to give to Martín.

Vano sat without a word, allowing Martín to absorb the discovery. Martín looked from the book to his pages and back. When the puzzle came into full view, Martín realized he was in possession of not only scripture which was illegal, but was in possession of Martin Luther's German translation of the New Testament. This was a death sentence!

"Do you read German?" Martín finally asked once the shock wore off.

Vano smiled. "Your Friar Tomás must trust you a great deal to give you the care of such valuable and dangerous scriptures."

Martín waited patiently for the answer to his first question. His slight squint broadcasted his desire to understand the scope of this situation.

"How much do you know of Friar Tomás' life?" Vano waited for Martín's knowledge of his mentor to register on his face. "I thought so," Vano said. "Years ago, he, with another man, a dear friend of mine, was invited to assist a young monk who was crossways with the pope. What has Friar Tomás taught you about the Diet of Worms?"

"Nothing," Martín said, but expecting to learn as Vano continued.

"With what's in your bag, he certainly felt you would learn about the Diet soon enough," Vano said. Sitting on the edge of the soft bed, he motioned for Martín to do the same.

"Our dear King Charles V found himself caught between the people and the Church. Heretics, which now you are one," Vano winked at Martín, "became the threat to the very power of the Church. One such heretic denounced the practices of selling forgiveness. His denouncement became such a hindrance to the inquisitors and the money collectors, the pope's holy chapel ceiling was threatened if he could not raise the money to pay the great painters to finish it.

"Under great pressure from the Church, King Charles commanded this heretic to appear before them. Everyone knew it was to be a fake inquiry and an excuse to capture and execute the heretic. In a bargain to lure the heretic from the safety of Wittenberg where Frederik the Wise, Elector of Saxony, protected the man, the king finally promised safe travel to and from this charade of a trial."

Martín was captivated with the story. Vano was a master storyteller. He now saw why people would pour in from the towns to hear the stories and enjoy the music of these Gitanos.

"After three days of trial, fear of the people convinced the inquisitors to release him."

Vano watched Martín intently and finally added, "The king's promised safety only pertained to his immediate area. Once out of that area, his promised protection could no longer guarantee the friar's safety."

As the story progressed, Vano's hands practically sculpted the words he used to dramatize the story. His head moved rhythmically, and his voice deepened with the drama. His eyes danced with his expressive eyelids and brows. Vano's face was a show all by itself. His narrative continued, and mesmerized Martín.

"Once in the forest, the small caravan returning the heretic to Wittenburg was attacked. They hooded the heretic, took him captive, and charged away.

"Everyone believed the order to capture and execute this heretic by the Church and the king was successfully carried out. The inquisitor's council was free to attend to other heretics and continue their persecution."

Vano paused. This was the climax of the story. Martín could see it on Vano's face. He held his breath in painful anticipation.

"The attack on the caravan was not an assault. It was a rescue. A rescue led by Friar Tomás."

Martín's eyes couldn't get any wider and even with his mouth wide open, breath couldn't escape.

"Tomás and his friends traveled through mountain, valley, and plain with the heretic until they knew no one could follow. They took the captive heretic and locked him up in the Wartberg Castle where they kept him prisoner for the next year."

"Who was he?" Martín whispered.

It was as if Vano was building the story in anticipation of that single question.

"That is where our Friar Tomás learned German, and where he got the very evidence you carry in your bag. Our Friar Tomás helped Martin Luther translate this New Testament from Latin to German."

"Friar Tomás knew Martin Luther?" Martín said. It was a breathless question. Martín's eyes were fixed on Vano's deep brown ones. "He never told me."

Martín ran his fingers over the pages with great reverence. "It looks like I am not the only heretic."

The camp had long gone to sleep. Vano pulled his copy of Luther's German New Testament from the shelf. In the darkness, he ran his fingers over the cover, reading "Die gantze Heilige Schrifft Deudsch" with his fingers. The words carefully etched into the leather reminded him of his time with the reverend. His mind traversed his own historic journey from these lands to Rome, and the revelations his time there with dear friends so mercifully provided.

Vano relived the heartache he suffered when he learned his two dear friends, Maria and Miguel, were slaughtered at the hands of the cardinal in Granada. He felt the love of God when years later his dear friend, very much alive, stood before him as Lazarus, raised from the dead, having been rescued from the cardinal's prison by a young monk. Years later, he was to suffer the heartache again when learning that this dear friend gave his life helping protect Martin Luther.

"Greater love hath no man than this, that he lay down his life for his friends." Twice.

Vano's whispered words startled his wife. She rolled over, pulling herself close, and rested her head on his chest. He set down the book. Vano wondered how long it took Tomás to suspect that this young boy was Miguel's son. When they meet Tomás in Toledo, he'd have to ask.

Tomás never knew Maria, but he did know Miguel and, in his communications with Vano, Tomás insisted that Martín was not only in the likeness of Miguel, but he carried Miguel's natural capacity for languages. Vano struggled with the irony and tragedy if this were true. It felt true right now. If it was, he wanted with all his heart to know all about Martín's mother who he hoped was his cherished Maria.

Auroral light began climbing its way over the horizon.

Though the bedroll Vano gave to Martín was more than he'd slept on in days, Martín spent a restless night absorbing the circumstances he found himself facing. A heretic traveling with another proud heretic. What Martín heard about the trials many rebellious clergy had, and were facing, troubled him greatly. His father lost his life protecting a people who believed differently. Clergy, lords, and citizens who shared even a slight disagreement with the Church were persecuted, hanged, burned, and garroted in the name of Christ. And Friar Tomás could never help Martín reconcile the demands of the pope and the king and their followers with the very teachings Martín read from the pages of scripture—the very pages he now possessed. Persecution was not at all what he found in the written word.

Morning came soon enough. Martín helped Faustino hitch the wagons and ready the camp to move.

"I see my father convinced you to join our little band of independent believers."

Martín tilted his head and squinted up at Faustino who now sat atop a rich brown Andalusian. With the horse's strong, elegant frame, Faustino looked like he was atop a statue. If its thick tail hadn't swatted at a fly disrupting his stance, Martín could have believed the picture a fine bronze statue in a city plaza.

Cautiously, Martín climbed up on a second Andalusian. Its dark gray mane and tail were thick and long, matching the gray of its lower legs. Its coat was motley white and dappled with gray. Martín ran his hand along the beautiful neck, almost expecting the ash to stick to his hand.

"We call him Adios," Faustino said. "Keep a tight rein, or you will learn why he got his name."

After a few jittery starts and stops, Martín pulled alongside Faustino. "And yours?"

"Babeica. A retired war horse. Sometimes he forgets we are not at war." Faustino winked at Martín and they led off, followed by the procession of wagons.

By mid-afternoon, Martín's seat and thighs were screaming for a rest, but he dared not admit it. Finally, the caravan slowed to a stop alongside a small rivulet. They loosed the horses and led them to water. After enjoying samples from a collection of cheeses and a variety of figs, grapes, and pomegranates, Martín shuffled toward the horses to help Faustino.

Faustino's mother, Mahala, walked up alongside Martín, took him by the arm and pulled him toward a small tent he hadn't noticed. She handed him a small earthen bowl filled with a cream-colored paste. "Use it liberally. If you do not, the next few days will be as miserable as can be." Mahala smiled at him and ushered him behind the curtain. Once inside, Martín realized it wasn't a tent, just a large cloth to provide him privacy. He rubbed the ointment on his chafing bottom and thighs.

When Martín made his way back to his horse, Carmelita watched with a smile. When she caught his eye, his embarrassment warmed his face.

Throughout the day, Martín noticed Vano's watchful eye. What was he thinking? Martín wanted to learn more about Friar Tomás, Reverend Martin Luther, and the story about a time in Rome that was mentioned only in passing when Martín asked where Vano met the reverend. The busy day never afforded that chance.

By the time the caravan stopped, it was dark and cold. They warmed up with a hard roll they dipped in a soothing broth.

"In the morning with an early start, we can reach Guadalupe by evening," Vano said.

Within minutes, the camp was quiet, and Martín fell into a deep sleep. More unanswered questions had piled into Martín's mind throughout the afternoon. Questions about the scriptures he held, the meaning of certain passages, how Gitanos reconciled demands of church and state. Too many questions. They'd have to wait.

Early the next morning, the routine repeated itself and the group continued their journey. Throughout the day, brief conversations failed to answer Martín's many questions. With new ones sprouting, the frustrations he felt reminded him how Friar Tomás often counseled patience as the virtue Martín needed most.

They arrived outside Guadalupe early in the afternoon, sooner than Vano had thought. Martín hoped to have some time to relax and spend a few minutes conversing with Vano, or at least a few minutes with Carmelita. That, too, would have to wait. The Gitanos had their work to prepare for. Martín mistakenly thought the preparation was the work. He was pleasantly surprised.

Only once when Martín was a young boy had his mother taken him to enjoy the lively entertainment of the Gitanos. This evening surpassed even the embellished memory of the color, the passion, the excitement, and the pageantry. People of all classes flocked from Guadalupe and surrounding villages to satisfy curiosity and escape mundane lives.

Bright, colorful skirts flew and bounced, legs kicked and intoxicated as Carmelita, accompanied by three other young Gitano women captured the eye and imagination of young and old, male and female. As the music faded and skirts came to rest, crowds roared in approval. Martín began to understand life was more than harsh labor to survive. Was he meant to become a Gitano?

Vano enchanted both old and young with stories of great exploits, shared with a passion and romance that turned even a mundane tale into an epic adventure.

Mahala told fortunes and filled heads and hearts with hope, fantasy, and caution.

The whole event mesmerized Martín. He'd spent days and nights with these welcoming people, and now seeing them in their glory dazzled him.

The music began again only to be interrupted by five horsemen pounding directly into the crowd, scattering onlookers and knocking gaming tables and food tables to the ground.

Martín's heart sank. From atop the massive horses, Guadalupe's Grand Inquisitor Bishop Dominguez, accompanied by the sheriff, two deputies, and riding a dappled gray Andalusian sat Gonzalo Pizarro. The sheriff turned to his two deputies, both on black stallions. "Close down this illegal gathering! By the order of Diego de Deza, the grand inquisitor, arrest this heretic."

Gonzalo wasn't looking at Vano or paying attention to the sheriff. With a hand on his sword at the ready, he stared at Faustino. Hunger in his eyes begged for retribution for the embarrassment he and his brother Juan suffered back in Trujillo. Martín could only imagine the pleasure Gonzalo would have if Faustino tried to defy these men and protect his father as he'd done with his sister. Martín didn't know how to pray for this. More than that, he wondered how they got to the sheriff and secured an accusation so impossible to rebut. And why not accuse Faustino rather than Vano?

Vano held up his hand toward Faustino who obeyed his father's objection to a bloody confrontation. Faustino was breathing heavily ready to pounce. Instantly, Carmelita came from nowhere toward the men. Martín expected the cat to pounce. Faustino put his arm around her waist and pulled her toward him, halting her advance.

How did they know? What do they know? Do they know he has illegal scriptures also?

Vano stood undaunted. "We have the laissez-passers, from the kings, our letter of protection from Pope Martín V, and validated with signatures from the kings of Aragon, Navarre, and Castile. We travel freely on our pilgrimages."

Vano knew the crowds knew nothing about the original letters of protection. He hoped these five horsemen did not know that King Ferdinand II had altered them. Ferdinand placed these wanderers under the supervision of religious leaders, which made it a more delicate balance to pit kings against popes. Vano was trying to set the crowd against the sheriff in case violence broke out. He also wanted to sepa rate his fellow Gitanos apart from the original accusation that he was a heretic, giving them a level of protection.

"That is no good. As a heretic, you have no license from the king. You will come with us or we will take leave to destroy you all." Bishop Dominguez was firm.

The crowd silently inched its way back at the command given in the name of the grand inquisitor. Martín thought they must know there is no opposition to the bishops and their ravenous hunger to cleanse Spain of heretics.

Vano turned to Faustino. "This will not hold. We have rights of passage from the king. Take our people to Toledo. We will remedy this mistake. Do not go via Buenasbodas; the road is treacherous and highwaymen plentiful."

Vano turned to the sheriff. "Let us be on our way. There is no fault in these people. They have earned an evening of diversion. May I say goodbye?"

The calm response kept the incident peaceful. All five riders remained mounted, finding no reason justifiable before the large crowd to become violent. Martín respected Vano's ability to protect his people with his calm response. "Blessed are the peacemakers," Martín whispered to himself.

Vano embraced Mahala and Carmelita, speaking quiet words to them as he did. He gave instructions to Faustino as they embraced—instructions Martín couldn't hear. He then stepped over to Martín who stood motionless struggling to understand this change in events.

"Remember this, my friend Martín, kings are nothing more than merchants, and for currency and merchandise, they use the lives of those they rule. You, my friend, are a product to sell, to trade, to use up, to wear out, and then destroy when your usefulness to the king is no more. Their partners in business are the cardinals, bishops, and friars. Your Friar Tomás may be one of the few noble exceptions. When you see him, and I pray that someday you do, thank him from the rest of us merchandise for standing alone on our behalf, for I am certain if he stands, he will unquestionably stand alone. God be with you, my new friend."

Faustino readied a cream-colored mare for his father. Vano mounted. The men turned to leave. Gonzalo gave Faustino a gloating glare, then joined the others to take Faustino's father to a likely death.

Once again, Martín stood helpless to object to or correct an injustice.

# Chapter Four

## Village of Waras, Chinchaysuyu,  Northern Tawantinsuyu

Cusimi bowed as she entered the small temple room. Sunlight crept through the eastern window, excusing the golden lamps that burned through the night where Sarpay petitioned Inti, God of the Sun, for patience while she prepared to give her life to him. As Inti now showered the small temple room with his light and warmth, the peace she expected did not accompany it.

Each time Sarpay supplicated the gods for peace, she was filled with foreboding for the future of her people.

Sarpay looked up as Cusimi approached. From the time they were young, Cusimi's companionship afforded Sarpay the luxury of sharing the quiet intimate burdens associated with Sarpay's role as First Priestess of the Empire. Cusimi's noble father gave Cusimi to Sarpay to be groomed and prepared as a capacocha, a pure child sacrifice. Cusimi soon demonstrated she would never be an appropriate child sacrifice to the gods. Yet, Sarpay loved Cusimi for her honesty, stubbornness, and loyalty. While growing up, few of Sarpay's many brothers came back for more after tangling with Cusimi the first time.

"Sarpay," Cusimi said, kneeling alongside her friend, "your brothers will not be content to each rule half the empire. Chasquis from Cusco and Quito report similar fears. Although they believe your father appointed Atahualpa to the northern empire and Huascar to the capital at Cusco, others say your father declared that if Ninan was unable to rule, then Huascar was to be the Sapa Inca. That rumor does not please Atahualpa." Sarpay knew Atahualpa clearly understood it was not a rumor. He started and fed the actual rumor that he was to rule the northern empire.

Could she reach the Temple of the Sun before a civil war consumed the empire? Sarpay closed her eyes and lowered her head. Cusimi remained silent.

Sarpay thought back how weeks ago she'd stood motionless in the shadow cast as the sun began its journey behind Pichincha, the sacred volcano rising on the western edge of Quito, the northern Inca capital. Her half-brother Atahualpa, from her father's third wife Tupac Palla, walked past her with his great general Quizquiz, leading a band of soldiers toward the bathhouse.

She heard Atahualpa say, "My father declared Ninan Cuyochi to succeed him as Sapa Inca before he died and if not, Huascar should reign."

Just before the two men disappeared out of earshot, she heard the general ask, "Can Huascar keep this empire together?" She didn't hear her brother's answer, but she doubted he would submit to Huascar.

Sarpay knew both these two half-brothers as well as anybody could. Of the many half-brothers she had, she felt Huascar the more diplomatic and generous with the people, but Atahualpa easily held a firmer hand with the several rebellious tribes in the north.

Atahualpa spent most of his life north in Quito, the second capital of the Inca Empire,  learning the art of war from his Sapa Inca father Huayna Capac. He and his generals, Quizquiz and Rumiñawi, led powerful armies. She knew Huascar was a brilliant administrator and dealt compassionately from Cusco. Her fear was that between the two, because they were from different wives, a competition had smoldered for many years. She feared the eventual collision of ambitions had arrived.

Each had been loved and honored by her father, and each were respected, hated, and feared by different lords, nobles, and enemies throughout the empire.

As she now contemplated on the potential succession of power, she appreciated her father's urgency for a great sacrifice to importune the gods for their favor when his heirs and the great epidemic challenged the very survival of the empire, an empire he and his ancestral Incas had fought to build.

Cusimi was patient. She sensed that Sarpay carried a burden she couldn't fully comprehend, but now was not the time to retreat into silence. There was an immediate responsibility — an entourage of nearly a thousand nobles, artisans, and lords who were accompanying Sarpay on her pilgrimage from the northern capital of Quito to Cusco, the heart of the empire, they needed Sarpay's leadership and strength.

At each village along the way, Sarpay paused to pray for the people and seek guidance from Inti on their behalf. From a young age, she had embraced her calling as a priestess with solemn devotion. Cusimi had often traveled with her and Sarpay's father across the vast Tawantinsuyu, witnessing firsthand her tireless dedication. In every community, Sarpay would kneel for hours, offering prayers to the sun god and his wife, the moon goddess, petitioning for abundant harvests, strong families, and healing.

Even in places where the Inca had conquered at great cost, Cusimi saw how the people revered Sarpay—not for her title, but for her gentleness and love.

But this time was different. Cusimi could see it in her face: a quiet despair that deepened with every village they passed. Sarpay could not offer hope now—not when a civil war was irrupting, and a plague was tearing through the empire.

She had lingered too long and served the needs of each village too faithfully. And now, Cusimi feared, time had slipped beyond their grasp.

Reaching out, Cusimi took Sarpay by the shoulders and gently pulled her close, inviting her back from the silence. "Time is short," Cusimi whispered. "If we delay, the procession with your father's body will reach Cusco before we do, and your sacrifice may be delayed even more."

Sarpay knew the large procession accompanying the Sapa Inca's body back to be memorialized in a grand funeral was several months into its journey. Would her procession arrive first? Chasquis reported that when Huascar learned his half-brother Atahualpa chose not to accompany his father's body, the insult was a spark that would ignite a non-extinguishable fire.

Sarpay took Cusimi by the hands and thanked her. She wrapped a warm vicuña robe over her shoulders, slipped her feet into her soft llama skin slippers, and stepped out into the brisk morning air. The small central plaza began to fill with local farmers bringing their produce to market. She felt her smiles were phony. She feared what a war between her two brothers would do to these peaceful, kind people. Their very survival would soon depend on which of her brothers they supported. A wrong choice would guarantee an entire extermination. Her heart wept. She knew the ambition of her two half-brothers. She knew the gods refused to give her peace. And she knew the declaration of her father, the great Inca Huyana Capac, was true that only a blood sacrifice of the firstborn could save the people. She loved her people, and she knew their survival depended on her blood. She would give it freely.

She entered a tall stone building which served as the nobles' bathhouse.

Fresh water from the hills ran freely, filling several basins before it continued through the central plaza and out to irrigate the many terraced fields. The water was clean and cold. She quickly bathed and prepared for the last stage of her journey to the Curahuasi Valley where she would first commune with the Apurimac goddess in the temple on the peaks of Choquequirao, rightly named the Apurimac temple.

From there she would go on to Cusco where she hoped to meet with her brother Huascar before she made her final journey to the Temple of the Sun, and give her life for the people.

If the reports from the chasquis were accurate, which she was confident they were, her brother Atahualpa, who had control of the three northern armies led by powerful generals, would soon be marching south. They could overpower and conquer her brother Huascar, who had the support of the people in Cusco. For those who stood against the armies, it would be a loss of life unparalleled. Her heart remained heavy.

Cusimi crossed the plaza, approaching Sarpay as she left the royal baths. Her large smile almost lifted Sarpay's heart.

"Sarpay, would you care for a surprise this morning? You have a visitor who is here to join you for breakfast." Cusimi's smile and tone was even a notch more positive than her typical happy and upbeat nature.

Since her father's death and his call for her ultimate sacrifice, she had little to smile about. Yet, in the past, Cusimi was the one who could make Sarpay not only smile but laugh out loud with her unique look at life. These past many months, Cusimi's efforts at instilling hope continued to fall short. This morning, she came close.

"A surprise? Promise me it is a pleasant surprise," Sarpay said.

"Oh, I promise. It is a man you love!"

"Cusimi, I am a priestess. I do not love men."

"Oh, yes you do." Cusimi grabbed Sarpay's hand and pulled her across the plaza and into a large building where sat one of the few men Sarpay actually did love.

"Sarpay, my dear priestess sister!"

Sarpay did indeed love this man. She rewarded Cusimi with a large smile, a smile long overdue. "You said a man. May I remind you this is a boy," she said. Her chiding did not dampen the smile.

She took the boy in her arms with a big hug. "Manco, my brother, what brings you here?"

"You."

In only his eighteenth year, Manco stood several inches taller than Sarpay. His long black hair was held back from his face by a royal band of gold proclaiming his royal lineage. The fine linen shirt hung open at the shoulders, revealing finely tuned muscles. Having participated in several battles with his brother Huascar, Manco was a proud warrior.

Being the son of Huyana made Manco a prince, but Manco's mother was of lesser nobility. Sarpay was no respecter of a person's lineage. Right now, she only cared about her own responsibility. Manco wore his princely title proudly. He knew he would never be in line to reign as Sapa Inca—to do so he would have to battle against both Huascar and the more aggressive Atahualpa, his half-brothers from two mothers more noble than his. But he did not care. He was about to receive his sister Cura Ocllo as a wife and to her he would add concubines as needed.

"You are here to see me?" Sarpay asked.

"Our brothers are preparing for battle. We need you. We need you, our oracle, to lead our armies," he said taking her hands in his and peering into her deep brown eyes.

"I have little I can contribute. I cannot stay with our armies. Our father required I go on a different path." Sarpay wasn't willing to share the details of her plan and the duty she was under to save the empire. As it was, she feared the sacrifice required of her had been delayed many months too long. If we'd gone immediately to the Temple of the Sun, this battle between my two brothers may have been averted, she thought. The gods are unhappy.

"But you know something," he said, "I see it in your eyes. Sister, I know you. What is it you see?" Manco persisted.

"I fear those who side with Huascar will suffer." She paused, closing her eyes, as she recalled earlier visions she'd received. She looked back into her brother's eyes. "We will all suffer. This war will weaken the empire, but there is a greater danger, I fear."

"What danger?" he begged.

"Like the illness that killed our father and Ninan and so many of our people mercilessly, another plague will reach our land." She paused again, looking into her memory. "You, my dear brother, will play a great part…" She faded off reaching into the depths of her memory. "That is all." She dared not tell his fate or that of her brothers who were now preparing for war.

Manco's youth and innocence kept him from feeling the sense of woe his sister felt. That was good, she thought. Why trouble him? He is so young.

A chasqui out of breath, interrupted their meeting. He knelt before Sarpay, gave a slight deference to Manco, and spoke, "The great priests from Cusco seek a blessing at your hand as they pass this morning. Their procession with the young pair of capacochas are sent by Prince Huascar seeking the gods' favor in his seizing the northern capital from the armies of Prince Atahualpa."

She cupped her face in her hands. Two young innocent lives are being sacrificed to the gods, for what? Only one life is required. Am I afraid? Is that why this trek is delayed? No! I am not afraid. I have prepared my entire life for this sacrifice.

She removed her hands and bid the chasqui to rise. "Who are the two chosen youths?"

"Qullana and Kuntari, led by the Priest Pantquinna."

She knew those two innocent children. As the high priestess, she knew most all the sacrificial children. They were chosen for their purity from the many tribes throughout the empire. They grew up in innocence, serving the gods and the people. Many had great talent. Untarnished from the world around them, they were unblemished. She knew Qullana came from Tiwanacu on the shore of Lake Titicaca. She was a fine weaver. The tunic Sarpay wore was woven by Qullana. She paused and ran her hands across the softness of the fabric, her fingers pinching it tenderly. Kuntari was a young boy from the Chachapoyas people recently captured by her father. His voice was that of birds. His natural harmony rivaled the gods' very expressions in the wind. It was magical when he sang.

She took Manco by the hand and led him from the room into the bright morning sunlight. The sacrificial procession was just entering the plaza. Sarpay recognized these Cusco-based priests and bade them forward. Taking them by the hands, she welcomed them. Carried on one sacred litter, the two youths smiled as Sarpay approached and they were lowered to the ground. She stepped up onto the litter and took the two children in her arms.

"How blessed are you to be joining the gods during these troubled times." She led the two children from the litter and motioned for the priests to follow. They accompanied her to the large stone building on the eastern wall of the plaza. She smiled as the two devoured a corn porridge sweetened by dark red berries. A glance at the priests expressed the question.

The taller of the priests bowed. "Armies have emptied the silos. We have rationed what little food that remained," the priest said.

"And your porters?" she asked.

"They have gone without food the most," he said, maintaining his bow.

"Bring them all in here. This is the work of the gods; though sacrifice is expected, it is not their sacrifice. I want them fed and you are not to continue until all are well."

His response to her questions about the chosen destination of this sacrifice made Sarpay realize it would be several months before these two children would be given a mixture of coca and fermented corn to help numb the pain and the fear. They would be so high in the mountains and would likely be buried alive. They would die of starvation or freeze to death. She refused to consider that, depending on how well the children reacted to the drugs, the priests may even hasten their sacrificial death with a blow to the head. Some priests felt it more merciful.

Sarpay wondered if she would join the gods in time to welcome these two children to the heavens. The very threat of war and the plague her sacrifice was to prevent continued to delay her sacrifice. She began to question her own dedication. Was she afraid? Her doubts continued to assail her.

Sarpay recognized how the porters and other followers were uncomfortable in the presence of the First Priestess of the Empire, the true daughter of the Sapa Inca. She didn't care. Soon, many of these very noble people would be dead.

Cusimi drew Sarpay's attention away from the sacrificial children, motioning her to leave the great hall and step outside.

"You have other visitors," she said.

Sarpay saw a small group of maybe twenty to thirty warriors standing at the entrance of the plaza. The leader of this small army stood proudly. His long black hair hung over his shoulders, reaching a well-muscled and bare chest. The scarlet band he wore on his head was decorated with bright yellow and red plumes of the beautiful parrots found in the jungles. In his hand, a tall spear was also adorned with feathers, and shells likely traded from the coastal villages. A bow hung from his shoulder and tips of arrows peeked above the plumes of his headdress.

These warriors did not threaten Sarpay. She had accompanied her father during some of the trading expeditions with the peoples of the jungles. Though the Shuar were a fierce tribe and were successful in repelling her father's armies in recent conquest attempts, other tribes of the jungle became part of the Inca Empire by trade. Life for them was better under Inca protection. Sarpay's father had even taken a wife from the jungles to honor them.

As Sarpay and Cusimi approached the men, the ceremonial patterns painted on the leader's face indicated he was not only of nobility, he was royalty, wearing the golden sun in his headband. This was Sarpay's half-brother, Urco. His smile broke through the seriousness of the meeting.

He bowed in respect; she did the same.

His serious countenance returned as quickly as it left. "Your father's armies have abandoned our people. His general demanded we join him in the march to Cusco. When we refused to leave our families to the mercy of the bloodthirsty Shuar, those of our people too infirm to flee were butchered by your brother's army."

"I am so sorry." Tears flowed over her bronze cheeks. Though inappropriate for a priestess, she pulled him close, his stiff body unflinching.

He released her grasp and looked down into her eyes. "You are our only hope."

Sarpay couldn't imagine how she could help a people scattered into the dense jungles.

"Lead us to Paititi." His eyes didn't leave hers. "You know we will be safe there. We will serve your people there."

For the people of the Inca Empire of Tawantinsuyu, Paititi was a legend, a myth, a city magnificent built along a river surrounded by such verdant fields, they practically sowed and harvested themselves. Paititi was a city of gold, populated by the gods' choicest children, where God himself walked the golden streets.

Sarpay knew the legends well. She'd heard her father talk about it, discuss the people who resided there, and then hope the gods would permit him to die there. But he never denied it was real. Was it? She wondered. If it was, how was she supposed to know how to find it? This was not her calling from the gods. She was called to save the empire, not a small people that may number in a few thousand if Atahualpa's army hadn't massacred them.

A scout from the Urco's group ran into the plaza and bowed before Sarpay. "Quizquiz, his army is approaching," he said, never looking up.

"You must go!" she said. "He will never let you live."

"You must come with us," Urco insisted, reaching out to take the priestess's arm. "There is no time."

"He serves me and my brother; he will not hurt me," she said. Even she recognized the lack of assurance in her voice.

Sarpay took Urco's arm and tried to turn him toward the plaza's opening. Urco stood solid. "I cannot lead you to Paititi, even I do not know where it is, or even if it is," she said.

"But our gods do," Urco said. "And our gods know you."

"Sarpay, you favor Huascar. You will be slaughtered! You know that. Come with me. NOW!" Manco said.

As word of the approaching army spread through the plaza, Manco and the men and women accompanying him marched quickly from the plaza away from the approaching army.

How could she leave all these people? How could she run? The procession she'd just fed was sent by Huascar. Could she save them? Sarpay knew Manco was right. She made the fateful decision to stay and try. The plaza emptied of all those who could flee. Sarpay insisted Cusimi go with Urco's people. Once the plaza was empty, she returned to the frantic people remaining in the citadel.

Minutes passed, then hours. She hoped all those fleeing were safely away. She gathered the priests and nobles into the great hall and together they spent their energies praying, supplicating the gods for deliverance.

The ground began to tremble. Conversations stopped. The sound of marching men grew louder. Commotion of an army entering the plaza struck fear into every heart. Quizquiz, one of Atahualpa's most brilliant and brutal generals, stood in the doorway.

Sarpay stood and approached him. She tried to carry an air of confident humility, hoping to encourage a peaceful encounter.

"Seize the priestess and kill the rest," he said.

Three men quickly took Sarpay, dragging her from the hall. Men poured into the great hall and began the work of slaughter. Cries and screams of horror echoed throughout the hall and poured out over the threshold of the great hall, reverberating across the plaza.

Once into the plaza, they released Sarpay. She turned and fought to return to the massacre, her heart ripping apart in her failure to protect the innocents. A powerful soldier knocked her to the ground. Again, she rose. Again, she was held back. Helpless, she crumbled to the ground in tears and petitioned the gods to accept her sacrifice right now. She knew they would not.

Her anger for the cruelty of Quizquiz was absorbed by her personal anguish of failing her father and the vision he had for her sacrifice. She buried her head in her hands. She knew she would now be a pawn in a deadly game. If they would take her life in a temple, would that fulfill her mission? She hoped the gods would accept her sacrifice, even if taken by the hands of wicked men.

The armies looted the citadel, taking all the food and other supplies for their march toward Cusco. Quizquiz's men dragged the stronger of the porters from the great hall and loaded them with the supplies looted from the remaining citadel buildings. This march toward the battle for Cusco would not be atop a royal litter. Following the massacre of the sacrificial children and all those accompanying the holy procession, Quizquiz's men continued their savage execution of Sarpay's entire company. She only hoped the few that Urco and Cusimi entreated to flee with them made it safely away.

The fierce army marched south. They tied Sarpay between two large soldiers. They moved at a pace she recognized would demand more than she could give. She didn't fear for her safety as much as she doubted the strength required of her body.

Even the tiniest shred of reverence and respect she received from many of the soldiers during the first days of the march toward Cusco evaporated to nothing over the following weeks. She felt like they considered her as livestock. Though she was not laden as were the pack animals, she felt her burden to save the empire with her blood outweighed them all.

Sarpay found she was fit enough, but now so many weeks into the journey, her feet were cracked and bloody. The comfortable vicuña slippers were long worn through. She'd begged for parts of a llama skin for which she traded her golden ear ornaments.

During the long marches, her mind and heart were caught up in the fate of those who fled the army, including Cusimi who she'd insisted leave with Urco. Her younger half-brother Manco gave her little concern. He was capable enough to take care of himself. As overly confident as he always seemed to be, she was certain he would eventually learn to temper himself.

Throughout the march, she was kept away from the other women who met the various demands of an army of men. Very little accommodation was made for her personal comfort or privacy. The personal humiliation she suffered became so common, she no longer clung to any dignity.

To the general and his captains, she had become invisible. They no longer spoke in private. She was a prisoner, a pawn in a larger game. Even if she survived the march, to them, she would be no threat.

Following a long hard march up over the Huánuco Pampa Mountain, ascending some eleven thousand feet, she was not the only person to collapse when the army reached the high Huánuco Pampa plateau.

The general and his captains gathered around a small fire, discussing plans for an upcoming battle they were certain Huascar would be ready for. A chasqui ran breathless up to the general, bowed, and told about a team of enemy spies who'd been following Quizquiz's camp's progress for several weeks. Quizquiz smiled. They were getting close. Soon he and his highly trained soldiers would begin to crush Huascar's armies.

Sarpay heard it all. She was too tired, disgusted, and angry to care. She stood and casually began to walk away from the camp. All she wanted was some privacy. Quizquiz noticed her movement and, with a motion of his head, sent three men to bring her back. They knew she couldn't get far. There was nowhere to run. There was no hurry. The three soldiers slowly closed the gap between her and the camp. The sounds of the men at the camp faded away. In the quiet, she heard her pursuers talk about what they would like to do with her. Their voices seemed to hang in the cool night air. She knew in a moment they would drag her back. She was too tired to care.

A sweaty hand grabbed her shoulder. Then it let go. It was too dark to see what happened, but a man fell at her feet. The faint moon barely reflected off the still body of the man who'd shown the most animosity toward her through the march. She stepped away from him when another arm reached out, and a strong hand grabbed her arm. It, too, let go as its owner dropped to the ground. The feathers of an arrow caught the light of the staff protruding from his chest. Before she could step away, jump or run, the third man crumbled to the ground. Three men lay still at her feet.

Which direction was safety?

In the distance, the figures silhouetted by the fire in the camp seemed not to move.

Looking into the impending darkness, Sarpay charged away from the three dead men and a camp of more than ten thousand warriors.

Her practically bare feet ignored the pain as they pounded on root and rock. She never saw the large, bare arm reach out and swoop her off her feet and toss her over a shoulder. For what seemed like miles, the shoulder pounded into her until she could no longer breathe.

# Chapter Five

## Gitano Camp Near Guadalupe, Spain

The arrest, which appeared lawful in form, accomplished just what the Inquisition was designed to do—it instilled fear and submission in the people. The excitement of the night waned quickly, and Vano's camp of Gitanos were soon abandoned. Frightened citizens returned to their mundane lives. Many whispered among themselves how poor Vano would never make it to Toledo and certainly would be hanged or burned long before getting an audience with the king.

On the road, tied securely to his mount, Vano hoped Faustino understood his instructions.

Now three days in a saddle broken up by miserable restless nights attempting sleep on the cold hard ground, Vano's captors were only kept from killing him by the reward promised by the bishop for returning the heretic for trial and burning.

This night, the sheriff insisted they ride through the night and lodge at Sebastian's Inn just outside of Toledo. They would arrive after midnight if they kept pushing. The men hungered for a bed, a woman, and a hot meal.

The moonlight cut through the canopy of trees from time to time, illuminating their way. The sound of horse hooves wearily clomping the earth and the rustle of fabric against the saddles was suddenly and sharply contrasted by a whoosh followed by a groan. A man fell from his horse, an arrow protruding from his chest, the thud echoing through the trees. With a second whoosh, a sharp crack, Vano fell from his mount, hitting the ground with a groan. A third whoosh and a fourth. Each delivered pain to a rider. Though hit and bleeding, those able to stay mounted bounded forward, leaving their captive and comrades lying motionless behind.

Arriving at Sebastian's Inn, the sheriff and his deputy helped Gonzalo from his horse. Gonzalo bled profusely from his chest. They carried him inside and put a stop to the bleeding. He might live. The sheriff was hit in the thigh but not deeply, and his deputy easily pulled an arrow from his hip. The arrow barely reached his flesh, his belt taking the brunt of its thrust.

The innkeeper approached the men. "Highwaymen. You should not be traveling these roads in darkness. They were sloppy tonight; you should all be dead," Sebastian said as he mopped up Gonzalo's blood from the table and chair.

"They got three of us!" the bishop said. "At first light we will go back."

"You will not find anything or anyone. They disappear and victims, stripped of valuables, are fed to wild dogs," said a woman bandaging Gonzalo's chest. "They keep the best horses, sell the rest."

The sheriff's bleeding leg was a lesser injury to the insult just levied by the woman. He was the sheriff, and his failure to provide safety to travelers was a threat to his success. Her matter-of-fact denunciation of the sheriff's competence was a disparagement, true but humiliating nonetheless. He blamed the Church for his inability to protect the people from highwaymen. The Church insisted that he chase down every alleged heretic accused of interfering with the dictates of the pope. And when the accused heretics don't obey the pope, they pay the bishops a handsome fee for forgiveness. Granted, all this padded the sheriff's pockets with coin, but the people didn't care about the heretics or the sheriff's pockets. They cared about their own safety. The sheriff was thus used by the Church and hated by the people. He loved his power too much to care. The sheriff changed the bloody rag on his thigh. He would get new pants tomorrow.

The next morning, the sheriff kicked dirt on the dried blood on the ground in disgust. "I still get my bounty," he said to the bishop.

"The Church does not pay for failures," the bishop said, unwilling to dismount.

"This is not a failure. The Church is free of a heretic, especially one who so cunningly taught against the pope."

"Even heretics deserve a trial." The bishop spoke with such piety, the sheriff nearly betrayed his disdain for the clergy and their pride.

"You mean a public trial and a burning?"

The bishop looked down at the sheriff with contempt, but the sheriff was counting the tracks of both men and horse.

"Are you going after them?" the bishop asked.

"Three bodies, dead bodies, pouring blood were dragged into those trees where they would be stripped of everything, and the horses were led off that direction." The sheriff pointed back behind the bishop. "You come with me, and we will see where the bodies were fed to the dogs."

The bishop turned his horse, kicked its flank, and charged back toward the inn.

"I thought so," the sheriff mumbled to himself, climbing back onto his horse.

They returned to the inn. The bishop confirmed the story with the patched-up survivors and mounted up to return to the monastery.

When the bishop was out of sight, the sheriff turned to Sebastian who was setting out breads, cheeses, and wine for the visitors. "Grumpy things, when they lose a trophy to extort, humiliate, and burn in the name of God."

When Faustino's Gitanos learned the sheriff and his men only stayed in Guadalupe one night and then rushed off toward Toledo, the Gitanos chose to hasten there as well. Under different conditions, they would have stopped in each town to work their magic, but they needed to get to Toledo and reach the king as soon as possible.

The group camped in a small valley southwest of Toledo. Faustino took Martín, who was becoming quite adept with the gray mare, and left the group and rode toward Toledo. They stopped at Sebastian's Inn, a substantial inn located prominently on the road leading into Toledo. As they entered, a woman stood in the doorway of a room off the side of the big hall. Martín could see past the woman and immediately recognized the man propped up on several pillows. He was shirtless, but a large bloodstained cloth was wrapped around his chest.

"Gonzalo," he uttered under his breath. He stepped back, cautious not to be seen, in case Gonzalo opened his eyes and looked past the woman.

Faustino walked past the door and approached Sebastian. "Good man," he said, "we are seeking a group of six or seven men, one a bishop, another a sheriff. They carried a Gitano captive heading to the Inquisition in Toledo. Might they have passed by here?"

"Which one do you care about?" It was an obviously unnecessary question. Faustino looked so much a Gitano that Martín well knew the man was just seeking to know where to stand with these two.

Faustino's clothes were simple but sturdy, a faded tunic tucked into wide, weather-beaten trousers, held up by a broad, colorful sash. His boots, though scuffed and worn, were clearly well made, built for the rigors of the nomadic road. But it was more than the clothes.

His skin was a deep olive, a tone that spoke of distant, sun-soaked lands. His hair, black as a raven's wing, hung long past his shoulders, tied back with a red bandana that added a flash of color to his otherwise dark appearance. Watching the innkeeper assess Faustino made Martín look closer too. He hadn't paid that much attention to Faustino's clothes even over these many days together. Martín realized he paid more attention to Carmelita's dress than Faustino's appearance.

Martín noticed he wore a few rings on his fingers, simple but displayed with pride. Around his neck hung a pendant, likely of little value, but clearly cherished. As the innkeeper looked his visitors up and down, Faustino's dark eyes, sharp and observant, scanned the inn as if weighing its worth, taking in every detail.

Faustino's gaze met the innkeeper's eyes, and for a moment, there was silence. The innkeeper smiled, realizing he was meeting an honest young man who carried his culture with pride, a man who had stories in his eyes and music in his soul.

Faustino confirmed the unnecessary question with a slight cock of his head.

"You're not seeking confession?" Sebastian asked. His big smile revealed not only a sense of humor, but three missing teeth among the somewhat yellowed ones remaining. Sebastian was a large man, round of chest and belly.

Faustino again answered with the tilt of his head.

"I am sorry, Gitano …"

"Faustino, my friends call me Faustino."

"I am sorry, Faustino. Yes, the men you describe came late last night. The one you seek was not with them. He and others were killed by highwaymen. He," Sebastian motioned to the room where Gonzalo laid, "may not live another day. The sheriff, unfortunately only slightly hurt, rode off just recently with a third man also wounded, in pursuit of the bishop who refused their bounty. The highwaymen were sloppy. Usually they start with the clergy, then the sheriff. But it was dark. The sheriff and the bishop returned to the site of the attack earlier today and confirmed the death of three of the men, one of which I assume is the man you seek—their prisoner?"

Faustino nodded.

"He must be someone of importance to the Church. The sheriff and the bishop are at such odds over payment. This man's death cost them both dearly."

Martín watched Faustino absorb the news that his father was dead, amazed how calmly he took the news. For Martín, though he'd only known the man a few short days, the loss was like another boulder of disappointment added to his short life of disappointments. His breathing became short and he wanted to plunge into the room where Gonzalo lay and finish him off. He knew it wasn't Gonzalo who killed Vano, but somehow Gonzalo was partially responsible. His fists clenched. It was time to do something against injustice. Sebastian's words brought Martín out of his spiral of thought.

"The highwaymen saved this friend of yours a terrible death. It was Bishop Diezas who led them. There is to be a public trial of six great heretics. Bishop Deizas boasted six will burn for their rebellion against God. Unless he finds one today, the people will witness an empty pyre. Embarrassing," Sebastian said.

"Where were they killed? Did the sheriff say?" Faustino asked.

"You won't find them. The sheriff and the bishop went looking and angrily returned, confirming the highwaymen destroyed the bodies."

Sebastian's wife offered Martín and Faustino a plate of hot bread, which they gratefully took.

"What about him?" Martín asked, pointing to Gonzalo's room.

"His friends left payment for his care, but we hope they will return for him."

Faustino tossed a few coins on the table and he and Martín left the inn and rode out toward Toledo.

The city of Toledo was surrounded on three sides by the Tagus River which provided the much-needed irrigation for the semi-arid city. Martín was surprised Faustino knew how to navigate the roads to cross the river at Puente de San Martín and enter the city through the western gate, Puerta del Cambrón. As they entered, Faustino pointed out that the bridge took its name from the local cambrón thorn bushes that lined the riverbanks, their tangled thorns snagging travelers' garments and drawing blood from careless hands. He said the Spaniards saw in them a fitting symbol to represent the resistance these people could wage against unwelcome attacks.

The city brimmed with so many people it became necessary to leave their horses at a livery and walk through the crowded streets.

"What's happening?" Faustino asked an old merchant selling melons.

"A great conquistador has returned and is impressing the king and his nobles. Gold is flowing."

As the two men worked their way through the crowds, they passed the plaza between the archbishop's palace and the Santa Iglesia Cathedral. Martín saw what brought so many from the country into the city. In the center of the square stood the staked pyres, towering structures of wood and kindling, carefully arranged to ensure a slow, excruciating death. The pyres were erected on a raised platform so that all could see, no matter how far back they stood. The wood was dry, chosen to catch flame quickly, yet burn long enough to prolong the suffering.

Martín once heard stories from travelers who witnessed burnings. They told of the screams, the unanswered prayers, and the stench of burning flesh. They told these stories in such vivid detail he knew the horror of what they had witnessed lingered permanently in their minds. The memories stood as a testament to the brutal consequences of heresy, a grim reminder of the price of defiance.

 He thought it true how the innkeeper Sebastian said Vano being killed by bandits was better than burning here in the plaza. The repulsiveness of the thought that tonight five or maybe, if the bishop was lucky, six people would burn as heretics wrestled with the curiosity to watch it for himself.

Faustino seemed unmoved by the sight. He was anxious to get to the Alcázar of Toledo where they hoped to petition for an audience with the Holy Roman Emperor Charles V who was receiving appeals. Martín struggled within himself to understand Faustino's urgency. His father was killed by bandits. To Martín it was just another proof that Friar Tomás was among the many deceived by the notion that there existed some merciful yet just God in heaven. How could a just god tolerate the injustices that never seemed to end?

What would Faustino accomplish? Was he afraid he was next? Did the bishop know about the hidden floor of the wagon and what it held? Martín was glad he'd left the copies of the New Testament, in both Latin and German, hidden in the compartment Vano showed only to him and Faustino.

Sticking close to Faustino, Martín found himself squeezing into the Alcázar palace among the throngs of people struggling to witness the spectacle.

A man accompanied by porters carrying baskets of golden statues, vessels, and pottery approached the king. Whispers echoed the name Hernán Cortéz. To his side stood a young man with strong, angular features. He was dressed in a colorful tunic and pants with fine leather shoes. His long black hair was pulled back and tied with a silken rope, exposing his rich brown complexion. Martín was taken with his innocence and confidence. When prompted by the king, the boy spoke broken and choppy Spanish but clearly enough to be understood, telling the king his people welcomed Cortéz's soldiers to help conquer their enemies. He bowed again and backed away slightly.

King Charles V, now the Holy Roman Emperor, stood and gave a slight bow back to the native boy. Martín felt this encounter was as unique to the king to meet the native Indian as it was for Martín, an insignificant orphan, to stand in the same room as a Holy Roman Emperor. Never in his life had he ever imagined such a thing. The king sat again, his large flowing cape bunching at his feet. The fur which lined it coiled as if it were a live fox trying to get comfortable.

Martín couldn't hear the discussion, but it was evident from whispers and quiet comments that Cortéz pleased the king. When Cortéz bowed to the emperor again, the large golden necklace hung free and glistened in the light that streamed through a tall window.

The king stood again and pronounced his acceptance of Cortéz's offering: "I accord you the noble title of don, but more importantly, name you Marques del Valle de Oaxaca." When Cortéz bowed again, the king stood and, with a wave of his head, excused the proud conqueror and his entourage. Martín had no idea what any of that meant. He did know, however, the name of Hernán Cortéz, for he was also from Martín's own Extremadura region of Spain. Everyone there knew the legends of his conquest of the Aztecs just a few years before.

As Cortéz turned to leave, Martín saw him nod and give reverence to another man surrounded by a group of like companions. He couldn't hear the words spoken, but it was evident the two men knew each other. Everyone watched the procession as Cortéz left the great hall.

When the last of Cortéz's group was gone, the king listened as a nobleman whispered in his ear. He looked up at the man standing with a strange, long-necked sheep, a short stocky Indian boy similar to the Indian with Cortéz, and porters with baskets of gold decorated with brightly colored feathers. The complexion of the young boy was similar to that of Cortéz's boy, but his chest was larger and his tunic much more colorful. His hair was shorter, but pulled back in a similar fashion. Martín wondered about their similarities and their differences. This whole experience was more awe-inspiring than he'd ever considered in his entire life.

Martín looked at Faustino to see his reaction. Faustino stood with a face so placid, Martín wondered if this was common among the Gitanos.

The aide to the king announced this second visitor. "Your highness, Francisco Pizarro of Trujillo, Extremadura, Spain, and most recently, mayor of your own Panama, in new Castile." The aide bowed and backed away.

Martín couldn't believe what he thought he just heard. Another Pizarro? Gonzalo's father, brother? It couldn't be. Martín knew there was another half-brother to his prime enemies, but he was certain it was Hernán, or Hernando, or Armando. Not Francisco.

Francisco Pizarro respectfully approached the king and presented his gifts with great reverence.

Without donning the Spanish helmet, Francisco stood in metal armor, not for battle but for show. The steel armor shined. Around his neck stood a crisp white collar and over his left shoulder a beautifully woven red silk cloak covering part of his left arm and tied on the right at his waist. His jet-black hair was cut short and barely crept below the band of his black felt hat, from which several brightly colored feathers added stark contrast to the shiny metal fortress he wore. A long black beard made the common leather-worn complexion of a Spaniard look pale.

Everyone in the crowd stood silent and motionless as Francisco introduced his young interpreter, then presented the beautiful textiles, golden plates, feathered cloaks, and a large golden medallion hanging from a golden chain.

Pizarro held more than just the king's interest. Next to the king sat his young new wife, Isabella of Portugal, who, with the great treasure just given her by Cortéz and now added upon by Pizarro, was like a little girl having just received everything a greedy little girl's heart could desire.

Martín looked from her to the king, amazed at the grandeur of his circumstance. Only weeks ago, Martín stood frozen in the hot sun watching two bullies accost an innocent young woman, unable to will himself to intervene. His only desire was to escape into the solitary and safe life of a monk. Now he stood in a crowded palace wherein two conquistadors promised the Holy Roman Emperor, Charles V and Queen Isabella, a New World with all the riches that New World would provide. From what Cortéz demonstrated and what Pizarro promised, that wealth was unlimited.

Charles asked questions, which were confidently answered by Pizarro. Isabella asked Pizarro to confirm a few of his promises. The monarchs whispered a few things to each other, then dismissed Pizarro and his retinue. The only part of this last conversation Martín understood clearly was there was a land across the ocean full of gold just like the one conquered by Hernán Cortéz. This land was called Peru, and Francisco Pizarro wanted it.

Faustino jostled for position to become the next in line to petition the king. The king stood, excused the court, and declared he'd seen enough for the day and escorted Isabella from the great hall. As he stood and took her hand, everyone bowed or knelt. Martín was in the presence of the Holy Roman Emperor and his queen, watching two conquistadors present priceless gifts, and he was so mesmerized by the spectacle, it took a yank from Faustino to get him on his knee.

Once the royalty exited the great hall, the crowd pressed closer to Pizarro to see for themselves the gold, the linens, and the tall, long-necked sheep. Faustino and Martín, who'd positioned themselves immediately behind Pizarro's procession, had the first opportunity to see and touch the fine fur of the animal. It was clearly finer wool than the sheep Martín had ever worked with.

The young interpreter who Pizarro introduced as Fillipinello, stood motionless, staring at Martín, his dark eyes locking on Martín's face. Martín stared back, not so much trying to recognize or memorize the features of his clear brown complexion or his young, innocent angular features, but because of the intensity of his stare. In broken and newly learned Spanish, the young boy struggled with what Martín recognized was a limited vocabulary, "How can you live be from Tumbes here?"

Martín leaned in toward the boy, seeking to hear the gentle words above the noise of the crowd pressing in to witness the spectacle.

"What did I hear you say?" Martín asked.

The boy repeated, again awkwardly, "Chimu kill you. Alive here over ocean. How?"

"You are mistaken, I don't know Chimu. I do not know any ocean," Martín said.

"No, you me help. Chimu kill you. Spanish leave you dead."

Martín was certain between the noise echoing through the large, crowded hall and the broken Spanish, he was misunderstanding the Indian. Martín's bewilderment was evident. Young Fillipinello did not release his visual grip on Martín's face.

"When yours took us, you not stopped them. You not fight them. Chimu take you to kill you. They us take," Fillipinello said.

"I have never seen you before. I am sorry," Martín said.

One of Pizarro's attendants pulled the young Indian away and into the crowd, exiting the great hall. Martín stood frozen in place.

The crowd dispersed. The sentries stood guard with no effort to show strength. The people seemed anxious to be on to their next spectacle. They moved like a herd of sheep, the chatter among them a low hum. Martín wanted to stop, assimilate everything he'd seen and heard and compare with Faustino what they'd witnessed, but to Martín Faustino seemed distant and unresponsive.

Just over the mass of people, Martín and Faustino could see the top of a large wooden cart pulled by two massive horses as it broke through the crowd, animating everyone.

"The heretic wagon," one in the crowd said.

"A full one," said another.

"A good night for the bishop," another voice said.

"He promised we could cook dinner over the flames," someone laughed as he pushed along.

"Word was the ol' bishop lost one. Might be short a flame."

The banter continued as if the subject were something less important than human life.

Curiosity was replaced with disgust as Martín recognized the sheer disrespect for life among these people. He reflected on what Vano told him before he was taken to his death. "People are just merchandise." These people might be merchandise, he thought. I hope I am not.

A small break in the crowd revealed the convicted prisoners standing in the wagon pulled by two powerful black horses. It cut its way into the grand plaza between the cathedral and the archbishop's palace. Again, Vano's words played in Martín's head. "With help from the clergy." Everything about this felt wrong.

Martín saw Faustino straining to identify the captives in the wagon. Finally, his tense shoulders and stone face relaxed. Martín realized this whole day Faustino hadn't believed his father was killed by bandits. Now that he confirmed Vano was not among the heretics who would soon be ashes, his hope could live on.

As they got closer, however, Martín's hope died. Within the wagon, he recognized Friar Tomás. Though not draped in the Franciscan robes, his brow, his mostly shaved head, and his long bare neck were certainly those of the one man who had shown kindness to Martín. He was the man who insisted Martín learn to read and write both Spanish and Latin. He was the one who successfully taught him about the Lord Jesus Christ and the Immaculate Conception, the life of miracles, and the great sacrifice upon the cross.

Friar Tomás was now a heretic? The seriousness of the word became more real. What does that mean? Is everything he taught me false? What is real? Martín was so shaken he stopped in his tracks. The crowd kept moving. As they pushed around him, Faustino turned back and caught him by the arm and pulled him forward. Though Faustino was taller than many in the multitude, and he could easily see above others, he didn't hesitate to force himself and Martín to the front.

From the archbishop's palace, out stepped the very bishop and sheriff who made the arrest back at the Gitano camp. Following them, the inquisitor wearing a tall red hat exited the palace to their right. Martín assumed he was the archbishop. He was accompanied by a dozen or so monks in their dark brown frocks with hoods over their heads.

Armed guards pulled five men and one woman from the wagon. Martín wondered which of these six victims was the substitute for the loss of Faustino's father, Vano.

Each was tied with hands behind their backs and shackles on their feet. The crowd hushed as each was led to one of the tall wooden stakes. The woman was dressed in a long white gown, her breasts and waist covered with metal bands. The executioner secured her to the stake with chains holding her tightly upright.

With helpers, the executioner continued securing each of the five men in the same way. One of the men was mumbling to himself, his volume increasing with each effort of the executioner to secure him. The woman began to sing a morose chant that had a disturbingly melodic cadence.

Martín could hear the soft words of a prayer coming from Friar Tomás as they secured his legs, waist, and shoulders to the stake with repeated loops of a chain. His prayer didn't cease even when the chains were pulled taut.

Martín recognized that prayer, a prayer they'd turned to a song that he'd sung with the friar on countless occasions. Almost automatically, Martín began to join the friar, slowly increasing the volume. When the friar heard he was not praying alone, he squinted to discover the source. A smile reached the friar's lips before his eyes met Martín's, as he recognized Martín's voice.

Their eyes, now moist with tears, remained locked. The tender smile on Friar Tomás' face seemed to feed Martín's hungry soul. A hunger for understanding in a world too inconsistent with the kingdom on earth as it is in heaven. There was no way for young Martín to comprehend any of this.

The smile instantly fell from Friar Tomás' face. Tomás' eyes opened wide, his cheeks flexed as he watched the sheriff silence Martín's singing, striking him with the hilt of his sword. Martín crumbled. Instantly, Faustino knelt and pulled Martín from the hard rocky ground. He pulled the scarf from around his neck and tied it around Martín's bleeding brow.

Martín shook the shock from his brow and ignored the pain. With all his might, he wanted to retaliate somehow. He had stood by his whole life, never exercising any courage. Life now held no value. He'd lost everything and everyone he'd ever loved. He had nothing left. Friar Tomás again locked eyes with Martín, and the slightest shake of his head called him off. Confused more than ever, Martín nearly collapsed again.

A strong arm pulled Martín close, giving him the power to continue standing. Martín's eyes couldn't focus though they tried. It was a friar holding Martín up, his face hidden under the hood. He seemed to be looking on as others did while the bishop offered forgiveness of their damned soul if the condemned heretics would recant their heretical teaching of liberty and independence for the people.

The woman denied she was a witch. Denied she'd cursed another woman to death and taken her husband. Denied she'd bewitched and seduced a priest. The faggots were stacked high around her, and when touched by the torch, burst into flame immediately. Her loose dress burned away instantly. Martín realized the need for the metal bands around her chest and waist. The priests in their goodness protected the onlookers from watching a naked woman writhe in pain as the climbing flames consumed her body and condemned her soul to hell.

Martín couldn't fathom the reality of the cruelty. He thought he had seen the depravity of humanity when men mistreated man and beast, but these flames seared memories into his mind that he knew would never be quenched.

Two other condemned heretics begged forgiveness. The bishop sprinkled holy water and pronounced their souls clean. He motioned for the torches to begin their work of purging the sins.

Martín, in his innocence, realized quickly this was a show, a perfectly orchestrated demonstration of the power of the Church to rule the thoughts and actions of the people.

He began to understand many of the subtle teachings he'd received at the feet of Friar Tomás. If teaching liberty, or freedom of conscience, or personal responsibility made one a heretic, then indeed Friar Tomás was a heretic. Again, the questions concerning Martín's possession of sacred texts raced through his mind. If he could just ask the only friar he trusted.

Friar Tomás stood tall and proud. His black hair hung loosely over his ears. It was longer than it had been back in Trujillo. Growth of stubble on his face was another indication he'd been unable to care for himself for many days.

It seemed the bishop took great delight demanding the friar recant his teaching that God gave man a mind to use in pursuing truth, that men are children of God on earth with a purpose greater than to be mere sheep.

Rather than refusing to recant while looking at the bishop, Friar Tomás looked directly at Martín.

"What I've declared I declare. I have only taught that Jesus Christ is my Savior and your Savior, and He alone can forgive sin. Men must appeal to Him for His mercy. Men must come to a knowledge of the Christ and choose to follow Him of their own free will."

"Burn him!" shouted the bishop. The torch hit the piles of dried faggots which seemed to be hungry for the flame, for they burst into hot orange, yellow, and red tentacles, each racing to reach the friar first. Just as the dress of the woman burned away first, Thomás' long, loose shirt was consumed in an instant.

He continued, looking directly at Martín. "Though I am unworthy, I give my life that others may live. Use what I have given you to free a people from tyranny. Help God's children take the sacred words of Christ and use them as

God intended, for as Christ declared to his captors, truth will make men free."

Flames climbed higher, consuming Tomás' flesh. The smoke choked his words as they became a prayer to heaven. "God, my mighty God, take me home to thee and be merciful to…" his prayer ended.

The crowd's jeering didn't seem to cease as Tomás proclaimed words about freedom. Martín wondered if any of these people even heard what Tomás' had just said, let alone understood it. He admitted to himself that though he heard the words, he hardly understood what freedom meant. And Tomás was speaking directly to Martín. Tomás' strong, proud neck could no longer hold his head high. It slumped and Martín's mentor, his adopted father, his only conduit to God, was gone, and had given Martín a personal charge to carry on his work.

The crowd turned their attention to the next condemned man. From his pyre, the flames licked at the man's feet. The pain, sudden and intense, ripped a scream from the man's throat. His cry was heart-wrenching. The smell of charred skin filled the air, but the nauseating stench failed to turn the crowd away from their grim fascination.

"Have you seen enough?" The friar supporting Martín, now providing almost all the power to keep Martín standing, looked into Martín's wet, burning eyes. "There is work for you to do, my friend," he said, taking Martín and pulling him through a feelingless, insensitive crowd waiting anxiously for the remaining executions.

Once free of the throng of people and smoke-filled air, Martín began to collect his strength and support himself. The strange friar relaxed his grip. Faustino was right behind them as they reached a small fountain surrounded by a pool. The friar lowered the hood of his tunic and, leaning into the pool, splashed his face with water and ran his fingers through long brown hair. This was no friar Martín had ever seen. It was the wrong haircut, the wrong complexion, and the robe hung too loosely.

Martín stood motionless, watching. When the friar's short exercise in hygiene ended, he turned to Martín and Faustino and confidently introduced himself.

"Humphrey Kynaston, at your service. We have a long way to go. If you care to refresh yourselves, we will be on our way."

# Chapter Six

## The High Plains Alti-Plano Tawantinsuyu - Inca Empire

Ever so gently, the same powerful arm that swooped her off her feet and tossed her over a shoulder, laid her gently on a warm llama blanket. In the darkness, she recognized no one. It wasn't until her body began to release its shock did she recognize a voice.

"You did it. You got her." It was Cusimi.

Sarpay's mind strained to grasp the situation, but her strength was not merely spent—it had been stolen. Worn thin by grief, duty, and the relentless toll of despair, she collapsed into unconsciousness.

Several times through the night, her eyes opened and tried to fathom what happened, where she was, and what would happen next. All she knew was she was no longer with the army, and Cusimi's gentle voice revealed she was probably safe. She drifted back to sleep.

Sarpay woke to a sensation she feared might indicate she was already in heaven with the gods. Urco stood next to a petite woman who might be old enough to be Sarpay's mother. The woman's hands worked magic with Sarpay's hard, bloody, and calloused feet. Sarpay dared not interrupt the heavenly attention. Tall, soft llama slippers were pulled over her feet and up her legs. The woman laced them up her calves.

Spoon by spoon, another woman lifted a warm broth to Sarpay's lips. The rest of Sarpay's body began to experience the overwhelming release of pain, anxiety, and hunger her feet had just relished.

Cusimi helped her sit up. The brisk air of the night before surrendered to a moist, warm breeze. She recognized her small band of rescuers had moved down off the high plateaus in the high Andean mountains. The threat from Quizquiz's men would be nonexistent here. Her father's army, led by Quizquiz and Rumiñawi, failed to conquer all the people of the jungles. By aligning with the Inca and providing a level of protection and trade, many of the jungle tribes became powerful allies with the Inca. Urco's people were one of those tribes. But many others, hostile to the Inca conquest, kept the Inca armies at bay.

She had refused Urco's urgent plea to guide his people to safety in Paititi. Yet, he rescued her from the war between her two brothers. She blinked her eyes and mouthed a thank you.

"They slaughtered everyone," she said. He bowed his head.

"Our people are gathering at Picchu and will serve your father's people there. It is safe there."

Sarpay's head jerked, her eyes squinted, as she looked directly at Urco.

"No, no, no, no, no. Not Picchu." She closed her eyes. A vision of the sacred citadel located at the base of the magnificent Huayna mountain rising majestically above the Urubamba River settled in her mind.

"They must not go there!" She was frantic. She tried to stand, but the pain in her abdomen from riding a shoulder several miles kept her from standing fully upright.

"They will destroy your people. Quizquiz sent Quichamba and his men to punish the people there. They support Huascar. They will be slaughtered."

Quichamba's name alone instilled fear. He allegedly served Quizquiz and Rumañawi, but mostly he served himself and Anchanchu, the demon of the underworld. Quichamba's job was terror. His brutality was credited for the surrender of rebellious tribes. Fearing his inhumanity, whole villages submitted to the demands of Atahualpa's generals. Quichamba never extended mercy.

Cusimi, with arms holding Sarpay steady, said, "You see that in a vision?"

"I heard them talking. They will cut down all who support Huascar."

She closed her eyes again, wincing in pain. "We must get there first." Sarpay was in no condition to run or even walk at any kind of pace to overtake an army that had several days' lead.

"We will beat the army," Urco said in his native tongue. "This is my jungle." He winked at Sarpay as he slung his bow over his shoulder, his puma skin pouch still full of arrows, and gathered his people. Sarpay understood what he said, though she didn't speak his native Aymara. When her father and previous Sapa Incas conquered or negotiated a people into the Inca Empire, they were taught Quechua, the common Inca tongue.

Assimilation gradually united the empire, but each tribe mostly maintained their native languages and dialects. It would take a master linguist to converse in more than their native tongue and one or two others.

Urco offered his shoulder. She declined with a smile and a nod. "We will keep up," she said, accepting Cusimi's arm.

The group dropped deeper into the dense forest. At times there was no trail at all. Sometimes they would emerge to find long bridges, woven from natural fibers of grass and wood, suspended across deep gorges. Sarpay had crossed these bridges before but still stood in wonder how their builders could construct them. It was easy to see how an invading army would not stand a chance if they attempted an open war in these jungles.

The heat became oppressive as they progressed deeper off the high Andean plateaus into the jungles.

Beautiful parrots of countless varieties adorned the trees. She recognized several whose kind provided the adornment for Urco's headdress. He stopped at one point as the group rounded a sharp mountain path. The trail was no wider than a single person or maybe two at times. He brought Sarpay up to his side and pointed at a large cat challenging their right to be using the cat's trail. The panther crouched, held still, and stared at them. His eyes glistened as sunlight broke through the canopy of vegetation. There was no fear on either side. Sarpay noticed Urco never reached for his bow or readied his lance. The two seemed to hold each other in high regard. Finally, it leaped from the trail and disappeared into the jungle. Urco smiled at Sarpay and they continued their journey.

"We are only a few days away from Picchu. Unless we have moved far faster than Quichamba's army, I expect to find evidence they will have crossed a path or two that we will eventually need to cross," Urco said.

Evening came. After several days of living on fruits and roots, they stopped to make a fire. One of Urco's men brought a monkey he'd killed. They skinned and cooked it over a small fire. The group settled down in the hot, humid air.

"As we climb, it will get cooler," Urco said. Handing a bow to Sarpay, he asked, "Do you know how to use one of these?"

"My father's wife, your mother, brought one to the palace. When I attempted to use it, my brothers mocked me so much that I never wanted to see it again."

Though the sun was well past the ridges of the looming mountains, Urco insisted she give it a try before darkness completely set in.

Sarpay followed Urco's instruction and pulled the string back as far as she could. She glanced up for his approval and let go of the string when she read a smile on his typically somber face. The arrow sailed only a dozen feet. She saw the dismal attempt and handed the bow back.

He refused it and handed her another arrow. Again, following instructions, she pulled back as far as she could. He helped her pull it a little farther and released his grip, giving her all the tension. "Hold it right there," he said.

Her strength gave out. The arrow took flight. This time it sailed much farther. Urco's fresh smile patched her wounded pride. She held out her hand for another arrow. It was accompanied with a third smile she never believed Urco could muster.

It sailed straight into a tree and shattered when it hit. "A man's or animal's skin will not shatter an arrow. That tree is now dead," he teased as he handed her another one. This arrow disappeared into the darkness. He reached out for the bow. She handed it to him.

Early the next morning when the sun awakened the camp, Urco raised to an elbow. A soft chuckle escaped his lips. He rose to his feet, walked over, and stood alongside Sarpay. "How many of my arrows have you lost?" She looked up into his teasing eyes. She pulled the last one back and let it fly. It flew wildly, but far. She turned back to Urco. "All of them." She handed the bow back to him and returned to the others who were now getting up and breaking camp. Urco called to a handful of his men to help gather the scattered arrows. There was little time to create more while they were on the run.

# Chapter Seven

## Toledo, Spain

The three men left the crowd of grim onlookers and circled back around the palace and toward the livery where they left their horses. Martín's shock faded so slowly he numbly followed, relying on Faustino to ask the stranger donning monk's robes the many questions rising in Martín's head. Faustino seemed to have the same ones.

The cobblestone streets were now mostly clear of merchants, shoppers, and onlookers who were busy watching the executions. Another monk standing alone in the recess of a large stone building looked out of place. Smoke from the burning wafted through the stillness of the hot evening air. The monk stepped toward them as they approached. He led the very horse Faustino saddled for his father back in their camp during the arrest. Faustino stopped suddenly and pulled a long dagger from his belt. With a laugh, the monk lowered his hood. A large smile reached from ear to ear.

In three bounding steps, Faustino took his father in his arms. This new shock was enough to cripple Martín. Did Faustino know all along? How? Or was he just hopeful? Was this as much a shock to Faustino as it was to Martín? What if Faustino had been quicker with the knife? So many questions piled up, Martín was surprised this fake friar Humphrey could keep Martín steady under the weight of them all.

"Let us be free of this city." Vano took Martín's arm and pulled him down a secluded alley. They reached the livery, then quickly saddled and mounted their horses. The four men galloped through Puerta del Sol, one of the city's majestic gates built nearly a hundred years earlier. They crossed the northern bridge, the Puente de Alcántar, and headed due east, the sun long set behind them, its brilliant orange cutting through the rising smoke of the heretical sacrifices.

Free of the smoke and forced to concentrate on his horsemanship,

Martín's mind settled and cleared itself of the shock. Yet his heavy heart would never be free of the devastating loss of Friar Tomás.

Humphrey led the foursome on a magnificent black stallion. Even in the lost light of the evening, the remaining sunlight glistened off its shiny coat. As Humphrey kicked the stallion into motion, he called the creature by name, "Beelzebub, be off!" What an appropriate name, Martín thought, especially after watching such satanic acts of horrible executions.

The men rode through the night. As the sun rose, they were well out of Archbishop Deza's reach, but would never be outside the reach of King Charles or the pope.

Martín wondered if he'd ever return to Trujillo. Did Señora Lopez know? Did she know by giving him Friar Tomás' illegal texts, she had branded him a heretic? Did she know the Pizarros would track them down?

After a long dusty day, the four men finally stopped at a small, remote inn, leaving their horses in the care of a young boy who led them away to a small corral.

Humphrey pushed open the heavy inn door that looked like it had withstood the battery of an army laying siege. The innkeeper's face lit up. "Sir Humphrey, you honor me!" The bright smile seemed to light the tired spirits of this stranger Martín was eager to know. The two men took one another in a bear hug. A small cloud of dust rose from Humphrey's shoulder when the innkeeper pounded on his back.

Vano and Faustino plopped into two large chairs, setting gloves and hats on the table in front of them. Martín stared in confusion. What should be an occasion of joy was too clouded by loss and mystery.

When Vano pounded on the table next to where he sat, Martín understood and left his stupor at the door and sat down. "Martín, you've been thrown into a world that will never make sense. Of the many questions in your eyes, I can only attempt to answer one. My dear Sir Humphrey is the feared English outlaw condemned by King Henry VII and pardoned by King Henry VIII. Henry thinks Humphrey is here hunting the dangerous heretic William Tyndale."

Martín looked from Humphrey back to Vano, absorbing every word.

"If Humphrey wanted Tyndale back in England, he would be back in England," Vano said. "Tyndale would not now be safely sitting in Germany translating the Greek Bible into English."

When Vano pulled the Bible into the story, his eyes twinkled, which sent a shiver up Martín's spine. Martín knew nothing of this Tyndale Vano was talking about. Up to this part of the story, he was just another accused heretic with a tragic future.

"Martín, you are now part of an important heretical work. I don't know your part in it, but your dear friend Friar Tomás convinced me you are chosen by God and blessed by Him with great abilities in languages. You can read and write Castilian and Latin. He encouraged me to continue your education."

Humphrey pulled back a chair and sat next to Martín who opened his mouth ready to ask a question, but closed it when Humphrey placed his large hand on Martín's arm.

"You, my boy, are coming with me," Humphrey said.

Vano pulled Martín's attention back. "The question I cannot answer is why Friar Tomás refused our offer to break him free and secret him out of Spain."

This was too much for Martín's mind to comprehend. Just weeks ago, he sat alone and desperate. Now he was a fugitive traveling with outlaws and heretics who, if kings and popes had their way, would all be in flames right now.

"The cunning and intrigue go both ways. The battle is a long one. It has continued for centuries. Liberty is not free." Humphrey put his hand on Martín's shoulder, turning him to be face to face. "The power of the Church and the kings is immense, but the power of the heart is unconquerable. Though fear and hate are found everywhere, there are those yearning, who sacrifice all to help our tiny work. But God's power is in our tiny work. It was He who brought me to Toledo. I had come to seek the help of my dear friend Vano when, by such a surprise, I came upon him in the company of the bishop and the sheriff. I followed and knew there was only one way to prevent him from becoming ashes. So, I "killed" Vano, and sent the sheriff and bishop running for their miserable and evil lives. I needed witnesses that poor Vano had been sent to hell."

Martín finally asked, "You tried to free Friar Tomás, and he refused?"

The joy and the boldness of their success dampened. Vano grew sober. "I told Friar Tomás we succeeded in bringing you to our camp, along with the manuscripts he intended for you to have. It gave him great peace. That is when his resolve to give his life for Christ as a testimony against the evils of the Church became resolute."

"You brought me to your camp?" Martín asked. "It was Señora Lopez—"

Vano cut him off. "I did not send Faustino and Carmelita to Trujillo for produce. I sent them to get you."

Martín's mind was reeling.

"Tomás said your gifts with languages were more important than his life. We needed to get you out of Spain," Humphrey said. "There are some men you need to meet."

Martín squinted one eye with a slight tilt of the head. He couldn't help but think how the bishop and the sheriff need another heretic to fill their quota, and yet they let the one they lost walk in and talk to one of their condemned? It seemed incredible. Was it true?

The innkeeper brought dinner to the table, and the men ate heartily. "Where are Titzel's boys cheating the people these days?" Humphrey asked the innkeeper.

"As you move north, you will meet their band of pious thieves in the Basque Country."

"Good, we will need to get young Martín financed."

Martín stopped in mid-bite, looked up, and decided not to add one more question to the tornado swirling through his mind. There were already too many. It had been too long since his mind rested, and he didn't dare ask one more unanswerable question. He welcomed sleep.

Early the next morning, rested and fed, the men saddled up and set off toward Zaragoza. Before long, they pulled up and Vano finally set forth the plans.

"My friend Martín, though my daughter Carmelita will be sorely disappointed not to see you again, here is where we part company. God calls you another way. Sir Humphrey here was sent to recruit help for a sacred work. It is you, not me, God needs."

Martín could not believe his ears, yet the feeling Vano spoke the truth was unmistakable. How could I help in a sacred work? Is it because I can read and write? In the nearly ten years since he and his mother journeyed from Bolibar to Trujillo, he had not given the prophecy made by a strange old woman a serious thought. It was a vague memory from his childhood, but it hadn't faded completely.

The old woman had shown great kindness. He recalled the words she said to his mother.

"God told me a young boy was coming and showed me where to find you. In a vision, I saw your boy help bring the words of Christ to common people. I saw him teach in foreign tongues and in distant lands."

Just as he and his mother rode away from the old woman those many years ago, she said, "You, my dear boy, have a sacred work ahead of you." Martín didn't understand those words back then, but now the words rushed back in perfect clarity.

I am to teach in foreign lands? Now, they must get me out of Spain? Is that what she meant?

"Faustino and I will meet our people in Ávila and flee the reach of the bishop for a time. We pray for you. Remember, liberty is a sacred work, God's work. We may never see it in our lives, my friend, but in His work, you are now enlisted," Vano said.

Vano pulled from his saddlebag a leather satchel and gave it to Martín. He opened the satchel and recognized these were the sacred texts given to him by Friar Tomás. "Keep these protected and hidden. You do not want Tetzel's dogs to know you are a heretic. God will protect you." He gave Martín another kind look and, turning to Humphrey, said, "You and Beelzebub have a mission. Do not risk his life!"

"You know me," Humphrey said.

"Yes, I do, and that is why I worry." Vano turned to Martín. "May God protect you when Humphrey fails to do so." He gave a wide smile and kicked the mare. Vano and Faustino were off.

Humphrey turned Beelzebub, looked over his shoulder to confirm Martín was coming out of his stupor, and headed toward a rise in the distant woods growing along a river that worked its way off the hills. Martín gave his mount a little kick, and took one more look back toward Vano and Faustino who were now out of view. He quickly caught up with Humphrey. He had nothing to say. Events of the past several weeks made no sense to him. He wondered if it even mattered if he knew where he was being taken. They rode for most of the day through the woods and from valley to valley, passing small settlements, homesteads, and barren land.

Martín missed Vano and Faustino. Though Martín spent only a number of days with Faustino and his family, he felt more welcome with them than with this new riding companion, Sir Humphrey. And his horse was a massive beast. When they stopped to rest their horses and Martín cared for his beautiful Andalusian, he felt like the judgement of Beelzebub was upon him.

The large horse scared him. Was it his evil eyes?

Martín was happy to be back on the move. At nightfall they reached another inn and again with few words they ate, slept, and were on their way early the next morning. Two more days and nights Martín wondered if he would ever return to Trujillo. He thought back to just weeks ago, when Faustino's mother Mahala insisted he apply generous amounts of her salve to his chafing thighs. He figured he was a seasoned horseman now. He was stiff after long days in the saddle, but had no raw, worn skin. Could he possibly turn and take this horse back to Trujillo? Did he want to? Where was this journey taking him? Would he ever have the safety and security he thought he wanted within the walls of the monastery?

"Vano tells me this is home for you," Humphrey said as they slowed to enter a small town. Martín looked around. A few simple stone buildings and a quaint church built along a small river made up the whole of the village. "Vano says you are Basque and if you are indeed Martín de Ziortza-Bolibar, as you told us in the tavern, this is home."

Martín slid off his horse and led it down to the river's edge. It greedily drank. As it did, Martín looked out toward the hills. He remembered they looked like giant mountains when he was so little. They were still the tallest mountains he'd ever seen, but they didn't seem as threatening as he remembered as a child.

Martín was so young when he and his mother moved from this town and traveled to Trujillo, he struggled to recognize anything. Then, in a dim memory, he saw himself walking past the church toward the river's edge and up onto the wooden bridge. He remembered the urge to plunge in and play. He recalled the feeling of frustration, even anger, when his attempt to jump from the railing into the water was halted. His mother swooped in and caught him almost in midair as his feet left the wooden beam.

In his frustration he turned, wanting to strike her for stopping him. His mother fended off the blow with a soft, loving hand. She easily caught his fist before it could find its target. In his struggle to be free, his elbow slammed hard into her chest. The blow freed her grip on him and she crumbled to the ground in pain. She was breathless, unable even to bring herself to her knees for many minutes. He remembered the guilt he felt years later when he learned about her fight to live following what should have been a life-ending strike from a soldier's sword. That feeling of guilt never faded, though she insisted he was just a child who knew no better.

She refused to divulge the details. Martín realized now he knew almost nothing about life, especially her life. He did know about death. He walked over to the bridge. Over the years, it had been fortified with new wood and stonework. He stepped up to the place where he'd tried to jump those many years ago. That vivid memory was so real.

"We have some work to do in nearby Bilbao," Humphrey said, interrupting Martín's drifting mind.

Martín stepped off the bridge, walked back to his horse, mounted, and the two men headed west. After several more hours in the saddle, they entered Bilbao. Martín's eyes darted from Humphrey to the citizens, to the merchants, to the buildings, and back. What did Humphrey have planned?

In front of the mighty cathedral, the plaza served as the major marketplace. Stands large and small featured every kind of produce. Breads and cheeses, fruits from local orchards, vegetables, from the nearby farms. The smells and sounds were familiar to Martín, the variety similar, but it felt different. Bilbao was nestled near a bay and sat at the base of the Artzanda Mountains. The air was moist. Martín felt perspiration form on his brow even though he hadn't done anything strenuous. The humid air cradled each scent and advertised every vendor's offering like an invisible sign, which changed flavor with each merchant they passed.

Martín followed Humphrey through the crowded square. Beelzebub received the respect he had grown used to. People moved to let him freely pass. At the edge of the market stood a collection of monks attending to a crowd of peasants. Beyond them stood an elevated platform surrounded by tall red banners. The peasants seemed to be waiting their turn behind a group of lords giving particular homage to a man behind a large table elevated on the platform.

Martín's blood ran cold, yet the perspiration increased. He didn't know the man but his tall hat, rich red cloak, and his very countenance broadcast, "I am more important than you. Approach me humbly."

Humphrey stopped, letting Martín pull up alongside. "I need to give penance to the good bishop. I feel a sin coming on that will need absolution," Humphrey said.

He casually slid off Beelzebub and handed the reins to Martín. "Secure the mounts over there." He pointed to a post several yards beyond the crowd, "then come watch but stay inconspicuous. We don't want these men snooping into what you have hidden in your bags."

Martín wondered if the manuscripts he had in his bags, and

approaching the men who would certainly joy in seeing him burn, wasn't an additional source of the sweat soaking the tunic he wore under his overshirt.

By the time Martín secured the horses and attempted to blend into the crowd surrounding the large platform and table, Humphrey had worked his way to the front of the line.

"You are an Englishman. What brings you to Spain and particularly to me? Your King Henry and our dear pope are not seeing eye to eye," the bishop said.

Martín had so little knowledge of the world's stage in which he now played a part. With almost every word or deed, he felt he was being educated. Martín appreciated Humphrey's accent, and he had learned Humphrey was from England. Vano said he had even been an outlaw but was since acquitted. Humphrey admitted Henry VII condemned him for murder, but King Henry VIII himself pardoned Humphrey when he aided the king in battle. Martín hadn't yet considered how Humphrey learned to speak Spanish so well.

"My heart is impure, my lord," Humphrey said to the bishop, "I fear my temper may get the best of me. There is a man acting unjustly to the poor. Should my forbearance falter and I abuse this man and then make good to the poor for the injustices they suffer, I seek penance and absolution for this sin."

Humphrey bowed, then knelt before the bishop in such contrition Martín blinked the sweat from his eyes and refocused to assure himself this was the same bold Sir Humphrey who defied the priests in Toledo by denying them their chance to punish Vano. He was giving himself to the mercy of the Church. Martín shuddered at the realization.

The gleam in the eye and the smile on the bishop's face contradicted the holiness that should have been present at this sacred confession.

Humphrey continued, not looking up, "What may I contribute to God's church that I may be free of guilt and punishment both earthly and eternal?"

"My good English son, such absolution is not cheap. I fear you may not have the means to receive such exoneration," the bishop said in a most somber tone.

Martín was learning quickly. Humphrey's facial expressions were convincing, the humility looked real, so real, Martín wondered if Sir Humphrey's earlier disdain for the Church was turning to submission.

"Anything it takes," Humphrey said, still bowed.

Martín couldn't hear the amount the bishop whispered to Humphrey, but those close by did. The jerks of their heads and the startled faces told Martín the cost was unheard of.

Humbly, Humphrey nodded, reached inside his coat and from a black leather pouch pulled gold coin after gold coin and placed them before the bishop, whose fake stern smile couldn't resist its conversion to greedy joy.

Humphrey looked up, perceived the greed, and placed one more coin on the pile. The bishop was as stunned as Martín and all the other onlookers. Humphrey waited quietly. It took several moments for the shock to wear off before the bishop pulled a certificate of pardon from a satchel. He filled in the alleged sin and signed it with a flourish for all to witness. Martín's eyes finally blinked to bring him out of shock.

Humphrey took the certificate from the hand of the bishop, but not until he kissed the giant diamond-encrusted gold ring. "My greatest thanks to a man of God!" Humphrey said with a flourish as grand as the display from the bishop signing the pardon.

Humphrey turned with head bowed, stepped from the platform, humbly walked through the crowd, and out of the plaza. Stunned, Martín watched him disappear. Leaving his stupor, Martín raced to the horses and led them from the plaza into the street where Humphrey vanished.

"Now, we wait." Humphrey's confident voice echoed down the alley where he leaned against the faded and dirty block wall that in its prime was white. The paint was failing as fast as Martín's innocence as to the working of men.

Martín, still afraid of Humphrey, wasn't quite confident enough to beg answers. Yet, it was time to learn about his destiny, which until a few weeks ago was to live out a life of miserable, lonely poverty as a monk. Now he feared he might join Friar Tomás in sacrificing his life at the stake for the crime of learning to read the holy scriptures.

"We wait?" Martín tried to stand confidently. It was hard to keep eye contact while waiting for an answer. "You gave that bishop more gold than I've seen in my life. What could you possibly be waiting for?" Humphrey smiled and accepted the challenge.

"Come with me," Humphrey said, taking Beelzebub's reins from Martín and walking back toward the plaza. They stood at the edge of the plaza looking toward the spectacle of common peasants standing patiently in line to confess to the priest and buy forgiveness.

"Look at them, standing in the hot sun willing to give freely of their money for the promise their sins or even the sins of their dead ancestors can be forgiven. For the poor ones who cannot buy freedom from purgatory, they will pay to shorten the time they will be condemned there." Humphrey talked as he and Martín watched the crowd.

"Martín, do you believe that priest has authority to command God to forgive sins or release a sinner from purgatory?"

Martín looked up toward Humphrey who continued staring at the crowd. He contemplated for a moment. Friar Tomás received sinners' confession all the time. He had even received Martín's confessions, as innocent as they may have been. But he always felt the friar was sincere when he told him to perform some form of penance to be free of sin. Then he recalled how Jesus forgave. Wouldn't a man of God have that same authority? He looked back at the crowd and remembered how the bishop's face changed as the pile of gold grew with each fresh coin Humphrey set before him. It was a different smile than what he'd seen on Friar Tomás' face when a sinner repented.

"Where do you think all that money goes?" Humphrey asked, adding another question to the previous one still unanswered.

Martín couldn't answer either question. He searched his memory of each of the stories of Jesus. Not one included the need for money. Not once did Jesus rely on the people's money for forgiveness, or buildings, or even a roof over his head.

"No," Martín finally said. "No."

"Is that repetition or two answers?" Humphrey said.

"Two answers."

"A second no is not an answer to the second question," Humphrey said.

Martín just stared.

"Let's answer one of those questions tomorrow." Humphrey gracefully mounted Beelzebub and led him very noticeably through the square headed back toward Bolibar.

They settled into a small inn near the church next to the river. Martín found sleep easily. As he fell asleep, Humphrey reached over and pulled the German pages of the New Testament from Martín's bag. To candlelight, he read aloud. "Niemand kann zwei Herren dienen: entweder er wird den einen hassen und den andern lieben, oder er wird dem einen anhangen und den andern verachten."

# Chapter Eight

## Urubamba River – Tawantinsuyu, Peru

Urco's men reached the Urubamba River and followed it for several miles. In places, the canyon walls rose so abruptly it became difficult to navigate the rocky edges. At other times, the valley through which the river made its journey spread out, giving the river an opportunity to relax and sprawl as it pleased. At the end of one lazy valley, the canyon walls narrowed, giving the river the challenge to charge through the tight confines. The rush of water became violent. The group clung to the steep rock face as the narrow path they followed wound its way in and out of sheer stone cliffs. They rounded a bend where the heavy vegetation was less dense. A bridge suspended high above them rocked gently in the wind.

"They will try crossing there," Urco said, pointing up. "They won't. Two or three archers up there on this side of the bridge can easily keep an army from crossing. The army will be forced to descend to the river bottom and cross these waters right up there." He commanded three archers into the thick vegetation, which quickly consumed them. She recognized those three were headed up and would be defending the bridge.

Sarpay listened carefully. The noise of the rushing water swallowed some of Urco's words.

They continued forward until they reached what Urco had described as the potential river crossing point.

"We will make our stand here," he said, as several more of his men disappeared into the jungle. Urco gave more instructions to others and ushered an older warrior forward to escort Sarpay and Cusimi along with several of the other warriors up another trail. She assumed it led up to Picchu, the citadel built on the plateau below the mountain Huayna, the citadel which housed the Temple of the Sun, the temple where she could soon give her life for her people.

Sarpay bowed to Urco, who would remain with those staying to protect this river crossing. She and the others followed the ancient warrior up the rugged hillside.

The small group with Sarpay and Cusimi had one responsibility—to reach Picchu to warn and gather the local citizens, along with Urco's people who he had sent to Picchu. They were all to abandon the citadel quickly before Quichamba's men could arrive.

The group climbed through a dense section of forest where, from a clearing in the canopy, she saw Quichamba's men already preparing to cross the bridge. Urco's men were not fast enough. The army, one man at a time, would be crossing the bridge within moments. Each crossing would take several minutes, but if any of Quichamba's men crossed successfully before Urco's men were ready, the three archers Urco sent would be no match for Quichamba's killers.

Without a moment's delay, Sarpay grabbed the bow from the older warrior. Securing his sack of arrows, she bounded up the trail as fast as she could run. She reached another clearing and looked across the chasm and saw the first of Quichamba's men cautiously crossing.

Was there to be any resistance? Were Urco's men aware they were too late? Would they charge into their own deaths? Was Urco looking skyward to see his plan was failing?

She increased her speed. She knew she couldn't stop a warrior. The most damage she had ever caused was when her arrow and a tree had an argument. The tree won. But she could warn them. Could she warn them in time? She reached the summit and ran along the ridge of the mountain toward the bridge. The first warrior had already crossed the bridge. As she got closer, she saw one of Quichamba's men pull a lance from the lifeless body of one of Urco's men, who was too slow to reach the protection of the forest. "Where are the others?" she whispered to herself.

Another man reached the end of the bridge, smiling when he saw the bloody lance and Urco's lifeless warrior.

His smile turned to shock. Wincing in pain, he reached to his chest where the long arrow entered. Even from the distance, Sarpay saw where the tip protruded out his back. Another arrow followed the first, and the man with the lance dropped to his knees. Were there others? Nobody seemed to notice Sarpay, but she saw seven men at various stages on the bridge. Urco's men were not in the open. They delivered death from cover in the heavy vegetation. Yet, Quichamba's men would continue to come. They would die on this side of the bridge if they continued, or the other side at Quichamba's hand if they disobeyed his orders and failed to cross. How long could Urco's men keep this up?

Sarpay readied an arrow. If she released it, they would immediately target her. She knew her arrow would hardly pierce the thick woven armor worn by Quichamba's men.

Unlike the men from Urco's tribe who wore clothes for adornment more than protection, leaving themselves bare chested and bare legged, Quichamba's men were like all Inca warriors. They wore the standard unku, the sleeveless tunic made from woven wool or cotton. Each warrior, including the two dead ones who were first to die, demonstrated their status and region from which they hailed by the geometric patterns and symbols that were intricately decorated on their unku. Each warrior's unku was belted at the waist with a woven sash, which held their pouch containing coca leaves for stamina during long campaigns.

These men were from the northern tribes. Over their tunics, they wore the chumpi, a wide belt made of leather and adorned with metal disks that served both decorative and protective purposes. The chumpi secured an open fabric wrap that reached their knees, which allowed for ease of movement in battle.

Sarpay had never seen Quichamba's warriors in battle. She always envisioned them to be a rough collection of the worst soldiers, probably without the pride of her father's warriors. Yet, these warriors donned the mascaypacha, just as her father's warriors did. The headdress was made from brightly colored feathers and adorned with a gold and silver plate. The feathers were arranged in various fan shapes, symbolizing the warrior's bravery and rank. With these warriors' faces painted in red and black war paint, Quichamba's men took pride in intimidating their enemies before massacring them.

Two more warriors reached the end of the bridge. The first of the two took an arrow in his chest, but before he could fall, his companion reached his arms around the man and using him as a human shield, charged toward the source of the arrow. A second arrow hit the human shield, and a third. The soldiers continued forward. A third and fourth man reached land and pushed forward.

Sarpay figured Urco's men could never hold out. All was lost. More warriors were crossing the bridge. Urco had sent three of his men to this side of the bridge. The slowest one was dead and Sarpay could only guess their supply of arrows did not outnumber Quichamba's army.

As she watched the men on the bridge, Sarpay suddenly realized that despite the brilliant engineering, this kind of bridge would be unforgiving if too many men strained its lashings.

With only thirty feet to go before the next soldier reached land, Sarpay, with readied bow, lunged forward and launched her first arrow. It bounced off the lashings of the bridge several feet in front of the first man. He paused just long enough to register from whence the arrow came. A wicked smile filled his face when he recognized the threat came from the priestess, who obviously had no mastery of a bow. As more men poured onto the bridge from the other side of the canyon, Sarpay realized all she needed was to stall the progress of the men approaching her side.

Hurry was not an option for the men. Sarpay was now at the head of the bridge. Oh, what she would give for a knife. She nocked another arrow and let it fly at the leading man. He leaned quickly to the side, dodging the arrow. It struck the second man, but not hard enough to even draw blood.

The dodge, however, began the bridge rocking. The ripple of the rocking gained momentum. It multiplied as it passed from man to man, giving each a little more reason to hold tight. Sarpay let loose another arrow. This time, it flew wildly above the charging men. But it was enough to make the men slow and cautious. The first man bore down on Sarpay, his threatening eyes burning into her confidence. The bridge groaned, a groan easily heard above the rushing water a thousand feet below.

Sarpay readied another arrow. Returning the threatening stare, she let it loose, this time aimed at his feet. He easily dodged the arrow, but as the movement shifted his weight, he amplified the rocking of the bridge. Sarpay didn't see the men on the opposite end of the bridge turning quickly, trying to get off the bridge. The shift in weight created another groan, louder than the first.

One more arrow. All she needed was one more arrow. The lead soldier was only a few feet away. Then everything went sideways. A large club hit Sarpay so hard she tumbled helpless to the ground. In her fog, she thought she heard a third groan scream through the canyon. In the instant she looked up, her assailant pitched forward, tried to retreat, and screams filled her ears. What happened? She couldn't collect her thoughts. She couldn't focus. Was she dead, unconscious? Everything spun. She closed her eyes, hoping when they opened again, she might recognize reality.

When she opened her eyes, she was again being transported by Urco, this time in his arms rather than over his shoulders. It was gentle and comforting.

"Hello." The word she heard matched the movement of the powerful warrior's lips.

She blinked a few times and returned the greeting.

"Hello. Are we alive?" she asked.

"Yes, but not for long. They will be here by nightfall," he said. "You and your new weapon bought us a day. Maybe more."

"Can I walk?" she said. Not that she wasn't minding the gentle movement of his gait. He stopped and helped her down to her feet. Her head ached terribly as she tried to steady herself. She held his arm.

"What happened?" she asked.

"You saved us all. You stalled the men on the bridge. When they began dancing to dodge your arrows, it was more than the bridge wanted to endure. It snapped. At least eight men went down with it, including your first dance partner."

She rubbed her sore temple. "And this?"

"One got away from Husquo's arrow before you joined the battle and he turned on you," he said.

She squinted up into his eyes.

"My man Husquo's second arrow did not miss," Urco said. "Your attacker joined the men in the river. We must all be gone by tomorrow," he said. "I have spies watching the army. We have already started the exodus."

"But where are we going?" she asked.

"Paititi." His answer was as confident as if Paititi were his own village. Yet she knew he had no more knowledge of where Paititi was than she did.

But she was not going to Paititi. The Temple of the Sun in the Citadel of Picchu was the chosen destination for her sacrifice directed by her father's vision those many moons ago. She would give her life there. The priests to perform the ordinance might have fled and the rites might be modified to the situation, but by tomorrow, her blood would be shed as a sacrifice to appease the gods' demands. The war between her brothers would end. The plague would stop and the invasion she'd seen in her vision would never happen.

As the day progressed, Sarpay's balance improved. Finally she, Urco, Cusimi, and several of Urco's men climbed the stone stairs that led to the Gateway of the Sun, which served as an entry to the Picchu Citadel.

It had been several years since Sarpay had been to the citadel with her father Huayna Capac, after whom they named the majestic Huanya Picchu which rose like a sentinel, its rugged silhouette stark against the sky. To Sarpay it was indeed where the earthly and divine intersected. She could almost feel the presence of the ancient spirits that dwelled there watching over the sacred city.

As she stepped through the Gateway of the Sun, the world unfolded before her like a tapestry woven by the gods themselves. Below her, the sacred city lay nestled within the embrace of the towering peaks, the stone terraces cascading down the mountainside like the steps of a colossal temple. The intricate masonry carved from the bones of the earth formed a harmonious blend with the natural landscape as if the city grew from the mountain itself.

Though she had been present from time to time and witnessed how each stone was meticulously placed, she was convinced the skill and energy of their ancestors guided and strengthened the workers that had shaped them.

Directly ahead of her, the terraces of Picchu stretched out in graceful curves following the shape of the land. The fields where crops of maize and papas flourished testified of the abundance provided by the gods. At any other time, farmers would be tending to their crops, the priests would be offering rituals to ensure a bountiful harvest, and children would be playing. But not today.

Further down, the citadel's central plaza came into view, a wide-open space where the people of Picchu once gathered for ceremonies, celebrations, and markets. The Temple of the Sun, with its curved walls perfectly aligned with the solstices, stood as a focal point, its presence commanding respect and awe. This is where her mortal life would end. She would finally fulfill her father's command.

Thousands of feet below the city, the Urubamba River wound its way through the valley. The river's journey from the high Andes to the distant jungles seemed to mirror her own path, one of purpose and destiny, flowing ever forward despite the obstacles in its way.

The air was crisp and clear, filled with the scent of wet earth and wildflowers, mingling with the distant calls of birds. They were unaware of her impending sacrifice and the danger of the imminent attack from Quichamba's warriors. As she took in the view, Sarpay felt a deep connection to the land and to her people, as if the very essence of the empire pulsed through her veins. This was more than just a city; it was the heart of a civilization, a place where the earth met the sky, where the living communed with the gods.

With each breath, she absorbed the majesty of this, her father's favorite refuge, feeling the weight of her heritage and the responsibility it carried. This was her home, her legacy, a place where history and destiny converged, and she knew that giving her life would echo through the ages, just as the footsteps of her ancestors had before her.

A train of heavily loaded llamas driven by a team of herders crossed the thick grassy sacred plaza toward a path that disappeared into a forest shrouded in clouds. When Sarpay was a young girl and visited the Picchu Citadel with her father, she climbed and followed that path so many times she followed it fearlessly, even when it was so often blanketed in clouds. The path led up a pass between the Huayna and Huch'uy mountains. It then looped to the back side and wound its way deep into the cloud forests. For someone inexperienced with these dense forests, the path would be impossible to follow.

Sarpay watched another herd of llamas led toward the path. She was impressed that Urco's urgency to escape an impending attack was internalized by the people of the citadel. Peasants, nobles, and lords joined with the recent refugees of Urco's jungle tribes to coordinate the exodus.

Despite the urgency of the exodus and her sacrifice, Sarpay reflected on the richness of her empire, not just in territory but in culture. The clothing of each tribe told a story, one of adaptation to the land, of traditions passed down through generations, and of the unity that bound them all under the banner of the Inca. Though the clothing and adornments from each tribe and people varied in material, color, and design, they all shared a common thread—a deep connection to the earth and a reverence for the forces of nature that sustained their way of life.

From the people living along the coast to the people of the Altiplano and those from the jungles, the kaleidoscope of fabric and form contributed to the vast tapestry of her father's empire woven together by the wisdom of her ancestors and the leadership of her father the Sapa Inca.

Once past the Gateway of the Sun and gaining confidence in her stability, she moved quickly toward the Temple of the Sun hoping to find and stall any remaining priest or priestess who might obey her, the First Priestess of the Empire, to offer the ultimate sacrifice. She glanced inside, but the priests and priestesses had fled.

She learned the priests led the first groups into the cloud forests. Disappointed, she pushed across the sacred plaza toward the Temple of the

Three Windows. There she found Cusimi arguing with a priest, trying to convince him to follow her to the Temple of the Sun. He was not willing to go. He knew there was no time. Word was spreading that Quichamba's army breached the small band positioned at the river's edge. The army had begun the climb up from the river.

Runners quickly spread the news. Panic set the once orderly exodus into chaos. The narrow path from the citadel between the two mountains could never accommodate a rush by man and animal. Sarpay insisted the priests from the Temple of the Three Windows come and perform one more ordinance. Despite her being the First Priestess of the Empire, dedication to the gods surrendered to fear and panic.

A second runner charged through the main gate and, spotting Urco, ran directly toward him. After a few quick words, the runner dashed from one side of the crowded plaza to the other. Urco's small band of warriors, who'd been doing everything possible to keep order with the mass exodus, assembled.

"It must be you," Sarpay demanded. "Come with me now." Sarpay took Cusimi's arm and nearly dragged her across the crowded and chaotic plaza toward the Temple of the Sun. They crossed the threshold and entered.

The air inside the sacred temple was thick with the scent of burning incense left unattended when the priests and priestesses fled. Cusimi, though not a priestess, felt the weight of unspoken prayers. She respected the rites and honored the rituals, but in her heart she couldn't accept the divinity of the Sapa Inca, that he who ruled was more than a mere mortal. Cusimi was the daughter of a noble from a Chimu tribe. As a young girl, her father gave her to Huyana Capac, the Sapa Inca, to serve the First Priestess in her sacred duties. Her father hoped one day she would be given the great honor of becoming a capacocha. If his daughter could serve the gods as a child sacrifice, her father believed he would win favor with not only the mortal god, the Sapa Inca Huayna, but with Inti, the God of the Sun, and Viracocha, the Creator God.

Cusimi had helped Sarpay prepare the young capacochas on several occasions, repulsed each time as she saw the innocence and purity of the young children whose lives would be taken to appease or please some unknown god. She never feared becoming one of them and giving her own life. She had long proven her capacity for trouble. Yes, according to Sarpay, she maintained her purity, but her lack of faith and her belligerent denial that man was God kept her just outside the reach of child sacrifice worthy. Now that she was a fully developed woman in her late teens, it was her downright dangerous ability to defend herself against the unwanted advances of even formidable soldiers that kept her close to Sarpay. The First Priestess loved her and now needed her more than ever. Cusimi knew she had the skill and power to carry out this sacred sacrifice. The intensity of Sarpay's belief and conviction that indeed this was demanded of the gods almost convinced Cusimi to believe it true.

Though it was past midday, sunlight penetrated the sacred space. The golden tapestries carved with images of the ancestors brought with them a darkness befitting a blood sacrifice. She imagined what it would be like at Inti Raymi, the Festival of the Sun, when the Inca celebrated the shortest day of the year, and this room was lit with direct blinding sun. She would never know. It would be forbidden for her to enter this temple. Without Sarpay's command, she would not be here now.

At the center of the chamber, the sacred altar loomed—a massive slab of polished stone, cold and unyielding. Upon it lay Sarpay, her body now adorned in a simple white drape. There was no time for ceremonial vestments. Gold bracelets she had hidden from Quichamba's soldiers encircled her wrists, and the royal delicate necklace of turquoise beads Quichamba permitted her to keep rested against her chest, rising and falling with each measured breath.

Cusimi knew Sarpay had been prepared for this, had accepted her fate, but still, a deep, primal fear gripped Cusimi's heart. It wasn't death that frightened her; she knew death. She witnessed death her whole life. It was the unknown that lay beyond. She feared the uncertainty and the darkness that would envelop her the moment the sharp obsidian knife in her hand pierced Sarpay's chest.

A coolness drifted through. She could see a thin sheen of sweat on Sarpay's face, neck, and bare arms. The tension made Cusimi's pulse quicken.

"I am ready," Sarpay whispered. Her voice was barely audible above the panicked commands and commotion out in the citadel. Cusimi had grown up with Sarpay; she felt she knew every emotion. She recognized a strength in Sarpay's words. There was resolve. How could she be so firm in her belief that her blood would ensure the salvation of the empire? Cusimi wished Sarpay might long to live, to feel the warmth of the sun on her skin. It seemed the air was cooling inside the temple.

Cusimi's hands trembled as she held the ceremonial knife. The blade carved from obsidian was sharpened to perfection. Cusimi's eyes were wide, filled with a mix of sorrow and disbelief. She had not been chosen to perform the sacrifice—a priest or priestess had this duty. How could she take the life of the one she had grown up with, the one she had shared every secret, every dream, every fear with?

Sarpay turned her head, her eyes pleading for Cusimi to plunge the knife and halt the destruction of her people.

The weight was too much for Cusimi. She feared her heart pounded so loudly it would echo through the temple. Cusimi's hand tightened around the hilt of the knife. She stepped closer. The coolness of the temple pressed against her and seemed to invite the blood. She felt the weight of the gods upon her. Were they watching? Were they waiting? Were they demanding? Then her own emotions asked, "Do they care?"

As she raised the knife, a sudden warmth flooded over her. Was it a sign of approval or rejection? She was not a priestess. She was not to be in the temple. She was not authorized to perform such a sacred ceremonial sacrifice. Was anyone on earth authorized to take the blood of the firstborn?

Sarpay closed her eyes. Cusimi saw a single tear slip down Sarpay's cheek. It landed and glistened on the golden covered stone altar.

Cusimi hesitated, the knife hovering above the First Priestess of the Empire's chest. The moment stretched, each heartbeat a painful eternity. The warmth in the temple became suffocating. Where was the coolness of just minutes before?

Then, with a shuddering breath, Cusimi brought the knife down.

"Not today." Urco snatched the knife from Cusimi and dropped it to the ground.

"I will take your life myself when the time comes. Until then, my gods need you more than your gods need you."

He pulled Sarpay off the altar and stood her on her feet. Her shock disabled any response. She stood motionless. Cusimi was seconds too late.

"They overpowered my men at the river. Our defense at the gate will last only minutes more. You must lead the people through the cloud forest! Once we get these people to safety, I will perform the sacrifice."

Sarpay wanted with all her being to force Urco to obey her command to take her life right there. Was she afraid of him? Was she afraid to die? Was she afraid of the gods? She was so overcome with Urco's demand and her failure, she couldn't form the words to protest.

Cusimi pulled Sarpay from the temple. Urco, Cusimi and Sarpay ran across the sacred plaza and into the pass. Once Sarpay fought her way to the front of the caravan, the speed of the exodus doubled and tripled. Her presence and support of the directions given by Urco's men instilled confidence and trust in the fleeing residents. Confusion seemed to vanish.

Sarpay's heart, which she wished to have sacrificed only moments before, was shattered. She had been prevented from fulfilling the single most important duty she had ever been given. If she could hate, she would hate Urco for stopping Cusimi. She would hate Cusimi for not being faster with the sacrificial knife. She would hate Rumiñawi, Quizquiz, and Atahualpa for destroying an empire. She would hate herself for failing her father and angering the gods. But she did not know how to hate.

Where could she lead these people where they would be outside the reach of the war? Urco's people in the jungles were friendly to Huascar and now enemies to Atahualpa's armies, but without the presence of her father's former protection, they were under threat by the Shuar tribes as well.

Never had she considered she would be leading a small community of her father's people to safety from the ravages of a civil war.

The cloud forest was always magical to Sarpay. The constant heavy mist around the treetops filtered the sunlight and provided ample moisture to the prolific plant life. As the caravan descended into the forest, the humidity which provided for the dense plant life also added to the slipperiness of the stone path. Throughout the empire, a great network of stone paths connected each of the four quarters of the Tawantinsuyu Empire. Though Sarpay had not followed this path farther past where it met the Urubamba River, she knew it followed the river until it divided, with one branch leading back up toward Cusco and the other branch dropping off into the jungles.

She knew another holy temple secluded deep in the Antisuyu jungle would provide her next opportunity. She felt The Sun Temple in Cusco would be closer but not safer. Premonition told her Quichamba and his army anticipated that her escape route would lead them back around and up to the southern capital. She also didn't know how soon Quizquiz's army would meet Huascar's army in Cusco.

Her only choice would be north toward the remote refuge of Chuqip'allta on the northeast slopes of the empire, where nobles often retreated to the palace of Vitcos. Her only risk would be any Cañari or Shaur they might meet. Though conquered by her father, both peoples refused Inca control. Should she meet either, there would be lives lost.

They broke through the dense clouds and dropped down along the river. The thick ferns which crowded the trail through their journey off the mountain gave way to prolific bright red orchids blanketing the hillside. With visibility now unhindered, Sarpay gave direction to Cusimi, who was with a team of shepherds leading the first pack of llamas. She led them north, deeper into Cañari and Shaur territory.

When the last of the exodus cleared the clouds and reached the river, Sarpay searched for Urco and his men. They were not there. She waited longer than she felt she should before trying to catch up to the exodus. She was on her own, now leading his people—victims of the Shaur, and her people, supporters of Huascar and enemies of Atahualpa, being hunted by the butcher Quichamba.

If they were successful in reaching Vitcos, she would sacrifice her life there. If they weren't, her life would have been taken by her enemies. She knew if her life were taken, it would not be considered a worthy sacrifice by the gods; it must be given. She and these people must reach the safety of Chuqip'allta and the Yurak Rumi.

With what she'd understood from conversations with other priests and priestesses, she felt if she were alone, she could reach Vitcos within four or five days. But leading several hundred refugees and hundreds of pack animals, she feared they would be vulnerable for several weeks trekking up and over snow-capped mountains and down deep gorges.

On the fourth day, the caravan reached what was once a friendly village. Where once stood finely crafted homes, built from stone and sod, smoke rose from remnants of the thatch roofs. Carefully cultivated fields, though not large, lay stocks of maize stomped flat. Beautifully woven fabrics which protected common areas were now burned away, exposing the bloody bodies that lay scattered throughout the village.

"Cañari."

Sarpay and Urco's captain stood next to the village chief, lying on his back. Dark pools of drying blood surrounded his head, which was nearly severed. It was the lance protruding six feet out of his chest adorned with the feathers of the macaw, native to the northern jungles, that gave Urco's captain his claim the attack was made by the Cañari. He pulled the lance free.

"They left the lance as their signature and warning," he said.

"Where are they now?" Sarpay asked. "They must know we are here."

"They do," he said.

"Why are we still alive?" she asked.

"You." He looked straight into her eyes.

She tilted her head, squinting up into his.

"You escaped Quichamba," the captain said.

"You said these are Cañari."

The captain lowered the top of the lance. Where the brightly colored macaw feathers adorned the deadly staff, he pointed to a golden ring that capped the top.

"These Cañari are traitors to their own. They kill for profit. They kill for amusement. These here, they killed for Quichamba," he said.

"What are they waiting for?" she asked.

"They thirst for terror. Death is only sweet to them if the prey is in fear. The fear they instill is much of the reward."

She ran her fingers over the gold band. She pulled it off and looked closely at the engraving. She recognized Quichamba's seal.

"So Quichamba did not pursue us because he has these Cañari in the jungles?" she practically whispered the words to herself. "Urco and his men never joined us," she said, not looking up.

The captain confirmed her conclusion. "Urco held Quichamba's army back. They have not caught up with us either."

An arrow ripped into the captain's shoulder, knocking him to the ground. She turned sharply toward the direction from where the arrow came. Wearing only a small puma skin around his waist, a powerful warrior stood at the edge of the forest. A tall lance in his left hand was decorated identically to the one the captain had just pulled from the village chief's chest. His other hand held the bow she assumed was the source of the arrow in the captain's shoulder.

His piercing black eyes bore into Sarpay. Not one of the several hundred people she'd just led into this death trap moved. The silence was surprising to her. Without even moving her head, her eyes scanned the edge of the trees. Warriors lined the forest's edge. With the intricate detail of the white paint on their faces, she recognized the intent of this war party. There was no interest in prisoners. Noting the golden band on the lance, she knew she might be the only exception. They would trade her for some favor only Quichamba could provide.

The warrior took one step toward her. He dropped to his knees, then to his face, an arrow protruding from the base of his head.

The shock was enough for both victims and warriors—hunters and prey.

Sarpay reached down and took the bow from the captain lying on the ground, snatched an arrow, and readied to send it flying. But where to?

# Chapter Nine

## Ziortza-Bolibar - Spain

Martín woke abruptly and wiped his eyes clear. Through a sliver of moonlight, he noticed Humphrey's bed was empty. He sat up, walked to the door, opened it slightly, and looked for light. There was none. He returned to bed, but curiosity refused him sleep. Sleep eventually conquered. When he woke, he realized Humphrey's bed had seen no use through the night. It was still empty. Martín made his way down the stairs to the dining hall. As he reached the bottom, he heard a commotion in the small courtyard outside. He went to the door and saw Humphrey dismount from an exhausted Beelzebub. Humphrey dusted himself off and came toward the door. Martín quickly hurried to the table and sat down.

"Morning," Humphrey said as he joined Martín.

He avoided direct eye contact with Martín, but signaled for breakfast. He ate ferociously.

"Today, Martín, you will replace one of yesterday's no's with a yes." Humphrey got up and walked up the stairs, where he climbed into bed, immediately falling fast asleep.

Humphrey's sudden departure left Martín in his own confused thoughts. No other guests stayed at the inn, so except for the innkeeper offering more to drink, nothing more was said.

Martín returned upstairs a couple of times throughout the morning, only to still find Humphrey asleep. He went out to the barn and brushed down Beelzebub. His initial fear of the beast had lessened, but the respect remained. As he groomed him, the horse received the care with gratitude.

During the years he'd helped his mother with the monastery's horses in Trujillo, he'd learned to recognize horses felt, thought, and recognized care. Martín wondered how hard or how far this poor animal traveled during the night.

It was nearly midday when Martín left the barn and headed toward the inn. A cloud of dust followed a group of men on horseback charging into the courtyard disrupting the quiet still air. Martín recognized a few of the men from the plaza, still in their monk's cloaks. The man in the lead had to be the sheriff and with him, three other men armed with swords.

"You! We are here to arrest your partner. Stand aside or we will take you as well," the sheriff said.

The sheriff dismounted. Martín was shocked to watch Humphrey enter the courtyard. "What is this?" Humphrey asked the sheriff, "You have no claim on me. I am an innocent man."

"Come with us, peaceably. We are enough to take you and, as you are unarmed, you know what I say is true." The men on horseback worked their way back around to flank Humphrey. Humphrey stepped away from the inn far enough for the men to easily surround him. Two men entered the inn and moments later exited with Humphrey's saddlebags in hand. They handed them to the monks.

"Humphrey, what are you doing?" Martín mumbled to himself. "You and Beelzebub could easily elude these men."

Martín watched, bewildered that Humphrey put up no resistance. Humphrey calmly approached the sheriff with both hands held up to be tied. Behind one monk was a saddled but riderless horse. The sheriff led Humphrey to it where, even with tied hands, he easily mounted.

"When is my trial?" Humphrey asked, loud enough to ensure Martín heard.

"Tomorrow at the Bilbao Cathedral Plaza. The good bishop is eager to be in Madrid. You delayed his journey, and he wishes to see you tried quickly."

No accusation? Martín wondered. It is as if Humphrey and the sheriff both knew Humphrey's alleged crime and it had to do with the bishop. Humphrey urged his horse up past Martín and, in what Martín assumed was Humphrey's native English, still foreign to Martín, gave instructions as they led Humphrey away.

Martín watched in confusion as the men escorted Humphrey from the inn. I don't know English. What did he say? What is the meaning of those foreign words? Was Humphrey confused? Was he drunk? He stood confounded at the scene of his companion led away by the sheriff, several deputies, and four monks.

Yet those English words would not remain in his memory long. He had to note them down, even if he could not understand them.

Martín returned upstairs to the room. He sat on the bed and pondered. As he sat and confusion turned to frustration, his focus eventually turned to the small table against the wall. On it were a large parchment, a quill, and a bottle of ink.

How strange, he thought. That wasn't there earlier. He stood and stepped over to the small table. He read the words written in Castilian: "Martín, do as I told you. I have confidence you will understand. You are gifted by God and called by Him to bring His word to the world. He and I need you."

"Understand?" Martín mumbled, "Understand? Understand what? Gibberish? I do not understand! You spoke in a language I do not know!" His mumbling grew into forceful words. He rubbed his hands over his brow, trying to get it to understand. This made no sense to him. "You planned this, or at least expected it." Martín sat back on the bed, thoughts racing. "Why did you expect to get arrested and then rely on me to do something told to me in a foreign language?" He opened the large window. Everything out in the courtyard was quiet. He went downstairs.

All afternoon, he repeatedly walked from the inn to the stable and back upstairs. He sat and thought. Suddenly, his eyes widened. Over and over, he read the words written along the top of the large parchment.

"Martín, do as I told you. I have confidence you will understand. You are gifted by God and called by Him to bring His word to the world. He and I need you."

Why had he not seen it? He shook his head in disbelief. A grin of disgust joined his shaking head as his eyes lifted to the heavens.

He took the quill and wrote as best he could the instructions given to him hours earlier as the sheriff led Humphrey from the courtyard. He then tried to read the words. They were more sounds than words when Humphrey said them. Martín tried to parse the sounds into words he thought he could remember. But they had no meaning. He voiced the sounds he had written, hoping they might be recognizable.

"Occultatum debajo matelas indulgencia pretiosa protect it llévelo con usted et Beelzebub a procès revelare when dicho prepare us dos Spain leave."

Again and again he vocalized. But no meaning emerged.

His memory was a good one, but Martín was certain there were sounds left out. But he thought he knew what he had to do. He had to learn

English today.

When his eyes returned to the page, he realized the words he wrote were not all English. He made out a blend of words, both familiar and foreign. "Is this English?" he said, "How strange. Is English simply a language borrowed from others?" Lazy Englishmen. He thought.

His eyes returned to the personal note written by Humphrey. It was clearly written in Spanish. Then he read aloud the words he tried to remember, spoken by Humphrey to him in the courtyard. No, even if Martín transcribed them wrong, there were at least three languages represented here. He began putting the words together. Mixing the Latin words with the Spanish words, if he remembered and noted them down correctly, he guessed at various possibilities that may have a basis in the Latin. Finally, he had a message that might be correct. It would be easy enough to prove.

A smile conquered the battle between frustration and despair. Martín understood.

"Hidden under the mattress is the indulgence I so expensively bought. Protect it. Bring it with you and Beelzebub to the trial. Reveal it when I tell you to. Be prepared for the two of us to leave Spain."

He knew Latin. The Spanish words were only variations of the Latin. The remaining words, whether English, French, Italian, or Greek, mattered not. He knew exactly what to do to prove or disprove his conclusion. He went over to the mattress, lifted it, and retrieved the large parchment printed so majestically and signed by the bishop himself. Martín's mind began putting puzzle pieces together. He realized and feared what was about to happen.

He read the message again and again. The trial was tomorrow. He would be ready.

Humphrey's bedroll also lay alongside the bed. It was evident the sheriff's men had already rummaged through it. They had searched for the indulgence. Not finding it, they left the bedroll and its contents scattered on the floor. Martín picked up its contents: a knife, dried meats, stockings, etc. Tucked behind the indulgence under the bed, he pulled out the pages Friar Tomás gave him through Señora Lopez just weeks earlier. Martín's smile carried both a sense of relief and fear. The men were looking for the indulgence, not this piece of evidence that could convict Humphrey of heresy. That evidence would convict Martín, if anyone found him in possession of these most sacred but illegal documents.

Yet he settled back and searched for the verses Friar Tomás had so many times repeated concerning Martín's duty to God. He read, "And he said unto them, Go ye therefore, and teach all nations, baptizing them in the name of the Father, and of the Son, and of the Holy Ghost: Teaching them to observe all things whatsoever I have commanded you: and, lo, I am with you always, even unto the end of the world. Amen."

Martín reflected on the scene from Toledo where Tomás cried out, condemning the clergy and calling Martín to do something about liberty. The words "I am with you always, even unto the end of the world," played over and over in Martín's mind. Where was God the Father when Friar Tomás needed him? Though Martín knew how to pray and prayed always, he could not resolve to fall on his knees and ask that question again. By nightfall, he was too mentally exhausted to think and too worried to sleep. He was grateful for the restless night to end.

As the sun broke over the distant hills, Martín carefully folded the indulgence and tucked it safely under his coat. He hid the sacred texts that could so easily condemn him to the pyre into a small blanket and tied it to his saddle. Then, Martín urged his horse from the stable. With Beelzebub's reins tied to his saddle, he left Bolibar and headed west to Bilbao.

Now on his own, entrusted with an important responsibility, a responsibility he had never experienced before, he struggled to understand the weight on his shoulders. This was new. He didn't know if he liked it. Yet he felt a sense of freedom, pride, power, a power that melted into worry. No, I don't like it, he finally conceded.

Feelings of inadequacy ran through him again and again. Those feelings fought against the sensation of being needed, being depended upon, being important. Somebody needed him. Someone trusted him. A person he met only several days earlier depended on him and believed in him. That somebody was brave. And though his only reassurance that this somebody was trustworthy came from Vano, a Gitano he had only known for a short time as well, Martín knew this was right. But could it be possible God had work for an orphaned peasant, with no more skill than to clean stables and feed herds of swine? But I can read. That thought shot through him so fleetingly it disrupted his self-deprecation.

The sun was now rising behind him. His heels tapped the horse, and it went from a casual trot to a gallop.

As Martín entered the great square in Bilbao, he led the horses around its perimeter, looking for a secure place to leave them tied up. A crowd was gathering around the large platform where just two days earlier Humphrey, along with countless others, gave hard-earned money to buy forgiveness for themselves or loved ones both dead and living.

That thought still struggled to find peace in Martín's mind. How could this bishop, dressed in the finest robes, surrounded by numberless attendants, parade across the country and extort money from the hungry, struggling peasants, as well as rich landowners, and nobility, and even men like Humphrey, who Martín suspected to be nothing more than a brilliant highwayman. Yet from peasant and clergy alike, Martín heard said over and again, "When in the coffer the coin rings, out of purgatory, the soul springs."

How could this bishop reach past the veil of death and offer forgiveness to the living and the dead?

Friar Tomás never justified indulgences to Martín, yet he had never seriously condemned them either. Until this moment, Martín hadn't seriously pondered the exact crime that cost Friar Tomás his life. Martín knew Friar Tomás believed the people needed to have access to read the scriptures themselves. Why else was he so insistent Martín learn to read and write Latin? Learning to read and write Spanish made sense, but the scriptures were only available in Latin, so why insist Martín learn to read and write Latin if it wasn't to study the Bible on his own?

But what was Humphrey's crime? Martín pulled out and read the indulgence several more times before tucking it safely away. It said nothing about heresy. It was about forgiveness for losing his temper, harming and robbing a man. A crime he was yet to commit. Then, as he secured Beelzebub's reins to a post, he saw it: a small bag of coins tucked carefully in a small pouch sewn into the back of the saddle.

Martín's eyes shot wide. Humphrey was a highwayman. While he was out the other night, he was robbing. This Humphrey was no more than a robber, a thief. He was going to use Martín in his crime. Martín's stomach churned. The thought of Humphrey's betrayal to Vano and pretending to escort this innocent boy on a journey for God made him sick. His hands trembled as he finished securing the horses to a post behind a shop that faced the plaza. He looked up into Beelzebub's eyes. Of course, a robber and thief would name his horse after the devil himself.

Yet, Vano had so much confidence in Humphrey. They had done some great things together, it was clear. But Vano's apparent piety and his hoarding of both Latin and German language Bibles was a ruse. Was Vano nothing more than a heretic who hid behind the facade of piety?

Martín believed Vano loved and respected Friar Tomás. At least he led

Martín to believe he did. Why did Vano escape the fire but Tomás burned? Why did the Church want Vano?

Too many questions. Why did Friar Tomás give Martín the scriptures? Why did Humphrey make sure Martín had them in his own possession? Of course, to ensure Martín was an accomplice, so Martín couldn't run without becoming a fugitive all alone in a strange land.

But could God really have a plan for Martín? Does God use outlaws in His work? Is the Church His work? Did Friar Tomás deserve to die as a heretic? Or was he a martyr? Martín had no one he could trust to answer that question.

He would talk to the bishop. Certainly, the bishop would know what Martín should do.

Friars, monks, priests, and bishops, each in their various cassocks, left the cathedral and marched to the platform which just days earlier served as the post of indulgences. Over the bishop's cassock, the full-length white cape of his white ferraiolo reached his ankles where it contrasted the bright red lining that shone brightly each time he moved. Martín counted the thirty-nine buttons which adorned the friars' and priests' ankle-length brown cassocks. Martín tried to remember if the red buttons belonged to the priests or the friars. The monks in their humble robes looked out of place. He only knew Friar Tomás' brown woolen robe had no adornment to draw attention. He smiled, thinking how the thirty-nine buttons represented the forty lashes minus one from the ancient rabbinical law. Martín pondered withholding the indulgence just to see how many lashes Humphrey's crime earned.

The sheriff, accompanied by two rows of armed men, swords at the ready, rounded a corner and entered the square, a dangerous prisoner between them. The crowd's attention left the men of the clergy who arranged themselves in two rows on each side of the bench Martín assumed would seat the judge in this trial. As the sheriff's column approached, onlookers stretched, moved, and shuffled to see the man accused of an unforgivable crime.

Whispers, not so quiet whispers, worked their way through the crowd. Murder, rape, robbery, drunkenness; all accusations assumed by the people. What about heresy? Martín wondered.

When the sheriff's column reached the platform, the crowd closed in around the platform. Martín edged his way close enough to hear the proceedings. When he got into a position where he could both see and hear, he saw a stout, dark-haired man sat confidently with his arms resting on a small table placed before him. Hair trimmed short, parted in the middle and each one in place as if obedient to the very respect this man demanded, accentuated his pale complexion. His cloak was jet-black in contrast to the shades of brown of the ecclesiastics.

The striking scene seemed like a staged theatrical pageant Martín had only heard people talk about. He realized the bishop planned every detail of this show to instill a fear of justice.

The sheriff's men stepped back, leaving Humphrey standing alone six feet before the judge. The crowd hushed, everyone eager to hear the proceedings. "Sir Humphrey Kynaston, they have accused you of attacking the good bishop, severely beating him and robbing him of the sacred donations gathered in the pope's name, donations given to secure the redemption for many of these before whom you stand today."

Martín expected the charge of robbery, but rob the bishop? Martín's eyes opened wide. Then he wondered how much of this rehearsed accusation was provided by the bishop himself. Did the bishop and the judge conspire to guarantee a guilty verdict?

The judge continued. Though he was not reading from a script, it was evident to Martín his statement was well prepared. "Citizens, both rich and poor, receive forgiveness of sins both grave and minor, both for the living and the dead, through the penance required by God as proclaimed by His holy servants, the bishops."

The judge lifted his arm and motioned to the bishop sitting apart from the other clergy on the stand. The bishop positioned himself for the crowd to see him clearly. His bruised face, lacerated cheek and bandaged forehead brought a gasp from the crowd. Even Martín took a deep breath when he recognized the damage Humphrey was being accused of inflicting.

Martín looked from the bishop to Humphrey and back to the bishop. What Humphrey did disgusted Martín. The charges were correct. He knew it. His hands unconsciously entered his coat and fingered the parchment folded there. He realized Humphrey depended on this trick to receive any kind of leniency. If I turn around right now and walk away, Humphrey will get just what he deserves. He moved to do just that, but with one glance back at the platform, he saw Humphrey staring directly at him. Their eyes caught, and Martín couldn't look away. Finally, his eyes drifted from Humphrey to the bishop, willing Humphrey's eyes to follow. Humphrey nodded ever so slightly, confessing to Martín of the crime.

There was no remorse in Humphrey's eyes. His face was triumphant.

Martín squinted, trying to read more from Humphrey's expression. The confidence unnerved Martín. He caught himself taking quick breaths, which he realized was his custom any time his fear took control. In his uncertainty, he began looking around, from the crowd to the judge to the bishop and back to Humphrey. Humphrey was now turned toward the judge as he continued his accusation.

"How do you plea?" asked the judge in triumph, having delivered more a sermon for the bishop to promote the importance of these sacred holy indulgences than an accusation of a crime. A sermon Martín mostly missed because of the battle waging between his heart and his head.

"I plead guilty!" Humphrey said. He said it so boldly the breath taken in by the crowd could have pulled clouds from the sky. There were, however, none. The sky was clear, blue, and hot.

The bishop stood triumphantly. He had won. The Church had won. The people had won. God had won and the devil lost.

Along with the rest of the crowd, who now breathed again, Martín stood in shock. Of course, he was guilty, but now what?

"May I address the court, your eminence?" Humphrey asked the judge, bowing in respect and submission.

The judge nodded his permission.

Humphrey took a step forward, bowed, and respectfully addressed the judge, but looking toward the bishop said, "This fine bishop and his holy men have traveled far to serve God in His holy work of salvation. They have sacrificed to provide these fine citizens…" his attention which was previously directed at the bishop and the other clergy, now turned to the crowd of people so it was as if he was addressing them, "…the hope that brings peace into their lives. The peace they deserve to know God has accepted their sacrifice and at the drop of the coin, sins both theirs and of their loved ones are now forgiven. These good people who have given so freely are forgiven of their trespasses against one another and against God, by this good bishop." He paused to give the crowd that peace.

"My sins, however, are now in a unique position. As many of you know, I too knew I depended on the mercy and forgiveness guaranteed by paying a penance for my sins. A sizable payment. A generous payment required by this very good bishop." He pointed back, acknowledging the bishop. Martín watched as the color drained from the bishop's face.

No, Martín could not walk away and leave the guilty to suffer his fate.

An unseen power moved him. He reached into his coat and began inching through the crowd toward the platform. Humphrey watched his every step. The tiniest smile snuck through the sober confession. Humphrey's lecture did not stop.

"Knowing the fallen man that I am, I knew the gold and silver was too much a temptation for a wretched man like me. I even refrained from the drink, trying to bolster myself against the temptation. Yet, I failed."

The crowd was silent. Each seemed to relate to the feelings of despair people feel when they recognize their weakness when faced with temptation.

Martín followed Humphrey's eyes as he looked around the crowd and to those on the platform, ending on the judge.

"Your eminence," Humphrey said looking directly at the judge, "knowing my weakness and knowing the grace and mercy afforded by our Savior Jesus Christ, and knowing the justice and honor provided by His chosen servant, the bishop here, I submit to you the holy pardon given me and duly signed by the bishop himself."

Humphrey knelt in reverence to the judge. The bishop's once pale face and wide eyes turned red; veins bulged with anger. Martín looked from the bishop to Humphrey, kneeling submissively. Martín approached Humphrey, uncertain if he needed permission. Half expecting to be stopped by the sheriff or one of the monks, Martín pulled the indulgence parchment from his coat and looked to the judge for permission to approach. A slight nod gave him courage to hand the parchment to the judge. He quickly withdrew back into the crowd where he felt he could hide. Having the eyes of everyone on him was unnerving. He caught himself breathing short, quick breaths.

The judge unfolded the parchment. Slowly reading each word, his lips betrayed him. As his lips mouthed the words, a smile grew. At one point, his eyes left the parchment. Without even moving his head, his eyes looked toward the bishop. The smile grew. He read again, this time not hiding his amusement. He turned his head to the bishop, whose anger and hate now blended with embarrassment begging for justice.

The judge motioned for Humphrey to stand. He did. Then the judge motioned for the bishop to do likewise and invited both of them to approach the small table. He turned the parchment toward the bishop.

"This is your signature?" he said, pointing to it. The bishop nodded.

"Sir Humphrey Kynaston, you are free to go. This good bishop in his benevolence and in the Holy Name of Jesus Christ gives you full pardon and forgiveness." The judge winked at Humphrey. Humphrey bowed to the judge, then to the bishop. He turned and walked humbly across the platform. He spotted Martín. The crowd parted. Martín stood motionless.

Humphrey put his arm around Martín. "I knew you would know what to do. I bet my life on you."

Martín looked up in amazement.

"Now let's get you to France," Humphrey said as they reached the horses. It was as if Beelzebub knew what had just taken place. He looked Martín in the eyes with an eerie glint of approval.

 Martín followed in silence, his thoughts unsettled. There was no doubt Humphrey outsmarted the old bishop, but he'd done nothing different from the man than take advantage, bully, and rob the Church of the money poor people paid in penance for sin.

Martín had experience with bullies. He suffered at the hands of the Pizarro brothers. He hated how cowards used physical superiority with such disdain for others. Humphrey was just a big, proud—but smart—bully. He knew how to get away with it. Even Beelzebub seemed proud.

What would the bishop do now? Did Humphrey rob him of all the penance money? Martín wondered where the money was. He packed the horses and knew they did not have the money. The few coins hidden in the saddle were certainly too meager to be it.

He also wondered if the crowd, once the shock wore off, would start wondering about the forgiveness they purchased now that the purchase price was in the hands of the clever yet forgiven highwayman.

If Humphrey had the penance money, would the sins remain forgiven?

These thoughts and many others so clouded Martín's mind as he did nothing but follow Humphrey and Beelzebub up and over hills, through valleys, and down to a small peninsula jutting out into the sea. How long had they been riding?

Martín pulled in a breath. It was the first time he'd ever seen the ocean. White waves crashed against the rocks. His mind had been so busy trying to understand the previous several days he had not paid attention to where they were going. It was afternoon, and the sun was high in the sky beating down on the craggy coastline.

Martín didn't realize they'd stopped. The scene captivated him. Finally, he closed his mouth, his breathing slowed, and he looked over to Humphrey sitting next to him on Beelzebub, enjoying the shock and wonder Martín was experiencing.

"I remember vividly the first time my father took me to the ocean." Humphrey's tone was calm, considering the moment. "I was younger than you are now. My father was the high sheriff in Shropshire. The first time our family went to the sea, it amazed me as it does you now."

The scene erased Martín's concerns, or at least pushed them to the side for the moment.

"Follow me. I think I can answer a few of the questions your poor little mind has been grappling with these past several hours." Humphrey pulled Beelzebub around and headed down the coastal path. As they neared the sea, their horses slowed to navigate the uneven and rocky ground. They reached a bridge that spanned an unpassable section of earth the waves had carved away. Martín was so taken with the sight of the vast ocean he hadn't paid attention to the church that sat atop the large rocky mount. On both sides of the stone bridge, waves crashed against the rocks. Beelzebub charged along as if he lived here and knew every stone. Martín's horse was a bit more tentative.

The bridge was barely wide enough for one horse. Martín wondered if two riders had ever met in the middle, which one had to back up? A cool mist climbed its way up from the crashing waves, cooling Martín's brow. He tasted it with each breath.

Once across the stone bridge, they faced an ascent up a zigzag stairway. Humphrey pulled up and dismounted. He tossed his reins over Beelzebub's neck and waited for Martín to do the same with his horse.

"There's nowhere they can go," Humphrey said, to answer the concern on Martín's face about the horses.

Except to plunge into the sea, Martín thought. There was only a steep, grassy outcropping which, if mishandled, would lead to a fall some two hundred feet into a perilous rocky beach.

Humphrey began the long trek up a sheer, winding set of rock stairs that sharply cut back and forth. Martín hardly dared to look back to see how the horses fared. The climb demanded his concentration and courage. The afternoon sun bore down as there was nothing to provide protection. Now above the sea, the oppressive heat displaced the cooling mist.

They reached the top to find two simple buildings that consumed nearly the entire top of the mount. Martín stood in awe once again. Breathing heavily and drenched with perspiration, he crossed the small plaza that separated a house from what he assumed was a chapel. Each step echoed back and forth between the two structures until the sounds found an escape riding the gentle and welcome breeze. He stood and stared at the front of the larger of the two buildings.

"A chapel?" he asked almost too softly to hear over the waves that crashed far below echoing up the rocky hill.

"San Juan de Gaztelugatxe," Humphrey said.

Martín turned, looking at Humphrey, leaning an ear to hear it again.

"Gaztelugatxe," Humphrey repeated, "it's Basque, your native tongue. I don't speak it either. No need for you to learn it. Your mother took you to Trujillo where there would have been no one to teach you."

The large wooden door creaked open and cut Humphrey's discussion short. A man stood in the doorway, no more than five feet tall, much shorter than Martín and more than a foot shorter than Humphrey. Certainly not a threat physically, Martín thought subconsciously, yet his piercing black eyes locked on Martín, pushing Martín back a few steps.

"You are from Ziortza," the man said as a statement, not a question. "You look just like your father."

Martín stood motionless, trying to understand this man. He knew what the words meant. His heavy accent was Basque. He was realizing there might be other people who knew his father. Those many years ago as a child, when Martín and his mother first arrived in Trujillo, Señora Lopez admitted to having known his mother when they were both younger girls. Other than his mother's sister, who he never met, there had been no other family relationship he'd ever heard of. When the horse thieves killed his mother, he was completely alone in the world. Martín concluded a family legacy did not exist. Martín lowered his eyes and, with his head slightly bowed, returned his eyes to the man's stare.

"I never saw my father," was all Martín could say.

"If you see yourself, you see your father."

The two stared at each other. How to react to that? Curiosity was building. Martín's father died before Martín was born. He never knew him. His mother loved and missed him, but she never told Martín many details about him other than that he was brave and gave his life to save a helpless man.

"A man no greater have I known," the old man said. The man stepped back, pushing the door wide open in a gesture, inviting Martín and Humphrey into the chapel.

Humphrey took the man by the hand with a big smile, looking from him to Martín. "Iñaki, my friend, this is Martín. The treasure you keep is for him. He has a work to do."

Iñaki led them into the chapel. Above the massive double doors, a large window shaped like a wagon wheel sucked in sunlight across the long narrow hall. It was complimented by the light tumbling through three smaller windows placed high above the rows of pews lined up so worshipers could face the altar on the far end of the hall.

Iñaki was not dressed like a friar. He looked out of place in this site of worship, Martín thought. Martín followed as Iñaki and Humphrey appeared to be whispering to each other. The words were soft enough to be erased by the echoing sound of their boots on the highly polished tile floor.

They stopped at the small landing that held the altar. Iñaki knelt and tapped the edge of a tile. It lifted, revealing a hidden cavity. Iñaki reached in and removed a large, roughly stitched cloth bag. Martín peered into the cavity and saw there were more bags beneath it.

Iñaki stood and handed the bag to Humphrey who untied the bag, reached in, and pulled out a gold coin, rotating it in his fingers like a goldsmith assessing its weight and value. As it turned, sunlight reflected off it.

Martín thought back to when Humphrey's bed sat empty through the night. His head shook slightly. Could Beelzebub carry Humphrey from the bishop's carriage to here and back to Bolibar in one night? He remembered how much Beelzebub seemed to enjoy Martín's care the next morning. Martín looked from Humphrey's eyes to the coin.

Humphrey handed the coin to Martín, who struggled to assess if taking it, certainly a stolen coin from the Church, made him equal in sin to this highwayman. Did Humphrey's indulgence transfer the gold's ownership to the robber who brutally stole it? Martín thought it likely this coin was even one of the many coins Humphrey used to buy his own indulgence.

Martín took the coin and held it carefully, as if it could singe his fingers.

Humphrey then tied the top of the bag and handed it to Martín. "This is God's money. He is making you its steward. This sacred trust you must never break."

God's money? Martín almost laughed. Did he mean money stolen from God? Money sacrificed by people in hope for grace, for mercy at the judgement seat? God's money? The bag was heavy. It was more money than Martín ever imagined was in one place at one time. A random gold coin was the most he'd ever seen and here Humphrey handed him a life's worth.

Humphrey's glare burned the words into Martín's soul. "This sacred trust you must never break." It echoed through his mind, erasing the thoughts of it first being plundered from the bishop. Humphrey then turned back to Iñaki. "You know what to do with the rest of those?" His head motioned to the opening in the floor. It was not a question as much as a confirming statement.

Iñaki gave Humphrey a slight nod, accompanied by an impish smile, as if he were part of a sinister scheme. Iñaki replaced the tile, and the three men crossed the chapel without another word.

They stepped into the open court. Humphrey leaned his ear into the wind and squinted into the distance. Martín couldn't see or hear anything unusual.

"Time we go," Humphrey said, turning to leave the plaza. Iñaki took Martín's arm, and pulled him square in front of him.

"Your father Miguel is proud of you," Iñaki said.

"My father never knew me. He died in Granada before I was born."

The old man shook his head almost imperceptibly. "No, he didn't. Your father was a gifted servant of God." Iñaki put his hand on Martín's arm as if commanding him to stay. He pulled Martín back inside, walked over to a box hanging on the wall below one of the high round windows. He pulled from it a leather purse. Returning to Martín, he opened it and pulled several sheets of parchment tightly folded. He dropped the purse onto a pew and unfolded one of the parchment sheets. "Your father Miguel served God alongside a humble monk. He taught me about God in my own tongue. He taught the Moors in their own tongue and the Spaniards in theirs. He was a man of God, who spoke for God. And he wore a sword in the name of God. He brought me to Christ. I owe my soul to him."

Iñaki handed the opened parchment to Martín. Martín examined the words. The handwriting and the words were foreign. He looked from the words to Iñaki, begging an explanation.

"You are holding the Book of Matthew from the Bible in your father's own hand. He was translating it into Basque for our people. He left this copy for me. You must take it. It belongs to you now."

Iñaki took the sheets from Martín and carefully placed them back into the purse. He offered the purse to Martín. The two men stepped back into the plaza.

Martín couldn't take his eyes from Iñaki. He knew so little of his father. A desperate urge surged through him to ask questions. Humphrey left the plaza, hustling down the steep stairs off the hill. It was then Martín glanced and noticed a cloud of dust off on a western hillside.

"Go!" Iñaki said, releasing his hold on Martín's arm.

Martín paused, wishing he could learn more. Then he bounded down the stairs, struggling to keep his balance with both arms needed to hold the bag of coins and the purse. By the time Martín finally reached the last stair, Humphrey had mounted Beelzebub and held the reins of Martín's horse.

Martín stuffed the bag and purse into a pouch and leaped onto his horse. The two charged across the bridge. The horses couldn't let loose until they reached the solid earth free of the stones. Rather than charge back up the long narrow road the way they came, Humphrey left the road and rode along the cliff's edge around the hill and out of sight. They paused behind a bend where, covered by a thick outcropping of vegetation, they turned and watched a dozen riders pound down the road toward the bridge. Just as Humphrey and Martín had, they slowed as they led their horses across the stone bridge. Once across the bridge, five of the men left their horses and hiked up the stairs.

Humphrey turned to Martín. "Iñaki will not be intimidated. Those men are looking for me, not him. The bishop is demanding the sheriff search everywhere."

"But the trial, the indulgence, the judge said…" Martín started.

"That indulgence means nothing to the bishop," Humphrey said.

Martín watched as the men reached the top of the stairs and disappeared. Humphrey turned Beelzebub and climbed up away from the coastline.

"We will find it friendlier going in France," he said.

Martín followed.

# Chapter Ten

## Cloud Forests - Peru

Urco's captain looked from the warrior to Sarpay and held up a hand cautioning Sarpay to wait. Another warrior took a step forward. He was the next in power, she thought. Her aim adjusted. This arrow wouldn't miss. She didn't frighten him. The warriors just lost their leader and the second in command would likely fall to her arrow, but these warriors would not waver. She knew that.

What did she expect, a massacre, like the one this village suffered? No. Now it was evident they wanted one thing. Her. Only then would come the massacre. Could she outrun them? No. Should she surrender in exchange for the lives of all these people? Would that be the sacrifice required by the gods?

She pulled the arrow back, its aim clearly directed at the first warrior. Still no fear. His eyes and hers locked. He stepped forward, not raising the lance or the club. He slowly advanced. None of the other warriors appeared to ready their weapons. She knew she was going to be taken. They would take her regardless if one or two or ten of them died. They would have their prize—the First Priestess of the Empire. The favor they would have with the mighty Atahualpa would guarantee their power over the many tribes of the Antisuyu on the eastern slopes of the mighty Inca Empire.

She no longer feared death, but what could she do to prevent the slaughter of these people and the slaughter of countless other peoples loyal to her half-brother Huascar?

She pulled her arrow back further. She knew it wouldn't stop the attack, but what would one more dead warrior mean?

Closing within twenty paces, the new apparent leader joined his former chief flat on his face, an arrow in the back of his neck. A second warrior approached and dropped next to him. Sarpay's bow began shaking. The string pulled so tightly, her muscles struggled to hold firm. A third warrior and then a fourth dropped. All hit from behind. Another warrior charged ahead, crossing the remaining few yards in just a few jumps.

Sarpay was quick enough to release her arrow, catching him square in the chest. His momentum carried him forward. Dropping his lance, which hadn't had time to threaten her, he tumbled over her, sending both of them sprawling into the edge of the river. She scrambled out from under him. His lifeless body was face down, his blood flowing into the current.

Two more attackers fell. The people from the citadel took courage and turned on the warriors, taking the lances and clubs from the fallen and wielding them on the assailants. Within minutes, the few surviving warriors disappeared back into the jungle.

Sarpay knelt to attend to Urco's captain, who struggled to stand.

"They will be back. This caravan is not safe as long as you are with us." A voice came from the forest. She recognized that voice.

Urco and three of his men came out of the forest. His men collected the arrows from their victims. He joined Sarpay and pulled the arrow still protruding from his captain's shoulder. He was not gentle, but as quickly as the blood flowed, Sarpay had the wound patched with coca leaves and wrapped it with a piece of woven fabric she tore from a blanket tucked in the pannier of a pack llama.

Urco stepped into the river to the warrior who Sarpay hit. He rolled the body over. The arrow buried into his chest had shattered when he fell and pulled her into the river. Urco yanked the broken shaft from the man's chest, retrieving the serrated tip of the arrow.

"I taught you well." Urco smiled, holding up the arrow, pointing the tip toward the dead man. He returned to where Cusimi and Sarpay were finishing their bandaging.

The captain showed little response to the pain when Urco had pulled the arrow free, but when his tense muscles relaxed, Sarpay knew the numbing properties of the coca leaves were at work. The captain said something in a language she did not understand.

Urco's solemn face turned more serious. He spoke directly to the captain. "Rumi, Tipaq, and Quizo are lost."

He turned back to Sarpay, "Quichamba promised freedom from the Inca to the people who bring you to him. This village refused to join him."

Cusimi leaned over to Sarpay. "You know what he wants. Can you stop him?" It was a statement more than a question. Sarpay shook her bowed head, slowly closing her eyes. Of course she knew. She was the only pure daughter of the Sapa Inca and his pure wife, both direct descendants of the sun and moon gods. She would make a grand prize for the conquering army in what was becoming the bloodiest battles the empire had ever known. She was First Priestess of the Empire who had proven her seership, leading her father's armies to victory through visions she received of the future. Her gift of seership caused so much death.

All eyes waited on Sarpay's response to Cusimi's statement. Sarpay hesitated, then looking up to Urco said, "Both of my brothers think I can assure them victory as I did for my father."

She lowered her head, willing herself not to cry. Only she and her father knew the future of the empire depended on her great sacrifice. Even Cusimi didn't understand the fullness of the imperative that her blood be shed for the salvation of the empire. Now was not the time to tell the complete story.

"Can you get us to Vitcos?" Sarpay asked. "The future for both armies depends on my getting to a sacred temple."

"Both the Cuñari and the Shaur are standing between us and Vitcos. If you travel with this group, they will never be safe," Urco said.

"Then we must get beyond their reach," she said, finishing the repair to the captain's shoulder.

"Paititi," Urco said. He helped his captain to his feet. "If we can get to Paititi we will be safe."

"What happened at Picchu?" the captain asked, changing the subject.

"Rumi and Tipaq were stationed at the entrance of Picchu. Securely hidden, they held Quichamba's forces at bay long enough to give our group time to disappear into the cloud forest. Quiz and I positioned ourselves above the trail leading to the entrance. Quichamba's men are not bowmen nor are they proficient with stones. With lances and clubs, their skill is unmatched. We simply had to stay out of reach. Together they might have totaled five hundred men; only three hundred now." He smiled.

Urco's people and the citadel's citizens who successfully escaped Picchu began collecting the animals and supplies from the massacred village and prepared to continue on. Collectively, they were not eager to remain in the now-desolate village and the surrounding farmland, though it was a choice land.

Urco continued his narrative. "Quizo insisted I take the rest of my men and protect the trail into the cloud forest. He stayed behind to help Rumi and Tipaq. When they were eventually overrun, nearly a hundred more of

Quichamba's men lay dead, but hundreds more pushed through, only to find Picchu abandoned.

"Though Quichamba's army, are the most efficient killers from all four quarters of the empire, Quichamba is unwilling to plunge into the clouds himself. He promised freedom to the people who bring the princess back to him."

Sarpay knew what this meant. She learned from her elders and from personal experience that over the past century as her father, grandfather, and generations before conquered a people, whether by force or by compromise, the people are assimilated into the Inca Empire. Yet most villages were permitted to maintain their individual cultures and customs and continued to worship their gods in their own way. She witnessed how they taught these people the common language, skills in farming, irrigation, and construction. As part of the mighty Inca Empire, most assimilated people flourished. Life became more prosperous, more productive, and more secure. Under Inca protection, that security promoted confidence to plan, and build, and prosper. Before the Inca conquest, insecurity held people back, and threats from enemies, famine, and other disasters destroyed whole tribes. Despite the prosperity enjoyed, several conquered people rebelled and resisted what Inca rule provided. Mostly, the rebellious were the powerful ones who themselves wanted to rule and subdue other tribes.

Therefore, Sarpay knew if any of the rebellious tribes were to deliver her and win their freedom, they would be free to continue their own conquests. Sarpay knew she was a thing to trade for liberty. Whose liberty and at what cost to the empire?

"I must go another way," Sarpay said. "I only endanger these, your people. They will be safe in Vitcos, but without me."

"Paititi," Urco said again.

"First, help me and Cusimi get to Cusco and the Temple of the Sun." Sarpay knew this was a half-truth. She hoped if they made it to Cusco, her sacrifice would end the war and the gods would lead Urco and his people to the safety of Paititi.

Urco reorganized the caravan, giving instructions to his men to guide this group to the safety of Vitcos. With nothing more than packs on their backs, He, Cusimi, Sarpay, and Cataquil, Urco's young brother-in-law, left the caravan and climbed north up toward the mountain tops, where they hoped to circle around Quizquiz's army, avoiding Quichamba's assassins and eventually reach Cusco. In Sarpay's mind, she realized it would take months for such a roundabout journey.

There had to be a better way.

# Chapter Eleven

Southern Slopes of the Pyrenees Mountains – Northern Spain

Hours passed. The setting sun turned the leaves to purple as they approached the summit of a tree-covered bluff. Humphrey pulled up through a clearing, and looked down upon what in the fading light appeared to be a small cluster of buildings struggling to become a village.

"Tonight, we will be safer out here than in there. I don't like the looks of it." Humphrey slid off Beelzebub, pulled the saddle, and left him free to forage. Martín followed, but hesitated to leave his horse free to wander. Humphrey, without looking up, said. "Leave him free. Beelz'll keep track of him."

The looks of what? Again, the mystery of this man did not settle with Martín. Nothing looked odd. He just stared at Humphrey. What did Humphrey know about the village but didn't share?

"Did God's money belong to the bishop three days ago?" Martín held the sack out in front of him, waiting until Humphrey, who was lighting a small fire, looked up.

"It never belonged to the bishop. Nor the Church. Nor does it belong to you. They gave it to God at great sacrifice in hopes of freeing a soul from purgatory."

Humphrey warmed his hands over the small flames. "Martín, you will soon understand."

He continued warming his hands without looking up at Martín. "They teach peasants that purgatory is like this fire. If they give money to the bishop, they won't burn for their sins. Do you think Friar Tomás didn't have enough money to pay for his sin of heresy, so the bishop wanted him to start purgatory before he faced God's judgment?"

Martín looked from the sack of gold in his hands to Humphrey, poking the fire with a stick, stirring the flames. The vision of Friar Tomás at the stake, flames consuming his body, came vividly back into his mind.

Humphrey continued. "No, my friend, Friar Tomás burned at the pyre because a bishop caught him giving copies of the holy scriptures to peasants. Martín, he gave his life for you. They did not take it from him. I regret Vano and I could not rescue Friar Tomás in time. The scriptures you have in your possession bring you in opposition to the pope and, thus, his bishops. They hate me and want revenge for embarrassing the bishop. If it was just about the gold you are holding, they would take it back and put you in prison. But if they found the holy word you have hidden in your bedroll, you would burn for it."

Humphrey pulled the stick from the fire and held it up against the darkened sky. Martín shuddered, too overwhelmed to understand his entire situation.

Martín lifted the saddle and tucked the gold underneath it. Humphrey pulled a flask of wine from his bag and handed it to Martín, who took a timid swallow and handed it back. Martín didn't say any more. He pulled a blanket over his shoulders, laid down, and once the events of the past several weeks finally played themselves out in his mind, he drifted off to sleep. Smoke from the dying fire wafted over the sleeping men.

When Martín woke, both Beelzebub and Humphrey were gone. He cleared his head, stood, and stretched. The morning sun crept over the distant eastern horizon. Its reflection on the water perfectly silhouetted his horse, drinking from a small pond he hadn't noticed the evening before.

Its head jerked up and looked toward Martín at the sound of pounding hooves. The sound was so sudden Martín nearly fell he turned so quickly.

"It's time to go," Humphrey said as he pounded past Martín to the small pond where he gathered Martín's horse and led him back to Martín, who stood holding the saddle ready. Once mounted, the two charged off along the ridge of a bluff, plunging into the deepest part of the forest. After galloping for a while, they slowed, and Humphrey let Martín pull up alongside. He handed Martín a bag, but kept the horses walking. The contents felt more valuable than the gold tied to his saddle. The bread was certainly the freshest it could be. He tore into it. The cheese and grapes did their job.

"Thank you," Martín finally uttered.

"Thank the farmer. You rewarded his kindness."

Martín's squint questioned Humphrey's statement.

"God's money," Humphrey said.

Martín reached back and patted the bag of coins.

"God's money?" Martín said.

"That is what it's for," Humphrey said.

With only a few rest stops, they traveled on. Martín realized the good farmer provided several days' worth of food—meats, fruits, cheeses, and even refilled Humphrey's wine flask.

They avoided the several small villages they passed, hoping to be free of the bishop's men. After several days, they stopped at a tavern. The innkeeper was a tall, slender Frenchman. He may have been the tallest man Martín had ever seen. Speaking what had to be French, since Martín didn't understand a word, the innkeeper welcomed them. Humphrey seemed to speak French awkwardly, and tried what Martín was certain was English. Then surprisingly, the innkeeper, in very poor Spanish, intermixed with French, came to an agreement with Humphrey for a meal and lodging. Once they got to Spanish, Martín realized French wouldn't be too far of a stretch to learn if he had someone to coach him a little.

The hot meal warmed every bit of their bodies. After what Martín felt was a sufficient number of refills of very fine French wine, Humphrey slowed. The way Humphrey was willing to spend it, Martín was grateful he had an ample supply of God's money.

Martín helped Humphrey to a room, which, for the second time in a couple weeks, they would share. With as much as Humphrey drank and with no bishops to plunder, he did not worry that Humphrey would have any midnight adventures.

Martín laid down on the most comfortable bed he believed he ever slept on. Wondering what lay ahead with this man, then wondering how Carmelita and Faustino fared, his mind drifted to Iñaki and his brief comments that he knew Martín's father. Oh, how he wanted to return and talk with the only man who ever made mention of his father. The interest in his father was new.

Refreshed and seemingly not being persued gave Martín a peculiar sense of hope. He was no longer wholly on his own. Though Friar Tomás had been a mentor and a teacher, when Tomás left Trujillo, Martín slipped into desperation at being alone. Little did he recognize at the time how Señora Lopez had repeatedly been there for him, and how Faustino and Carmelita so immediately befriended him, and how their father, Vano, so directly supported him. These series of events began erasing that despair. A small speck of faith that God did know him and cared began to grow.

Now, as they saddled their horses to begin their trek across France, Martín felt less suspicious of this highwayman who so cunningly outsmarted the pope's agents. And today he carried on his horse copies of the holy scriptures, manuscripts he could not merely read, but had read, a handwritten copy of the Book of Matthew allegedly translated by his father, and an uncounted variety of coins looted from the Church.

Martín had no reason to feel hopeful, but he did. So, he asked. "Were the contents under the alter tiles with Iñaki the rest of your plunder?"

Humphrey smiled. "Not plundered, my young friend, rescued."

Martín smiled at the response to what Martín thought was a valid question. A cloaked accusation he tried to craft carefully for days.

"Rescued from God?" Martín asked.

"Rescued for God," Humphrey said.

"Iñaki will take the gold and silver plundered from the common people by the bishop and return it to the honest in heart to relieve their poverty. God does not need another monument in Rome built for the glory of man. He needs only the heart. He approves of and appreciates chapels and cathedrals, temples and synagogues where his children may come to worship Him and learn His holy word. But He does not always need them."

They rode along in silence for what seemed like hours while Martín processed the realization that Humphrey thought of himself as a philosopher as well as a protector.

The road narrowed, and Martín fell in behind Humphrey on a trail that ran along a small river. Crystal clear water tumbled over moss-covered stones, gently filling the air with peace. When the trees parted and the river widened, they plunged across, water splashing. On the other side, they climbed up through a heavy forest. At the summit, the clamor of pounding hooves echoed through the trees. Less than a hundred feet away, a coach pulled by six powerful horses bounded past, its driver urgently pushing them as fast as they could run.

Both men looked at each other, sharing the same quizzical expression. Moments later, the pounding of hooves from horses carrying a dozen men chasing the coach sent a billow of dust to join the cloud kicked up when the coach passed. A quick glance to catch Martín's eye, and Humphrey had Beelzebub at a full run. It took Martín's horse only slight encouragement, and he, too, was at a full run. But why were they running? What did Humphrey see? Who did he see? Was it the coach? Or the men chasing it?

Martín wondered if the look Humphrey gave meant to follow or wait. He kept following.

Beelzebub soon caught up with the last of the pursuing horsemen. Within seconds, Martín passed two of them who had tumbled to the ground. A quick glance back and he noted they were moving. At least Humphrey didn't kill them, Martín thought.

Martín reached a large clearing. He could see the coach, its teams still at a full run. Several of the horsemen were closing the gap. Within minutes, whoever these men were would catch the coach. It then disappeared over a rise. But where was Humphrey? Martín's Andalusian couldn't match the power or speed of Beelzebub, but Martín figured he could follow Humphrey's lead and continue on. Martín surprised a horseman when he pulled up alongside. Without knowing what else to do, he reached out and punched the rider in the face, knocking him back and off his horse.

The action stunned Martín as much as it did the man now tumbling on the ground. His riderless horse slowed and galloped off. The next rider turned, noticing his companion's horse veer off to the right without its rider. With his companion on the ground, the rider reached to pull a sword on this stranger who was clearly disrupting their charge. Just as the blade left its sheath, the Andalusian of its own volition pushed into the horse, throwing the man off balance. The Andalusian kept pressing, causing the opposing horse to stumble. To keep from toppling, the horse jerked left, unsettling the rider, who, with sword in hand, tumbled to the ground.

Could Martín keep this up? No, he knew he couldn't, but what else should he do? Where was Humphrey? Do I charge ahead? Pull back? Who are they chasing? Am I interfering with the French law? Did Humphrey realize he was on the wrong side of this chase and run for his life?

Well up ahead, Martín saw the fastest of the men overtake the coach and bring it to a halt. The remaining men circled the coach. Martín was not about to stick around all by himself, waiting for the men to take him prisoner, regardless of whose side he was on. He turned and charged up and over a small hill, hoping to disappear before the four men who'd been de-horsed collected their mounts and joined their companions.

Martín slowed, letting his horse catch his breath, and carefully climbed down into a hollow, out of sight. The horse did all the work, yet Martín's heart was doing all the pounding.

His heart slowed, as did the heavy breathing of his horse. He knew it. He knew as soon as there was real trouble, Humphrey would save himself and abandon Martín. Feelings of anger gave way to frustration. Did Humphrey take this chance to flee?

The more he thought, the more he hoped that was not true. But where did he go? The calm was as unnerving as the chase. He remounted and slowly climbed his way back the way he came, dismounting as he reached the top of the small hill. Carefully peeking over the ridge, he saw no sign of the men or their horses. Yet the coach stood there alone. Its two teams of horses were gone. It wasn't going anywhere. Martín searched the horizon for any sign of friend or foe. He remounted his horse and headed over the hill.

Eventually, he made his way down the hill to the coach. All was quiet. Except for his heart. When he reached the coach, he found its driver lying dead, cut deeply in the chest. He stepped up into the coach. He'd never seen one this finely appointed. Rich purple cushions were connected to the bottom and back of the bench, tied with golden strings. Its builders padded the walls with complementary velvet lining, secured with silver buttons. Iridescent white drapes, now torn loose, hung raggedly from brass rods. This was not the coach of the common, nor even of nobility. Though Martín admitted he'd never seen a royal coach, he concluded this was one.

He stood alongside his Andalusian looking over the saddle to where they'd come, then in the other direction where the coach was originally headed. Where to now? He mounted and circled the coach, looking for a hint of where the coach's passenger or passengers were taken, now obviously on horseback.

His horse was sound, God's silver was safe, so he chose to return to the inn where he'd spent the previous night. When he reached the place where he and Humphrey joined the chase, he left the road and went up through the woods. It wasn't long before he wasn't sure just which way he'd come. As he turned and returned, he decided he'd never follow the back of a horse again. Next time he followed someone he would watch where he was going. Evening came. This was going to be a lonely night.

Martín gave his horse a nudge to climb one more hill to see if the other side offered a clue. Voices pulled him to an abrupt stop. He listened intently, leaning his ear toward its source. French. Angry French. Threatening Spanish. Then a sweet unfamiliar voice wafted through the trees. This voice was magical. The passenger, Martín thought. Was there more than one? Where was Humphrey?

He secured his horse in a dense thicket and, as quietly as possible, climbed through the trees to see from whom and from where the voices came.

Martín's heart stopped in mid-beat. Chills raced horror up and down his back. He recognized a voice. By the light of a small fire, sat Humphrey, arguing with the man who had led the group of horsemen chasing the coach.

Seated next to Humphrey was a woman Martín guessed was the passenger of the captured coach. Oh how he wished the light were better so he could see her more clearly. As much as the flickering light permitted, he watched how gracefully she moved. Her dress was as fine as he'd ever seen. Even in the darkness he assessed the woman was elegant.

Then Martín realized he understood the argument. The first words in this heated argument were unfamiliar to him. Since he and Humphrey had been headed to France, he assumed they were speaking French. Now he recognized most of the argument was Spanish. Maybe he just misunderstood, but these were Spaniards! The argument centered on the several profit options concerning the fate of their captive.

It appeared someone hired this band to capture and return the woman to Madrid, and paid dearly up front, with a handsome reward added to the bounty following a successful return. The woman, Martín learned, was a relative of the King of France who was being held prisoner in Madrid by Charles V, the Holy Roman Emperor. The emperor promised her safe passage to and from Madrid to visit the imprisoned King Francis. Once outside Spain, she was to be kidnapped and returned as a political pawn to be used against Francis in Charles's demands for France to surrender Burgundy.

The English accent clearly separated Humphrey's argument from the rest. Martín realized Humphrey was arguing to secure a ransom from Francis's followers in Paris. He insisted it would be much more lucrative. Why was Humphrey even part of this discussion? Again, Martín still wondered if Humphrey was nothing more than an opportunist highwayman. But if so, why was a lifetime's worth of gold and silver coins hidden in Martín's saddle and not Humphrey's?

Martín counted the men surrounding the fire. Where were the rest of them? He leaned in, trying to see between two trees that kept him hidden; as he did so, his eyes met Humphrey's. They locked. Humphrey smiled, turned to the woman and in Latin, English, and Spanish quickly spoke in what the men around the fire thought was riddles. To Martín, the message was perfectly clear this time.

"This very night, one of God's chosen will deliver you. Please be ready to ride," Humphrey spoke softly to the woman.

Me? Martín wondered. Was this another coded message asking Martín to do something? To rescue this woman? She was definitely someone of consequence. Humphrey then continued his multi-language message. "Buy her freedom with God's silver."

God's silver? How do I buy her? Martín's thoughts and the mystery of Sir Humphrey were exhausting. He crept back away from the small camp and crawled his way back to his horse. No horse. It was gone. He knew he tied it up right here. He knew it! It was secure. It didn't wander off. His heart pounded so loudly in his chest he felt the men in the camp might hear it. He dropped to his knees to beseech God's help. Before he could utter a word, a deep, gravelly voice rumbled through the grove.

"Missing something, boy?"

Martín turned, but the light of a moon barely cut through the canopy of trees. The dark figure stood accompanied by an even larger figure. The man held the reins of his horse and the slight glisten of steel beckoned Martín to stand.

Martín stood, and as he did, he felt the steel on his chest.

"To the fire," the shadow said.

Martín, the man, and the horse worked their way back to the small clearing which hosted the many men surrounding the fire.

In Spanish, the man who Martín assumed led this band, said, "Is this God's chosen one, you so carefully tried to infer would rescue the princess?" The man was speaking directly to Humphrey. "Where is God's silver to be used to buy her eminence's freedom?" the man asked, mocking Humphrey's riddle.

Martín realized, however cunning Humphrey was, this man was besting him. Did the man know how he'd outsmarted the bishop and must now be in possession of a king's ransom's worth of gold and silver coins? Already wide, trying to see every detail, Martín's eyes got even wider when the man walked over to Martín's horse and pulled the bedroll and bags, dropping them to the ground. With a slight motion of his head, he directed the man holding the reins to lead the horse away.

The man pulled open the satchel tucked in the bedroll. He pulled the manuscripts free and held them up to the light. His wide grin sent icy chills throughout Martín's entire body. He looked from the scriptures to Martín and back to the woman, and then to one of his men.

Holding up the bag with God's sacred gold and silver given to Martín's care, the man grinned. "Oh, how our fortunes have changed," he said.

"The most highly prized prisoner in all of Europe, the very highwayman wanted dead by our good bishop, his indulgence, and the heretic who carries with him all the evidence needed to light the pyre's flames." A deep growl of laughter escaped his lips.

Martín longed for the lonely, hunger-filled poverty of Trujillo. He lowered his head. Why wasn't Humphrey doing anything? Of course, he was one of them. Martín looked back up and into Humphrey's eyes with disdain. He wasn't ashamed in the least. How could Humphrey do nothing? This man, who Martín assumed was the captain, just included Humphrey in his list of prizes. Had Humphrey been one of them? Did the captain just turn on him? And Vano trusted this man!

When the man who led Martín's horse away returned, the sword was still at the ready. He pointed with the sword for Martín to join Humphrey who sat next to the woman. Rather than sit next to Humphrey, Martín's disgust drove him to sit next to the woman. At least there was no question of her loyalty. Yet. But who was she?

He plopped down and watched the firelight dance on her cheeks. She was elegant. Of course she would be. A relative of the king, the French King, he thought—King Francis I. A king who Martín understood was only a dozen years his senior. The irony amused him. The King of France, barely in his thirties, imprisoned by the Holy Roman Emperor, King Charles V still in his twenties. Did God ordain these men to rule and control the lives of countless citizens? To amass armies and conquer, destroy and control? His head shook ever so slightly in wonder.

When the woman looked at Martín, even in the fire's light, her radiance shocked him. Her violet-blue eyes seemed to instill peace. His heart slowed. She gently placed her hand on his trembling arm.

"My young friend, you will not burn in the pyre." She spoke so gently, so confidently, that his heart calmed. "Though these men may appear to control our destiny, there are powers greater than what we see. Take heart."

With swords drawn by nearly all the men, the captain approached Humphrey and secured his feet with a cord which wrapped around his waist and secured his arms behind him. If Humphrey was at one time in league with these men, he was no longer. It seemed like justice to Martín.

The men congratulated each other, boasting to be more cunning than the legendary Highwayman Humphrey Kynaston.

The revelry slowly subsided as man after man dropped off to sleep. Two men sat alert, swords at the ready, watching the captives. The guards were too close to miss any conversation, so the captives remained silent. One man stood and went a few steps away from the fire and turned his back to it.

"Show some decency, man," Humphrey bellowed, waking several of the soldiers who stirred and, noticing nothing of consequence, tried to return to sleep. The man retired deeper into the woods.

"You will never get me back to Toledo," Humphrey said flatly to the man remaining awake at the fire.

"Maybe not alive. But be assured your body and the bishop's gold will make it to Toledo," the man said.

"Diego, don't be a fool. Take the money and go. You'll never see your share of the reward. How many times have the bishops cheated? Let Santiago take the heretic and the princess. He and the rest of these will have their hands full with these two. He'll never risk chasing you. Just leave Beelzebub loose a few miles out."

Martín's droopy eyelids sprang open. Not just a relative of the king! The princess? King Francis' sister! His eyes couldn't stop staring. He wondered if she knew the treachery Humphrey was committing. Leave the princess and the heretic? Martín shuddered.

Diego was considering it. The bishop's bag of indulgences lay next to Santiago, who appeared to be soundly sleeping. All thoughts of sleep were long gone. Martín sat silently. A slight breeze changed direction, taking with it the near constant smoke from the fire and sending it away. Martín hadn't taken a truly deep breath since he sat next to the princess. With the smoke gone, the flavor of sweet lemon wafted past Martín, alerting his senses even more.

If he was being taken to his certain death, he realized it wouldn't be so unpleasant traveling with this woman. Might she plead for clemency? Again, the tiniest of breezes brought the sweet lemon scent to linger with Martín. He again fixed his eyes on this remarkable woman as she lay so regal and calm.

The second guard returned, and they said nothing more. Sometime in the night, Martín drifted off to sleep. He woke startled at the yells and cursing of Santiago. The princess was standing still, silently watching the chaos of the camp. It took Martín a few minutes to get his mind clear.

He noted the smile on the princess's face. She seemed to enjoy the crisis. As Martín stood, he recognized the crisis meant they would all be on foot. Diego and Humphrey were gone; as was the indulgence money, Martín's scriptures, and all the horses.

Why hadn't Humphrey taken the princess with him? Then he

remembered Humphrey told Diego that Santiago would be too busy to seek retribution from Diego. But the horses? The princess turned to Martín as the cursing yielded to demands. Santiago was sharp with his commands. Within minutes, hot cider served as a breakfast and they began what Martín estimated would be a journey of several days until they reached Lesaka, where they could hire a carriage for the prisoners. Martín had wondered why they abandoned the coach. Now, he realized they wanted to move much quicker than a coach would afford. On foot, they were not quick at all. The morning march continued until the sun stood tall in the clear sky.

The caravan of bounty hunters stopped at a small spring being fed by the glaciers of the nearby Pyrenees. Martín offered a hand to help the princess to her knees to get a drink. He didn't know how a princess would do fetching water on her knees. Until now Santiago had kept them apart, with several Spaniards between them as they marched throughout the morning. For only the second time since they took him captive, the princess spoke to Martín.

"Are you able to read those texts they took from your horse?" she asked.

Martín nodded affirmatively. He didn't know how to speak to a princess.

"Who taught you?" she asked.

This time he couldn't answer with a head motion.

"Your, um, your highness," he began, stumbling over himself, "a friar, Friar Tomás of Trujillo. He insisted I learn. Yet he paid for it with his life."

She took his offered hand, helping her kneel next to the spring where she dipped her delicate hand and brought handful after handful to her surprisingly red lips. He'd not seen a woman of this caliber up close like this. It was an adventure just watching her.

Ready to stand, she offered her dry hand to Martín, who automatically helped her to her feet. She left the wet hand free to dry. A small curtsy accompanied a gentle, "Thank you." Now in the full light of day, her violet-blue eyes sparkled. Though she'd traveled several days in a coach, survived a vicious attack, spent the night on the ground, and been forced to march for hours, her regalness was undaunted. Her long black hair glistened in the sunlight. She wore it uncovered, braided with ribbons and pinned up; it was puffed over the ears before being drawn back at chin level into a braid.

Martín wondered how she would have managed on a horse with the long gown she wore. The dress was loosely fitted to her body and flared from the hips. Under the square neckline was a white undershirt of some sort. Martín wondered how many layers there might be. Her sleeves were wide at the wrist, which made it hard to drink from a stream. Oh, how Martín wished he could have offered a goblet or something when she stooped for a drink. The gown fastened in the front and its slits revealed more layers of soft white fabric.

In perfect Latin, which both she and Martín knew these highwaymen would not understand, she said, "So, as a heretic, taught by your friar, have you read those selections of scriptures we saw last night?" Her smile carried the tinge of sarcasm as she said heretic.

"Many times, your highness." Martín bowed.

"Marguerite," she said. "We two seem to be companions in some crime." Her smile warmed him.

"Martín." He returned the introduction with a bow. The brief rest ended. A Spaniard pushed his way between Martín and Marguerite, with Martín taking the brunt of the separation, nearly tumbling to the ground.

Marguerite smiled and winked as Martín regained his footing and looked back at her. He returned the smile, which melted the suppressed hate which always simmered below the surface at the mistreatment by bullies. The few times that hate got the best of him, he suffered the more. He'd learned to suffer in silence.

The rest of the day was a non-stop climb as they worked their way through the foothills of the Pyrenees approaching the border of Spain. The closer they got to Spain, the more worrisome Marguerite became entering that country. The climb was taking its toll on everyone. As the sun lowered in the sky, temperatures dropped. Martín realized the princess, with her layers of clothing, would soon have the advantage.

By evening, the small band reached a summit which looked down into the small village. "Saint-Jean-Pied-de-Port," Marguerite whispered. A French village, Martín thought. Martín wondered if anyone here might recognize the princess and seek to help her.

The company worked their way past a few small buildings as they descended the hill toward a slow, winding river. They approached a stone bridge that led to a freshly painted two-story building on its opposite side, which, as far as Martín could assess, led into the village's town center. As they neared a small tavern on the closest side of the river, two of the Spaniards held Martín and Marguerite back while the rest of the men continued into the tavern.

A small empty shack which seemed to cling on for its life hung out over the river. The two men ushered Marguerite and Martín into the shack and out of sight. One man stayed inside with them, the other remained outside.

It was evident these men were taking no chances of someone recognizing a French Princess. The night got cooler. There was no fire, but after a while, Santiago brought food and drink. They ate in the darkness. The moon was rising and gave enough light for Martín to see a small corral holding horses. At least tomorrow they would be riding, Martín thought. His feet were sore enough, but he imagined they did not design whatever footwear the princess wore for hiking. But he was still curious how the large gown would fare on a horse.

Under guard, Martín stepped outside to a small privy, eager to find relief. Returning to the shack, the sword at his back, the guard poked and pushed. The pain from the sharp jabs hurt less than the insult that he was weak and harmless. Suddenly, there was a hard thud and the guard dropped to the ground. Martín turned quickly. The guard lay motionless.

Behind him stood what the moon made look like a giant ghost.

"Time to go," the ghost whispered.

Martín froze, dumbfounded.

"No time to think, no time to wait. Go!" The shadow disappeared.

Martín knelt. The guard was motionless, unconscious. Now alone, Martín looked every direction. Who was watching? He quickly stole away to the corral, considering a quick escape. There were plenty of horses. All of Santiago's men were in the tavern with more than enough to drink. This was his chance.

Just as he was ready to hop into the corral and choose a fast horse, he could not will his legs to move. Too many thoughts crowded in.

He couldn't leave the princess, even if he was a heretic and would soon burn for the crime of possessing and reading the holy word of God. But there was no evidence, he reasoned. Humphrey saw to that. He smiled at the one thing Humphrey did for his benefit. He could lie, and he wouldn't burn. Then he thought back to when Friar Tomás commanded him to do something. No, Martín thought, he couldn't lie, and he would burn. He had to run right now so he could fulfill Tomás' admonition. His legs let loose, and he climbed into the corral and quietly mingled among the horses looking for the one he felt might outrun the rest.

He couldn't leave the princess. But how could he best the man guarding her? He put his arm on a horse he knew could save him. He could ride away right now. He could tell someone and they could rescue the princess. Who would he tell? Who could he trust? No one. Martín had been on his own most of his life, but this was the first time he thought of someone else. That thought stalled his self-preservation.

He dropped his arm from the neck of the animal he was certain could take him far away, far from the bishop's fire, far from this woman, a real woman, a lady that was so fine, so regal, yes, he could burn for her.

He made a choice. As he worked his way past the other horses toward the gate of the corral, he envisioned Marguerite and her long gown struggling to get on a horse and staying on. Could she ride? Had she, in her fine royal life, ridden a horse? He slowed, put his arm over the back of another horse and wondered.

As he stood there, the door to the small shack opened. In shadow, he saw the second guard looking about. Then out stepped the princess. The two shadows looked like a dream. A man wielding a sword ushered Marguerite directly toward him. Martín pulled close to the horse out of sight.

He waited, realizing they would soon reach the fallen guard. Then what would happen? The sword. Why didn't he grab the sword from the fallen guard? The guard poked the princess in the back. That was enough. Martín scaled the rails of the coral and lunged toward the guard. Just as Martín leaped into the air, the guard turned and pointed the sword upward. The guard's aim was as poor as Martín's. He missed the sword. He also missed the guard, landing hard on his face.

Martín instantly wanted to yell for the princess to run. He had no breath to do so. Fighting for air, he struggled to his knees. The guard stood above him with sword raised. He suddenly dropped to the ground. Martín looked up, finally getting enough air to tell the princess to run. But he didn't need to. She stood calmly, sword in one hand and with the other, reached to help Martín to his feet. Martín looked to the guard lying unconscious face down, and back to the princess.

It was too dark to see her smile, but he could feel it. Now back on his feet, they hurried toward the corral.

A tall shadow of a mountain on a demonic horse stood between them and the corral. The horse, with its devilish eyes glistening in the moonlight, erased the pain Martín felt in his chest and in his pride.

Beelzebub. Never had Martín welcomed the sight of the devil like he did tonight. Without a second thought, Martín helped Marguerite up onto a horse. Yes, this princess could ride. She tucked and pulled the gown with such expertise, Martín's concerns with it vanished. Humphrey collected two other horses upon which they tied the two unconscious guards. Martín was up on his own horse with his own saddle and saddlebags in an instant. The five horses charged along the river, away from the stone bridge, past the town and up into the forested hills.

In the darkness, with the moon occasionally peeking through, the horses served as navigators. Eventually, they reached a clearing where the welcome moonlight signaled they were safely away.

Humphrey pulled around to face Marguerite. "Your Highness. This is where I leave you." He looked over to Martín, her eyes followed. "You are in expert hands for now." He rode back toward Martín, pulling the two horses carrying the unconscious men with him, and stopped facing Martín.

"You could have run," Humphrey said. "When you had the chance."

Martín knew it was Humphrey who had told him to. But wondered what Humphrey meant.

"You could have, and I would not have stopped you." Humphrey paused for a moment. "But you did not. You did not because God chose you for a work, a work for liberty."

Martín still didn't answer. He just stared into the shadowed face.

"My friend, even in the darkness, I can see your face asking questions. When Diego realized his greed would get him killed after I caught him, he fled, embarrassed and afraid. You will never see him again. Santiago will suspect these two as traitors as well. These will never come after you in fear of Santiago. They too will run. But they cannot know by which way you and the princess travel. I will help them on their way and will meet you at Les Salces. I heard the princess say she has friends who were waiting for her there."

Martín still had no words to express his gratitude, his wonder, nor his confusion. He was supposed to escort a princess across a country he knew nothing about? And after she had just saved his life?

Humphrey seemed to read his very thoughts.

"You have money enough. I have only spent God's gold to buy your freedom. These horses were worth the price you paid for them. It was with God's help I found your horse."

Martín almost unconsciously reached his hand back and touched the bags tied to his saddle.

"It is time you took the princess home. Her brother, King Francis I, will be grateful you did." With that, Humphrey led his two prisoners away toward the sea.

# Chapter Twelve

### Antisuyu, Tawantinsuyu, Peru

Sarpay held the tip of an arrow in her hand, rotating it slowly. She ran her finger over its edge. Touching her finger to her tongue, she licked off the drop of blood. She looked to Urco, who was tying a similar tip to a shaft with a bright red cotton thread.

"How has your tribe become the finest experts with an arrow?" she asked, complementing Urco's tribe as the empire's deadliest archers.

Though unsaid, she knew that was the reason Atahualpa sent Rumañawi to constrain Urco's people to join with his army. Atahualpa wanted their deadly skill as archers. Other tribes from the Anitsuyu were proficient archers, but none were like Urco's people. Where most tribes had skilled sling men and modest archers, Urco's warriors depended solely on the bow. Their challenge was keeping supplied with arrows. With the cork-like Isana wood plentiful in Urco's region and the flexibility of the chonta wood for the bow, Urco's people had a natural advantage in becoming skilled masters. But their accuracy went beyond the primitive use of local woods.

Urco dipped his finger into a tree tar he kept in a small pouch and sealed the string in place. He looked back to Sarpay, shook his head and said, "The yuraq yana qari."

Chills ran up her back. The yuraq yana qari was a rumor, a myth, a story that grew over the past few years. It was told that men, white and black with hair on their faces, flew upon the waters by the wind and met the people in the coastal city of Tumbes. When the strange visitors kidnapped the Tumbes noble's sons, the Tumbes warriors captured two of the strangers. The local Tumbes people called the prisoners the yuraq yana qari, the white man and the black man.

She asked, "You've seen the strangers?"

"They lived in my village. They showed us how to make the bow more resilient, how to feather the shaft to fly faster and straighter. The yuraq yana qari is the reason the Shaur fear our warriors. They taught us where our aim is most deadly."

"And why Atahualpa wants your warriors," she added.

He nodded.

"Where are the strangers now?"

Urco tilted his head, raised an eyebrow, and with a tiny smile said, "Paititi. Lead us there and you will meet them."

"Paititi? I cannot lead you there, even if it existed, which I doubt. If it did, my father would have found and conquered it!" Sarpay's frustration was evident to everyone.

"The Cañari bought these two men from the Chamaya. In both tribes, these men heard the legend of Paititi…"

Sarpay interrupted, "They understood Cañari and Chamaya? Those tribes speak different tongues."

"They grasp languages fast. These men are not the gods promised to return, but they are wise beyond our learning. In a battle against your father's army, the white one captured a chasqui who was taking a quipu back to Atahualpa. The chasqui could not read the quipu but from it the yurak qari learned it was a communication about the battles and the strength of the Cañari army. He deciphered its code and kept your father's army at bay."

"How did he get to your village?"

"It was written in the quipu."

"He could read the quipu? There were no quipucamayocs among the Cañari. How did he learn?"

Urco simply shrugged. "You teach quipu keepers in yachay wasi, your house of learning."

Sarpay heard rumors about the strange intruders. The one with white skin grew hair on his face and was tall, like Urco's warriors. The black one, his partner, was quick and powerful. But they were captive slaves that somehow gained their freedom. She never heard that they became proficient in native languages, yet, understanding the quipu made the story sound too fantastic to believe. Though the quipucamayocs were not the only quipu keepers, only members from noble families enjoyed the education that included the quipu. How could the man learn how to read a thousand knots?

Sarpay considered herself proficient in reading the quipu, but had seldom found the need to do so to any great degree. Quipus were mostly used to keep track of peoples, populations, taxes, and harvests. Sarpay's interest in the quipus focused on the few senior quipucamayocs who used them for keeping records of times, seasons, and sacred events.

As a child, when Sarpay learned about the Creation God Viracocha, she thought it was part of the oral history passed from father to son. Vivid images of her father's priest those many years ago came clearly to mind. He was holding a colorful quipu in his hand when he taught her about the creation of the world. Now, these many years later, and with Urco's claim that the white man read a quipu, she wondered if whole stories were contained within the knots.

Her mind raced back to her childhood. Carried on her father's royal litter borne on the shoulders of powerful nobles, Sarpay traveled from Cusco to the shore of Lake Titicaca to worship at Tiwanaku, the great temple of a people of ages past. This was part of her preparations to become the First Priestess of the Empire. The journey, though many weeks long, had filled her with excitement. She was just a young girl at the time, yet the experience profoundly affected her view of her world. The priest's deep, warm voice captured her imagination. She visualized in her mind the actual creation of the world as he spoke to his young priestess.

She remembered back how the sun dipped low in the sky, casting long shadows across the massive Gateway of the Sun. They sat around a crackling fire. The evening air was cool. A soft breeze drifted off Lake Titicaca. Adding peace to her heart was the distant melody of cannas played by the llama keepers to their animals as they settled for the night. Her father's priest, draped in richly embroidered robes, settled comfortably beside Sarpay. His eyes reflected the flickering flames as he began to weave the ancient tale.

"Listen well," he said. His voice was full of reverence. He then insisted she needed to understand what he was about to tell, for it was the very essence of the Inca's existence. It was the foundation upon which the empire stood.

"In the beginning," he said, "there was only boundless darkness and chaos. The world was not yet formed, only energy and potential. The great Creator God Viracocha descended from heaven. Viracocha had great power and wisdom. From the chaos, He organized this world. He brought order. With his powerful voice, He summoned the sun and moon gods, Inti and

Mama Killa. He commanded them to light up the heavens. Inti's golden rays pierced the darkness and cast its light on the world He formed.

"Viracocha," the priest said, "placed each star in the sky to give us guidance in the nighttime." Sarpay remembered staring up into the sky watching the stars begin to twinkle in the darkening sky. The priest continued, pausing from time to time, letting Sarpay absorb the story.

"With the world now illuminated, Viracocha continued forming the earth. He shaped each mountain, dug the deep oceans. He carved valleys and made beautiful sacred rivers. With His holy divine hands, He was an artist at work."

In Sarpay's young mind, she thought about her favorite places and how she loved each place for its own beauty. The priest interrupted her drifting thoughts.

"Young princess, even with all the beauty and wonder, the earth was still empty. There was no life. Viracocha knew that this new creation had no use without life. He wanted a living earth, so He breathed life into the soil. Soon the first plants sprang forth. This pleased Viracocha. The earth became more beautiful. The mountains became clothed with forests, grass, and flowers. The world came to life. He filled the flowing rivers and oceans with fish. He placed animals large and small upon the hills and valleys.

"Viracocha saw there was something still missing. There was no one to see the beauty of what He had organized out of chaos. There was no one to appreciate Viracocha for what He created. There was no one to enjoy this new world. There was no one to honor Him and give Him reverence. So He took from the rocks and formed the first humans and breathed into them life. These first humans began to grow and to fill the earth. They failed to glorify Viracocha. The humans did not appreciate the beauty created by Viracocha. They did not honor their creator. They did not give reverence to Him for his creation. He was sad. They became a selfish and angry people. The whole earth was filled with unhappiness. The people grew large and strong and hard.

"Viracocha loved the humans He created, but they did not serve Him. He commanded the rains to fall and the oceans to rise until all the people drowned. He washed the earth with a great flood. When the world was once again clean, He began again to place animals upon the land and the forests and valleys began again to become beautiful and green.

"Then instead of from rocks, He took of the clay and formed people. He hoped these people would have softer hearts and would love and honor Him, and love His creation."

The priest paused, letting the significance of the moment settle in.

Sarpay thought of the massive Gate of the Sun only a few hundred feet away with its carved image of Viracocha holding thunderbolts in each hand and wearing a crown with rays of the sun. She wondered if the tears were caused by His sadness at having to destroy the humans He created and start again.

"But Viracocha's work was not done," the priest continued. "He divided the humans into many groups: some to live in the highlands and some to dwell in the lowlands, some to live near the deserts, and some to live on distant islands. To each people He gave gifts of crops and animals and taught them to thrive and be happy and to fill the earth."

The priest's voice took on a tone of deep reverence. "And so, young Sarpay, First Priestess of the Empire, you have an important work to help our great people, the mighty Inca, to honor our great Creator Viracocha. With his creation complete, Viracocha departed from the world and returned to the heavens where He could observe the fruits of his labor. He left behind the sun god, Inti, to light the day and the moon goddess, Mama Killa, to guide the night. And He entrusted us, His children, with the sacred duty to honor and care for the world He had so lovingly crafted."

With his gaze steady and full of pride, the priest concluded. "We, the people of the Inca Empire, are the descendants of those first humans, and it is our sacred duty to remember this story and to live in harmony with the heavens. We are the stewards of Viracocha's creation, and through our actions, we honor His divine vision."

Urco was patient with Sarpay's mental journey back into her past.

Sarpay wondered if her mighty Inca Empire was honoring Viracocha's divine vision. Was conquering other peoples and destroying one another, living in harmony with the heavens? She realized that indeed the Creator God Viracocha, and the sun and moon gods, Inti and Mama Killa, were requiring her blood as a sacrifice to bring harmony back into the world.

Sarpay had always felt a deep sense of connection to the world and its origins, a profound understanding of her place within the grand tapestry of the cosmos. Her mind cleared and she focused on Urco, who was securing a fresh tip to another perfectly straight shaft. As if she hadn't just journeyed back twenty years to relive a very sacred part of her life, she calmly said, "And your yuraq qari did not tell you where to find Paititi?"

Urco looked from his arrow and into her eyes. "He found a prophesy on the quipu, a warning about a people who, in the search for gold, will leave a trail of blood so wide and so deep the rivers will weep in sorrow."

The vision her father saw just before his death and the subsequent visions she received concerning the Inca Empire supported Urco's claim the yuraq qari indeed found and deciphered a quipu.

Who was this white man? Was he a spy? Did he find Paititi and was he going to lead the invasion she'd seen in vision to the great city of gold? For the first time, she felt an urgency to find Paititi and warn the people. She didn't even know if it was real. If the people of Paititi were Inca, wouldn't her father have known them? Wouldn't she know where Paititi was? Or was it like the people of Tiwanaku down on Lake Titicaca, a mighty empire of ages past, now only a remnant of glory?

Urco handed her the finished arrow, pulling her from the mental battle raging inside her. He began assembling another.

# Chapter Thirteen

Pyrenees Mountains, France

Though the moon knew which direction it needed to travel through the night sky, Martín simply assumed if he set the moon over his left shoulder, they'd at least be in France. The two horses were likely rested before they undertook this trek upward. Martín let them work their course north through the night.

The oncoming dawn added detail to the shadows in the east and rimmed the horizon in a delicate pink glow. The sun ultimately cracked over the eastern horizon. Flashing lights glistened through the woods. As Martín and Marguerite reached the rim of the tree line, the sparkles became blinding. Opening before them, an iridescent alpine lake produced a dazzling vista. Martín was oblivious to his horse's defiance to advance. Marguerite's horse stepped backwards in somewhat of a panic.

A great brown bear intent on his breakfast stood at the edge of the lake and tore into a thick growth of berry bushes, burrowing fiercely for a breakfast. At the whinny of the horses, the bear turned. Irritated by the interruption, he opened his massive mouth and bellowed a frightening growl. Both horses, now giddy, anxiously backed up. The bear returned to his scrub. Determining it barren of any nourishment, the massive furry arm gave it one swipe with his mighty paw, claws shooting leaves and wood sailing. He trudged off along the shoreline toward the waterfall that was feeding the lake its crystal pure water.

Ultimately, he lumbered up and away from the lake. The horses settled down, and Martín led his horse along the opposite shoreline. He dismounted and offered a hand to ease Marguerite down.

"First time in the Pyrenees?" Marguerite asked as she untucked, unfolded, and straightened her gown.

He couldn't pull his eyes off the glory of the setting.

"First time anywhere," he said, eyes glued to the wonder of it all. He reached into the pouch on his Andalusian and drew a cup from the handful of utensils accompanying a selection of dried meats, fruits, and cheeses. Martín wondered if the farmer who provided these much-appreciated supplies knew of their generosity, or if God's silver provided. Humphrey had prepared them well. Martín also wondered how he knew the captives would arrive at that village and subsequently prepared for their escape. Who is Humphrey? That question still troubled Martín.

Martín dipped the cup into crystal clear water from a spring emptying into the lake and handed it respectfully to Marguerite.

"Martín, Humphrey said you are Basque. Your father never brought you to these mountains?"

Martín shook his head. "I never knew my father. Until an old Basque caretaker at the Gaztelugatxe claimed he knew my father and said he might still live, I was certain he died before I was born. That's what my mother said."

Martín took the cup and refilled it for the princess. She welcomed it and quickly emptied it again. He repeated the gesture. When she raised her hand, he nodded and filled and emptied the cup again and again himself.

"What took you to Trujillo?" she asked.

Martín told the story of how, when his mother was widowed and wanted to raise Martín with family in Trujillo, they left their homeland. He talked of her death, how Friar Tomás took him in as an orphan, and even how Señora Lopez became a type of caretaker.

As they enjoyed the warmth of the rising sun, Martín told of the Gitanos, how he accompanied Faustino and Carmelita to their camp, and how Vano introduced him to Humphrey. When he shared the antic of the bishop's indulgence funding his adventure, she laughed out loud, startling a doe and her fawn, who had cautiously come to the lake for a drink.

Martín recognized the princess was at odds with King Charles, and that she was not overly disturbed Martín had in his possession copies of the holy scriptures which undoubtedly made him a heretic. He wanted to trust her but was unsettled about all that had developed the past many weeks. Too many conflicting parties. There was no way his short, meaningless life equipped him for this.

"Humphrey called that silver tied to your saddle God's silver. He insists you have a calling from God. Do you know what that calling is?" she asked.

Martín shook his head. "God does not talk to me."

"Do you talk to Him?" she asked.

He hadn't held eye contact with Marguerite for more than a glance until now.

He looked into her eyes, trying to read the question behind the question. "No. Not since Friar Tomás made me recite the Lord's prayer," he finally confessed.

"That is not what I asked," she said. Her eyes remained fixed on his.

Again, he wondered what she meant.

She expanded her question. "I grieve men such as Friar Tomás suffer at the hands of wicked men who claim God's authority. If you have read the holy words of Christ as you say you have, did you find in them justification for man to do anything other than forgive and love?"

She didn't wait for an answer. Martín realized she didn't plan to.

"Friar Tomás must have felt something special in you. He prepared you for something. Your Gitano patron Vano perceived it as well. Even the highwayman Humphrey, who risked his life to provide you the means to carry out the work…" she looked over at the bag of silver tied to Martín's Andalusian, "senses God knows you."

This was all too overwhelming for Martín's young mind to fathom. Finally, his mouth found itself.

"Who are you?" His mouth hung open, but his eyes never left hers. Her gentle smile sent an affection through his body.

"I think…I am a tutor…your tutor."

"No, who are you?" This time, Martín tried to exert some tenacity, which was still a new struggle for him.

"I am French. I am considered royalty. I own land. The king gave me to a man for a political alliance. Which one of those do you want me to be?" Her smile grew.

Martín knew so very little about the workings of the royals. He didn't know what to say.

"Martín," she said, "I am Marguerite d'Angouleme, daughter of the Duchess d'Angouleme, Louise de Savoy and Charles de Velois, d'Orléans, Duke d'Angouleme. As wife of Charles IV, Duke of Alençon, I am also

Duchess of Alençon and Berry. I was once promised to several royals, including the English King Henry VIII, to the Constable of Bourbon, and to Philip of Austria."

Her beautiful dark eyebrows lifted slightly, affixing exclamation marks to her introduction.

She paused, giving him time to absorb these names and titles. "What you may have been asking, and what matters the most right now? I am sister to Francis the First, King of France, who currently is held prisoner by our dear Holy Roman Emperor, Charles V."

Even with so little experience with politics, things became very clear.

"Will not your husband the duke come to rescue you?" Martín asked.

"Not right away. He died last year. We were married only a few years, yet he would never chance challenging these Spaniards. Martín, God sent you to rescue me," she finally said. Martín couldn't tell if she was serious or not. Technically, she rescued him, he thought. He let it lie.

Again, he turned his attention to the majesty of the water cascading into the crystal-clear alpine lake. Never had he seen such majesty. Yet never had he stood in the presence of such majesty.

Marguerite began tucking and poking and folding her gown, readying to mount her horse. Martín gave her a hand up, swung up onto his own mount, and they proceeded around the lake.

By late afternoon, they dropped out of the more rugged terrain. It wouldn't be long until they were out of the cover of the woods. The dense forest soon gave way to foothills. They continued until the sun, which greeted them in the morning, bid them a peaceful good night. They found a small grass-filled meadow where the horses earned their night's rest, and quickly ate from the provisions provided by Humphrey. As the moon rose, Marguerite and Martín were both too tired to do any more exploring into Martín's purpose of life. He was grateful.

His sleepy eyes made their last attempt to fathom the majesty of the stars above, stars he'd never tired of watching.

# Chapter Fourteen

## Pyrenees Mountains, France

Martín and his hostess were awoken by a gentle breeze quaking the leaves. The leaves joined in with the rhythm of tumbling water from the nearby spring. Together they performed in the orchestra accompanied by the early morning chorus of swallows, snow finches, and jays, calling, replying, and gently waking the visitors.

Martín still wondered about his hostess, the most valuable prize ever hunted by an emperor. What would this new day bring?

The near icy spring water forbade anything more than a quick splash to rinse the sleep from their eyes and faces. They ate a paltry breakfast, preserving the stores Humphrey had so considerably packed. Those stores, Martín appreciated, would only last another day if they ate any more robustly. Would a princess be satisfied eating so scanty a meal? He wondered.

For most of the morning, they rode along a ridgeline that overlooked a fertile valley. In the distance, small clusters of buildings came and went, but none of them appeared to be anything resembling a village.

When they stopped to give their horses another break, a break both Marguerite and Martín also needed, Martín noticed her frustration with the awkwardness of the gown, which by the day looked less regal.

"How did your brother become king?" It took a bit of courage for Martín to begin his own questions of the princess.

Marguerite smiled. "I wondered how you were going to begin your education." Her eyes danced perfectly with her smile to put Martín's uneasiness aside in questioning a lady of Marguerite's stature.

"Friar Tomás said our belief that God destined certain men to rule was foolish. He said if God so intended, why would kings worry so much about an heir to whom they could pass the throne?" Martín's question added raised eyebrows to Marguerite's expression.

"I like your Friar Tomás." Marguerite started, "He is right. What they profess and what is real are two different worlds. The professed world is based on the belief that the land belongs to God. Kings rule by divine right. They manage the land and use it as they wish. They consider it their land."

Martín interrupted her. "Where does the pope fit in? Is he above the king, between the king and God?"

Martín understood her slightly raised finger meant she was getting to that relationship.

"The power of a king is only as strong as he can influence the citizens over whom he reigns to follow the laws he establishes and enforces."

Martín squinted in slight recognition of the fact.

Marguerite climbed back onto her horse. Martín handed her the reins and hopped up onto his. They rode along the ridge.

She continued, "Land. It is all about land. Everything depends on who owns it. The land is the provider of life. Since the king claims ownership, land becomes the source of his influence. The king grants the land to important people. These people pledge loyalty to the king and swear to serve and protect him. These people we call nobles.

"The king also grants land to lesser important people he calls knights. These are military men. They agree to fight for the king in exchange for their lands. The lands are no good if there are no people to work them. Since only those to whom the king grants land can own it, all the rest of the people must work the land if they are to eat. Thus, most of the people are what we call serfs or peasants. Literally, they belong to the land. When a king grants land to a noble or a knight, the peasants who belong to the land essentially become property of those to whom the king granted the land."

So far, this was easy to understand for Martín. Friar Tomás used a similar reasoning to help Martín understand why he was a peasant and how his family fit into the bottom of the functioning societal order.

"The pope," she continued, "is in a unique position. He wields tremendous power, yet he doesn't claim to own the land as does the king. The pope claims the right to challenge a king's right to own the land, since the people accept him as the representative of God. The pope is God's vicar on earth. He claims—and the people accept that claim—that he has the God-given responsibility to intervene and impose sanctions on an unjust king. If indeed the pope has power to pronounce judgement against a king, he may depose a king, forfeit the king's kingdom and put another king in his place, or excommunicate a king. He may also endorse the actions of a king."

Martín hesitated for only a moment, considering the statement about a pope's endorsement. Then he blurted out the question.

"If a king committed a horrendous act, contrary to the commandments of Jesus Christ, commandments that you and I can read in the very words I have here," he patted the bundle on the back of his saddle, "but the pope says it's God's will, then the king will never be punished, and he can keep his lands, and thus his power?"

Marguerite slowly nodded her head. "Sadly, yes."

"Then all the king has to do is keep the pope happy, and if he helps the pope get whatever he wants, both of them can sin with immunity," Martín said with confidence.

"An unjust king and a corrupt pope make a terrible pair," she admitted.

"What about your brother?"

"Am I still answering how he became king? Or am I now answering if he is an unjust king?"

Martín paused, fearing he may have been too bold. "I don't believe I have the right to ask you, as his sister, to judge your own brother." Martín toned back his words.

Marguerite switched from her delicately accented Spanish, which Martín felt might have been her weakest language, to Latin. Though he'd learned Latin from Friar Thomás and felt he could read and write it proficiently, he had very little practice using it in conversation. He was surprised when she so naturally continued this conversation in Latin. Yet, it seemed logical.

"Tell me Martín, how you would define primogenitura."

Much of this conversation had taken place as the two rode side by side. At this question, Martín slowed his horse to a stop so he could think it through. Marguerite did the same.

Martín struggled at first, composing his response in Latin.

"primogenitura, probably comes from primogenitus, which I believe comes from primus and the past participle gignere and genitus."

So many Latin words were similar in Spanish, Martín often mixed the two with little notice.

"You were paying attention." Marguerite's expression displayed her surprise. "That law and variations of it have ruled the succession of kings for centuries. How much do you want to know?" she asked.

"How long do we have until we are safe, and you no longer need to pretend I rescued you?" he said with a joking smile.

"Well then," Marguerite launched into a lecture on the law of firstborn inheritances. "This rule of primogenitura developed among successions in France over centuries. In 1316, they debarred Joan from the throne, the only surviving child of Louis X of France, in favor of her uncle, Philip, Count of Poitiers. After this, they declared women could not inherit the French throne. Then in 1328, after the death of Charles IV, his paternal cousin, Philip, Count of Valois, became king, notwithstanding the claims of Edward III of England. By proximity of blood, Edward was the closest male related as the eldest son of Isabella, the sister of Charles. The assemblies of the French barons and prelates and the University of Paris resolved that males who derive their right to inheritance through their mother should also be excluded. This ruling became a key point of contention in the subsequent Hundred Years War. Over the following century, French jurists adopted a clause from the 6th century Pactus Legis Salicae, a century ago, which asserted that no female or her descendants could inherit the throne. And that was the governing rule for the French succession."

Martín just stared at Marguerite. She burst into laughter at his shock.

"When you are a woman and you cannot join with your brother jousting, fighting, or enjoying sport, learning obscure history becomes your sport," she said.

Martín realized her teasing him was her sport. He liked her. She was fun.

"I just wanted to know why your father was not the king before your brother," he said.

Marguerite laughed again.

"Before my brother became king, King Louis XII reigned from 1498 to 1515. He did not have any direct male heirs. He liked my brother and so he chose my brother to be king."

Martín didn't want to accept that answer, but she offered no more. They continued along.

Martín finally asked, "Do you believe God chose him? Or King Louis? Why not choose me or Humphrey?"

"It is the bloodline," she said. "Neither you nor Humphrey have royal blood. King Louis XII is our cousin. Without an heir, Francis became a natural choice," she said.

"Is he the only cousin?" he asked. "Certainly, you know of a few other cousins."

She laughed. "Oh, I know of a few other cousins. How about you, how close are you to your cousins?"

"I don't have any cousins that I know. My mother's family from Trujillo were gone when we got there, and I never met anyone from my father's family. How many cousins do you have?"

"Hundreds," she said. "Francis and I, and King Louis XII share a fourth great grandfather. King Charles the First had eleven children. Only one son could follow him as king. The other ten are still royalty. They marry royalty from other lands, or at least nobility from other lands, and mostly so that the kingdom remains strong or can grow."

"Do you get to choose?" Martín asked. He knew better. Friar Tomás never liked how the royalty bartered, traded, or aligned their children for alliances between kingdoms. It was one of the many opinions that crept into the lessons Martín received from the friar. Martín was curious how Marguerite would answer.

"No."

Martín noticed her answer had lost its playfulness. She had been so upbeat, almost happy to share her sport. So he left his next question for later, that of her late husband.

"What does a king do with his ten royal children?" he asked.

"They get lands, estates. And they grow. The next king does the same. Each has a few more children and soon, some of the royal children have been married to the royal families in other kingdoms, all in hopes of unifying to strengthen a king's power and influence."

Martín noticed this was almost a mechanical presentation of her family tree with no passion.

"How do you keep track of them all?" he asked.

"We never can." She paused, "Well, we have scribes keeping the royal records. Clergy also keeps records, births, baptisms, marriages…"

"And it was your sport to study those records?" he teased. "And that's how, from your hundreds of cousins, your brother became king? You helped position him?"

Martín regretted the statement as soon as it left his lips. It wasn't his own thought. Jockeying, manipulating, and positioning people for titles was another of the offending practices Martín learned about from the friar. In one of the many lessons, Friar Tomás told Martín about the pope's rise to become the pope. The pope had purchased, at the age of thirty-seven and not even a priest, the papacy by securing votes with promises of position and wealth. Martín still wondered, however, from the hundreds of cousins, why Francis?

Marguerite's eyes had widened and her face flushed. That was the second line Martín crossed that was out of bounds.

He quickly tried to recover. "I'm sorry."

She looked at Martín for a long while. He became uncomfortable having offended the king's own sister at least twice now. He wondered if he kept it up, if she might turn him over to the clergy after all. The scorching sun on his back would be nothing compared to that of the pyre.

Her face softened. "Martín of Bolibar, your innocence and honesty are refreshing. I believe Humphrey and what he told me your friar and your Gitano friend Vano claim about you. I hope you find the work God has for you."

He tired of hearing about God's future for him. He changed this line of thinking, "Each new king has a royal family with princes and princesses who marry and make kingdoms of their own?"

They both relaxed. She continued the lesson. "As I mentioned, it's about land. But along with lands come titles. Though land is the same everywhere, if it is worked, people eat, if it is not worked, they do not eat; titles vary from kingdom to kingdom. With royal blood, princes and princesses maintain those titles when needed. More commonly we give them titles of duke and duchess. Some of those princes and princesses marry royalty, some marry nobles."

"Hereditary titles, such as count, duke, and earl are often linked to lands, power, and responsibilities. My father, four generations from King Francis, was a duke. My mother was a noble, not royal. Francis and I have royal blood through my father."

Martín followed her explanation easily. Yet, he was waiting to learn why Louis chose Francis and not one of the many other cousins.

He posed another question. "You said there are hundreds of cousins. There would have to be hundreds scattered over four generations." Then

Martín paused and squinted, pondering how to rephrase his delicate question, a question which could undo the current calm. "Why Francis?"

Marguerite opened her mouth to answer, when both she and Martín turned to see a cloud of dust in the distance along a road far to their left. They quickly pulled their horses behind one of the few stands of trees that grew along a spring flowing down from the snows in the Pyrenees. They watched as the horsemen came into view. It didn't look like they were following Martín and the princess, but they were certainly in a hurry, heading the same way.

During the few days Martín and Marguerite traveled, they'd kept their distance from villages and settlements. A young Spaniard traveling on horseback with a lady dressed in a princess gown would create too many questions and would be hard to forget.

"It is time we make some changes," she said as they watched the horsemen slow, nearing a distant collection of buildings. "Are you willing to spend some of God's silver to buy yourself a peasant woman?"

"If I spent the whole of it, I could never turn you into a peasant. I've known peasant women. They are nothing like you."

"Then we two will become troubadours on our way to King Francis's court," she said.

"And should someone ask us to entertain?" he asked.

"Then we entertain. Do you sing?" she asked.

Martín sat up so quickly and stiffly in the saddle, Marguerite struggled to hold back the laughter.

"I will compose for you an epic poem. It will impress, inspire, and entertain. It will be of such harmonious majesty you will draw all attention away from the scullery maid traveling with you."

Was this her idea of sport? Yes, words are her passion, he resolved. But he didn't relax.

"Of course, your epic poem will be in French. Yes, Martín, you will learn French. I will see to it."

Though Martín guessed that Marguerite worked out her plan perfectly in her head and was keen on sharing it with him, the two kept a careful eye on the band of horsemen who disappeared into the small settlement.

"Who are they?" he asked.

"Likely the Constable of Bourbon's men, a traitor to France." She said it so dispassionately, it surprised Martín there was no anger in her tone. His attention turned from the settlement to Marguerite, who continued watching through the trees. She spoke as if this revelation were nothing more than small talk. It was her casualness that amazed Martín.

"The Constable of Bourbon, Charles III, was the Duke of Bourbon. Smart, rich, handsome. Owned lots of land he inherited through his wife's family. In fact, he is in line to be king if my brother's sons do not. He is the very reason the emperor, Charles V, holds my brother prisoner in Madrid. We just call him the Constable."

"He betrayed your brother?"

"And my mother. She was going to marry him."

If Marguerite had turned to look at Martín, she would have laughed out loud at his gaping mouth and stupefied look.

"My mother wanted his lands and thought if she married him, she could settle the question of who those lands belonged to. Remember, Martín, it's about land. When the Constable did not want to marry my mother, and I do not fault him for it, she is fourteen years his senior, Francis took the land from him anyway."

Marguerite still watched carefully, moving her head between the trees to maintain a careful view of the settlement.

"The Constable was and is a cunning general. When Francis stripped him of his command and titles, he became a traitor and secretly joined with your Charles V, the Holy Roman Emperor, and Henry VIII as they try to partition France."

Was she composing the epic story already? This was fantastic. Martín had to interject a question just to keep the story straight.

"Did your brother, the king, strip him of the command before or after he refused to marry your mother?"

"After." Again, she never turned her attention from the horsemen in the settlement.

"Well, I can see how that might be difficult," Martín muttered.

"But it was during the battle of Pavia, where the Germans and the Spanish defeated the French badly, and they killed many of our great nobles. That is when Charles V took my brother prisoner. The Constable led the Spanish and German forces."

Martín couldn't help but wonder how such a chain of events eventually resulted in one king being held prisoner by another king, and the commander responsible was at one time invited to be the king's father-in-law. Being poor and hungry in Trujillo was so simple.

"And now he is after you?" Martín asked.

She nodded.

"Do you think he regrets not marrying your mother?" Martín couldn't make himself not ask.

Finally, Marguerite turned to see Martín's giant smile bringing her out of the concentration on the chain of events. Events that turned her from a princess once offered to the King of England into a fox being chased by a pack of hounds out for blood.

They both laughed at the thought.

"For many, revenge is sweet balm to the wounded soul. But it seldom stops the bleeding and always leaves a scar," she said.

She turned back to watch the horsemen dismount and enter various buildings. They were searching, it was clear. Eventually, they all mounted and continued their trek northward. Martín wondered how many villages would they search? How far would they dare to travel before admitting failure? Will they have hired spies in each village they visit? For certain, they would fail. They must fail.

# Chapter Fifteen

## Urubamba River Crossing - Inca Empire

"Do you have a wife?" Cusimi asked Urco.

Very little personal information had been shared since the group fled from the Picchu Citadel, and very little before. Now, as time stretched from days into weeks and then months since leaving the palace in Quito, she hungered for the genuine companionship she and Sarpay shared for so many years. The pain of failing to take Sarpay's blood to satisfy the gods contrasted with her gratitude for Urco's strength in delaying the sacrifice until another day.

Though she knew that Sarpay believed it was a sacrifice needed, her love for Sarpay overshadowed her desire to appease the gods. Would her rebellion against the will of the gods bring on the destruction of the empire?

She concluded it was time to be a person, a living, loving human, a woman again. Not just a fugitive. If they were going to die, she wanted to live first.

"Not anymore," Urco said.

Cusimi hadn't thought she might open a wound with such a simple question, but what did she expect? A yes or no? Her eyes begged him for more.

Urco's eyes were kind. "My wife, given to me by Sarpay's father, was a daughter of a noble from Cusco. She died giving birth to my son. Our village was attacked and several of our people taken captive. Cataquil and I and a few others went to rescue our people. When we returned, my wife had given birth but bled to death because our village shaman was one of those taken captive. When we returned, our shaman, one of those we rescued, tried to save my son. Yet my son also died. My wife and my son should be enough of a blood sacrifice to appease the gods."

There was no bitterness as Urco spoke. But the sadness seemed to provide a level of determination. Cusimi began to sense the urgency in Urco's desire to find Paititi and leave a world of blood and war behind. It was not the gold that drove Urco. He sought safety for him and his people. Cusimi could feel his love for them.

"I am so sorry," she said.

Cataquil, who never spoke except to Urco about the defense and escape said, "I am sorry too." He spoke so softly, it was hardly audible.

Cusimi turned to Cataquil. He was looking down. She had never made eye contact with him in all this time. She had never spoken with him actually, and he never spoke to her. She wanted to ask if Cataquil was his real name. The God of Thunder and Lightning was named Cataquil. Was this a formal name or a nickname given for a power and temperament she had yet to see?

"You loved Urco's wife?" Cusimi couldn't resist trying to spark a conversation. It flickered and died. Urco spoke up.

"Cataquil came to our village with Tica, my wife. Tica is his twin sister, born of a noble mother. When I married Tica, I married Cataquil. They were inseparable. I believe sometimes they still are one. I often feel Cataquil's wisdom comes directly from Tica. When he speaks, I listen."

Cataquil never looked up, but Cusimi knew he was listening. Did the conversation offend him? She watched him closely as she asked her next question. "Cataquil, did you know the yuraq qari?"

Cataquil looked up quickly. His eyes seemed to want eagerly to respond, but he remained silent. Cusimi, Sarpay, and Urco said nothing. Finally, Cataquil, in practically a whisper said to the ground, "They promised to come back. They never did. My Tica is dead."

Urco caught Cusimi's eye, and his slight nod of the head confirmed that was all she would get from Tica's other half.

"You promised to sacrifice me yourself when we reach the temple in Cusco. Will you keep your promise when we reach the Apurimac temple instead, if there are no living priests or priestesses to be found?" Sarpay asked.

"Apurimac?" Urco repeated.

Cusimi gave Sarpay credit for remaining focused. She realized Sarpay's resolve to give her life stood directly in opposition to Urco's design to find Paititi. And without Sarpay receiving a vision from the gods as to where Paititi is, he had no chance of ever finding it. Cusimi hoped Urco would keep the priestess alive, Paititi or not. Yet, the Apurimac temple, if they found no massive armies standing between them and it, was less than a few weeks away.

Cusimi whispered a prayer to the gods, to inspire Sarpay to believe they, the gods, accepted Urco's wife and son to be blood enough. Though she knew they wouldn't.

"Cusco will take too long. There are too many armies between us and Cusco," Sarpay said.

Cusimi shuddered. She knew Apurimac was closer and had a very sacred temple. It was a temple Sarpay favored with great reverence. If there were one, Cusimi knew the Apurimac temple would be Sarpay's choice. Several times, Cusimi had accompanied Sarpay when she served as the oracle of the Apurimac. It stood above the Apurimac River Gorge, looking down nearly two miles into the violent rapids of the Sacred Apurimac River. The rapids were believed to convey divine messages. The priests there were certain to fulfill Sarpay's directive. Cusimi felt she needed to impede Sarpay's journey. Though betrayal was not in her character, she turned to Urco and whispered.

"When we reach the Apurimac, and Sarpay fulfills her duty to the gods, how will you find Paititi?" Cusimi didn't care if she revealed a part of herself that boarded on apostasy from the workings of the gods.

Urco smiled, "Our priestess Sarpay will not disappoint the gods. I will not disappoint her, and she will not disappoint my people. If we are to find Paititi, the gods will make it possible."

It was clear to Cusimi her question struck an offensive tone with Cataquil. He brought his head up and glared into Cusimi's eyes.

"We will find it," Cataquil said, "I know."

Could Cataquil be a god of lightning and thunder? Not so far, she concluded.

Throughout Cusimi's effort to bring the small four-person consort of pilgrims together, Urco finished tying several arrows, bundled the supplies, and readied the group for the journey from the safety of his jungles through the rugged mountains and across the Apurimac River.

There were three passable rope bridges they might cross. They all knew it was likely each would be either guarded by Atahualpa's soldiers or destroyed by them. Urco and Cataquil were certainly not dressed for the high Andes mountains.

Urco and Cataquil now had the challenge of finding a friendly tribe or visit an unfriendly one by stealth to secure more provisions and appropriate clothing. Urco took no offense to Cusimi's curiosity. He appreciated it. She was truthful and open. He shared her skepticism about the gods requiring blood. The battles between the tribes in the empire, not to mention between the Incas and outside tribes, should provide enough blood for all the gods, yet somehow it didn't. Could only the blood of the firstborn satisfy them?

Urco led the small group, and Cataquil, carrying the largest bundle, followed in the rear. As they climbed up out of the thick jungles, evidence of a passing army gave them peace, along with horror. The armies had moved on; they were safe for now, Yet, the first village they approached still smoldered. Bodies laid strewn and charred.

"Quichamba," Urco said. The stone and mud buildings stood lifeless, charred, with their thatch roofs burned away. Urco knew he would find more bodies trapped by a murderous army, suffocating smoke and flame inside. The gentle, innocent conversation of only hours before about families echoed through his mind. He rummaged through the carnage from house to house searching for life. This village, on the edge of the Antisuyu jungles must have resisted or even just existed as it stood in the path of a locust-like army devouring every living thing in its path.

Urco stood in the doorway of the village's largest structure that he figured was the home of the village's noble. A large woven alpaca tapestry still hung on a wall. An image of Inti the sun god was woven into the fine fur. Only singed by the flames and matted with smoke, it hung defying the inferno. Did the gods have more respect for their own image than they did for humanity? He shook his head. He wondered if Cusimi, who he was learning wasn't as resolute as her mistress Sarpay, might also question the gods.

"Urco, come!" Cataquil called. There was urgency in his calm request. Urco followed past two burned shells of homes. There at the edge of the village where a large field of corn had been trampled, a young child no more than four or five years old lay clinging to the body of a woman who appeared to have been attempting to flee the village but whose progress ended with a spear to her back. Standing next to the scene was a young man not even in his teens. He stood defiant with a lance in one hand and an obsidian club in another. His tunic and sandals told Urco he was a chasqui, one of the empire's thousands of runners. A sling common to a fighter hung from the boy's leather belt. Urco wondered if the boy could wield the weapons. He hadn't run. Or maybe he did, but he arrived too late.

Sarpay quietly and tenderly knelt next to the child. Sarpay was no warrior and gave no threat to the young chasqui who kept his eye on Cataquil and Urco. Sarpay pulled the child away from the woman and into her arms. Urco couldn't hear the words she whispered, but he saw the peace settle the child's shaking body. The memory of his own lifeless Tica and his beloved baby melted his heart. But it didn't purge the anger. He looked upwards, and whispered, "Inti, God of the Sun, is this not enough death for you?"

Fearless, Cataquil approached and put his arms around the young runner and held him tight. Cusimi stepped up alongside Urco and the two watched two pure souls comfort two suffering ones.

"I will help you find Paititi," Cusimi said. Her eyes filled with tears not willing to fall.

"Where is my sister?" Atahualpa sat calmly carving slices of roasted llama. From a silver cup, he took a long drink of his chicha. He never looked up.

Quichamba never flinched as he answered. "When we caught them at Picchu, savages held us back long enough for her to disappear into the cloud forest. The Shuar failed to stop them. Your priestess sister, with some others, then disappeared. We believe they are heading to the protection of Huascar in Cusco. We have spies in every village. They will never reach Cusco."

If Quichamba was any other warrior, he knew a report like this one would end his life. But he was not like any other warrior, and he knew Atahualpa knew it. Quichamba was too valuable an assassin, and he was confident with his network of spies the priestess never would reach Cusco. And he would be a vital necessity to the future Sapa Inca. Quichamba knew it. Yet a second such failure might be too much.

"Our spies recovered a quipu with your brother Huascar's battle plans. A young chasqui is carrying the quipu to Quizquiz who is approaching the Apurimac," Quichamba said.

Atahualpa listened but never looked up. "You trust the young chasqui?"

"We destroyed a neighboring village and threatened to do the same to his village if he failed. He will not fail."

Nothing more was said. Quichamba retreated. Atahualpa cut another slice of the tender meat and filled his mouth. Juice ran down from the edge of his lips. A young girl, using a bright crimson cloth, caught the drip and stepped back ready to hand her master the silver cup.

# Chapter Sixteen

## Pyrenees Foothills, France

"Martín, are you ready to visit France? And become a Frenchman? I am certain the Constable's men are looking for a princess, possibly accompanied by an Englishman and a young Spaniard, not an old scullery maid accompanying a French troubadour."

Martín shuddered at her plan.

The horsemen they'd watched seemed to head north by northeast. Marguerite and Martín circled around the village and went a more westerly direction. It was late in the day when they reached a small town bustling with people. It was market day. Clusters of houses and businesses surrounded the monastery. There were enough people coming and going that two strangers were not a unique occasion. Yet they knew the Constable's men wouldn't miss a town like this one. Marguerite slipped off her horse and led both horses along a small stream that stunk with human refuse. She pulled a kerchief free and held it over her nose and mouth. They'd planned their approach as they rode. Marguerite would keep out of sight while Martín would shop for the right change of clothes for them both. Martín needed to look the traveling troubadour and Marguerite, though a bit older than him, a maid of no consequence. A bit of God's silver could make them into whatever they chose. They stopped between two secluded buildings.

To Martín, what goes on beneath a woman's outer gown was still a mystery. Marguerite told him that when he found a tailor's shop, a seamstress inside could help him find the right chemise and kirtle. With these two fresh items, Marguerite assured him she would look less the princess and more the maid. From there, she would secure the rest herself. When she referred to the rest of the clothing she needed, his bright red flush brought her to laughter.

He was also to secure a change of clothes for himself, which he welcomed. The only time he'd had relief from what he was wearing was a quick dip in a spring three days ago before they left the Pyrenees.

Locating a fabric shop that sold ready-made clothing wasn't always easy. Martín passed two drapers but felt their trade in fabric held little hope of finding something ready for Marguerite to wear. He wondered if she'd had a fine tailor make her clothes or if she was proficient at making them herself, as she was not only noble but royal.

A small sign hung beside a door with an emblem of needles and thread and the French word Mercier. Martín stepped inside. Martín had performed small services for Señora Lopez many times that required his delivering various woolen and linen cloths. This shop was not much different, with the exception that he didn't know the customers or workers. Though Marguerite coached him through the words in French, he'd never been on an errand for a princess hiding from evil men. He was more worried about his nervousness at speaking French than dealing with a crowd of women.

There were two large tables, one attended by five women spinning thread and the other covered by several piles of woolen bundles, where three women rolled out and measured with a long wooden measuring stick. The more matronly of the three women rolling out blue cloth looked up at Martín and, with a smile, nodded to a young maid to attend to him.

The maid happily left the other women to attend to the young handsome man. Martín was first taken by her striking blue eyes and red lips, contrasted by her pale pink complexion. When she opened those smiling lips, the words flowed out like music. He understood few of them but felt their friendly tone. He stood next to a tall counter upon which were scattered sewing threads, needles, and pins. Unconsciously, he reached over and picked up a pair of finely forged scissors and began squeezing them as if he were cutting the fabric, just as he'd done so many times before in Señora Lopez's friend's shop. He bowed and practiced his first French with this pretty young stranger.

"I am in need of a chemise and a kirtle for my sister."

Again, her musical words held him transfixed, but he gathered enough to understand she was asking the size. He held his hand about the height he thought Marguerite was and with both hands intimated her shape. Noticing the shears in his hand, he quickly set them back down, and with a wavy motion, illustrated Marguerite's curves. When he realized all the women in the shop were watching him describe a woman's shape, their chuckles generated a warmth in his face.

His French accent fled as he tried to recover from his embarrassment.

In broken Spanish, the matronly woman said, "Your sister? Cannot she come in herself?"

Recognizing he'd done a poor job masquerading as a Frenchman, but trying anyway, he said, "She is back home in Bolibar and I promised her something sewn of your fine French cloth."

The older woman, speaking still in Spanish smiled and asked, "Then why not take her our French silk chemise? If she is worthy of your affection, she is worthy of silk."

The matronly woman pointed to an area toward the back of the shop, returning to French said, "Show our friend here the fine silk."

The young French maid gladly ushered Martín to the back of the shop, away from the other women. Once alone, she pulled a large sandalwood box from a shelf. As she did, it nearly slipped from her hands. Martín instantly snatched it from her and gently placed it on a table. Her beautiful blue eyes blinked a thank you.

She opened the box and pulled a sheer silk chemise and, holding the thin shoulder straps, let it unfold, its hem tumbling to the ground. She held it up against herself to display its size compared to her. Again, Martín felt his face flush, this time much hotter. He could practically see through it. Slowly, he shook his head. Was that what a princess wears under a kirtle? Not if he were buying it, it wasn't. He hoped the young maid's impish smile was meant to tease and there was a more modest, more practical French chemise available. After all, Martín knew enough that most kirtles wouldn't completely cover the chemise.

After her jest, she pulled a fine linen chemise with sleeves and embroidered yellow pattern along the collar. She held it up as well. He nodded an approval. She then pulled another box from a tall shelf. This time, Martín reached up to help her set it on the table.

Several items sat inside the box. Martín pointed to the dark green one. She pulled it out and in like manner let it unfold as she held it up by the shoulders. As its hem touched the ground, Martín's nod signaled his approval.

The front door to the mercery banged open, startling everyone inside. From where the young maid and Martín stood, they couldn't see the commotion. The maid took a few steps to peer around the small partition that separated her and Martín from the front of the mercery.

A strong male voice cut through the light chatter of the women in the shop's front and yanked the smile from the young maid. Martín concentrated with all his might to understand.

"Men from Spain, under command of the king are seeking a noble woman, kidnapped by two men, one Spanish and the other English. The king offers a handsome reward for their arrest. If I were them, I'd be trying to disguise her so as not to be recognized. If they come here, I must know immediately."

Martín's wide eyes locked onto the young maid's eyes, begging. Her tiny smile revealed nothing. His breathing froze.

The women in the shop looked from face to face and then, almost in sync, looked toward the back of the shop. No words spoken. The man charged around the partition where he found the young maid folding the silk chemise and putting it back in its box. She secured the lid, put the box back on its shelf, and returned to the front of the shop where the other women continued measuring the cloth.

The man looked about the area and, seeing nothing out of the ordinary, commanded again, "Anything you suspect, I must know immediately." He stomped out and slammed the door behind him.

All eyes turned to the young maid, who quietly walked from woman to woman, placing a silver coin in front of each. No words said, she returned to work.

Grateful for a back door, Martín stood nervously as a cart passed, being pushed by two monks paying him no attention. Martín hung his head as they passed. Did they see the rush of red in his face? He softly touched his cheek where the maid kissed him as he escaped out the back. The more robust of the two monks, speaking in Latin, complained of the prior asking them to assist the bakery on their day of fasting. Martín smiled at the complaint, remembering the monks who'd served with Friar Tomás. Though servants of God, they were men with appetites, weaknesses, and passions.

His thoughts quickly turned to Marguerite. Did she know this small town was now aware of her escape—kidnapping? Would this town recognize their own king's sister, their princess? Where could he and the princess be safe? He kept the new chemise and kirtle tucked under his arm and followed the monks. If they returned to the monastery, and if it were typical, he would be on familiar ground.

He followed as carefully as he could. The two monks crossed a small bridge and passed through an arched entryway into the cloister. They immediately turned right, and because they'd mentioned working for the bakery, Martín hoped they headed to the kitchen, Martín's favorite part of a monastery. His stomach would have to wait. Seeking the dormitory and hoping all the monks would be attending to their various assignments; Martín passed the laundry. Even better, he thought. Several dark brown robes hung in the sunshine, newly washed and ready for a fugitive and kidnap victim. Martín quickly pulled two robes from the line and ducked back out of sight. With no one watching, Martín wrapped one robe around his middle and secured it with a rope. He then pulled the second robe over himself and secured it with a second rope. He wished for a mirror to admire his new shape. Pulling the hood over his head, he turned his back to the two monks who'd loaded the cart with bread and reentered the cloister.

Speaking now in slow deliberate Latin, Martín, with his face somewhat covered, said, "Good brothers, may I take my turn with your cart? Permit me to take it back to the market for you. You two may rest out of the scorching sun."

"Who are you?" asked the round monk.

"Friar Martín visiting from Pau," Martín said.

"Thank you, but Prior Phillip will not look kindly on us having a visitor serve us and us not him," the taller monk replied.

"May I at least earn a loaf for the end of my fast?" Martín said.

"That you may." The robust monk stepped away from the cart and let Martín pull. The three monks proceeded from the monastery toward the market.

Martín asked about Prior Phillip and other monks, their monastery, town, and market. He concluded Prior Phillip was a man of God like Friar Tomás. But he concluded there was no sense in taking any risks when the conversation turned to heresy and word that a robber escaped from the Church in Bilbao, and that the pope sent personal emissaries to capture a heretic and a tall Englishman with a devilish black horse who was traveling with his mistress accused of being a witch.

Even the Church was now in on the hunt. If these two innocent monks were aware of Marguerite's escape and his and Humphrey's part in the escape, this was becoming a dangerous journey.

Martín knew he had to get Marguerite away from here as quickly as possible. Martín feigned a knowledge of the chase, having heard of it from the bishop's men and hinted he'd heard the pope's emissaries knew the heretic, the Englishman, and his witch had actually gone south into Spain with a band of Gitanos.

When the monks and Martín reached the market, Martín politely thanked the monks for letting him serve them. He received two loaves gratefully and excused himself. He worked his way through the crowds. Few paid any attention to another monk. He walked confidently, keeping his hood over his head.

The stench of human refuse soon overpowered the smoke of the cooking fires, which until now masked the general odor of a crowded market. It quickly erased the welcoming smell of the fresh loaves in his arms. He left the market and rounded the edge of a building. From the corner of his eye, he saw a figure dart around its corner. His horse stood saddled next to hers.

"Milady," he whispered, "it's me, Friar Martín." Marguerite peeked out from the corner as he lowered the hood.

"Even the Church is hunting you. Your Constable of Bourbon is very thorough. They think you are a witch traveling with the English heretic Humphrey. The people think an English highwayman and a young Spaniard robbed the Church."

"Oh, Charles, Charles, Charles," she said. "I am complemented by the Constable's earnestness, but I laugh at his foolishness."

Martín handed the loaves to her and loosed the rope holding her new wardrobe. He pulled both the robe and her new clothes free. "I think we start with this." He handed her the robe, leaving the chemise and kirtle tucked under his arm. Fortunately, the robe was large enough to cover her dress with plenty of room. He smiled, recognizing there were monks even larger than the robust monk he assisted with the cart.

He helped Marguerite onto her horse and together they rode back along the small yet foul canal. Martín wanted to laugh at the hooded monk riding alongside him. Marguerite's voluminous dress, now accompanied by an oversize monk's robe all piled upon a horse gave the appearance of a giant bulbous spider carried by its tiny spindly legs. He'd feel sorry for her horse if he didn't know the giant bulbous body was just fluff and fabric.

# Chapter Seventeen

## Small French Town – Southern France

As they crossed the bridge leaving town, few people gave them any notice. Two monks on horseback were common enough. They soon were away from the town sufficiently to give their horses the freedom to charge away. Eventually, they slowed and walked their horses around a small, abandoned chapel, the far side having given its life in God's service and then tumbling in reverence to the newer chapel across the river. It stood silently in the center of the ruins of an ancient village, abandoned when the new monastery invited the people to migrate to more favorable lands.

Martín helped Marguerite untangle the mass of cloth holding her prisoner on the horse and she slipped down. Once free of the monk's robes, Martín readied to give her the new items of clothing. Before he could even pull the package free, Marguerite slipped out of her gown and stood before him in a tight, form-fitting chemise. His gaze froze, and his face flushed with heat. Marguerite laughed, stepped toward him, and almost had to pry the bundle from his stiff hands.

She stepped around the horse and used it for privacy. Martín watched as one chemise dropped to the ground, reheating his flushed face. At the sight of her bare legs, the monk's robe he wore became unbearably warm. Marguerite transformed from princess to maid. She gathered the changed items, tossed them over the saddle, and came back around the horse. The transformation was amazing.

The beautiful dark green kirtle laced up the front. Where the fresh white chemise was visible through the sleeves and waist, the seams of the kirtle, embroidered with yellow threads, accented the contrast between the two. She pulled it tight around her waist and, unlike the larger gown she'd been wearing before, she now looked a bit more plausible to be on horseback.

Marguerite held up the pair of leggings Martín included with the other items and, looking over the top of them, asked, "And these?"

His face flushed red again, "I thought that since you're riding astride, well…" He didn't know how to finish the statement. Again, she laughed out loud.

"Very thoughtful." She put them with her changed clothes and rolled them into a bundle, along with the monk's robe, and tied them to the back of her horse.

They rode off, now in disguise, and over the next two weeks as they traveled together, Martín learned of Marguerite's family, how years earlier she'd been offered to King Henry VIII, Prince Phillip of Austria, and then, to make a political alliance, King Louis VII gave her to Charles IV of Alençon, who died only two years later. Martín spent hour after hour learning and practicing French. After a time, she insisted the rest of the trip they only speak her native tongue.

Martín was getting an education unparalleled. In turn, Martín shared his story about living in Trujillo, his experience with Friar Tomás, how he'd been pushed along this unknown path with seemingly no choices given him.

Marguerite assured him several times that though she couldn't tell him what his role in current world affairs might be, she felt certain God did.

Each day, they'd stop only after dark and with an occasional fire. She insisted he read to her from the selections of the Bible that, for an unknown reason, Friar Tomás, even in his absence, arranged for Martín to have. Several times he questioned why he hadn't lost these sacred texts during all the time he was on the run as a heretic.

Only a few times did Marguerite and Martín feel confident about stopping at a small farmhouse and asking a family to host them for the night. Each time, though the families requested nothing in return, Martín saw to it they'd find a small thank you. A miracle he hoped they would consider their good fortune. A miracle he hoped they wouldn't share until he and Marguerite were far, far away.

"We should reach safety by nightfall," Marguerite said as they mounted up, the sun making its morning debut. The sound of horses in the distance interrupted the otherwise quiet dawn. Martín quickly pulled around and led both horses into a thicket, out of sight.

"Le roi Charles doit vous vouloir très mal." In his newly learned French, Martín's attempt to tell Marguerite that King Charles V must want her badly brought a welcome smile.

She chuckled. "Or you. You are the heretic, and they do not know Sir Humphrey abandoned us long ago. And I think by now King Charles does not care. It is the Constable's own vanity that drives this search."

Martín stood between the two horses with his fingers running through the manes, calming both horses. He turned from the upcoming horsemen and squinted at Marguerite.

Two horsemen passed. Interesting, he thought, a monk and an escort? What could be their hurry? They were too far away and through the cover of trees, Martín couldn't make them out, but there was a familiarity. Their cloud of dust settled, and the two fugitives waited several more minutes until the sound of beating horses' hooves was gone.

"That horse makes me think of one the Constable was so proud of. This story will interest you," she started. "The Constable is Charles III, Duke of Bourbon, as I mentioned. When his parents died, he was the sole heir to the family's titles and extensive lands in Auvergne. But it did not end there. He married his cousin Suzanne, Duchess of Bourbon. Now, as the Duke of Bourbon and with the death of Charles IV the Duke of Alençon, he was in line to become King of France, after my brother's sons."

They mounted up and carefully left the cluster of trees and followed the same direction as the horsemen.

Marguerite continued, "When Suzanne died, his lands were too much a temptation for my mother, and when the Constable refused the offer of marriage from my mother, she coerced my brother, the king, to confiscate the lands."

Martín's attention left the road ahead. He stared at Marguerite as she unraveled the tale. She told this so matter of fact. Having heard much of this earlier, the shock was gone, but his dismay at the behavior of people with power continued.

"When the Constable then betrayed France and joined with the Holy Roman Emperor Charles V and England's King Henry VIII to partition France, my brother stripped the Constable of lands, power, and titles, and rightly so."

"Naturally," Martín muttered in French.

Marguerite smiled at his attempt to solidify his language lessons.

"His treachery delivered my brother into King Charles V's hands. And it is his passion that is certainly behind our pursuer's relentlessness," she said calmly.

"I now see why he cares so deeply about my heresy," Martín said.

She turned to Martín, and her smile yielded to laughter as she realized how silly Martín's wicked heresy could ever compare to the intrigues and betrayals of kings and nations.

"Just confirming, he did not want to be your father-in-law?" Martín asked.

"Well," she said, "my mother is fourteen years his senior."

"Ah." Martín muttered nodding his head, "Still?"

The story continued about the families, relationships, and marriages between kingdoms, alliances, lands, and inheritances. Martín's tutor shared everything. She told story after story of men falling in love with the wives of other men. About wives and daughters falling in love with soldiers, servants, knights, and knaves. How kings seemed to own women and could use them as political capital, giving and taking for strategic gain.

Though Martín had no experience with women or their place in society, and his own mother passed away before he even reached the age of ten, he felt something about this was wrong, unjust, unfair. And there he sat, riding side by side with a remarkable woman who seemed to accept her strategic role without bitterness or anger. His mind reflected on Friar Tomás and how between lessons in reading, writing, the teachings of Christ, and the intricacies of the Church, Friar Tomás interspersed lessons on the ways of man. Oh, how he wished he'd understood then how little he knew, so he would have tried harder to learn.

Now, as he accompanied this brilliant woman, he wondered how little a person can know, or even how much a person can know.

# Chapter Eighteen

## The Kingdom of Navarre – South of France

Marguerite assured Martín they were now safely on the French side of the Pyrenees and were traveling in the Kingdom of Navarre. Speaking mostly French, she translated only new words so Martín could understand. She told how the Kingdom of Navarre straddled both the north and south sides of the Pyrenees and had once been part of Martín's own Basque homeland until Ferdinand and Isabella, whose passion to own the small country, drove them to conquer and make Navarre Spanish lands. They only succeeded in conquering the southern half.

She went on to describe Navarre's king. King Henry II d'Albret. Only a few years older than Martín, he was vivacious and creative, she said. As Marguerite described him, Martín recognized the respect in her tone. Her accents on various words tipped and raised and her eyes danced with delight when she explained how Henry fought alongside her brother Francis in the Battle of Pavia. During that battle, when her brother's army faced defeat by the Spanish, both Henry and Francis were taken captive. That's when Charles V, the Holy Roman Emperor, successfully carried Francis back to Madrid as a political prisoner. Henry, however, cleverly exchanged clothing with a page, escaped, and slipped away, eventually making his way across the country on foot to safety. Now as King of Navarre, Henry ruled this small kingdom with tremendous respect from both nobles and peasants. Martín's smile grew through the telling. It wasn't just respect from nobles and peasants. Martín knew one member of royalty who held Navarre's king in the highest regard.

The couple reached a summit. Martín's breath escaped when they looked down upon the sparkling diamonds created as the sun danced on the Gave de Pau, a winding river that crawled its way through a beautifully lush valley floor. Small collections of buildings accented the valley, a steeple here and the rising smoke from a building there told Martín they'd reached civilization and, if Marguerite was right, safety.

Martín couldn't take his eyes off the scene unfolding before him. The worry that had consumed him ever since leaving Trujillo seemed to be lighter with each step he took. It felt like this could be home. Maybe he was a native of Navarre.

As they entered the first cluster of buildings, the smells reminded him that the several weeks on the run had afforded them few savory meals. Like sirens beckoning the Argonauts to their doom, a bakery begged Martín's attention. His attention quickly turned to an open-air fire over which an enormous pig rotated. Its sweet aroma practically erased the memory of the hunger and cold they'd experienced crossing the rugged Pyrenees.

Martín turned away from the pig roasting, unwilling to admit to the battle between his hunger and his somewhat self-imposed responsibility to care for the most precious fugitive in the entire Holy Roman Empire.

They rode past a small rock church which was doing its best to stay upright, as many of its foundational stones appeared to be crumbling and failing.

Next to it, the foundation of a much larger replacement chapel had reached about chest high. Workers were cutting stone in the yard between the ancient church and the one hoping to one day serve as a worthy replacement.

They dismounted and led their horses into a small market. The clangs of a blacksmith's iron mallet, ladies exchanging goods, laughter, and the noise of mothers directing children hung in the air. The sounds of community felt good to Martín's ears.

On the opposite side of the small market, a man saddling his horse stared at the peasant woman riding alongside a priest. When the priest caught him staring, the man turned quickly and spoke to his younger companion, who was struggling to tighten the cinch on his saddle.

"I believe that is her," the older of the two said, a smile revealing perfect white teeth. "Cunning, very cunning."

"The peasant woman and the priest?" the younger man said, squinting to get a better look. The couple had passed. He could only see a man in a dark brown robe tied at the waist with rope who accompanied a maid, whose long dark hair fell loosely down her back. The priest turned one more time and caught the two men staring. They quickly turned away.

"No one would suspect a lowly maid traveling with a monk," the older man said. "Follow me. We may make this journey worth our time."

The two men carefully followed the monk and the maid as they left the small cluster of buildings and crossed through the market. The men kept their distance but the older of the two caught the attention of a young boy, whispered in his ear, and gave him a coin.

As Martín and Marguerite walked their horses along the banks of the river, something felt amiss. His eyes darted each direction, searching for any indication there might be trouble. Yet, he knew nothing about French cities or markets. He tried to tell himself to relax. They approached the stone bridge that spanned the river and led to the heart of the city, in the center of which stood a majestic château.

A boy raced past Marguerite and Martín, up and over the bridge, and then disappeared.

When the young boy passed in such a run, Martín watched him for a moment, then turned to see where he might have come from. It confirmed his suspicions. They were being followed.

"Two men I saw staring at you back in the market are following us," Martín said.

Marguerite casually looked behind them. "We will continue forward but not cross the bridge, then see if they continue to follow," she said.

What was she thinking, Martín wondered. Wouldn't they be safer in the city as opposed to out here alone, along a riverbank?

They passed the bridge and casually increased their speed. The two men passed the bridge as well and seemed to close the gap. Marguerite and Martín recognized they were not just being followed, they were being pursued.

"Do you still have Humphrey's sword?" she asked.

Martín wanted to chuckle that Marguerite referred to the sword Humphrey gave to him as Humphrey's sword. He knew Humphrey would never part with his own sword. The one strapped to Martín's waist under the cloak was probably taken from one of Humphrey's victims. Martín's hand gripped its handle, his eyes darting down to where she could see it under his robe. Martín had spent little time with a sword. He never owned one and only used this one to clear brush and prepare the ground for sleep and protection from the weather. None of the vegetation he slayed had the intent to fight back. Could he really put up a defense?

With a quick glance behind them, Marguerite stopped, smiled at Martín, then laughed out loud.

# Chapter Nineteen

## Henry's Castle, Château de Pau, Navarre

As the two men approached, Martín noted Marguerite's hands regain their pinkish color, her shoulders lower, and the tightness of her cheeks relax. Even her horse seemed to relax.

She recognizes these two, Martín realized. Her lips gave way to the broadening smile.

"Princess Marguerite of Angoulême," the older of the two men exclaimed as they approached. His smile matched hers. A grin followed his bow. His raised eyebrows posed the question why a princess traveled on horseback dressed as a maid with only a young priest no older than the man's young traveling companion.

"Gérard Calvin de Noyon," Marguerite said as Gérard and his companion pulled up their horses, bowing in respect to the princess. They dismounted and joined Marguerite and Martín on foot.

"You are a little far south. Might this be young John?" she asked. The young man bowed again.

"John, last I heard, you were under the tutelage of the famed Mathurin Cordier in Paris at the College de la Marche." She paused just a moment for him to confirm her comment. "And you have completed your studies?"

John, also giving respect to the princess, bowed as he said, "My studies still continue…"

Gérard interrupted, "John is too smart to waste his life in traditional studies. I have enrolled him at the University of Orléans to study law. He will certainly make more money at the law than as an ecclesiastic."

Martín thought, not if he sells indulgences.

Marguerite nodded agreement. "But still, Navarre seems the long way around to get from Paris to Orléans."

"Because our good friend King Henry d'Albret of Navarre spent considerable time with us in Noyon, John wanted to return the honor. At the long-standing invitation of Henry, we felt now was the time to come pay a visit in Pau."

Marguerite turned to Martín, "Martín, may I introduce you to Gérard Calvin and his willful son John. Old friends from years ago. From what I hear, young John is much like you, a fellow heretic."

This statement produced a shock among all three men. Marguerite's tiny smile registered that she succeeded in creating the reaction she wanted. Still addressing Martín, she continued, "John here has some strong opinions concerning God's relationship with man. Those opinions run contrary to those of the Church."

Of all things to include in an introduction, Martín wondered why she would instantly categorize John as a heretic. Yet knowing that these two men were not a threat to him or Marguerite did put him at ease.

"May we accompany you to Henry's court?" Gérard asked. They turned their direction back toward the bridge. The sun reflected off the copper roofs of the majestic Château de Pau, which rose majestically above the city.

Gérard and Marguerite walked side by side leading their horses and Marguerite began telling Gérard about her journey and Francis' health and the ordeal with Charles V in Spain.

Martín reflected on the variety of people he had encountered over the past several weeks, and now, added to the mix, was a young man traveling with his father before he left one university to attend another, and who was considered a heretic. Who was this John Calvin?

"Martín," John said, "the princess called you a fellow heretic. You a priest and disagree with the pope?"

Martín didn't consider himself a heretic at all. And the priest's robe was merely a disguise. He had been taught by a wonderful monk and by some strange occurrence, he possessed unlawful holy scriptures, and he could actually read them. The bold actions of an English highwayman had entangled him with the Church. And now, by no act of his own, he had escaped the decree of the Holy Roman Emperor to capture the King of France's own sister and had accompanied her to France. Speechless, Martín just looked at John.

This young man, about his same age, a large forehead and auburn hair grown over his ears, carried an aura of confidence. His piercing brown eyes remained fixed on Martín. Martín wondered what it would be like to attend a college. *I have never been able to choose anything. What would I choose if I ever could? My only choice, to enter the monastery, was taken from me. How can I even make a choice? I didn't choose to be a heretic.*

Finally, in his new language of French, Martín constructed his response.

"I have in my possession copies of several sections of the holy scriptures given me by a friar who also taught me to read and write both Spanish and Latin."

"And French?" John asked. John was patient with Martín's French. It was evident to him that Martín's somewhat limited vocabulary, but proper grammar, revealed he was new to it. John smiled and switched from French to Latin.

"So you did not attend a university to learn your Latin? You learned all this when you became a monk?" John asked.

Marguerite, overhearing this discussion, chuckled, turned to John, and said, "Martín here is better set to be a priest and smarter than any I have known, but no, the Church is not worthy of Martín. The robe is a ruse to protect my honor."

Martín bowed his appreciation to this gracious lady. It was as if she somehow knew he was struggling to explain why he was impersonating a priest. "I've not attended any school," he said. "A humble monk, Friar Tomás, is my only tutor. And the kind princess afforded me some hours to learn your language."

"You have copies of the scriptures?" John asked.

Martín nodded.

"May I?" John asked.

As they walked, Martín reached up onto the horse and pulled the manuscripts from the bedroll tied to his saddle. He handed them to John, curious why he was at ease doing so.

"Ah, the gospels of Mathew and John," Calvin said as he shuffled through them, "and the epistles of Paul."

Martín felt proud to be in the possession of something garnering him some respect from this new acquaintance, a college man with what appeared to be a quick and capable mind.

"Martín," he asked, "What are your beliefs concerning our standing with

God and His judgements?"

Martín was so shocked by the question, he couldn't even begin to process the question, let alone understand from where John's reasons for asking it came from.

"You have read these, have you not?" John asked with a raised eyebrow.

This was an interesting way to begin a conversation, Martín thought as he gained his composure and quickly reflected how he'd responded to Friar Tomás when the friar quizzed him on his reading. This was one point of doctrine Martín challenged the friar on several times.

How could God know us from the beginning, know what our future was, and we still have agency to choose our life's path? These questions took on more relevance as Martín now experienced the injustices being inflicted on innocent people. The injustices were even supported by men allegedly chosen by God to lead his church and bring men to Christ. He saw the injustices also inflicted by kings who claimed to rule by the ordination of God. Martín saw firsthand these men were not the infallible men they claimed to be.

John pulled a sheet from the manuscript and said, "In Roman 8, Paul writes, 'We know that in everything God works for good with those who love him, who are called according to his purpose. For those whom he foreknew, he also predestined to be conformed to the image of his Son, in order that he might be the firstborn among many brethren. And those whom he predestined he also called; and those whom he called he also justified; and those whom he justified he also glorified.'"

Again, Martín's mind raced. He knew this verse. It was one he and Friar Tomás discussed often, but never to Martín's satisfaction. Martín concluded it must be a tricky one for John as well.

Martín cautiously began, reflecting back how Friar Tomás, while perishing in the flames, and Vano both insisted there was a work for Martín, a work ordained by God. Still uncertain of his own beliefs or understandings of man's relationship with God, he prepared to speak.

John didn't let Martín answer. He continued, "God preordained, for His glory and the display of His attributes of mercy and justice, a part of the human race, without any merit of their own to eternal salvation, another part in just punishment of their sin, to eternal damnation."

This is not a discussion, Martín thought. It's a sermon. John's conviction impressed Martín. His confidence, his skill with words. But he was wrong. Martín felt it and knew it. Martín's mind wandered, realizing the truth of what Gérard said about how John would do better in the law compared to the clergy. As John continued, Martín's mind wandered back into the sermon.

"By predestination we mean the eternal decree of God, by which He determined with Himself whatever He wished to happen with regard to every man. All are not created on equal terms, but some are preordained to eternal life, others to eternal damnation; and, accordingly, as each has been created for one or other of these ends, we say that he has been predestinated to life or to death."

Martín chose not to refute this claim. He knew it couldn't possibly be true that we live the way we live because God decreed it so. No, that could never be so.

Marguerite, though in conversation with Gérard about nothing of consequence, understood her young student's apprehension to participate in the very one-sided exploration of God's work with men. When Gérard paused for just a moment, Marguerite took the opportunity to help Martín out again.

"So, John, do you insist this doctrine you profess, that everything is God's predetermined path, is authentic enough to preach it against the will of our great and holy pope and the Church?"

Martín mouthed the words thank you.

Marguerite turned to Martín before John could launch into another sermon. "Martín, you see why I introduced you two as fellow heretics."

She laughed, as did Gérard. John only chuckled, realizing Marguerite respected his divergent views but did not necessarily need to agree or disagree.

"How do you think John's sermon would endear him to the very bishops who entrusted you with their holy work?" She winked at Martín as her eyes shot toward the holy work in the shape of gold and silver tied to his saddle.

"Pau," Gérard said as they reached the bridge and faced the city, "safety for you, your highness."

Martín had not been listening to Gérard's and Marguerite's conversation, but he concluded she'd shared their story with him.

"It will be my privilege to present you to King Henry II of Navarre. We have been friends a long time. Marguerite, he needs a queen. May I propose such a union?" Gérard's smile betrayed the innocence of the poke at her being husband-less.

"I was not so fond of the choice King Louis XII made for me. I certainly will not put my future in your hands," she said curtly, "and I do not need any introduction."

Gérard's smile aside, he turned to Martín, "Martín, I don't know just how well you might know the princess here but I do tell, that if you were a duke, or a prince of some fame, she would make you a wonderful wife. Considering her many potential matches over her years, I must say I agree that the match made by Louis XII to Charles, Duke of Alençon was nothing more than a land transaction for the king. By marrying him to Marguerete, she would receive the county, plus 60,000 crowns, as her dowry. The hardheaded Louis used her to retain possession of the county and its revenues. Alençon might have been considered a worthy husband since he was a direct descendant of Charles, brother to Philip the Fair, King of France, but he was far from being a suitable mate for this intelligent, quick-witted, liberally educated Marguerite." Gérard paused to let that sink in, then added a last poke at Marguerite's former husband. "Charles was a dull, melancholic man with a mean, bad-tempered disposition."

Gérard turned to Marguerite and asked, "Did I get that mostly right?"

Marguerite just nodded. That nod gave Gérard permission to continue. He did.

"This traveling companion of yours was named as a possible bride for Arthur, Prince of Wales, as well as his brother Prince Henry before Prince Henry became King Henry VIII, and even Charles of Austria who you know as Charles V, Holy Roman Emperor. I assume she did not share all that with you."

Marguerite never attempted to interrupt or correct Gérard. Martín knew she was very special. Now he knew he wasn't the only one that thought so. It became clear why Charles V had extra incentive to capture this particular princess.

The group led their horses across the stone bridge that led into the proper city of Pau. They made their way to the château and entered a large courtyard surrounded by young walnut trees. Opposite the courtyard stood a large, finely built home. On the right corner stood a tall turret, yet there were no battlements saying keep away. From the high walls, large windows accented the smooth, cream-colored stone placed symmetrically to give the appearance of moving clouds. Beautifully sculptured shrubs grew all along the base of the walls, ending at the large open door.

This large château was like the few he'd seen back in Spain, but it felt less threatening. Maybe, he thought, it felt more friendly because he was walking alongside a princess, the sister of the nation's king.

News of their arrival must have been made known, for as they approached the large open door, out stepped a tall, pale man no more than a few years Martín's senior. His confidence, accompanied by a smile, radiated a welcome as he opened his arms and embraced Gérard. He then gave a warm nod to John and turned to Marguerite. His smile turned to shock and then, taking her with both hands, bowed respectively.

"Princess Marguerite, what have these men done to you?" He looked her up and down.

Martín knew these two were well acquainted. The description she'd offered of him as they wound their way off the mountain toward the city made that clear. She had portrayed him perfectly. Henry called several young attendants to care for the horses, but before they led them away, Martín quickly retrieved his bundles. The king welcomed them into a large hall and insisted they rest while he provided nourishment to keep them until a proper supper could be prepared. Martín welcomed the rest and the plates of breads, cheese, dried meats, fruits, and wine. Compared to the past few weeks, this alone was a feast.

Following an afternoon of rest and spirited conversation, Henry provided a sumptuous meal like Martín had never even imagined. Though Marguerite felt confident in Martín's newly learned French, from time to time during the many varied discussions, she clarified an individual concept when she perceived Martín might struggle with a point in French being made concerning politics or religion.

Martín realized when she made these points, he did recognize the meaning of the words being used. He just couldn't accept some of them aligning with his own personal belief in God. He knew he was not educated or trained in theology, but he knew in his very soul God did not suffer any infants to be automatically damned if they were never baptized, and as John was saying some infants were among the elect and would be saved and others were predestined for eternal death. But who was Martín to argue with scholars of the law and the scriptures? There he sat, a poor orphan. He was in no position to discuss politics and religion with kings.

As the evening ended, Henry's servants ushered the group to individual lush sleeping quarters. Martín was certainly tired enough to sleep, but as his mind reflected on the evening's conversations, he tried to plug holes in the reasoning with the meager things he'd just recently learned from Gitanos, highwaymen, his beloved friar, and now a fellow heretic.

As John insisted that since the very word baptize means to be immersed, the early church at the time of Christ certainly baptized by immersion just as John the Baptist took Jesus down into the River Jordan to baptize Him. Martín realized though John would indeed be a heretic with that belief, it resonated true to Martín's heart. Other points, though made confidently by John, couldn't find a place to peacefully dwell in Martín's soul.

When John's claim that the Church should be ended rather than reformed, and there was only one true church, and the restoration of the true Church shall be of such a nature that it shall last forever, Martín felt like an innocent compared to this true heretic. "Until then, kings should make an end to popery," John claimed.

With these statements presented so sharply, even Henry agreed it was time to leave the pope out of their kingdom's affairs.

The night ended on a high note when the king asked John what God had done before He created the world. John smilingly said, "He was building hell for the curious."

Martín's mind pondered on that curious claim. He smiled and drifted into the deepest sleep he ever had.

# Chapter Twenty

## Edge of the Antisuyu, Tawantinsuyu - Peru

Of the hundreds of dead scattered throughout the destroyed village, the group attended to only one. Sarpay collected small pieces of cloth that survived the fatal fires and ceremonially wrapped the young child's mother. Cataquil cleared an area of brush from a small hill overlooking the burned village. He then gently laid the body and one by one gathered stones and covered it, creating a tomb from the stones.

As Cataquil worked, and Sarpay performed her sacred rituals, Cusimi cared for the young child, permitting him to remain close to his mother's body and Sarpay. Urco learned all he could from the young chasqui. He was young but claimed to have run the thousands of miles from one end of the empire to the other. He even claimed to have once seen the floating houses driven by clouds upon the great ocean. There would be time to learn more from this brave boy, but the immediate need was to get away from this village and avoid the next one.

Sarpay knelt next to the mound of stones. She handed the child one last rock carried up from the village. She helped him place it on his mother's final home. Hand in hand, Sarpay and the child returned to where Urco and the chasqui were speaking.

"You will never reach the Apurimac," the young chasqui said. "Quichamba, Quizquiz, and Rumiñawi each have their own eyes and ears crisscrossing Tawantinsuyu."

"We have no choice, it is Apurimac or Cusco," Sarpay said. "Is the way to Cusco better?"

"Or Paititi," Cusimi said.

All eyes darted to Cusimi who was now kneeling next to the child, braiding his long black hair into a tail.

The chasqui's smile consumed his narrow face.

It wasn't a typical smile. Urco saw there was a whole mountain hidden behind that smile. He read into it more than happiness. The boy was not more than a decade old; what could he know? Yet an army just plowed through a village. How many more villages received this same treatment? Where was this boy when the village was attacked? Did he watch it? Was he from this village? No, his headdress was not from a village this close to the jungles. He wore the tunic of a coastal region with tassels from the desert and feathers from the northern jungles.

Urco wondered how the boy confidently said they would never make it to the Apurimac. As he considered, Urco realized this boy probably knew very well every road between this village and Apurimac. He was a runner, a chasqui, of course he knew every trail across the Inca Empire. How much did he know? Why was he here now? Was this a stop or his destination? Was he left behind by Quichamba to finish any survivors? Did he kill the woman? Did he try to save her? Was his heart softened at the sight of the child mourning his mother's death? Urco had second thoughts about how much the two discussed while Sarpay had been preparing the dead.

# Chapter Twenty-one

## Château de Pau - Navarre

A young man gently shook Martín awake. "It is morning, sir. Your friends are dining without you."

Martín's mind struggled to process the words. He blinked his eyes, struggling to open them. He thanked the young page and hastened to dress. When he reached the dining hall, the shock of what he saw drowned out the very active debate taking place.

"There has to be a way to know for sure!" demanded a robust friar seated next to John. But it wasn't his rumpled robe or disheveled hair hanging over his ears that surprised Martín. It was the smile on Humphrey's face. The man sitting next to Humphrey turned quickly to see what Humphrey was smiling about. His eyes met Martín's.

All were staring at Martín. The friar was the first to attempt an explanation of the group's appearance in Pau.

"I come to collect the robes you stole from the priory," he said.

Humphrey shook his head. "No, you were following these two, hoping to lead the Constable's dogs to the princess. When the princess joins us this morning, you will apologize, seek forgiveness, and take your fat carcass back to Spain," Humphrey said.

John didn't revel in the banter. "Martín, your interesting friends here do not understand the scriptures. Especially your spiritual leader here, Friar Fernando."

Martín did not know this friar was his spiritual leader. He didn't even know the friar. But he now knew his supposed friend's name. The friar turned back to continue the debate Martín interrupted. Humphrey pulled Martín to the table. "You will love this. The friar here insists John is a heretic for believing God predestined each of us to heaven or to hell."

Martín nodded subtle agreement.

Friar Fernando continued, "If I'm destined for heaven, I want to know. If I'm destined to hell, I want to know. I refuse to spend my life resisting temptation if I'm going to hell, anyway. I want to enjoy this life now if I'm destined to burn in hell."

"Believe me," Humphrey said before John could answer with a more respectful answer, "you are going to hell, you and all your pious cheats, so you might as well quit pretending that you are not."

"Well, well," a melodically female voice said, "I have never heard such talk." Marguerite entered the hall, accompanied by Henry. "What has raised such a discussion? I fear I might have missed something interesting."

All five men stood and bowed both to Marguerite and Henry. Henry waved them all to be seated. He clapped to a page standing at attention and as he and Marguerite joined the table, Gérard entered and a cadre of servants served the large group a rich, hot breakfast of eggs, pork, and a variety of breads.

"Henry," Marguerite began, "are you going to introduce me to your guests?"

He said, "I believe you know Sir Humphrey. When he arrived last night, he claimed to be in your service." Marguerite smiled and nodded, then winked at Humphrey. "Humphrey," Henry continued, "will you be so kind as to introduce your companions?"

"The well-behaved Gitano is Faustino, sent by a dear friend to assist me with your young protector Martín. The friar here," Humphrey said, "is nothing more than a thief and a liar, and likely a fornicator, too. I caught him following Marguerite and Martín. Figured he was looking for a way to lead the Constable's men to her and collect the bounty. So, I invited him to travel with me."

"You brought him to my home?" Henry asked.

"I was confident you would have him executed for his crimes," Humphrey said, "which I will enjoy watching."

The friar didn't protest at the words thief, liar, fornicator, or even seeking after a bounty. But at the word execution, the friar choked on his wine, which dribbled down his chin. Marguerite kindly handed him a kerchief.

Marguerite's smile told Martín she wasn't taking Humphrey too seriously. Martín still wasn't too sure about Humphrey, especially since he abandoned them back in Spain. Martín well understood execution was not a word to take lightly.

With all eyes on the friar, the friar began his defense. "Until this good John Calvin of Noyan confirms which side of heaven I am destined to be on, I bet against hell and deny the charges laid before you by the self-proclaimed judge and jurist, and his devilish mount, Beelzebub," Friar Fernando said.

All eyes remained on the friar. His attention went to Marguerite. "Your own constable, Charles of Bourbon, and his men arrived in Saint Louis de Larrau, just hours before you. Our prior commanded me to watch the bridge for three travelers; a lady, a simple young man, and a warrior riding a tall black devil of a horse."

"Well, I just knew, even without the devil horseman," his eyes motioned to Humphrey, "it was you, Princess. I knew it. But I could not help myself. I followed you 'till I was certain you were safe, then I ran to see what the boy was doing. Clever getting you a new riding outfit, and a pretty one too. I do apologize for watching you change. Could not help myself. But I promise that is the closest I ever come to fornicatin,' though."

The pink of Marguerite's cheeks turned to a brighter red.

"Right then I decided celibacy weren't for me. I had to leave the monastery and get me a wife of my own, and an honest job."

This confession brought raised eyebrows, shocked faces, and smiles all around. Marguerite's color returned and in a mix of pride and shame, she said, "I am not sure if I should be honored or embarrassed to have influenced your life's change."

"Honored, m'lady. Honored. Do not be embarrassed at all. I seen the light. I was going to make a poor priest."

"You saw more than the light," Humphrey said. Then he turned to Henry, "I think you should still execute him for peeping on the princess."

The friar choked again. They all laughed again. Except John, who with a tight smile said, "Right now, I am leaning toward hell for you, friar. Then again, if you leave the clergy, seeking another road, which I myself am doing, maybe I am not as certain."

"So what do we call you?" Henry asked.

"In the church I am Friar Fernando," he said. "Nando to everyone else."

Henry, resuming an air of nobility, which of course he was as King of Navarre, said, "Friar Fernando, I reverse the sentence of death and give my executioner the day off, and as for your sin of appreciating the beauty of the princess here, that is up to her."

All eyes followed the confession, then the king's pardon, and now turned to Marguerite, who, with a wide smile and red face, confirmed the pardon. "I am honored to have provided your life a new direction. I pray you will not waste it."

Marguerite spent the rest of the day with Henry and issues of state. When the group reunited after a day of caring for horses, weapons, and sharing sordid tales of their exploits over the past weeks, Marguerite again looked the part of one king's sister and another king's devoted friend.

"Friar, did you come closer to your quest to learn your destiny?" Marguerite asked.

Nando squinted one eye, "Still hedging my bet on heaven. At least until my next temptation. These two do not make it easy. Gunna miss 'em though, when I am the only one in heaven."

The banter continued through the evening, a welcome rest from several weeks of an intense and risky journey.

In the morning, Humphrey, Martín, Nando, and Faustino left Gérard and John with King Henry in Pau and accompanied Marguerite on her way to Amboise. Henry provided a comfortable carriage for Marguerite. With four horsemen as protection, Marguerite was again treated as if on a royal mission, appropriately so.

Over the past weeks, as Martín and Marguerite had traveled through Spain and over the Pyrenees, Marguerite included great segments of poetry she'd quote and require Martín to repeat as part of his French lessons. She regretted her inability to write these verses due to their speedy travel and lack of quill and parchment. But now, fully equipped at the kindness of King Henry, Marguerite set ink to paper continuously throughout their journey northward. She cherished the occasional stretches of smooth roads, which made her writing more legible.

From time to time, to learn of their various adventures, she invited one of her four companions to accompany her in the carriage. In the evenings, they gathered in the various inns and dined together. She insisted the key to teaching and learning was through stories. As she listened to the various tales told by Friar Fernando and Humphrey, she often took notes, and her interest never waned. Martín wondered at the tales. His puny life seemed so little compared to Humphrey's, who fought battles, seduced women, both noble and peasant, rescued heretics, and defied bishops. Humphrey compared the different peoples, but insisted how the weakness of humanity was universal and the grand character of both men and women could be found just as universally, yet not as plentifully. With the exception of female-crazed friars.

When the friar began sharing stories about life in a monastery and how he ended up in the robes of a friar, laughter filled the great dining hall. Martín concluded Nando, as they now all called him, did not need John Calvin to proclaim his destiny of heaven or hell; it was quite clear heaven would have to wait.

"My father was a baker, highly respected and needed in the coastal village of Cadiz." Nando said, "He taught me to make the dough, to mold it, to leaven it, to heat the ovens, and to rotate and tend the dough during the baking." Nando talked so purposely none expected the story to do anything but ramble. "As you know, the holy Eucharist bread, the host, is made with only fresh ground wheat and pure water." Smiles replaced glares.

"The prior asked my father to provide the host for an important mass." Nando paused. "Did you know that white capsicum powder is fine like flour? Chuckles started. "My father asked me to deliver the hosts for the special mass honoring Holy Thursday and the end of Lent. I was proud to be part of the special mass. I now believe it would have been wise to test the potency of capsicum powder I put in the holy wafers."

"The prior never asked my father for holy Eucharist wafers again. Those wafers were as hot as the devil hisself." Nando completed his tale as if it were as normal an event as watching the sunrise on a cloudy day.

"Some say Elena de Zargoza drank the entire vessel of wine because she was thirsty. Others respected her humility. But it was more wine at one time than I think she was accustomed to. When the prior left the confessional that night, his face was red as I ever saw it. I rightly think I was on God's errand helping Señora Zargoza come clean."

"Can a priest confess to hisself?" Nando asked between bites. "I hope so, or toting this robe around all these years will be for nothing."

Though Martín, now after these many weeks away from his lonely existence in Trujillo, felt comfortable and grateful to actually associate with and have friends, he felt he had nothing to contribute to the stories. Ambition, dreams, and anticipation had long been starved out of him. He had no exploits, no triumphs, no successes to even exaggerate. His only consistent desire was to avoid being pitied by others. Yet, these people accepted him, and claimed he had a divine purpose, something to contribute.

Though he couldn't imagine what that might be, he wanted it to be true.

The next morning as the group readied their horses, Marguerite joined them dressed in the chemise and kirtle Martín had secured for her in de Larrau where he purchased the maid's chemise and where Nando chose to leave the priesthood. Humphrey secured a horse from a local livery for her.

"If you will indulge my desire to lead this band, we can arrive tonight at Amboise. The carriage will arrive tomorrow and then I will return it to Henry." Marguerite accepted the surprised looks and nods as approval, and she quickly mounted and charged from the yard and across the fields.

For several seconds, the men stood motionless, with the exception of blank stares at each other. Humphrey was first up onto Beelzebub, followed by Faustino, Nando, and Martín. Marguerite led the group relentlessly throughout the day. She was close to home and pushed to arrive by nightfall.

As they crossed the narrow rock bridge over the Val de Loire, a lazy, deep blue river near Blere, Marguerite seemed to push even harder, forcing her train of escorts to keep up.

Martín began to feel abandoned, even as he rode side by side with the other men. For weeks, he had the princess to himself. Her attention and appreciation gave him purpose. With her, he was somebody. He was needed. In his heart, he knew this independent woman actually didn't need anybody. It was her brother, the King of France, who needed her. With the death of their mother, Claude, the king's children needed Marguerite. It was all of France that needed her. It was the collection of scholars, heretics, peasants, and orphans from Trujillo who needed her.

Nando interrupted Martín's thoughts when he reached out and took hold of the reins of Martín's horse. "Quick," he said, "trade me clothes."

"What are you doing?" Martín said, trying to slap Nando's hand away.

"I cannot let her see me like this," Nando said.

Martín looked at Nando, panicking as if a monk in his long dark robe, astride a cream-colored stallion, was a crime. Thinking Nando was maybe joking, Martín said, "She has seen you like this for five days. Why is now different?"

Nando pointed with his eyes to a woman standing alongside the road talking with Marguerite. Marguerite had stopped and was climbing down off her horse.

Martín's heart nearly stopped when he focused his eyes on the woman who had caught Nando's attention. Immediately, Martín understood. Almost subconsciously, Martín sat up a little straighter, dusted his sleeves, and slowed his approach. Nando did the same, resigning to this first impression he was about to make.

The men on horses gathered around this young woman and Marguerite, whose embrace seemed far more than customary.

Martín was the first to his feet. Taking the reins of Marguerite's horse, he bowed as Marguerite turned to introduce the woman to her horsemen.

"Gentlemen, may I introduce the pride of England and a favorite of France, and my adopted daughter, Mistress Anne Boleyn, returning from England to help my mother, the regent of France, with Francis's children while I was away?"

This young woman's beauty was not lost on any of the horsemen. Martín understood Nando's interest and smiled broadly as Nando fumbled over himself to pay his respect. "Mistress Anne, may I offer you the humblest welcome as a new convert to the world where appreciation of God's loveliest creatures is not pushed aside over the archaic rituals of piety for the clergy? M'lady." When Nando ended his statement, he took Anne's hand, kissed it, and bowed.

Anne looked the friar in the eyes and, as if she was confused not knowing what she should do next, she gently retrieved her hand, bowed, and said, "Thank you. I think."

Humphrey said, "M'lady, I believe our good friar here was trying to say, a lady as pretty as you could make a man forget his vows to the priesthood."

Humphrey remained on his horse and chuckled as Nando slobbered over Anne's beauty. Then he said, "Mistress Anne, I applaud your generosity to leave Henry's court, yet I am surprised he let you get away." Martín realized Humphrey, as a fellow Englishman, knew King Henry VIII and probably knew what was happening at court.

Marguerite grinned at the attention Anne received. She returned her attention back to Anne and, taking her hands, said, "Forgive my dear protectors here. They have been solicitous to my every need, and I credit their valor alone for my safety and protection. You will love them as I do. Yet, knowing Henry's interest, I too wondered how you slipped across the channel."

"I am embarrassed to say, my interest in helping your mother with Maude's children, while you risked your life to aid your brother, is not as noble as you might think. The king is relentless and makes life unbearable. I wonder why Catherine is not as anxious for a divorce as he is. Yet, she and the pope are the only hope I have."

During his journey with Marguerite, Martín began to understand the drama of the courts of kings. Now he realized it was an impossible task to keep the relationships clear. He wondered if Nando and Faustino were as confused as he was.

Nando came to the rescue, for which Martín was beginning to love the man. "Mistress Anne, if I may be so bold, as it is not my natural disposition to pry into the trials of a lady, might I inquire which Henry you are referring to?"

Not giving Anne the chance to answer. Humphrey turned to Anne and said, "Pardon me," then back to Nando, "One thing you Spaniards must learn is how to keep our Henrys straight." Humphrey winked at Anne and Marguerite. "In England, we have eight of them now. Number seven condemned me to death, number eight pardoned me. Here in France one of them was Marguerite's first husband, and the one whose generosity you just enjoyed, King Henry of Navarre, is another. Seems nobody having babies can think up a new name anymore. And if they do, as soon as they're made king, they change it."

Anne smiled, nodded thanks to Humphrey, and looked at Nando, "He is number eight."

Marguerite, seeming to enjoy this lesson on the royalty, put her arm around Anne and began leading her back along the river. Until now, the vibrant young woman who captured the attention of the men had to share the attention. They'd been oblivious to the monumental Château Royal d'Amboise that rose majestically across the river. Martín again caught himself breathless as he took in the scene.

Another magnificent monument to architects and builders. It again struck Martín with awe. His thoughts raced through the images cemented into his mind. Each was grander than the last: from the churches in his home of Trujillo, to the cathedral in Guadalupe, and the palaces in Toledo, the plaza in Bilbao surrounded by glorious churches and palaces, Henry's château, and now this.

Nando saw none of it. His eyes focused forward to where Marguerite and Anne were leading the group up onto the rock bridge leading to the château.

Three little children escaped a large outer door as the group entered the courtyard. Marguerite dropped to her knees as the children smothered her in hugs.

"Meet the royal children," she said, turning each child toward the men. "This is Margaret," young Margaret, only about three years old, curtsied. "This is Francis," he bowed respectively to the men, Martín guessed him to be five or six, "and Henry."

Henry bowed less than his two younger siblings but still respected Marguerite's introduction as important.

When Marguerite said Henry's name, all eyes turned to Humphrey to quickly validate his statement of the royal naming convention.

"Number nine?" Nando asked.

Marguerite introduced each of her chaperones to the children and ushered the group into the large hall, leaving their horses in the hands of two young men who led them to the stables. Martín quickly retrieved his bag before they led the horses away.

# Chapter Twenty-two

## Château Royal d'Amboise

Martín saw very little of Marguerite over the next several days. Henry's carriage that Marguerite abandoned for a horse, arrived two days later with a report of having been held up by highwaymen, but with no passengers, there was no harm. The four horsemen appreciated the rest, but after one day of it they were eager to be doing something that mattered.

Nando had the opportunity to spar with some of the court's swordsmen as they were training young men. As Martín watched, Humphrey joined him and said, "That one has not always been a friar. Those are not moves of a religious man."

Martín said, "I don't believe he has ever been a religious man." He turned to Humphrey and asked, "Where again did you find him?"

"I didn't," Humphrey said. "He claims to have found Marguerite and you in Saint Louis de Larrau when he was watching her undress. I caught him following you two when I was hoping to meet up in Pau. He is just a man, like all of us. Just as corruptible, just as lustful, but I would be careful with him when he has a blade under that robe."

Just then, Nando parried with the swordmaster, driving him back against a stone archway, his blade glistening in the sun. The swordmaster did not give way. He pushed forward, and both men seemed to enjoy having a battle with talent that met their own.

"Lose that robe, and he might make a fine highwayman," Humphrey said, as Nando and the swordmaster stopped the battle and congratulated each other's skills.

"Lose that robe and he would not be here with us. He would be in with her," Martín said. He motioned toward Anne who was watching from the other side of the courtyard.

Martín wondered if Nando was aware of his audience and if she had been some of the inspiration for his valiant swordplay. Too bad about the robe, he thought. Yet, how could a friar swordsman compete for the hand of a woman like Anne when the lustful King of England was moving heaven and earth to divorce his wife so he could have her?

All Martín could do about it was smile and shake his head.

Marguerite and her mother Louise, who was serving as regent of France while King Francis was a prisoner in Madrid, were anxiously engaged in negotiations with Charles V. Progress was mostly nonexistent. With this intrigue consuming the attention of the court, her rescuers spent little time with Marguerite. Nando, however, had the uncanny ability to be wherever Anne just happened to be.

"I think that robe is Nando's secret to Anne's heart. Makes her think the wolf is just a kid," Martín said as they watched Nando teaching the young dauphin, Henry, how to handle a sword parry as Anne looked on.

"Well, he knows it's useless," Humphrey said. "We're leaving tomorrow. We need to get you to Wittenburg. Having not been beheaded, the good Friar Nando is coming with us, and Anne is not."

Ever since Vano insisted God had a work for Martín, and Humphrey committed to assist his safe passage to Germany where that work would take place, though the journey was not a direct one, it seemed one event after another moved this tiny band in that direction. Martín's mind couldn't shake the thought that maybe Vano was a type of prophet. Yet, what could God want with me, a poor insignificant orphan?

In the morning, as the group was readying to leave, Martín stood alone in the library staring at a painting of a woman sitting alone. The woman in the painting looked back at Martín. The background of the painting depicted a serene countryside. Martín was so captivated with the singularity of this woman's countenance and how she seemed to look into Martín's soul, he didn't hear Marguerite enter the library and walk up beside him.

"Beautiful, is she not?" Marguerite said, breaking the silence.

"Is this you?" Martín asked.

"I like to think so. But no, she is much more than me."

Martín gave Marguerite a long look before slowly turning his attention back to the painting.

"This is you." Martín's words were no longer a question, they were a solid confirmation.

"Thank you," Marguerite whispered.

"I know nothing about art, about women, about princesses and queens. I don't know anything at all," he said. "But I think this woman does. I think she knows everything. And now, after more than a month with you, I think you do too."

Marguerite remained silent.

"This is you. Who painted it?" he asked.

"A dear friend of mine," she said. "An Italian by the name of Leonardo. A homo universalis, if I might say so in Latin. A polymath, a man whose knowledge spanned the universe but more than that, a staunch friend. Leonardo's fame in the Italian courts for his unique, refreshing style and curious mind captivated our interest, and he willingly came to France and spent his last years here with us."

Marguerite spoke with such admiration about this Leonardo that Martín wished he could add this interesting character to his quickly growing list of unforgettable acquaintances.

"When Leonardo came to us, this painting came with him, unfinished, but Leonardo started it at the same time an Italian nobleman commissioned him to paint his wife, Lisa. I believe he worked on this painting for nearly twenty years. He was still working on it when he died here a few years ago."

Martín listened to every word, captivated by both the reverent voice of Marguerite and the beauty of this woman depicted in the painting.

"I believe this painting represents the beauty Leonardo saw in every woman." Marguerite continued, "So yes, I like to think it is me, or a bit of me, a tiny bit of my bit of goodness made it into this painting."

Martín turned his attention from the painting to Marguerite. "What will happen to you now?"

Her eyes widened. "Pardon me?"

"You, what happens to you now?" Martín became more intent than he'd ever been. The intensity surprised her. "I am serious. Kings claim to own the land and thus they own the people on them. They own the women who they take and give for their own pleasure and benefit. The number eight Henry in England has a queen for a wife, but now he wants Anne instead. He is fighting the pope for permission. You even told us so. Anne does not want him. In fact, you can see how Nando would have her in a minute. He would drop that lousy robe and run off with her if he could. And I believe she might be happy about it."

Marguerite's tiny smile confirmed this surprising conjecture was not far off.

"So what happens to you now? You will get your brother Francis back. He will not appreciate all you have done for him, and he will find some nobleman, or rich man with royal blood who owns some important piece of land, and he will marry you off to him and you will remain gracious and honorable, probably more so."

As Martín continued, Marguerite's eyes widened with each pronouncement.

"So, what about you? Why have you no choice? You are not his property!"

Silence returned to the library. The only sound was Martín's heart pounding in his chest, trying to keep the blood flowing so it wouldn't explode in his head.

This may have been the first time in his life his true feelings had ever poured out, and to a woman of such noble position. He'd just condemned her brother, the King of France, along with the very fabric of the world.

He woke up that morning a mere heretic. Now he was a heretic against God and His church and a dissident against the most powerful men in the world. He didn't care. It was wrong. He knew it in his bones.

Marguerite watched him calm down. As his blood slowly returned his face to the kind, meek young man she tutored these many weeks, the admiration shown in her smile and her slow, almost imperceptible smile seemed to condone his feelings. A smile Martín recognized in the very painting they stood before.

"Martín, come with me." With no immediate response to his charges against the kings, Marguerite led Martín from the library across the plaza to the Church of Saint Florentin. The two stood before the beautifully carved white marble sarcophagus.

"Martín, inside this church lies Leonardo, one of the greatest men the world will ever know. I am certain even five hundred years from now his thinking, his work, his discoveries of the world will be credited to saving the world from pain, from hardship, and from the toils of life."

Martín followed Marguerite as she led him from the chapel to a room furnished with a large table lit by a large round window. She pulled a sheet from a painting secured to an aging easel. Martín stared with reverence at the painting of two women and a child grappling with a small lamb. Instantly, Martín recognized the style as similar to that of the painting of Lisa.

"King Louis XII commissioned this painting following the birth of his daughter Claude, my brother Francis's wife. Leonardo never finished it until he came to live with us," Marguerite said.

"The Virgin Mary and child Jesus are the answer to the question you asked," she said.

Martín wasn't sure she understood the question he meant to ask back in the library. The question about her future. It was his expression of confusion that led her to continue.

"Martín, the virgin did not seek her own. She was submissive to God's will. She was called to give birth to God's son, serve that son, prepare that son, to sustain that son so he could grow up perfectly and give his life for the world." Marguerite paused, giving Martín time to understand.

"I am not here to seek my own. The kings of France, or of Spain, or any kingdom on earth can never be expected to be anything more than mortal, with all the weaknesses that come with mortality. But I believe despite their failures, God, who knows all, moves His work forward."

Martín understood her meaning, but it didn't sway his feelings on life's injustices. Martín saw what kings, popes, bishops, and sheriffs, anyone with power, did to people. It was not God's work. Until now, as he pondered, he hadn't appreciated how Humphrey outsmarted them all with their own false proclamations. Is it possible to outsmart God? No, it can't be.

"My good friend," she said, "just as I feel the works of my dear Leonardo were inspired by God for God's own purposes, I too may contribute to God's purposes, and you will too, if you follow Him."

What Marguerite said wasn't wrong, but it was incomplete. It didn't satisfy as an answer to his question, so he pressed forward.

"I cannot claim to know what God wants or even if he wants anything from me. But as a heretic, I learned to read the holy scriptures and I can in two languages. On my horse are sections of those same words of Christ in German as well. Do you remember what Christ said to Pilate? 'The truth shall make you free.'"

Marguerite nodded, but didn't respond.

"Today, the truth will get you executed, put to the flame like my beloved Friar Tomás. How can God expect us to come to Him if we cannot choose otherwise?"

Marguerite's eyes widened, urging him forward.

"Choose ye this day, Joshua said." Martín's hands shook. Not that he forgot the rest of the verse, but he realized even this verse from the Old Testament would fail to make his point.

Marguerite finished the verse, "Whom you will follow, but as for me and my house, we will choose the Lord."

Martín pondered a few moments. His eyes wandered the room, looking at nothing in particular. When they settled back on the painting, he found the word he'd been searching for during the entire conversation.

"Libertas," he said, "it's freedom to choose. Libertad," he repeated in Spanish. He was speaking to himself as much as to Marguerite.

"Your friend John Calvin is wrong," Martín said as he looked from the painting to Marguerite. "God did not choose who He will save before we are even born. He gave His only begotten Son so we can choose. John gets to choose. Friar Tomás chose. He chose to die for Christ. I get to choose. But I want to live for Him. Not for the kings, not for the nobility, and not for the pope."

Thoughts raced through his head. "It's not choose or die, choose or be driven out. Your choice has to be free, or it is not a choice. When that choice is made because of fear, threats, lies… anything but love, it's not choice, it is manipulation." His voice became animated.

"People need to know the truth and they need to be free to choose." Martín finished his exposition. It had come to him like a light bursting upon him through a cloudy sky.

His eyes went from the painting of the women with the Christ Child to Marguerite. Her smile was the very smile from the painting of Lisa.

"I am so sorry if I offended." His eyes dropped to the floor. He realized he'd just chosen to be heretical.

"I see you have become the heretic we mocked you of being. Welcome." Her teasing smile broadened.

She continued, "We are born in a great time. I recognize the injustices. And many others with courage do as well. They are standing against those injustices. Though I am among the most privileged, my influence is limited. I stay the hand of the injustice when I can. My brother and I are often at odds concerning the affairs of the kingdom. Several of the men you have met these past many days are as heretical as or more so than John.

"When the common people can read the very words of Christ as you do, and if they will, they will throw the control of wicked men off. There will be a spiritual revolution. Do you remember how John felt a reformation of the Church was inadequate?" she asked.

Martín had pondered on that statement John Calvin made. It was one of the few that resonated because it was so out of sync with his others.

Marguerite continued, "John said God would not reform the Church, He would restore it. I do not know what that means, but I do know John and many others are all working toward that end, whether they know it or not. Kings, popes, bishops, knights, inventors, thinkers, and young orphan heretics are part of that march toward your libertas, your libertad, liberté. Martín, if you are right and God cherishes our liberty to choose Him, can He stop evil men from choosing otherwise, from actually choosing evil?"

That question dove deep into Martín's soul.

"Martín, you said you know nothing. Neither do I, but I know I love God and I pray I may contribute to God's effort to help His children march toward your vision of liberty."

She slipped the sheet back over the painting. Marguerite led Martín through the chapel and into the courtyard where Humphrey, Nando, and Faustino were readying the horses.

"Do you think Anne might be interested in Nando?" he asked.

"Do you believe Nando is really a friar?" she said.

Martín watched her smile transform from the one in the painting of Lisa to a big grin. She winked.

# Chapter Twenty-three

## Central Peru

"You believe he knows where the armies are?" Cusimi asked.

Urco nodded.

"Could he know where we find Paititi?" she asked.

Urco shook his head. He watched intently how the young chasqui remained close to Sarpay and the child as they searched the buildings that were less damaged during the attack.

Sarpay and Cataquil found enough provisions and some remnants of some nobles' wardrobes that soon the small group felt ready to move on. Urco and Cataquil looked better prepared for the highlands wearing soft llama-wool tunics over their bare bodies. Sarpay smiled at how they still wore the wraps around their waists.

Urco deferred to Sarpay to interrogate the chasqui even though he felt the young man might be more truthful if Urco asked the questions. He hoped that through her divine nature as the First Priestess of the Empire that she would assess the truth correctly. He wondered if Sarpay and Cusimi had the same feelings and misgivings about a young chasqui, who was seemingly unaffected by a village's complete desolation. It was with Cataquil that Urco wanted a private conversation. But Cataquil stayed too close to both the child and the chasqui who accompanied Sarpay. Maybe that was the clue.

The boy claimed he was in the service of the priests in Tumbes, though he was born near Cochabamba, down off the altiplano from Lake Titicaca. Urco had never been to Cochabamba, but Sarpay described it as a verdant plain between the high mountains and the jungles. Her father had turned Cochabamba into one of the most productive agricultural regions in the empire. Conquered by her grandfather, Topa Inca Yupanqi, it was inhabited early by the people of Tiwanaku. Sarpay had only been there twice that she could recall, but she remembered the massive fields of maize, which were harvested and carried by large caravans of llamas to supply the empire. The great harvests of maize were stored in many of the thousands of qullqas—storehouses built throughout the empire.

She remembered Cochabamba was in eternal spring. Summer or winter, it was comfortable. It was one of her father's favorite parts of the empire. She once asked why he kept his second capital in Quito rather than Cochabamba. She was young, but she remembered him telling her that if he stayed in Cochabamba too long, he would get fat and lazy living in luxury and drinking too much chicha. It was in the high altiplano where he was the sharpest. The empire depended on his leadership too much for him to waste his life selfishly, he had told her.

The young chasqui introduced himself as Achata Naku. Sarpay couldn't remember specifically, but she thought the name of the tribal chief in Cochabamba was Achata, or something like that. That information gave Urco some peace, at least to the origin of this boy. His tunic did reflect the colors and patterns of the coastal Tumbes. Urco finally chose not to judge the boy by his clothes. As a runner, he, of course, would add accessories to it from every region he passed through.

Urco felt until he had more reason to distrust, he would watch and pray that between Sarpay as a priestess, Cusimi as a skeptic, Cataquil as a pure soul, and himself as a warrior, they might sense the time when they would have reason to doubt his motives.

"You say there are three armies prepared to meet Huascar's forces?" Urco asked. The group, now made up of six, one being a young child, was ready to move south toward either the Apurimac or Cusco or some other temple once a safe one could be identified.

Naku looked into each of their eyes. Could he sense the feelings of mistrust? Urco wondered.

"The armies are positioned south of us now, with only small forces north. You are anxious to reach the Apurimac, which is impossible. Rumiñawi is in the way. To reach Cusco, you must go through or around Quizquiz," Naku said.

What Huascar wouldn't give for this information, Urco thought. But if Huascar didn't have his own host of chasquis crisscrossing the empire, he was a fool. But how did Naku know if he was not affiliated with Atahualpa's armies? Suspicion returned.

The child did not speak. Repeated gentle questions to him revealed no hope of a name. Sarpay chose to name him Topa, after her grandfather Topa Inca Yupanqui. With Topa in hand, the tiny band chose to follow the roads off the altiplano and travel along the coast. They risked encountering fewer villages along the way and hoped to find priests in the Pachacamac Temple. It was farther away, but a much safer journey. Even though it was not a major temple like the Apurimac or the Temple of The Sun in Cusco, Sarpay decided not to risk encountering the armies in order to reach those two more significant temples. She would rely on the gods to accept her sacrifice in Pachacamac or intervene on her behalf.

Urco quickly removed the tunic and high altiplano clothing once they began the descent down to the coast. He had never trekked from the jungles over the mountains and down to the ocean. He was pleased how well the roads connected the four suyus of Tawantinsuyu. In the early years of the Inca Empire, Pachacuti had organized it into four suyus or regions. Quito, Huayna Capac's northern capital and where he died was in the Chinchaysuyu in the northwest. Urco's tribe and other jungle tribes hovered off the mountains in the Antisuyu. Kuntisuyu was farther south but included the western coastline. Quilasuyu, which covered the southeast, included the lands of Cochabamba and Lake Titicaca, which Naku claimed as home. And Cusco sat right in the middle where each of the four suyus met.

In all of Urco's searching and with what little he learned from the white man, he felt he was going the wrong direction and away from possibly finding Paititi. The western coastlines could not possibly hide the great city of gold. Yet, he was certain he saw in Naku's face a spark of recognition of its existence. He was sure Naku believed Paititi was real. He hoped to find the right time to ask what Naku knew. Did Naku know where to find the white man? Or was he leading them to Quichamba's forces?

# Chapter Twenty-four

## Château Royal d'Amboise

When Marguerite and Martín left the church and reached the large courtyard, Humphrey was securing the satchel of God's silver to Martín's horse. Several members of the royal family and staff were bidding farewell as the men prepared to leave. Anne kissed Nando on the cheek as he prepared to mount. It was enough to halt his movement, and he dropped the reins of his horse. He turned and took her hands in his.

"Nando," Humphrey said, "she is promised to a king. What are you thinking?"

Both Martín and Marguerite saw the gentle show of affection. Wide eyes met as they looked at each other confirming what they just witnessed was real.

Marguerite said, "You'd better get him out of here, or the pope will not be the only one after your heads. England's number eight Henry will rescind Humphrey's pardon, and four heads will roll."

Beelzebub seemed the most impatient to be on the move. Once the men were mounted, Beelzebub took it as permission to charge off leading the band of misfits along the Loire River and north toward Saxony to meet a friend of Vano and Humphrey, a friend so important to Martín's destiny that they'd risk their own lives to get him there. A destiny Martín still knew little about.

Humphrey promised he'd have them to Metz within the week. And if Nando didn't find another female to distract him, they'd be to Wittenberg within two. He assured Marguerite with God's help they'd be clear of the bishop's men who they'd learned were still seeking retribution for his turning the indulgence tables on the church in Bilbao.

With the afternoon sun at their backs, the four horsemen, as they'd been called, cleared a small, forested hill overlooking the Meuse Valley where the Vair River meandered its way, flowing in and around rich green meadows. Beyond its banks, if you could call them banks, for the river created for itself channels and pools as it wished, rose gentle hills, two to three hundred feet high.

Just at the foot of the low, sloping wall of hills and on the very edge of the meadows, lay a little village of maybe forty or fifty houses. It was evident the village was never important enough to be walled. The houses were of stone with thatched and tiled roofs. They didn't appear to be much more than one or two rooms in size.

The spire of a small church rose above the cluster of houses. Small gardens were tucked around the houses. An elderly man and his wife stepped aside as the men approached. Even with his limited experience, Martín was the most fluent in French. Nando had spent time in the French monastery and Humphrey had some skill, but they hadn't been tutored in proper grammar as had Martín.

"Forgive us for this disruption, but pray thee, what village is this?" he asked, bowing his head to show deference to the couple.

"You do not know? Why it is Domremy, the birthplace of the Maid of Orléans," the old man said, eyeing each of the men looking for any recognition.

Humphrey's smile, accompanied by a subtle nod confirmed his recognition.

Martín's French was clearly not his native tongue, but the Frenchman understood well enough. Yet Martín recognized a bit of caution that accompanied the proclamation of the alleged fame of this tiny village. Martín noted Humphrey knew of this maid and asked Humphrey, "Is this Maid of Orléans someone of consequence?"

Humphrey nodded. "Martín, if you needed a witness of your call from God, this may be the place, for God Himself and His Holy angels have been here." This proclamation raised an eyebrow.

Nando, in his native Spanish asked, "Do we get to meet this maid?"

The old man watched and listened carefully. "What brings an Englishman, a Spanish friar, a Gitano, and a French student to Domremy? Most of our visitors are pilgrims, highwaymen, soldiers, or lost."

Martín smiled, shaking his head at how the old man so quickly and accurately recognized his companions. This is a wise one, Martín thought, wanting to give the man even more respect.

"You are observant," Martín said. "The Englishman is indeed a highwayman, who, for a reason only God knows, is between robberies and is dedicated to accompanying me to Wittenberg. We hope to reach Metz tonight. As to our friar, he is lost to his cause and is simply hoping to protect me from the Englishman. And our Gitano is simply wandering." Martín winked. He felt comfortable with the old man for some strange reason. The gentleness in his eyes exuded a meekness and a confidence, yet this man was a fellow peasant, a man and his wife who were like Martín, nobodies.

"You will not reach Metz tonight. Even that horse," he motioning to Beelzebub, "cannot reach Metz in less than a very long day." The old man looked from rider to rider, whispered something to his wife, then said, "Please follow me. Tonight, you will be our guests and you will learn of our maid."

Martín turned to his friends and even though they understood enough French, in Spanish he translated, "We are invited to enjoy the generosity of these fine people."

Holding hands, the couple led the men from the main road up to a small farmhouse surrounded by well-kept gardens behind which was a large meadow where a small herd of cows grazed lazily.

"It surprises me that your English friend here did not tell you about our Maid of Orléans. After all, it was his people who murdered her," the old man said as he ushered the men to a barn where they could care for their horses.

"My friend the friar will be disappointed your maid is no longer living," Martín said jokingly. "I am sure he was anxious to meet her."

"Oh, he would have loved her. Yet others of his kind did not. They had her burned at the stake as a heretic a hundred years ago."

That revelation stopped Martín cold. He turned to Humphrey, who was listening intently to the discussion.

"You know this story?" Martín asked Humphrey in Spanish.

Humphrey nodded. "I know the English side of the story. I am eager to learn what the French think. I am surprised our good Friar Nando does not know it from God's perspective."

"My new friends," the old man started, once the saddles rested idly on a long fence rail. Martín translated as he talked. "I am François Paré and my wife is Melina. If you have come from Amboise, it has been a day or two since you have eaten like you will tonight. But for now, come with me."

They followed François past a large garden and into a sloping meadow that led them back to the road where they had just been. They continued their descent toward the river and followed along its meandering banks.

François didn't say more than a few unimportant words until they entered the village. As they stood looking up at the cross that stood atop the single spire, he said, "This is where Joan was called by God to free France."

Martín had yet to connect the references made to the Maid of Orléans to the young peasant girl Joan, whose legend of heresy reached even to Trujillo. Martín considered the story more a fable told to prevent the peasantry from thinking God might expect more than their servitude to the nobles. And certainly to keep them from thinking for themselves.

"It was here in her father's garden between the house and the church when the archangel Michael, accompanied by other angels in a great light, visited young, thirteen-year-old Joan." François paused to let the story rest.

"You can imagine the fear Joan must have experienced. Yet, Michael promised her that others would visit, including Saint Catherine and Saint Margaret. Michael repeated this message enough times, her fear was followed by great comfort and peace. She claimed the angels bade her to be a good girl and in time God would bring her to save France from the English." When François mentioned the English, he looked toward Humphrey as if he represented the afflictions his country suffered during the Hundred Years' War.

The men stood silent. François continued, "Young Joan was undaunted. Think of the persecution she suffered. A peasant, an innocent teenage girl, expected to save France from the English?"

"Was she pretty?" Nando asked. The men just stared at him. François ignored the question.

"The French suffered defeat after defeat, yet, and following the direction of God and His angels, it still took Joan years to finally get an audience with the dauphin Charles. When she met with Charles, she claimed God called her to finally get Charles crowned king and then help push the English off French soil."

François led the men into the church where he began outlining Joan's journey from Domremy to Orléans where her leadership turned the tides of a war that the French had been losing for nearly one hundred years.

"Joan seldom spoke to us villagers of her visions. These deep religious experiences were too sacred for her common conversation. It was later that we in the village learned she only shared the instructions received from the heavenly visitors when it was necessary to fulfill their commands. Her reluctance was even more evident as she was questioned by the judges."

Nando interrupted, "What did the visitors tell her?"

"What she saw, or how she heard them speak, she never told anyone. What we know for certain is that she was sincere throughout her entire journey, and she never showed any evidence she was tricked or misled."

"François, I take no pride in how our English judges and Church treated your young maid, the now famous Joan of Arc, who gave her life defending what she knew was true," Humphrey said. "But as I have crossed the expanse of this Holy Roman Empire, I assure you it is not that holy. Yet I commend Pope Callixtus III for the retrial those years later, which found her innocent."

"How is the pope at resurrection?" Nando said.

All eyes turned to him.

"Well, it appears to me, men, great and small, are anxious to accuse and condemn in the name of Christ. Yet when they are later found to be wrong, which is almost always, people are dead, murdered, and their lives are ended for righteousness' sake. How do the dead ones, innocent ones choose to follow our Savior?" Nando asked. "And there's no punishment for the murderers?"

This may have been the first time Martín heard something so heartfelt or passionate from the friar. The words echoed the thoughts troubling Martín throughout this journey as he watched very pious men condemn and destroy.

Following several moments of silence, Martín said to François, "Forgive us, please continue."

François turned to Humphrey, "You are familiar with Joan's story? You have read the records of the trial?"

Humphrey nodded.

"Our good friar here asks a perfect question," François said. "In your travels across the less-than-holy empire," he smiled, "is there a king, a noble, a bishop, or even a pope who reigns or rules like the great king of us all? Even Jesus Christ?"

"Not that I have yet seen," Humphrey said.

As the men slowly walked through the chapel and out into the yard, François continued to share the story of the village's, even France's, most notable person. He told them how, even though Charles VII was her ruler by divine right, to Joan he was just the heir to the throne. She only ever called him dauphin. Since his coronation could only be had at Rheims, which was in English hands, Joan said God called her to help the king-to-be push the English back so the dauphin could get crowned. Yet those so closely associated with Charles worked to prevent her audience with him. François told how the most revered bishops, knights, advisors, and nobles interceded to prevent her from fulfilling her mission given to her by God.

As Martín listened, his trust in man's divine roles edged closer and closer to an abyss he feared might eventually swallow his very hope for mankind, and faith of a redemption which seemed to grow further and further out of reach. François had just said Joan, who had visitors from God, felt the dauphin was her ruler by divine right. Divine right had become a troubling concept for Martín. If the dauphin was divinely called, why didn't God push the English from France? Why would God call a little peasant girl to free His chosen king?

Martín's thoughts were interrupted when Nando asked François what the voices told Joan to do after she broke the siege of Orléans and led the dauphin to Rheims and saw him made king.

"Joan never revealed if she heard other commands concerning what else might lie in her future. Following the great victory of Orléans and her success in getting the dauphin crowned, future successes were clouded with betrayal, mistrust, and envy from some of our own people. After that, her capture by the Burgundians, her traitorous betrayal by the French bishop delivering her to the English led to a trial that, to many of us, displayed the truth of Satan's power over man."

Then François talked about the trial and the mistreatment by the very men of God, who of all people should be receptive to the spirit of God. More questions flooded Martín's mind. What happens to God's eternal purposes when He chooses a person like Joan to lead an army against the English, yet His divinely chosen king fails to support her, and she is tried, murdered by men of God, and she doesn't succeed?

"Did she ever plan to marry, have a family, and live like other young girls?" Nando asked.

"Many boys were interested in Joan. Her father wanted to marry her to a boy in the village, but she refused, knowing she could not accomplish her mission as a wife or mother. Her life was consecrated to obedience to God."

"Which is precisely why you will never have a wife, Nando,"

Humphrey said.

"God would never punish a woman or children with a rascal like you. It is better that you forget women," Faustino winked at Nando.

Martín turned to François, "Why would God call a young girl, a peasant girl, an innocent girl, to lead an army which for nearly a hundred years had been fighting and losing? And when she obeys, and triumphs, she is betrayed and murdered by those who claim to be God's very servants?"

The answer hung unanswered in the air. François looked into Martín's pleading eyes, then looked from man to man and shrugged his shoulders.

The men made their way back to François' home. Indeed, the meal was every bit as delicious as they anticipated following François' earlier declaration of his wife's cooking.

Faustino, in crude French, asked François how he knew about the difficulties Joan faced after she left Domremy.

François sat a little taller, his shoulders pulled back and his chest filled with air. "My grandfather was a knight who served alongside Joan. He knew she was called by God. He claimed he did not need to protect her from the English. That was God's job."

François' wife Melina, quiet up until now, looked Faustino in the eye and said, "His remorse was he could not protect her from the French nobles. We are ashamed of our own people."

The sadness in Melina's face prompted Martín to repeat a question of his own to which he had for weeks, and for which he never received a satisfactory answer. Maybe in Melina's simple world an innocent question may provide the answer. "Does God have a plan for everyone?"

After a few moments, she said, "I want to believe God has a work for each of us, large or small. Here in Domremy we are simple people, but I want to be part of a grand masterpiece. The masterpiece may be ages in the making. My tiny part may be finished by another, but I need to play my part. Joan was only called to start the freeing of France. She completed that journey. She then was called to serve in the condemnation and exposition of evil that had crept into the Church. The world will one day see her sacrifice play a considerable role in the eventual success of God's glorious plan for His children. I pray that one day people will be free to learn God's will for themselves and then choose to serve God without fear."

Melina's answer surprised Martín. Its depth illustrated she was not a mere simple soul. He pondered that thought. Where in the world were people free to choose their own destiny? He wondered if he would ever be free to choose to follow his heart. He didn't know who he was following. But he hoped he was following God.

The discussion waned. Melina and François made comfortable sleeping arrangements for their visitors.

The next morning, the men busied themselves helping François with his morning chores, and following another wonderful meal, they saddled their horses and prepared to go.

François refused Martín's offer of payment for the generous hospitality, not to mention the incomparable education. Yet in the quiet of the morning as the men almost reverently rode through the town of Domremy, Melina's words resonated in Martín's heart and mind.

He was glad he hadn't been called by heavenly visitors. Can you refuse to obey angels? It didn't work out well for Jonah when God called him to Nineveh. It took a whale to persuade him.

Throughout the rest of the day, Martín's mind wearied, rehashing Joan's life, her treatment by the king she had coronated, her accusers, and their very denial of God's ability to call a young girl. Their insistence that she deny what was real. Was her claim of angelic visitations real? Maybe it took an innocent maid to listen because others refused to obey.

Martín was grateful for Nando's interruption, which revealed he, too, was pondering Joan's life and sacrifice.

"After all she did for France, François said her reward was simply to have her village be tax exempt," Nando said.

Of all the obscure tiny pieces of François' story, Nando pondered this one? Martín just stared at Nando.

After the dizzying day, Martín was grateful to fall into a deep sleep in an inn they found in Metz.

# Chapter Twenty-five

### Altiplano – Tawantansuyu – Central Peru

Naku should have been as surprised as any of the group to find the qullqa empty. It was the third storage warehouse they found cleaned out. Sarpay stepped inside as if to breathe the rich organic air that clung to its roots as a provider of life.

The armies had wiped it clean days earlier, if not hours before. No maize, no papas, no dried llama. Sarpay's father was not the first Sapa Inca to begin establishing the qullqas strategically across the empire. They benefitted every member in the empire. Wise leaders assured that great amounts of maize, papas, dried meats, and fruits were brought from throughout the empire to fill the qullqas to sustain the population in times of famine, droughts, the frequent earthquakes, floods, and even attacks from outside armies. In times of surplus, the qullqas were packed full, so that in lean seasons they sustained both the high-born and the peasants. With more than two thousand qullqas, no one went hungry in the entire Tawantinsuyu empire.

Huayna Capac positioned many of the qullqas along the thousands of miles of roads. The well-constructed roads made life easier and more efficient for all of Tawantinsuyu. Products were easily transported and stored throughout the empire. These roads now facilitated the swift movement of armies. Which army came this way? Urco wondered. And when were they here?

The fact that Naku didn't seem surprised bothered Urco. He looked at Naku and without words raised his eyebrows. Naku understood the question.

"Quichamba's men," he said.

That was not the answer to bring peace to anyone's heart. But Naku was not looking into Urco's eyes when he spoke.

"Urco, are you proficient with that bow?" Naku asked.

Cusimi gave Naku a look that said, if you only knew what a master Urco is.

Naku said, "Give me your bow and two arrows. I want to see what it feels like to be a warrior." Naku dropped his lance and reached for the bow. Urco hesitated. The fact that Naku was not looking into his eyes unnerved him.

In a firm but quiet tone, Naku said, "If you don't give me the bow and two arrows, you will be dead, because behind you are Quichamba's spies. If they do not see you surrender your bow to me along with arrows, a lance and deadly stones will kill you first, then your brother. They will take and use Cusimi before destroying her, and then they will take the priestess back to Quichamba. They will leave Topa to starve."

This was exactly what Urco feared. Why hadn't Sarpay with her divine access to the gods recognized the betrayal, the treachery? He wanted to stare into Naku's eyes and see how deep the young chasqui's evil ran. Could he let Naku and his partners kill them and take Sarpay? Unarmed, wouldn't they kill them all anyway? Did Naku think that if he disarmed me, I would simply let Sarpay become a hostage once again?

"Please. Now," Naku said.

Urco believed there were men capable enough to cut him down with one nod from Naku.

Naku reached out a hand. Urco hesitated for several seconds more and carefully lifted the bow and arrow off his shoulder. He hesitantly offered it to Naku. Naku didn't close his hand on the bow. He took one arrow in his hand and held it still.

Hardly moving his lips, Naku's words climbed gently out of his mouth. "Over your left shoulder is their leader, you will not see him. His feathered headdress imitates your yellow macaw. Put the arrow three inches below the feathers. Turn back around, smash my face as you rip the second arrow from my hand. You will see a bowman launch an arrow at you. Kill him next. With two dead, I hope the rest will run."

The movement was instantaneous. Urco's first arrow met its mark three inches below the yellow feather. Apart from the yellow feathers, the man was perfectly invisible one second before. He fell forward, shattering the arrow protruding from his eye. Naku tumbled to the ground as Urco turned and smashed Naku's proud nose. As he fell, Naku released the second arrow he was holding. It hung in midair. Urco snatched it. The bowman Naku warned about was quicker than Naku indicated. An arrow buried its copper tip into Urco's bare shoulder, and he dropped the bow.

Three warriors charged forward. Sarpay grabbed the bow, nocked the arrow, and released it dead into the leading man. He fell at Urco's feet. The next warrior was on Urco, pulling him to the ground. Urco's shoulder took the full weight of both men. The pain nearly sucked Urco free of consciousness. Just before the attacker plunged a razor-sharp obsidian knife into Urco's chest, Cataquil yanked the man off and with one arm around the attacker's neck laid him motionless on the ground. A warrior had Sarpay, quenching her efforts to snatch another arrow. The last man, reaching to help carry Sarpay away was caught by Cataquil's club square in the face. He tumbled to the earth. It was now one against six if you counted the child who clung to Sarpay. The man holding Sarpay chose to fight another day. He released Sarpay, dodged Cataquil's second swing which didn't quite miss Sarpay, and disappeared into the brush.

Cusimi helped Sarpay to her feet. Topa clung tight to her legs. Cataquil went to the spot where the first man fell. When he returned with the weapons from the man Urco killed first, he carried with him a sling, a lance, a bag of perfect stones, and a colorful macaw headdress. A golden medallion hung around his neck. Sarpay, shaken and with bruised ribs from Cataquil's club, cared for Urco's bleeding shoulder. She could do nothing for his pride. Cusimi was wiping the blood from Naku's broken nose.

"Next time, I smash your face, and I take the arrow," Naku muttered as blood soaked the cloth Cusimi held to his mouth.

The arrow's copper tip dripped with blood when Sarpay pulled it from Urco's shoulder. Urco took it from her and examined how it was attached to the broken shaft. Their lives had just been preserved by the awareness and warning of the young chasqui, yet Urco was interested in the arrow. It was tribal. Each of the Antisuyu tribes developed their own styles of weapon manufacture. This one was Shuar. It explained the feather headdress as well. How many other hunters have been sent to capture the princess?

Urco motioned to the four dead warriors. "You know these?" Urco asked Naku.

Naku nodded.

"You were part of them?" Urco asked.

Another nod.

"Have they been following since the village?"

A third nod.

"Yet, you betrayed them. Why?"

Naku didn't shrink or hesitate. "The priestess."

All eyes were on Naku hoping for more. He said nothing. A tiny shrug of his shoulder was all he gave. It wasn't enough for Cusimi.

"The priestess? What do you mean the priestess?" Cusimi said.

Naku nodded toward Sarpay.

"I know who the priestess is," Cusimi said. "Why did you lead these men here, and then why did you betray them? Or did you betray them? Or were they betraying you?"

Urco appreciated Cusimi speaking up. She asked each of the questions running through his mind.

"Quichamba spies watch every qullqa. I knew this one had no spies. If I led Unay and his men here, we would not share the bounty with this qullqa's spies. I would be rewarded by Unay, and Quichamba would let me join his men. I could fight and kill in Prince Atahualpa's army."

Urco tried to reach into Naku's response for the answer to Cusimi's question. Naku hadn't answered the question. What was his plan now, to lead them into captivity and claim the entire bounty? Or to sacrifice any future as a warrior? Urco pondered if Cusimi and Sarpay wondered the same thing.

Urco sensed in Naku the same feelings he felt as a young man wanting to become someone of significance, to be needed. Now, Naku was just an invisible messenger, a chasqui running namelessly across the empire. Would Cusimi understand that? Would Sarpay know what irrelevance felt like? According to quipu keepers, over ten million Inca citizens were scattered across the four suyus. Were there enough quipus to record their names? Did even the Creator God Viracocha know their names?

There was no time to let his mind delve into the mysteries that many times generated more questions he knew would never find answers. But he knew he was not the only Inca to feel dispensable. Urco's people were survivors. During some seasons, though too short, they enjoyed joy and peace.

During other seasons, harsh seasons, families, villages, and towns suffered the intense heartache of illness and brutal death. One tribe destroying another. Urco's mother was a young girl when Sarpay's father laid siege to Urco's village. The fear had swept through his people many days before. The threat of utter destruction erased all hope. Urco's grandfather, the chiefest among the tribal leaders, chose to align with the Inca Empire in peace and unity. Many of the leaders argued that with such skill as had their warriors, they could defeat the Inca. Others tried to convince the tribe to retreat deeper into the jungles.

Urco's grandfather prevailed. A certain massacre was prevented. Urco's mother, along with many other tributes, were given in exchange. Urco's mother was given to the great Huayna Capac. Urco's village enjoyed greater peace, and they prospered under the protection and well-organized administration of the Inca.

Urco's mother became one of Huayna Capac's many wives and soon Urco was born, followed a year later by a sister. When his mother gave birth to a third child, a boy, she and the boy fell ill and died. Urco and his sister were sent back to the tribe in the Antisuyu, where his grandfather prepared him to rule all the tribes of the jungle people. Though Urco and his sister were of royal blood and were respected in the village, they were merely two more among ten million.

Urco grew strong and wise. He was favored by the people for his goodness more than for his ancestry. He learned from the finest archers and slingmen in the tribe. When he reached the age of twelve, it was his time to journey with his tribe's nobility to Cusco for the most sacred festival in the empire, the Inti Raymi, to pay homage to Inti, the Sun God, the divine protector of the Inca people.

As a young boy, he looked forward to the festivals. The celebrations of their ancestors, the harvest vigils to the Sun and Moon gods, to the god of the soil and rain. The memory of his first Inti Raymi, the Festival of the Sun, played slowly through Urco's mind. Though Huayna Capac, the Sapa Inca, was his father, Urco seldom saw him.

It was the winter solstice, the rebirth of the sun, the day when their god began his journey back toward the earth, bringing longer days and the promise of abundant crops. From the highest peaks of the Andes to the lowland valleys and coastal plains, the entire empire gathered in sacred local festivals to honor Inti. And this time, Urco would celebrate Inti Raymi from the very center of the world, Cusco.

The empire's finest temples and palaces ringed the central plaza. Vibrant colors transformed it into a visual circus. Tapestries, woven in bright colors and patterns that told stories of past victories and conquests, hung from balconies and walls. The sweet perfume of the flowers strewn across the ground mingled with the smell of roasting llama, maize, and the sacred nectar chicha.

Towering and resplendent, catching the light of the morning sun, stood the golden statue of Inti. Everyone gathered around it in reverence.

Huayna Capac himself stood on a raised platform. Urco's grandfather took him past the platform. As they passed, they stopped, knelt, and bowed in honor to Urco's father, Huayna Capac, the Sapa Inca. They then proceeded to the palace of the Sun, where Urco joined a group of around fifty other boys. These were the young sons of the great Sapa Inca, born from the emperor's many wives.

This was the first time Urco came to know how many half-brothers he had. The boys were divided up into groups that represented the various regions of Tawantisuyu and also by the royal standing of their mothers. Urco's mother was of noble birth, so he received the honor of wearing the brilliant golden headdress lined with alternating yellow and bright blue jungle macaw feathers.

Breaking through this fond memory, Urco's mind inserted the vision of the first time he saw Atahualpa and Huascar. They were two of the older brothers, but they were of royal birth along with Ninan, the half-brother who they all knew would be the next Sapa Inca. Huascar was kind but confident. He walked smoothly and calmly and spoke softly with the younger boys. Atahualpa seemed more determined. He stomped more than walked as he moved around the palace. Ninan never spoke. Ninan watched the boys, yet never interacted with any. Urco remembered wondering if these three royal sons were friends with each other or if they fought, as siblings often do. Urco had no brothers other than the several dozen from as many different mothers. But he knew none of them.

Once the young sons of the emperor were organized and adorned, Ninan led them from the palace back to the central square where their father stood in the midst of the crowd. He was draped in the finest deep royal red tunic, embroidered with golden suns. A crimson fringe, the majestic mascaypacha, of the Inca emperors, adorned his brow. It was a symbol of his divine connection to the Sun God. He raised his arms to the heavens, drawing every eye to him. Urco felt frozen in place. Deep and rhythmic, the ceremony commenced as drums began to beat. Processions of priests made their way toward the altar. Their robes flowed like the sacred rivers. Urco remembered the thick, heady scent of burning herbs. Like prayers rising toward the sky, the smoke drifted heavenward. The priests bore offerings for Inti: golden chalices filled with chicha, baskets of maize, and the most sacred of all—an immaculate white llama, its perfect, blemish-free wool a symbol of purity.

Urco left his memory and focused on Sarpay for a few moments. Perfect, blemish-free, pure; she was to be the ultimate sacrifice. He felt the gravity of her determination to get to the sacred temple, but in his weak, mortal state could not envision himself taking a knife to her perfect chest. He shuddered at the memory of the llama being led to the altar. As it was led, a quiet anticipation seemed to hum through the crowd. The high priest raised the ceremonial knife. Gleaming sunlight reflecting from its blade drew every eye. Everyone in the crowd knew the sacrifice was not only for the festival—it was for the prosperity and health of the entire empire.

Once spilled, the blood of the llama would ensure that the sun would continue to rise, the empire would continue to thrive, and crops would continue to grow.

Were there not enough perfect llamas to satisfy the gods? Did they now demand this ultimate sacrifice? He wondered.

Urco remembered how the priest made a swift, precise cut. Would he be as precise plunging a knife into Sarpay's perfect body? The llama's crimson blood flowed onto the sacred stone. The crowd took a collective gasp as the blade stopped the perfect heart of the perfect animal. Urco remembered looking up at his father who stood resolute, his gaze fixed on the sacrifice.

And now the same Sapa Inca, Urco and Sarpay's father, commanded that Sarpay, his only pure and perfect daughter, his firstborn, sacrifice her perfect life for the empire. But this time there would be no priests chanting, their voices rising and falling in harmony with the rhythm of the drums, their words ancient and powerful, connecting earth with divinity. If there were priests, they would be hesitant, resentful, even cowardly. If there were no priests, he would require Cusimi to provide him courage. Could Cataquil help?

Unlike the sacrifice of the immaculate llama, Sarpay's sacrifice would not give way to a joyous celebration. Dancers would not take to the plaza, their every movement graceful and full of meaning, with each step representing the cycles of life, birth, death, and rebirth. No one would be wearing brightly colored garments, woven with feathers and gold.

The sound of flutes and drums would not fill the air, their melodies echoing through the mountains and valleys. There would be no cheers and song, no exchanging of gifts of finely crafted jewelry and textiles among the nobles. The common folk would not be gathering to feast and share stories of God's blessings. Children would not be running through the streets, their laughter complementing the music, their faces bright with promise.

There would only be death, blood, and sorrow. Urco knew he would not pass cups of chicha around, toasts to the Sun God, the Sapa Inca, and the future of the empire.

"Naku," Urco began, "you were very brave. We thank you. But more, the gods thank you. I believe the gods know you. You may have sacrificed your chances to fight and kill with Quichamba, and you have now enlisted in a work for the gods."

Urco knew Naku hedged his bets by sacrificing his face. Urco admired the fact that Naku wanted to appear as a victim in an attack gone bad or as a martyr if the attack succeeded. He smiled to himself. This is a cunning young boy, Urco thought.

Naku seemed to sit a little straighter under Urco's praise.

"Can you lead us safely to a temple?" Sarpay asked.

"Not safely," Naku said.

# Chapter Twenty-six

## Wittenberg - Saxony – Holy Roman Empire

As the days passed and the men got closer to Wittenberg, the discussions revolved around what Humphrey knew of the villages and peoples in Saxony. It was evident Humphrey's journeys put him in contact with every sort of people.

Like so many times over the past weeks, each new hill or valley revealed a fresh vista for Martín to savor in an ever-growing catalog of unique and beautiful countrysides. Wittenberg was no different. Built on a small rise above the Elbe River, which sustained life in the surrounding countryside, the city of Wittenberg was nestled in lush green orchards and fields. The Castle Church, with its four gables and tall spire, stood majestically on the low tree-covered hill, reaching to heaven in reverence for God. On the opposite side of the city, the double stone towers of the parish church, the Stadtkirche of St. Mary's, framed the city as if serving as sentinels protecting the citizens of Wittenberg and calling all to come unto Christ.

The clatter of the horse hooves became more noticeable when the riders left the quiet of the dirt road and moved onto the heavy wood bridge spanning the lazy Elbe River. Humphrey led his band through the bustling streets. Each clomp of Beelzebub's large hoof on the cobbled streets vibrated down the narrow alleys, bouncing off the walls of the stone buildings.

The four men stopped at a small grassy area bordering the plaza. Leaving their horses there, Martín, Humphrey, Faustino, and Fernando walked across the plaza. Humphrey stopped some ten feet in front of a large wooden door. "That is the door," he said reverently. A smile accompanied the slight shake of his head. "The trouble started right here."

"There are a lot of doors behind which trouble starts. Believe me, I know," Nando said. "But a church door? What kind of trouble started here?"

Humphrey closed his eyes in disbelief, head shaking. He took a slow deep breath. "And you, a man of the cloth. I wonder." Humphrey approached the door and pushed it open with his shoulder. As he did so, he said, "The Ninety-five Theses." He raised his eyes to heaven and entered.

A monk met the men as they entered. Humphrey whispered something and the monk ushered the men up the tall stone staircase and into a small library where two men argued.

"Wycliff's translation was made from the Vulgate; it is not the same, it is not enough."

An animated, brown-haired man stood leaning against a pillar arguing with a monk sitting at a roughhewn desk who seemed exasperated with his companion.

"I will say it again." The man standing against the pillar blocked Martín's view of the monk's face. But he could tell from the brown robe the man was a monk. He spoke with a deep bass voice, "The problem is not the Vulgate, nor is it Wycliff. It is your weak excuse of a language. English needs to grow up and become a proper language before it will ever be worthy of the word of God." The monk leaned back in the large wooden chair and when he did so, he noticed he and his friend had visitors.

An enormous smile appeared on the monk's face. He looked up at his companion and motioned with his head to draw the man's attention to the visitors. Both men were now smiling at the four intruders.

"Humphrey, my man, they have not caught and hung you yet?" The man Martín assumed was an Englishman and who confirmed it when he spoke to Humphrey in English, took Humphrey in his arms and gave him a giant hug.

Over the past several weeks, Humphrey tried to do as well teaching Martín English as Marguerite did with French. Several times, Humphrey promised that if Martín could learn French so quickly, he could master English in half the time. Martín was convinced that was not true. Having mastered Latin and Spanish, thanks to Friar Tomás, and becoming somewhat proficient with French, thanks to the princess, stumbling through English convinced Martín that either Humphrey was a terrible instructor or indeed this monk who just condemned English was right—English was a challenging and unworthy language.

Yet, the debate between the two men was in Latin. An Englishman and a German? How else would they communicate?

When the man released his embrace, he said to Humphrey, "Introduce me to your companions. Do I take it that since they are with you, they are heretics, or outlaws, or both?"

Humphrey pulled the three men forward. "William, meet Martín, Faustino, and Fernando. Our friend Vano made me promise to bring them to meet the good priest here." Humphrey motioned over to the monk sitting at a large desk.

The priest stood. "Vano? A scurra fidelis if e'er there were one! A rogue and wanderer, yet with a soul more steadfast than many a cloistered friar! Would that all villains had such a heart. He has not burned yet?"

Martín immediately loved this priest. His expression of love and teasing felt comfortable landing in Martín's heart.

The priest stepped over and greeted Humphrey with another embrace. He took Faustino by the hand warmly and asked, "How is my good friend?"

"Father is well," Faustino said. "He will be pleased to hear you have stayed ahead of the Church."

"You mean outside the Church," the priest said.

"Yes, we heard that," Faustino said. Faustino became somber. With moistened eyes he said, "Father wished for me to tell you, your friend Friar Tomás gave his life on the pyres of Toledo. They did not take it. No flame would convince him to recant, and we failed to help him escape."

A blanket of sorrow smothered the joyful banter which echoed against the stone walls just moments earlier. The priest slowly closed his eyes, head bowed. The silence felt heavy, pulling tears to Martín's eyes. Though the weeks had turned to months, Martín's healing heart required little to tear open.

The priest's deep, sorrowful eyes fixed on Martín's. "So you are him?" He seemed to examine Martín's face. Breaking the stare, he turned to William. "Remember when I told you of Frederick's men who kidnapped and imprisoned me at Wartburg?"

William nodded. The priest continued, "This English outlaw who we both know and would never trust with our purse, but we trust with our lives…" he winked at Humphrey, "was assisted by two great defenders. Friar Tomás was one of those defenders."

William nodded his head slightly. The priest continued, "Tomás must think this is the boy. And if the Gitano Vano sent his son here to accompany the boy, he must agree with Tomás."

Martín's eyes followed the conversation back and forth between these three men, but he bristled when they called him "the boy." With what he'd been through, hadn't he proved to be a man, even a young one at least? He squinted his eyes.

"Martín," Humphrey said, "meet Martin Luther and William Tyndale, two of the most hated and hunted heretics in the empire. You will fit right in."

Nando, feeling left out of this introduction, said, "What about me?"

Humphrey nodded to Nando, "You don't fit in anywhere. Not even the ministry, the way you chase women."

"A friar who likes women?" Luther said, "Trust me, you fit in more than you know."

It did not surprise Martín to meet the famous Martin Luther. He knew they were traveling to Saxony for this very purpose, but the actual event was more subtle, yet more awe-inspiring, than he'd imagined. Friar Tomás spoke of the heretic monk, Martin Luther, with such great respect, Martín couldn't believe he was now in his very office. The fact that Friar Tomás tucked several pages of the Luther German Bible into his satchel supported Martín's realization a great rebellion against the Church was taking place, and Tomás threw Martín into the middle of it.

Luther returned his eyes to examine Martín. Martín didn't dare look away. He felt a love, a peace like he'd known during times with Friar Tomás when they'd put the studies aside and speak of life and the Savior. It was a peace he'd yearned for, but hadn't found since Friar Tomás left. Even the security that his time with Marguerite afforded didn't provide this inner peace, this comfort.

"You cannot help but be hungry and confused," Luther said. "Join William and me for supper. And for my good friar here, you will see us men of God are lesser men without women. You will love my wife," Luther said.

The men followed Luther across the large open grounds from the main university building to the Black Cloister. Luther told the story of how the Black Cloister, a former monastery, was given to him and his wife Katharina as a wedding present from the elector, John the Steadfast.

Speaking specifically to Nando, Luther bragged of his wife, "My Katie is in all things so obliging and pleasing to me that I would not exchange my poverty for the riches of Croesus."

When the group arrived at the Black Cloister, his Katie, Katharina, quickly went to work preparing a simple supper.

With her unflappable nature, Martín figured this was not the first time Luther's wife entertained a group of hungry men with nothing more but a moment's notice. Her movements were confident, un-flustered. She moved with grace. The only hint of rebellion to the immediate expectations to host the four visitors and William was a strand of her auburn hair that fought its way clear of the white lacy cap that held its companions captive. As the rebellious lock of hair hung directly over her eyes, she continued to sweep it aside as she set plater after plater on the table. Her round pink face retained just a handful of freckles. Martín wondered how much younger than Luther she must be, ten, fifteen, even twenty years?

The great dining hall of the Black Cloister, just as Luther described it, could certainly accommodate a large gathering of monks in its day, but as Martín looked around, he felt its open spaciousness made the one large table look small. As Katharina came and went from the kitchen, he recognized a regalness in her. Her long red dress, faded from years of wear and washing, so contrasted with those worn by the Princess Marguerite, it gave Martín pause to compare the two. This woman, despite her poverty, as Luther had described it, displayed just as much grace as Marguerite. He concluded, the woman inside the layers of fabric determines her value.

She placed a platter of herring on the table. As she moved to return to the kitchen, her striking blue eyes met Martín's. Her gentle smile confirmed to Martín this was an extraordinary woman. His respect for Luther grew. What had he done to be worthy of having a wife like this?

Once the table setting was complete, Katharina joined them as comfortably as if she were one of the special guests. Of course, she would. Martín wondered why he almost expected her to stay in the kitchen. She was not a servant, yet she was serving. "The greatest among you," ran through Martín's mind. He smiled at her.

When their young son Hans, who Martín guessed to be only three or four years old, entered the room, Luther proudly introduced him to the group.

"Martín, you couldn't have been but a few years older than this when your father left us. I credit him, your mother, and Faustino's father, Vano, for my split with the Church. Tomás was right, you look just like him."

When Luther suggested earlier that Martín might be confused and hungry, it was nothing. This new level of confusion swallowed the hunger. His mind, which had been struggling to swim upstream after meeting the famed Martin Luther, then learning he was married, nearly drowned when Luther confessed to know his parents.

"Martín, the time we spent together in Rome changed my life and consequently that of many others." Luther paused, his eyes fixed on Martín's face. "You look just like him. I am sure Friar Tomás thought so too. When he told Vano about you, he insisted you come here. They both felt you are destined to finish your father's work. And that is why he insisted Humphrey bring you here."

Martín knew nothing of this work attributed to his father. His mother loved Martín's father and was lost without him, but Martín knew no details, only that his father was a good man who was murdered before Martín was born. He always hoped the picture was true that his mother painted of his father as a great, valiant warrior for God. But he struggled to believe it.

"I never knew my father," Martín said. "He never knew me. He died before I was born. My mother told me a few stories, but I was only nine when she died. I barely remember her."

Luther leaned forward and looked directly at Martín. "Your father was chosen and taught by a good man, Cardinal Talavera. When he became Archbishop of Granada, he called on your father to help convert the Moors to Christianity. Following the Granada wars, the Alhambra treaty provided for freedom of religion to the Moors but exile for the Jews. The exile bothered your father. Because God gifted your father with languages, as we read about in Paul's letters to the Corinthians, he could teach the Moors in their own language, but this slow conversion was not good enough for Cardinal Cisneros. The cardinal and Isabella violated their own Alhambra Decree, which resulted in deadly uprisings. Your father stood against Cardinal Cisneros and Queen Isabella in this betrayal of their own treaty."

Martín had never heard this story before. That his father was gifted with language was a surprise. His mother never mentioned that, nor that his father was in the direct service of powerful men like Archbishop Talavera, Cardinal Cisneros, not to mention Queen Isabella. All Martín ever concluded from his ancestry was that his father was murdered when he tried to defend an old man, and his mother struggled to provide for Martín and died young, leaving him an orphan.

After letting Martín absorb this news, Luther continued, "Along with Talavera, your father and several other clergy learned the Arabic language. The Moors loved and respected your father and Archbishop Talavera. The break came when Cardinal Cisneros ordered the public burning of all the

Arabic manuscripts in Granada. Your father became hostile."

Quietly, almost to himself, Tyndale said, "Interesting how consistent tyrants become in destroying history and culture in their quest to dominate others."

All eyes turned to Tyndale. "When you destroy or at least confuse the roots, you can better manage the fruit," he said.

Martín didn't try to decipher what Tyndale said. His mind was busy absorbing Luther's news about his father. His shock began to melt his lifelong timidity, his self-loathing for being nothing but a poor orphan, a nothing. The news of his father's rage against injustice could not be more surprising. Yet, he knew what that rage felt like. He just never knew what to do with it.

"Why have I never known this? Did my mother know?" Martín turned to Humphrey, "Did you know?"

Humphrey slowly nodded.

"What happened to my father? What did… Why was… Did my mother…" Martín's questions poured out. Luther held up a gentle hand to slow the torrent of passionate pleas, which had been dammed up inside Martín his whole young lifetime.

"There is a great price paid in fighting against powerful people. It cost you a father. It cost the Moors their homes. It cost Talavera his respect, his position, and his life," Luther said.

Katharina refilled Luther's cup. He lifted it and drank. The pause in the story nearly opened the question floodgates again. Luther continued.

"Cisneros and the notorious inquisitor Rodriguez denounced Talavera. Everyone around him was arrested, including your father. Without the protection of the queen, who had since died, Cisneros arrested Talavera. It was your father who secured Archbishop Talavera's release. For doing that, your father was struck down, tortured, and imprisoned. The archbishop died shortly after."

"They killed Archbishop Talavera," Humphrey said. "Cisneros stripped him of everything he had or had done. It killed him."

The story had everyone captivated. Katharina sat next to Luther. Little Hans sat quietly on her lap.

Luther's eyes surveyed the group as if he were seeking the right words to finish the story.

"Do you remember your mother struggling to breathe?" Luther asked.

Martín's mind raced to the day she died. They didn't kill her. She died trying to defend the priests. She died trying to defend Martín. The struggle for breath was too much; her illness killed her. Yes, he did remember. He remembered watching her fight for air. He nodded slowly as he looked into Luther's eyes.

"The day your father defended the archbishop, your mother fought side by side with him. They were both struck down by the cardinal's guards." Luther paused again.

"They both lived," Luther said.

"Why…?" Martín's mouth couldn't complete the question. His mouth hung open and his head shook from side to side, his eyes almost looking into nothing. His breathing became shallow and rapid.

"Neither one of them ever knew the other survived. Your father watched one of Cardinal Cisneros' guards pierce your mother's heart with a sword. He watched her die before he was finally knocked unconscious and dragged to the Alcazaba prison and tortured. The last things your mother would have seen were the many times a sword pierced your father before he fell. No one survives that prison, especially a heretic."

Martín felt the heat in his face. He felt dizzy. The once spacious room began closing in. Katharina slid over next to him and gently pulled him close as if he were a child. His breathing slowed. Finally, deep, slow breaths cleared the vision.

"How do you know this? Who knows this?" Martín asked.

Luther gave plenty of time for Martín to absorb this news. "Somehow, your father survived the torture chambers in Cisneros' prison. For seven years, he remained a prisoner. A young guard, in conversation with your imprisoned father, became a convert to Christ. That convert became a monk. That monk eventually helped free your father."

"Friar Tomás," Martín's words were barely a whisper.

"Tomás and your father eventually connected with Faustino's father, who told them about my rising conflicts with the Church. That is how I met Friar Tomás. That is how we learned your father survived."

Martín's mind could hardly absorb this tale. If it wasn't about his own father, it might have been easier to keep it straight. The story was playing tug-o-war with his emotions, his previous perceptions, and misunderstandings. He was having to dislodge and discard eighteen years of misconceptions to make room.

"Where is his father now?" Nando asked.

Humphrey leaned forward to answer Nando, but kept his eyes on Martín. "Regretfully, I failed to protect him. He gave his life again, protecting another."

Humphrey turned to Martín and said, "Your father and Tomás thought it important to renew an acquaintance and visit Luther here in Wittenburg. On their way, they stumbled upon a tavern where I was finishing quite a fine meal. Before they could eat, several of King Charles' elite guards bounded into the tavern. I watched as your father and Tomás practically melted out of sight and out of the tavern. That was my clue. Enemies to the king and his guards were my kind of men. I followed them out and when I found they were looking for the reverend," Humphrey pointed to Luther, "we took it upon ourselves to stick our noses into the Church's business."

Humphrey gave Martín more time to absorb the story, then added, "Luther was not in Wittenburg. Has Tomás told you about the Diet of Worms?"

Martín nodded. The story of Luther's trial and the triumph over the inquisitors had pleased Friar Tomás so much, he shared it several times, and in great detail, with Martín. "Friar Tomás told me about it. He loved that story."

"Because Tomás lived it. It was your father, Tomás, and me who outsmarted the king's guards. The guards were said to have been sent to protect Luther. We knew better. They were sent to execute him. We got there first. Did you ever notice Tomás could not raise his left arm?"

Martín thought back. He never noticed at the time, but now remembered there were times when he asked Martín to do something that required both hands above the head. Martín nodded slowly as the memory surfaced.

"He took an arrow to the shoulder that night. Nearly bled to death. Your father saved Tomás' life, he saved Luther's life, he saved my life." Humphrey raised a sleeve and showed a long, jagged scar that ran from above the elbow to the wrist.

"Your father took on three archers and five horsemen by himself, killing half of them before they killed him. In the attack, Luther, Tomás, and I escaped. In truth, Tomás and I were so badly hurt, it was the reverend here that saved our lives."

Silence again filled the great hall. Nothing could be said. Martín had just learned his mother and father both survived murderous attacks, only to live apart for nine years before they each suffered violent deaths. He wanted to scream at heaven. He wanted to scream at Humphrey. He wanted to scream at Friar Tomás for never telling him that he knew his father. He wanted nothing. He wanted to return to the monastery to live and die alone. Even his tears were too shocked to fall.

Luther's story held the collective hunger at bay. All attention focused on his next words.

One more time, the silence gave the group time for their cups to be refilled and for the men to readjust on their uncomfortable hard wooden chairs.

Martín broke the silence with words pinched with bitterness, "Why would God do this? You all say my father was noble, my mother was valiant, that I have some mission. Following God seems to cause nothing but pain."

After a few moments of continued silence, Martín asked, "What makes you believe this great man you describe is my father? My mother, who died so many years ago, knew nothing about her own husband being alive? She watched him die. I think Humphrey here kidnapped the wrong orphan!" Martín's boldness was growing.

Luther smiled. He looked over to Humphrey, who'd just been accused of a kidnap rather than a rescue. Humphrey was on the brink of laughter. Luther turned back to Martín.

"Friar Tomás."

"Friar Tomás?" Martín repeated.

"Friar Tomás. He traveled with your father. He knew your father as well as anyone. After the king's guards killed your father, Tomás spent months healing here. When he later showed up in Trujillo, he recognized so much of your father in you, with a little research, he became convinced your mother was indeed Miguel's wife and you, his son."

It was the first time his father's name was mentioned during the entire conversation. With the exception of Iñaki's mention of it, he had not heard it said in over ten years. It echoed in his mind. Could this all be true? If it wasn't, how would they know his father's name?

Martín had no argument. Friar Tomás, for as long as he could remember, treated the memory of his mother with great respect and insisted Martín complete his lessons with precision. Martín always believed it was simple charity. His eyes were opening with the revelations from Luther. Friar Tomás taught him more than simple lessons other boys received. Martín was not only fluent in two of the prominent languages in the Holy Roman Empire, but he'd also been taught how to learn languages. He reflected on how easily he learned French at the tutoring of Marguerite and how English was no longer a foreign language, even at the encouragement of a harsh English highwayman.

Martín broke from his pondering.

"You say my father taught the Moors in their own language?"

Luther nodded. "He taught himself so quickly, Talavera insisted they all learn Arabic. He pushed so hard the philosophy that we must teach a man the gospel of Jesus Christ in his own tongue that many of the lazier and more indignant clergy fought back."

Tyndale, who sat quietly during this entire conversation, now entered the discussion. "I never knew or met your father, but what I now know of him encourages me to invite you into a growing collection of heretics who believe that to truly worship God and follow His Son Jesus Christ, a man must make that choice personally. It is impossible to preach Christ, except you preach against anti-Christ. That is to say, them with their false doctrine and violence of sword enforce to quench the true doctrine of Christ."

What did that mean? Martín wondered.

He well knew of the famed Dominican Friar Martin Luther, but his companion William Tyndale was still a mystery. With genuine curiosity, he wanted to ask, but was afraid it would be rude. He didn't have to. Tyndale continued.

"I perceived by experience, how that it was impossible to establish the lay people in any truth, except the scriptures were plainly laid before their eyes in their mother tongue, that they might see the process, order, and meaning of the text."

Humphrey spoke up again. "There's a great work to be done. It may take centuries, or more before it is complete, but as we heard that nut Calvin say, a restoration of the ancient church is required. We are part of a larger work than our own. The bigger problem the world faces is that great men like these two here just can't get to the point without frosting it with their philosophies of life. Martín, they need you. They need your talent. Friar Tomás recognized early on you have your father's gift. That is the reason they sent Vano to recruit you to the work."

Humphrey's little commentary raised an eyebrow on each of Luther's and Tyndale's faces.

Nando turned to Humphrey. "What is this, you ran out of purses to snatch and have become a reformer?"

Humphrey's face danced with delight. "These two are giving their lives so the people, common people, peasant people, may have the liberty to read, know, and understand God's words. It is just that they get in their own way. They need a fresh set of eyes, a new perspective. I do not know what their current disagreement is about, but I guess that Luther still has his disdain for my old English language, and that the English people deserve to live in ignorance, since their king refuses to permit them a Bible in English."

Humphrey was still curious about the discussion he, Faustino, Nando, and Martín interrupted. He brought the conversation back around to the insult cast by Luther. "Luther, you claim my language is not worthy of the word of God." He turned to Tyndale and finished his query. "And you didn't seem to reject that claim."

Tyndale tried to bring the prior discussion to a clean point. "The good reverend here is simply having fun with my claim and challenge that a translation of the books of the Bible from the original Hebrew or Greek will be a considerable challenge since our old English does not have the vocabulary for a clean, direct translation."

Luther tried to defend himself. "All I was trying to say to Wills here is that he will need to teach English to the English if he hopes to have a translation that will last, and that the translation will hold faithful to the meaning God intends."

"I admit," Tyndale said, "among many trained in Latin and Greek, and others with whom I have become acquainted, they consider English a barbaric language without the grammatical nuances necessary to express the word of God accurately."

Luther's smile showed his joy. "That is why Tyndale is here with me."

"I concede," Tyndale said. "Luther's German translation of the New Testament is of great use to me not only for its grammar and vocabulary, but for the theology."

Martín certainly didn't know enough English yet, but with the three languages he thought he knew, this was a viable discussion and challenge. "Are you trying to re-translate Wycliff's Bible?" Martín asked. "Is there a problem with how Wycliff translated it into English a century ago?"

Tyndale leaned forward and began arranging plates and cups on the table, preparing for a discussion. Martín had a plate in front of him already,

Tyndale took it back.

"On this plate we have the Jewish Bible, what we call the Old Testament. They wrote it almost entirely in Hebrew." He tore and placed a large piece of bread on the plate. Placing a small piece of white crumbly goat cheese next to the bread, he said, "It included a few short elements written in Aramaic."

He added several grapes and slices of apple, then took the plate and centered it on the table. "This is the Hebrew Bible," he said. "The Pentateuch. The first five books of the Old Testament, written almost completely in Hebrew."

He took Nando's plate, still empty, and repeated the process, putting bread and goat cheese on it. When he got to the grapes and apple slices, he paused.

"When the Persians controlled the whole of the eastern Mediterranean basin, Aramaic became the lingua franca, the common language between cultures in the area. For Jewish communities, in order to have the Torah, it became necessary to translate from the traditional Hebrew. As centuries rolled past, Greek became the dominant language. Jewish scholars began translating the Hebrew into Greek. By the time the New Testament was being recorded, it was mostly in Greek."

Then he added a herring, some figs, and some nuts on the side of the plate. He held up the second plate, obviously much fuller. "This is the whole Bible as we know it with both the New Testament and the Old Testament."

He set the plate down. Nando reached for it. A raised finger from Tyndale stopped him.

He took Humphrey's plate and repeated the process, but he replaced the apple slices with slices of dried pears and the figs with dates. He continued, "As Latin eventually became the lingua franca, St. Jerome completed the Latin translation, or Vulgate, as we call it." Three plates now stood side by side, looking very similar but with several differences. Tyndale's point was becoming clear.

Luther then continued the example by taking his own plate and imitating the Greek plate but replacing the white crumbly goat cheese with a local Brie de Meux. "My German Bible is as close as possible to the original Greek text as I can make it. Yet, it is a constant work in progress. It will be years before completion and refinement."

Tyndale then took his own plate and said, "This is the discussion you interrupted in the library," he placed the bread, the cheese and the herring exactly as was on the Hebrew plate. He then added the grapes, apples, and figs. The plate looked identical to a mix of the Hebrew and Greek plate. "This will be the English Bible. You cannot translate from the Latin to get this plate," he said.

Five plates stood loaded with food. Martín noticed Nando's hands doing their best to restrain themselves.

Everyone approved with slight nods of the head and tiny smiles. Luther then interrupted the acceptance.

He pulled the apples, the figs, the cheese, and the grapes from Tyndale's proposed English plate. "The English do not have the words to represent what we believe the original authors meant."

Martín squinted at the challenge translators face. He nodded his head, revealing he was understanding the problem.

Tyndale added to Luther's challenge, "When you render a text from one language to another, inevitably it involves interpretation and the changing of meaning. The choice of words may be theologically loaded. I have to stay as pure as possible. These are God's words we are dealing with, not the pope's or even St. Jerome's."

Luther then said, "As rude a language as is English, the properties of the Hebrew tongue agree a thousand times more with English than it does with Latin. With help," Luther looked directly at Martín, "our good William Tyndale may stumble his way into some English prose that might even teach a plowboy what God expects him to become."

Katherina interrupted the demonstration and passed the plates of food back to the hungry men. Nando mouthed a "thank you" to her. Martín, Nando, Faustino, and Humphrey ate in earnest.

Luther was evidently not ready to end the discussion. He picked up a slice of pear from the plate representing the Latin Vulgate version of the Bible translated by Jerome.

"Martín, how can Tyndale here talk about Christ's sacrifice and forgiveness when the English have no word for it?"

Martín's mouth was too full to answer. He wasn't sure if Luther expected an answer or not. Luther continued.

"How should he render 'to do penance'? Humphrey said you have a little experience with the Church's approach to penance and indulgences." He winked at Martín, then answered his own question.

"To do penance has sacramental implications. It requires the need of the

Church. We reject that. But are we right? What Tyndale and I were debating when you met us in the library was the term repentance. We feel confident the word repentance more closely reflects an act that an individual can do themselves before God, without the need of the Church."

"That was the debate? Seems simple to me," Humphrey said between bites.

"The debate was whether Tyndale wanted to burn at the stake for it," Luther said.

Tyndale said, "I will not always have a protector like Frederick or Martin Luther."

Nando, with a full mouth, muttered, "But if you are right, you will have God's protection."

All heads turned to Nando. Still with a full mouth, he said, "Right?"

Everyone around the table, with possibly Hans the only exception, knew even with God's direction and approbation for your service in His holy work, it didn't guarantee God's unlimited protection. They all knew the great sacrifices of life made by common and eminent men and women in God's work.

Martín's mind shot back to the scene of his mentor and protector, Friar Tomás, bearing witness to God's work as he burned to death. His mind then reflected on the young Maid of Orléans burning at the stake after dedicating her life to a country that betrayed her to the very enemy she helped defeat.

It was Martín's turn to ask the questions. "Why did God save France?"

With the abrupt change of topic, all heads turned to Martín. Nando almost spit out the wine that filled his mouth.

"God calls a young girl to lead the armies of France. He guides and protects her. She succeeds and leads from victory to victory, only to be betrayed by the very people she served. Her own countrymen sell her to the enemy, who, on false accusation, brutally burn her to death."

He paused long enough for Nando to compose himself and for the group who, in recalling the tragic story of the young Maid of Orléans, were curious about this strange change of topic.

Katharina broke the long silence.

"God's timetable is much longer than ours," she began, "I am certainly not a scholar like Luther and Tyndale. I lose the subtle meanings of words and sentences. But the Spirit of God that is moving a great work forward is not lost on me. I do not understand it, but I know God has a greater work than preserving France. But France is an important part of that greater work."

Every set of eyes focused on Katharina, yet she seemed to be focusing elsewhere. Every word seemed deliberate; this was not a casual answer for her.

"A hundred years from now, two hundred, maybe even five hundred, when all of us are long forgotten, the battle for liberty may still rage on. A battle for the hearts of men. A battle where one man does not control what another man thinks or says. A battle where both man and woman serve God with all their hearts. Where they love and raise children up to God without fear of a king or pope and his selfish whims."

She paused again looking to collect more words, words she claimed were not her strength.

"The very Bible my husband and dear Tyndale here are dedicating their lives to make as correct as possible, even in its most incomplete form, declares that Christ came to earth to liberate each and every one of us. That liberty only comes at the price of blood—His, Joan's, your dear friend Tomás, probably ours, and maybe yours."

She paused once again.

"Only when a man is at liberty to choose to serve God can he truly become what God wants him to become. Until every man can read, understand, and choose to follow God, there is no chance for Christ's words to inspire men to throw off the yoke of bondage as the Bible promises."

Everyone around the table sat silently. Martín's mind began racing again. He wondered about this woman. Maybe she was like Joan. Was she called by God to marry Martin Luther, to help him in this great work she described? What was Marguerite's part in the work? What was his? Why was he here?

Katharina turned directly to Martín. "Christ was betrayed by his own people and suffered death. He was not the first, nor was Joan the last. But remember, Christ's sacrifice was the ultimate sacrifice. Whatever part you are called to play in this march toward liberty, Jesus Christ is at the center of it."

Her intensity softened, she stood, took Hans by the hand, and left the great hall. The men looked from one to another in shock. Nando was the first to return his attention to his plate—the Hebrew and Greek plate.

So many thoughts converged, clashed, melded, and burned in Martín's mind he didn't taste the food on his Hebrew plate. The question that kept struggling to find resolution in Martín's young mind was that of his role in this grand work that Katharina and the French peasant woman Melina proclaimed might take centuries to complete. And second, if God really is omnipotent why is the grand work so difficult?

"But I do not know Greek, or Hebrew, or even English, with the exception of the English vocabulary of a robber who beats up innocent bishops," Martín said.

Humphrey didn't look up from his plate. His defense was simple. "Believe me, the bishop was not that innocent. I believe God has plenty of robbers pretending to do His sacred work. Maybe you might do more for God's kingdom as a partner with me."

Humphrey shared the detailed story of the indulgences in Bilbao to the group. Katharina, who returned from the kitchen to clear the table, asked, "How much of God's silver do you have left?"

Martín didn't know Katharina well enough, and he wondered if she needed it, wanted it, or was just curious. Humphrey answered, "If old Nando here did not eat so much, he would have much more."

Nando's plate was empty. It was evident he was ready for more, but he handed the empty plate to Katharina. "Thank you," he said to her.

"A man has to stay fit and strong if he expects to stay ready to serve God," Nando said. He patted his belly.

"I feel there is enough for whatever God wants. The purse feels no less weighty than when we began this journey. I have wondered if it was like the woman's cruse of oil, blessed by Elijah," Martín said.

Humphrey nodded and said, "Well, I have never been compared to Elijah, but I will accept the compliment."

Tyndale took Martín's reference to Elijah as an invitation to move the conversation.

"How well do you understand Elijah's story?" Tyndale asked Martín.

"I read it with Friar Tomás."

"You just referred to the woman's cruse of oil. What else do you remember?" Tyndale asked.

"He was fed by a raven," Martín paused, "he called down fire from heaven and torched the priests of Baal." A tiny smile made it to his lips.

Nando's eyes opening quickly caught Humphrey's attention.

"During the famine, the woman gave Elijah her last meal, and he blessed her oil to never run out," Martín said.

"And?" Tyndale said.

"He went up to a mountain where fire, earthquakes, and wind howled. He expected to hear from God in some mighty way, but he didn't. God talked to him in a still small voice," Martín said.

"Exactly," Tyndale said. "Do you remember when Christ asked his disciples who they thought he was?"

"In Matthew?" Martín asked.

Tyndale nodded.

Martín quoted, "Thou art blessed, Simon Bar-jona, for neither flesh nor blood hath revealed and showed this to thee, but my father that is in heaven?"

A large smile filled Tyndale's face. Martín's confidence grew.

An elbow poked Nando. "Do you remember any of this?" Humphrey whispered to Nando, whose attention was like that of a young child hearing an exciting adventure story for the first time. "Have you even read the holy scriptures?"

Nando waved Humphrey off like he would a bothersome fly. Humphrey smiled and returned his attention to Tyndale's inquiry.

"God spoke to Elijah with a still small voice. The Father, as Jesus said, revealed the fact that Jesus was the Christ, the Son of the Living God to Peter. Later, when Paul wrote to the Corinthians, he said that no man can say that Jesus is the Lord, but by the Holy Ghost," Tyndale said.

Luther watched with rapt attention, his elbows on the table with his hands cupping his chin, Katharina leaning against him. Faustino hadn't said a thing, but just watched. The interchange was more like a one-sided discussion than a lecture. Martín's eyes and nods confirmed his understanding. Occasionally, his eyebrows dropped as if inviting a bit more clarity.

"And in John we read that those who have the commandments and keep them are those who love Christ, and they will be loved by the Father, and Christ will manifest Himself to them," Tyndale said. His enthusiasm grew with each reference he shared.

"Martín," Humphrey interrupted, "this is what I said earlier. Luther and Tyndale here get so caught up in their brilliance and debate that they get in their own way, and soon they are more confusing than a Latin mass presented by Nando here."

"What are you saying?" Humphrey continued, turning to Tyndale.

"Revelation is available to all of us. We don't need the priest or the pope to tell us what the scriptures say and mean. People can read the words themselves. If they have the words in their own language, the Holy Ghost can reveal what the words mean," Tyndale said.

"But Elijah was a prophet, Peter was an apostle, Paul was an apostle," Nando said, "they're different."

A quick nod of agreement was all Nando got. "James knew you were going to say that."

Nando's head jerked back in surprise. "He did?"

"He knew most of us would say that," Tyndale said.

Luther smiled, lowered his hands to the table, and said, "If any of you lack wisdom, let him ask of God, that giveth to all men liberally, and upbraideth not; and it shall be given him."

"All men! That is why you are here right now. Martín, I need you. God needs you. Our English King Henry needs you. The English world needs you," Tyndale said.

"I do not read or even speak English. I barely understand Humphrey when he speaks it. Forget Greek, or even Hebrew." Martín held up the two empty plates used to demonstrate the difficulty in translating. "I still think Humphrey robbed a bishop for fun and then kidnapped the wrong orphan. I am not who you think I am," Martín insisted.

Luther's glare bore into Martín's soul. "Your father had a singular skill with languages. Latin, Basque, and Spanish were native to him. He taught himself Arabic and then he taught Archbishop Talavera's priests so they could teach the Moors in their own tongue. He knew people need to know the word for themselves. He taught himself Greek so he could translate the Bible into his own Basque. When Friar Tomás began teaching you, he knew you were Miguel's son. He told me you not only look just like him, which I now see for myself that you do, but that you have his gift. Tomás quoted Paul where Paul wrote to the Corinthians and exhorted them that the gift of tongues is only good if the words are understood. Your gift, Martín, is a gift, and as Paul said, 'except ye utter by the tongue words easy to be understood, how shall it be known what is spoken?'"

Martín's mouth hung open, his eyes squinting as if trying to filter the power of Luther's declaration.

Humphrey interrupted the staring contest. "Words easy to understand! That is why I dragged you across France to bail these two out of their lair of confusion. Words easy to understand. That is why the good bishop contributed God's silver to save the English."

Humphrey turned to Tyndale. "You and the high chancellor still sparring?"

Tyndale lowered his shaking head, and his eyes closed slowly. He breathed out through tight lips.

"Ever heard of Thomas More?" Luther asked Martín, Nando, and Faustino.

"The Lord High Chancellor of England!" Humphrey added the title to Luther's question.

All three men shook their heads.

"He thinks I am here looking for the heretic William Tyndale," Humphrey said.

Luther looked Martín directly in the eyes. "Thomas More is Tyndale's nemesis. Thinks us apostates misunderstand the meaning of God's words, says our translations are heresy. He and Henry will do anything to silence Tyndale and me."

"The number eight Henry?" Nando whispered.

"Sent me here to drag old William Tyndale back to where the Church can get their hands on him," Humphrey said. "But I don't think More is the worst threat. He is a bit on the outs with the king. More is currently siding with the Church. Henry doesn't like that. Henry has his eyes on Anne." Humphrey looked at Nando and winked. "Would not surprise me if More gets invited to the tower before you do, Will."

Martín's eyebrows rose and fell, betraying his failing attempt to follow the conversation.

"We talk about a man's agency to choose," Luther said. "You probably think we are mad. You accused Humphrey of kidnapping the wrong orphan. He got the right orphan, and maybe it is kidnapping. But we need your skills. God needs your skills. But you get to choose. Humphrey is returning to England… empty handed. When Faustino and the good Friar Nando return to Spain, you are free to return with them. They probably want you to. You still have enough of God's silver to get you all comfortably home." He paused, head tilted toward Tyndale, "But William here could use an assistant. He is not remaining here. He thinks he can be safe in Belgium, and has some friends there."

Martín said nothing. His face stoic, his eyes focused on each face one by one, reading one thought he knew they each shared: "Will Martín be selfish and go home, or sacrifice his life, make very deadly enemies, and probably die in prison or on the pyre?"

Katharina reached out and took Martín's hands. His shoulders softened, his breath slowed, his eyes rested on Katharina's. He blinked to clear a tear.

"These two are genuine heretics," she said. "If you join them, there is no going back. I had to make that choice. When a nun marries a priest, it's a lifetime choice. This choice for you is a choice you and God together must make."=

Her eyes remained fixed on his. His eyes moistened.

"But, neither of these two are Jesus. And you are not Simon bar-Jonah, nor are your two companions here the Sons of Thunder. For you, this is not a straight away decision. Spend a few days or weeks before absorbing all this. You do not have to make that choice alone, or now."

Martín decided he not only liked this woman, he loved her. She was like his mother gone these many years, full of kindness and understanding. She was confident, like Marguerite, and at peace. Where would he find peace, this confidence? It seemed that everyone had confidence but him.

The words echoed through Martín's mind, "Except ye utter by the tongue words easy to be understood, how shall it be known what is spoken?" Could I truly be needed? I have never been needed.

"I will stay. If you are right, if you are all right and God actually needs an orphan, He will help, or I will join Friar Tomás." While it felt good to make a decision, it felt horrifying to consider he just offered to die for his friends. They seemed so valuable since he had so few of them.

# Chapter Twenty-seven

## Pachacamac, Central Peru Coast

Cusimi convulsed. Had her stomach not been empty, it would have become so. Naku turned, not stepping inside. Urco took Sarpay, her body frozen stiff with shock and horror, and carried her from the scene. As First Priestess of the Empire, she had entered the unforgivably defiled temple first.

Once a place of pilgrimage and prophecy, where the high priests interpreted the will of the god Pachacamac, it now reeked of blood and desecration. The intricate murals that had once narrated sacred myths were splattered with blood. Quichamba's assassins had stormed the sanctuary, dragging the temple priests through its grand thresholds before executing them without mercy. Severed limbs and crimson stains clung to the finely carved stones. The air was heavy with the scent of death and smoke from smoldering offerings that would never be completed.

Pachacamac itself had once been a jewel of the coast, an ancient city of temples and terraced streets perched above the vast sea, gleaming like gold in the afternoon sun. Now it lay silent, a monument to ruin. Naku walked slowly from the bloodstained temple toward the sea, the rhythmic whisper of waves breaking on the shore a soft contrast to the horror behind him. His shoulders trembled with each step. He bowed his head in grief. Sarpay stepped beside him and wrapped her arm gently over his back. Her voice, heavy with sorrow, trembled in the salty air: "Is there any place, any city, where my warring brothers have not carved a path of tears?"

Too softly to hear, a word escaped his lips. Sarpay leaned closer. Naku repeated, "Paititi." Sarpay looked over her shoulder toward Urco. She knew that was precisely what Urco wanted to hear. Was there a sacred temple in Paititi? Was Paititi real? Could they ever find Paititi if it did exist? Would the empire fall before they could find it?

"Have you been there?" Sarpay asked. Her voice was nearly as quiet as his. Naku slowly turned to face Sarpay. He shook his head.

"Do you know where it is?"

He shook his head again. "I know who does," Naku whispered.

Sarpay could not balance the hope with the despair. She waited. She said nothing. She stared into his eyes when he looked up at her.

"The yuraq yana qari," Naku said.

"The black and white strangers?" Sarpay said. "You know them?"

Naku nodded.

Cusimi, with Topa in hand, stepped up just as Naku said yuraq yana qari. She leaned into Sarpay to hear more.

"Naku says they can lead us to Paititi," Sarpay said.

The whispering was gone. Urco joined the conversation with the word Paititi.

Urco looked to Sarpay for clarification.

Cusimi spoke up, "Naku thinks the black and white strangers can lead us to Paititi."

Urco let his eyes ask the question. He knew Naku understood.

"I was there at Tumbes when the bearded white men came. Their people took my brother. We captured two of their men, the black one with white teeth and the white one with hair on his face. When their people took my brother, I tried to stop them. I failed. Our nobles in Tumbes sold the white man and the black man as slaves. I saw them again in Cochabamba much later. The black one remembered me. By then, he could speak. I learned they found an ancient quipu and the white one learned to decipher it. People say it told them how to find Paititi."

Naku paused. He wasn't sure how much to tell. Even in his young life, he'd learned to be careful with information. Urco's eyes didn't release him from the telling.

Naku continued, "I helped them. I know the empire as well as anyone. Even the emperor does not know more." He looked over to see how Sarpay took that. She said nothing. He continued, "The quipu talked of valleys, rivers, and mountains that I did not recognize. I believe Paititi is not in Tawantinsuyu." He looked toward Sarpay. "Your father never found it. It has never been conquered."

"That is why it is only a legend," Cusimi said. "Maybe it is only a legend; a myth; a story for children."

"Did the strangers ever share their names? They had names, didn't they?" Urco wanted to know if Naku really met and conversed with the yuraq yana qari. The legends never referred to them by name. Remaining nameless, they were considered mythological to many.

Naku smiled, "Alichu is the black one. Miquai is the white one."

A smile slowly formed on Urco's face. That was close enough, he thought.

"You said you helped them? And where do we find Alichu and Miquai? They may be more elusive than Paititi. Perhaps they have been lost in this war?" Urco said.

"No, they have not. They are too smart. They speak many languages. They understand war. They make friends. They are protected."

"Where do we find them?" Sarpay asked.

"Cochabamba."

"Cochabamba? A journey to Cochabamba will take many months. We cannot wait! The empire will be destroyed by then, either by war or by plague," Sarpay said. Her tone surprised Cusimi and drew a sharp look from Urco.

Cataquil stood innocently throughout this discussion, listening and watching silently. "How many temples are between here and Cochabamba?"

Naku looked up to Cataquil, who was still wearing the golden medallion he took from Unay's dead body. Naku thought for a few moments, pulled a simple quipu from his belt, and counted the knots in the strings. He tucked the quipu away. "Nine. That includes two in Cusco, one in Pichu, the Apurimac and three more, all impossible to reach without passing through the war."

"So there are two we can reach?" Sarpay asked.

"Ari qhipay and Tiwanaku on the great lake. But Tiwanaku is deserted. There is a temple in Cochabamba," Naku said. "And Cochabamba is months away only if you travel on a litter. We can be there much faster."

"Why do you think Alichu and Miquai can be found in Cochabamba?" Cusimi asked. "Is that where you helped them?"

"The quipu led them to Cochabamba. From there, the quipu's directions were unclear. The quipu described mountains, rivers and valleys

I did not recognize."

"Maybe there is no Paititi," Cusimi said.

"There are some in Cochabamba who claim their ancestors traded with Paititi," Naku said.

Sarpay knew she would never make it as far as Cochabamba. Her life must necessarily be given before this little flock could reach Cochabamba. How she would love to visit this beautiful fertile valley again. Cochabamba and the surrounding valleys served the empire with its massive maize farms. Her father brought farmers from around the empire to colonize the rich, fertile land. The colonists they called mitimas practically fed the empire.

Sarpay knew Cochabamba was far enough away from the battles waged by her two brothers to be safe. But she worried that either of her brothers might send an army to capture the very source of the empire's food. No other area was more vital. The strategic move of controlling the food could be used to starve out the opposition. Right now, however, her little flock would never make it to Cochabamba or anywhere if they couldn't find something to eat today.

Sarpay turned to Urco. "When we abandoned Pichu, did Quichamba destroy it?"

Urco shook his head. "There was no reason. They certainly wiped it clean of provisions, but with no one to punish, they would abandon it and concentrate their forces on Cusco."

"With Atahualpa's forces aimed at Cusco, the Temple of the Sun in Pichu might be the fastest and safest. You then can proceed to Cochabamba." Sarpay's suggestion was aimed at both Urco and Naku.

"Not Pichu. Tiwanaku. Come," Naku said.

Naku led the little group from the shoreline, through the square, past rows of burned-out houses, across fields destroyed by marching armies, and into a thick forested hillside. They arrived at a well-hidden stone building not much taller than Urco and no more than what he could stretch his arms across. A small door easily hidden with the heavy growth was exposed when Naku pulled away the vines and ferns. He reached inside and dragged two roughly woven sacks into the sunlight. Maize and chuño brought relief to the hungry.

"Small emergency qullqas also scatter the empire. I helped build this one," Naku said.

"Do the armies know about them?" Urco asked.

Naku shook his head and grinned. "Nobody but the local villagers." He paused, his eyes twinkled, "And some of us chasquis."

Urco fully understood private stashes. He winked at Naku.

"Priestess, back in Pichu I promised to take your heart myself, a promise I will keep, though unworthily. To Pichu or Tiwanaku?" Urco asked.

Sarpay looked at each face, then up through the trees to the sky. She turned back toward the temple which had been desecrated. Was she already too late? Tiwanaku was far closer to Cochabamba and would be the smart choice, but backtracking to Pichu, though shorter, required them passing back through dangerous tribal territories.

"Tiwanaku," she said.

# Chapter Twenty-eight

Wittenberg, Saxony – Holy Roman Empire

Over the next several days, discussions focused on the challenges Martin Luther and William Tyndale faced with their efforts to translate God's word into 'words easy to be understood.' Martín, Nando, and Faustino were captivated by the intrigues, hypocrisy, evils, and opposition faced by men anxious to further God's work. And not men alone.

Martín thought about the Maid of Orléans, betrayed by her own country. He would never be able to forget Friar Tomás who suffered as did so many other martyrs. He considered how God rescued the English heretic John Wycliff from the flame by calling him home before the Church could execute him. The tiniest smile, tinged with disgust, crept across Martín's face when he recalled when Luther told how the Council of Constance couldn't let Wycliff's heretical body rest in peace. Wycliff died of a stroke and yet some forty years later they dug up his body and burned it. Martín shook his head.

Martín wondered why God let so many sacrifice so much for His word. Many times, he reflected on God's own Son, betrayed and murdered. As his thoughts contemplated Christ hanging on the cross, his mind flashed again to the scene of Friar Tomás who he watched voluntarily giving his life for Christ's word and admonishing in his very last words for Martín to "Use what I have given you to free a people from tyranny. Help God's children take the sacred words of Christ and use them as God intended, for just as Christ declared to his captors, truth will make man free."

Like Christ Himself, who forgave from the cross, Tomás showed no bitterness or hate, only encouragement for Martín. I could never love and sacrifice like that, Martín concluded.

It was apparent Martín wasn't the only one reflecting on these peculiar times. The ongoing debate between Tyndale and the Englishman Thomas More captivated Nando. He found it fascinating that through letters, pamphlets, and books, two Englishmen carried out such a debate over the translation of God's words.

Innocently Nando asked, "Why doesn't More side with you two in questioning papal authority and help King Henry's quest to get Anne?" That question launched an additional debate over the motivations of those who keep the histories and more specifically those who translate, interpret, or teach those histories. Tyndale insisted More's writings, though sincere, could easily be understood to either pardon or condemn the king. Martín's respect for the sacredness of his newfound responsibility caused him to once again doubt his ability to contribute anything to this sacred work. The heaviness of this responsibility pulled on his spirit.

Humphrey couldn't let Nando's innocent question rest. "Like I said before, Sir Thomas More must tread lightly. He and the king do not sit on the same pew. Tyndale here renders the word ekklesia as congregation. More claims the English translation of ekklesia is church. One lends more power to the pope, the other lends more power and authority to the people. Which one do you think lets King Henry marry Anne?"

"And which one gives Thomas More the axe?" Faustino asked.

"Well, my English friend," Luther said, "Humphrey, maybe you did not need to kidnap the orphan. Maybe Tyndale here only needed a fellow Englishman to help sort this out."

"Not me," Humphrey said, "I am soon back to England." He leaned back on his chair and patted his sword, which interestingly, he always had nearby. This time it was comfortably sitting on the table behind him. "This does my talking, and with words easy to be understood. And God willing, I'm taking Nando with me. I will teach him some words easy to be understood by a few shapely young ladies back in Shropshire. They will help Nando forget about Anne. And they won't cost him his head."

Faustino said, "I suppose then that Nando will not return with me and meet my sister? If she cannot have Martín, Carmelita might settle for a man of the cloth. We could fit him into the family."

"No, thank you to these kind offers, but I think God calls me another way," Nando said.

"What way?" Humphrey said.

Nando reached across the table and pulled a pear from a bowl of fruit, which had kept his attention from the moment Katharina placed it there when the morning's debates began. "I think God wants me to stay right here and help the good reverend." He took a bite, and juice escaped the corner of his mouth.

Preparing for a second bite, Nando paused, ready to expound some bit of wisdom, when one of Luther's young students charged into the hall. Out of breath, he handed a hastily folded note to Luther.

Luther squinted at the young boy then began carefully unfolding the note, his eyes focusing on the face of his student. "Is Frederick well?"

"Well enough. But he insisted I get this to you immediately," the boy said.

All eyes turned to the note and Luther's apparent lack of urgency in opening it. Luther held it out where his eyes scanned from side to side, line by line. As he did, muscles tightened around his temples. One eyebrow twitched. The room was silent. The only sound was the breathing of the young student, still catching his breath. Martín wondered how far he ran to bring these tidings to Luther.

Luther looked up. His eyes scanned the curious faces.

"Frederick received news that despite our Holy Roman Emperor Charles' tolerance of the protestants here in Saxony, he does not want this apostasy spreading. He approves of and encourages Tyndale's arrest and trial if Tyndale is found in Charles's jurisdiction." Luther pondered for several minutes. The room remained silent. The group sensed some idea was taking shape.

"Antwerp," Humphrey finally said. "A trusted friend there is supportive of the protestants. He is well connected and has no use for Charles, Henry, or the pope. Nando and I can get you there, William." He patted his sword again, then knocked his hand against Nando's sword under his cloak. It clanged.

"Frederick thinks you need to be away today. He says men are on their way from Worms. He is not sure how close they are." Luther stood, handed another pear to Nando, and said to Katharina, "Please bundle up what provisions you can. These Ritters Ketzers need to be gone when the king's men arrive."

"Antwerp?" Tyndale said. "You want me closer to the fire? I was teasing when I said I would be safe in Belgium."

Humphrey stood and declared, "God will be with William and Martín. I will report to King Henry's men that you fled the continent to Egypt. I look forward to a rendezvous with one of the women at court. God willing."

Nando said, "God willing?" Nando looked from Tyndale's face to Martín's, his eyebrows raised.

"I will give your regards to Carmelita. Though she will be heartbroken," Faustino said.

Nando squinted at Martín. Martín tilted his head, winked, and said, "Nando, no matter how Sir Thomas More insists Henry can't marry Anne, chasing the king's mistress will give you more trouble than your thick neck will bear."

Humphrey asked Nando, "Second thoughts?"

Nando paused only seconds. "No, I will miss Katharina, but Shropshire sounds interesting. English women surely need the word of God."

"Nando and I will accompany Martín and Tyndale as far as Antwerp." Humphrey gathered his sword. "Am I fleeing alone?"

Faustino stood. "I will join you as far as Leipzig."

Within the hour, they had the horses saddled. Katharina provided four sizable bundles. The men thanked her generosity and Nando, accepting a kiss on his cheek and a brief embrace, mounted and the men left Luther, Katharina, and Wittenberg behind.

The initial seriousness of the journey relaxed with every hour they put between them and Wittenberg, a welcome relief for the Ritters Ketzers, as Luther called the band of five men when he bid them farewell with a prayer and blessing. Humphrey particularly liked the title, Ritters Ketzers. Being called The Knights Heretic seemed to give substance to his self-proclaimed duty to get Tyndale safely out of the Church's reach.

Eventually, Martín broke the silence. "Will you really tell the king you failed to capture Tyndale and could not bring him back to face the Inquisition?"

"I'm not going to tell him anything. Henry is too busy with the pope and trying to rid himself of Catherine of Aragon so he can marry Anne. I fear that if he doesn't succeed, he'll dispose of Catherine, marry Anne, and start his own church. He is not a follower of Christ. He is a follower of himself," Humphrey said. "Me and Beelz, we'll stay clear of ol' Henry."

Humphrey's smile relaxed Martín. "Martín, I worry more for Nando here. I doubt he is any more a monk than you are. But he has a pure heart. A man who loves women can't be so bad. I do not know if I can keep him away from the wrong ones. But if we get into trouble, I will be happy to have his blade close by. It's fast and true. You saw it back in Amboise. I would not challenge him in a serious duel."

Miguel liked feeling like a friend, an equal in many ways. He was on his way to help in a sacred work, with a good man. Yes, it was dangerous, but it felt good to finally have a purpose, a valid reason to live.

"And maybe after you help Tyndale, you can return to Carmelita. She would welcome your return if you chose her," Faustino said as he rode up alongside the two men.

The afternoon sun struggled to slip below the tree line. As the day wore down, the men sheltered in a small inn. God's silver still provided well enough. The next morning, before being joined by the others, Martín and Tyndale sat at a thick, round table. A candle resting on the edge had long melted away. Papers from his own satchel spread out alongside a handful of manuscripts Tyndale asked him to read. Tyndale sat quietly, watching Martín compare texts.

Reading aloud, powerful words, poetic words, rolled from Martín's lips, "'Let there be light, and there was light,' 'male and female created he them,' 'who told thee that thou wast naked?'" Martín was nearly speechless. He looked up into Tyndale's eyes. "With your gift for sublime prose, I can be of no use to you. These words are magic to me. I could in no way create this transcendence in my own tongue, let alone in yours."

Tyndale said nothing.

Martín made notes on a sheet of parchment, then lifted the sheet and held it before him and read, "'Thou shalt love the Lord thy God with all thine heart, with all thy soul, and with all thy might,' 'the salt of the earth,' 'the powers that be,' 'a law unto themselves,' and 'fight the good fight.'"

"These words pierce my soul," Martín said. "Humphrey did kidnap the wrong orphan."

"You say you cannot create words of this beauty?" Tyndale said. "That is not why you were kidnapped, if kidnapped is the word you wish to use. You were called. These are not my words. They are God's words. His words will set man free. It is His responsibility to enter them into the hearts of man. My duty is, with His guidance, to translate them in such a way as not to interpret them. God is not obligated to tell us everything. He is not obligated to our need to know. Martín, our darkness cannot perceive His light. Let us therefore give diligence rather to do the will of God. The mysteries are mysteries for a reason. We must not pretend to interpret God's mysteries, for he will do so for each sincere seeker of His will. Just as Simon Peter received a knowledge of Christ's divinity through the spirit, so we may all receive that knowledge individually in ways that will move us individually."

Martín listened carefully, yet felt he hardly understood what Tyndale was saying. He understood each and every word. But what did they mean to him? The question of his own value in this work still hung in the air.

Tyndale asked, "Martín, do you realize much of this conversation has been in my native tongue, not yours? You are the man for God's work now and here."

Martín hadn't considered they'd mostly been speaking English, blended with Spanish and Latin. His mind rushed back to the coded message Humphrey gave back in Bolibar when he wanted Martín to bring the indulgence to Bilbao for Humphrey's trial. "What is it you want? What possibly could I contribute?" Martín asked.

Tyndale smiled, eyes twinkling. "I need fresh unencumbered eyes and an open heart. God does not need scholars with set ideas to debate His word. There are plenty of those. He calls young, unqualified children so He has a clean canvas on which to work. Think of Daniel, Josiah, David, Joseph, Esther, Joan, Mary. He calls you."

Martín listened, hoping to place himself alongside the great young servants Tyndale listed. He shook his head. He was not a David, a Joseph, or even a Daniel.

"When you arrived in Wittenberg, Luther and I were engaged in a vigorous debate. Do you remember?"

"Something about English being a rude language that cannot sustain God's words," Martín said.

"I am struggling with my own temptation to interpret rather than translate. Especially when no current word exists. Please follow my thinking," Tyndale said.

Martín cleared the pile of sheets in front of him. He pulled one clean sheet free.

Tyndale began, "Those words that sounded so magical to you, 'let there be light,' and 'male and female created he them,' and 'who told thee that thou wast naked?' Those words are simple and few. Those few words lead us through the creation and fall of mankind."

Martín's hand held a quill ready to make a note.

"Reconciliation between humanity and God is my struggle. That is what Luther and I were debating. Write down these words; kippur, the Hebrew word; and katallage the Greek word. They refer to covering, expiation, and the restoring of a relationship. I want to capture this multi-faceted idea in one single English term," Tyndale said. "After all the preaching is over, that is the core of Christ's gospel."

Martín stared at Tyndale. He squinted and leaned forward, then looked down at the two words he just wrote. He said nothing.

"What are the Latin words?" Tyndale eventually asked.

As much as he thought he remembered from Tomás' teaching, this was a serious challenge to remember more than just the stories from the scriptures.

"Reconciliatio or propitiation," Martín said.

Tyndale nodded. "These words are accurate, but will require familiarity with Latin theological terminology. The common English reader will not fully understand. We must make it simpler. That is why I need you, Martín."

Martín's shoulders seemed heavier. He moved in an attempt to knock the new load free. "What do you want these words to mean?" Martín asked, pointing at the words he'd just written.

"The Hebrew kippur refers to covering or purging of sins. Katallage refers to reconciliation. Our new word or term must bring together not only the forgiveness of sins but also the restoration of unity between God and humanity through Christ's sacrifice."

Again, Tyndale paused so Martín could fully absorb the gravity of the challenge. Martín slowly nodded, though slightly. He began to remember discussions with Friar Tomás, discussions he hardly understood. This is one which Friar Tomás struggled to help Martín understand. Friar Tomás taught how Adam and Eve's disobedience in the Garden of Eden broke the perfect relationship between humanity and God. Sin became a barrier. Only through a mediator could reconciliation take place. This all came freshly into focus. The thought that surfaced was how much better Tyndale would be if Tomás was sitting here instead of him.

Countless verses from both the Old and New Testament flooded into Martín's mind. It shocked him how so many came to his memory. Tyndale waited patiently.

"Is there no English word to describe becoming unified with God through repentance and forgiveness?" Martín finally asked.

Humphrey plopped himself next to Martín. "Maybe ol' Luther was right, English is not ready for the word of God,"

Following Humphrey in, Faustino said, "No Nando yet?"

"Probably busy with prayers," Humphrey winked.

Nando finally joined the group and soon the band of five Ritters Ketzers were back on the road. Martín was anxious to spend more time sitting with Tyndale. Though he felt he was useless, he loved the spiritual stimulation. The word unity played over and over in his mind. He tried to visualize the many times Christ spoke of Himself being one with the Father. Oh, how he wanted to read the pages to get the words right. In his mind flowed the words of John; I and my Father are one, and in Christ's prayer for his disciples, That they all may be one, as you, Father, are in me and I in you. Was that what Tyndale meant by unity?

Another day wound down, the sun dropping off the tree-covered horizon. In the darkness, a flickering campfire cast shadows on colorful wagons and worn tents. The scent of smoke and roasted meat enticed the Ritters Ketzers forward. Murmured songs and the faint strum of a guitar and the floating melody of a flute accompanied hushed laughter drifting into the still night.

As the five men neared, the camp quieted. Horses let out low, wary whinnies, a snort, and muffled nicker. Was it a greeting or warning?

A figure wrapped in a blanket sitting at the fire stood to face the travelers. Others sitting around the fire focused their eyes on the strangers, some inviting and others guarded.

"Welkom, reizigers. Wat brengt u hier?" The man said. Humphrey raised a hand. The men pulled up alongside Humphrey. This spokesperson, who Martín assumed was the elder of the group, smiled broadly and bowed.

Tyndale returned the bow and smile, then said, "Win Zijn, op doorreis naar een andere stad."

"You are English and speak my Romani Dutch?" the man asked.

"Spanish and Basque as well," Tyndale said, gesturing to his companions. He bowed again.

"These are my kind," Faustino said to Martín.

Apparently assured of no immediate threat, the man repeated, "Welkom, I am Viktor Zigeunerhart. Join us at our fire."

Respectfully, the men slipped to the ground. A young man seated by the fire quickly helped Faustino with the horses. Martín noticed an almost immediate bond. He doubted Faustino spoke Dutch, nor the fellow Gitano Spanish, but they seemed to communicate regardless.

"Please enjoy food and drink for the horses and a warm fire and warm food for you." Martín sensed an air of guarded friendliness. As Tyndale spoke with members of the group in their native Romani Dutch, there grew an atmosphere of mutual respect.

Martín appreciated Viktor's charm. He seemed to evoke the charisma Martín assumed it would take to be the camp leader. He smiled, recalling how Faustino's father, Vano, exhibited this same manner. Following a welcome yet unexpected evening with fresh, lively friends, a few accommodations were made. Shuffling folks from one tent to another, the group settled in for the night.

Martín slept soundly under the 'balvalengo teló' as Viktor described his blanket of feathers. The next morning, after Faustino finished his third cup of hot horchata, he insisted on learning how to replicate it. Like his family's brew, the steam rose from the cup accompanied by the sweet smell of cinnamon and lemon, but there was something extra.

Martín attempted to share some of God's silver, but was firmly rebuked. As the men moved on, Martín concluded he might just take Faustino up on his invitation to return with him to Vano's family following completion of his tasks with Tyndale. He loved the feeling of family.

He wished he could stay and enjoy these free-spirited outcasts. He wondered how free they really were. They seemed to govern themselves and always be happy. Could an entire society govern itself? Could a civilization make its own laws and choose who would rule over them? Would they need anyone at all to rule? Could a people live without a king? Without a pope? Freedom, liberty, freewill—did these actually exist? It seemed that they were lofty dreams. Could it ever be?

The mental exercises distracted Martín. A branch bent as Tyndale passed; it flung back and slapped Martín in the face, yanking him from his tunnel of thoughts. He looked around and realized he had no idea where they'd been. His mind snapped back to the time when he blindly followed Beelzebub and Humphrey only later to regret not paying attention. The sun was now peeking over the tree line. Its warmth helped relieve the tension locking Martín's muscles. Martín kicked his horse and pulled up alongside Tyndale with whom he'd not really spoken at length since they left the Romani camp earlier.

The night before, when Martín turned in, Tyndale and another sat at the fire, blankets over their shoulders, talking quietly. Martín tried to listen until sleep had taken its toll. This new day finally provided the opportunity for Martín to ride alongside Tyndale.

"How late did you and Viktor continue sparring? And is his name really Firedance?" Martín asked.

"I knew you would pick up Dutch quickly. What else did you learn?" Tyndale asked.

"I learned common people are commonly kind. Rulers seldom are."

"That is what you learned last night?" Tyndale asked.

Martín didn't respond for several moments. "You and Luther believe people, common people, uneducated people, powerless people deserve to know God's words as purely as God intended them to be understood. Kings, popes, priests, people with lands and titles will arrest and execute anyone who seeks to bring truth to their people."

"You learned that last night?" Tyndale asked.

"No, but what you are trying to do became more important to me."

"You had a busier night than I did," Tyndale said.

"Do you believe, I mean deeply believe, that the simple act of reading the word of God, for yourself I mean, will throw off the dominion one man holds over another?" Martín asked.

Tyndale smiled as if this was his favorite question. "Personal access to God's word will bring enlightenment, justice, and freedom from political and ecclesiastical tyranny. It will be literacy, learning truth. Just as Christ said, truth will make man free. Yes, Martín, with all my heart I believe it. I may give my life for it and if so, I willingly do so."

As conversations continued, the sun gradually made its way from behind the men, and was now leading them forward. As afternoon began ebbing toward evening, Martín began discussing the various words from his limited vocabularies in several languages that might mean unity, becoming one. He finally asked, "Do you want the word to be a verb or a noun?"

Tyndale almost slipped from his saddle he turned to face Martín so quickly. "Say that again."

Martín said, "This word you are looking for that combines forgiveness, repentance, and unification with God, do you want it to be a final act, an act in process, a final status, or a future hope?"

Tyndale pulled up his horse. Martín wondered if he said something offensive. He also repeated the words in his mind to see what language he'd just been using. He concluded it was English. Nando, Faustino, and Humphrey rode on for several minutes before they realized Martín and

Tyndale had stopped.

"Repeat what you just said," Tyndale asked.

"Unity, you want a word that means we destroy the barrier between humanity and God. Do you want a word that means we are at one with God like Jesus says He and the Father are one, or do you mean we can become at-one with God?" Martín hesitated, concerned he may have used his limited English poorly, even offensively.

Tyndale said nothing.

Martín reworded the question. "Are you wanting to capture the action of becoming one with God, the result of being at one with God, or the state of reconciling our sins with God?" Martín watched to see if this time his question was better understood. He thought back to how the object they all discussed was 'words easy to be understood.' Right now, he doubted his questions even rose to that level. Then he asked, "Or do you mean the actual act of Christ atoning for our sins?"

Tyndale sat silent, still, staring at Martín. A tear rolled from Tyndale's eye. It disappeared into his short beard. One word rolled over Tyndale's lips, "Yes."

Martín thought for several seconds. It felt like minutes. Warmth filled his body. It washed over him. It was peace. It was love. It was as if the entire world became clear. He saw himself approved of by God, known by Him. He never wanted this feeling to leave. He then remembered a discussion with Marguerite where she taught him how French sometimes combines an ending to a word to transform it.

He asked Tyndale, "Is there an English word like one in French taught to me by a princess that she used to turn a verb into a noun?"

"Do you remember the French word?" Tyndale asked.

"Ment," Martín said.

Tyndale sat motionless. A second tear quickly chased the first, then a third. Almost in a whisper, as reverently as any word ever spoken, Tyndale said, "Ment."

Martín leaned in to hear better. Tyndale repeated, "Ment."

Tyndale's lips quivered. "Martín, do you know why they brought you to me?"

Martín shook his head. He wished he did.

"For this."

# Chapter Twenty-nine

## Duchy of Guelders - Southern Netherlands

For the rest of the late afternoon, the Ritters Ketzers rode directly into the glare of the bright sunlight. When the sun finally dipped and the glare fled, two rows of soldiers pulled from hiding onto the road. A second collection of soldiers came in from behind, surrounding the Ritters.

A uniformed Spaniard sat atop a charcoal gray stallion. His piercing eyes looked from man to man. They paused when they met Martín's. He squinted and blinked. Humphrey saw the connection. This man recognized Miguel in young Martín's face. He wore the scar on his cheek given him so generously by Miguel's whip. He looked back at Tyndale. With sword drawn, he proclaimed William Tyndale under arrest and demanded the other four men to peacefully slide off their horses, or his archers, six of whom were mounted behind him with arrows nocked and ready to draw, would drop each man dead to the ground. "All we want is the heretic," the Spaniard said.

Beelzebub, apparently taking offense at the threat of the man and his stallion, snorted, nostrils wide, and reared up on his powerful back legs, his front legs clawing at the air. Almost in unison, the archers in shock released their arrows. Where each had taken aim at individual riders before Beelzebub's demonic challenge, the startled archers' arrows flew randomly past the men, only one meeting its mark which knocked Nando from his horse.

Beelzebub launched forward and just as his front legs hit the ground, Humphrey's sword was free, spilling words easily understood.

The instant chaos shocked the gray stallion. When Beelzebub charged, the horse had already unsettled his rider, whose sword missed wildly. Humphrey's sword did not. It sliced cleanly, nearly severing the rider's arm and knocking him to the ground.

The arrest attempt became mayhem. Faustino, not nearly the swordsman as Humphrey or Nando, charged into the line of archers, keeping them from launching a second volley at the Ritters Ketzers. Faustino yelled to Humphrey to take Tyndale and Martín to safety. He and Nando would keep the soldiers at bay. An archer pulled another arrow and aimed at Tyndale. Two powerful hooves met the archer square, sending him flying from his horse. He hit the ground and never moved again. It was as if Beelzebub and Humphrey were taking turns in a game. Rider after rider with sword or bow found themselves on the ground. After Beelzebub dislodged a few more soldiers and Humphrey dispatched several soldiers to the other world, Humphrey, Tyndale, and Martín charged away.

Martín turned and watched over his shoulder as Nando pulled himself up, yanked the arrow from his thigh, and put his sword to vigorous use. The battle was sword to sword. Faustino charged in and out of the archers, and kept them in disarray as Nando dodged and parried. Wounded and on foot, it took all of Nando's strength to deflect each blow.

Martín slowed, heart aching. He was again cowering, running from trouble. What did God want? Did God want anything? Did God care? He stopped and turned around. An archer pulled an arrow and readied to launch it into Faustino's back while Nando's sword battled on both his left and right. Turning just in time, Nando's sword cut through the archer's bow and caught the archer in the stomach. Its force knocked the man to the ground where Nando put an end to his sojourn in mortality.

Two soldiers turned and charged from the battle, heading directly toward Humphrey, Tyndale, and Martín. Martín sat frozen. The leading soldier fell from his horse just feet before reaching a paralyzed Martín. As the second soldier lifted his sword, he tumbled to the ground, rolling into Martín's horse.

Faustino, now with bow in hand, waved and yelled for Martín to run. Martín couldn't make his numb body move. Tyndale and Humphrey had long since been swallowed in the cover of the forest.

Faustino screamed for Martín to run. Then the whole world slowed. Everything became perfectly clear. An arrow caught Faustino squarely in the chest. His eyes opened wide. Still pleading for Martín to go, Faustino dropped to his knees. The bow fell from his hands. A second arrow tore through his shoulder, twisting him around.

Sounds of steel on steel and cries of death echoed inside Martín. Faustino was down. His first true friend giving his life. The Savior's words

"No greater love!" screamed through every fiber in Martín's being. Martín wanted to charge back toward the battle. But what could he do? A third arrow pierced Faustino's back. Faustino crumpled to the earth. The world was no longer slow. It stopped.

Decades of never-used courage pulsed down Martín's legs. He kicked the horse into action and charged back toward the battle. He jumped down to Faustino's motionless body. Almost too light to hear, Faustino's words, "My friend, you..." Martín couldn't hear any more. Faustino winced, took a shallow breath, and exhaled two words, "serve God."

Everything fell silent. Martín turned. The battle was over. He expected to see a triumphant demon of a horse proudly proclaiming victory with its invincible rider. It was not to be.

Surrounded by archers, dead, wounded, and bleeding, with arrows drawn, several swordsmen and their leader nursing an arm with a partially severed hand, Nando leaned on his sword, and breathing heavily, pulled away his cloak to reveal a large patch of blood oozing red as if it were a volcano encouraging molten lava toward a valley. Nando dropped to a knee; his pale face met the dirt. Martín was at Nando's side in an instant, applying pressure to choke the flow. He tore a strip from his tunic and wrapped it tightly to dam the bloody river. He scanned the many fallen bodies. Where was Humphrey? Where was Beelzebub? He never got to ask. All went dark.

The sound of wooden wheels crunching the ground pierced the pounding in Martín's head. The darkness of the night battled with the darkness in his mind and heart. Martín tried to sit up. The body lying next to him took short shallow breaths. At least it was alive. Was it Nando? He moved the robe aside and felt the cold caked bandage he'd wrapped around Nando's bleeding leg. Somehow, his captors hadn't removed the bandage he ripped from his own tunic to stop the bleeding.

The nightmare played over and over in Martín's mind. Watching a friend, possibly his first and only true friend, sacrifice his life for a work he proclaimed was God's work, ate a hole in Martín's soul. Where was God tonight? The enclosed wagon was barely large enough for two men. Martín knew he wouldn't find Faustino's body with them. Where was Humphrey? And, did Tyndale get free? The questions bounced from one side of Martín's brain to the other. Eventually, other questions wedged their way into his mind. Why was a Spaniard leading this group of soldiers, and in the Netherlands?

The morning light that crawled into the wagon attempted but failed to climb into Martín's mind. After several hours, the wagon stopped. Muffled voices made their way around the wagon, accompanied by heavy boots on gravel. The wagon door swung open, letting in a burst of light. Martín squinted, his eyes focusing on the same face that called for the arrest of the heretic William Tyndale. He held Humphrey's indulgence in his left hand. If he had the indulgence, Martín knew he also had the remnants of God's silver and likely enough evidence for a grand fire.

"If you want your friend to live, tell me where your little group of heretics were headed," he said. "The bishop will not care if your friend dies and I bring only you back to burn." Martín realized this soldier was in the employ of the king and the Church. Humphrey had explained what a prize the heretic Tyndale was. The reward, he said, would bring mercenaries not only from England but from throughout the Holy Roman Empire to find him. Martín realized he and Humphrey were just a bonus. Faustino and Nando were disposable. Martín, though he understood perfectly the Spanish spoken by the soldier, shook his head.

The man's eyes bore into Martín's. Martín couldn't take his eyes off the scar on the man's cheek. The man tucked Humphrey's indulgence under the arm with the bandaged hand. He slammed and locked the wagon door. The wagon continued forward. Thirst eventually carved away at the unanswerable question and Martín's growing bitterness against Humphrey, the Church, Friar Tomás, and even God. Darkness eventually claimed the day and the wagon stopped. In the darkness, the soldier demanded once again to know the heretic's intended destination. Martín once again refused. Nando's short shallow breaths eventually lulled Martín to sleep.

Martín woke to the voices of several men giving and taking instruction. He deciphered enough words to understand a traveling Belgian Romani camp admitted to having hosted two men the night after the attack. Martín's heart carved out just enough mercy to whisper a thank you to heaven. He hoped those two men were Tyndale and Humphrey, but feared those two men were Tyndale and Humphrey, for now this group of mercenaries knew which direction to hunt.

The wagon door pulled open; a small cask of wine landed at Martín's feet and the door slammed shut. The wagon continued on its way. Martín wanted to consume the entire cask both to quench a crippling thirst and to drown his anguish. He first lifted Nando's head and carefully dripped the wine into his mouth. Short, involuntary swallows seemed to sooth Martín's concern for his only remaining friend, who he wondered if he were still alive despite the beating heart and static breathing.

Short sips failed to keep Martín's thirst at bay.

After four days of nursing Nando's leg and drip feeding him daily rations of wine, Nando woke. "Am I dead?" Nando's eyes struggled to focus. They opened, closed, squinted, and finally rested on Martín's face. "Am I dreaming?"

"If you were dreaming, you would be looking at Anne's face, not mine," Martín said. "And I would be back in the peaceful security of the monastery."

Every muscle in Nando's face tightened. A hard breath escaped his tightened lips.

"No, my friend, we are living a nightmare. If living is the right word." Martín lifted the nearly empty cask of wine to Nando's lips. Nando took it and wet his parched mouth.

"Where are we?" Nando asked.

"As best as I can figure, France."

Nando lifted his head, looked around the dark confines of the wagon and back to Martín. "Can you have them drop me off at Amboise? I would very much like to check on Anne to see if she has changed her mind about my offer."

"Your offer?"

"Well, my proposal," Nando said.

"You never said you proposed."

"Matters of the heart are not for the heathen."

"Me, the heathen?" Martín asked.

"I don't know yet." Even in the darkness, Martín made out a smile on Nando's pained face. "Why does my body hurt so much?" Nando asked.

"Because you refused to die," Martín said.

"Am I given a choice?"

"Not for long."

Nando eased back, and with a labored breath laid still.

# Chapter Thirty

## Pachacamac, Central Peru Coast - Tawantinsuyu

Naku handed a sack of maize to Cataquil, who tied it over his shoulder. He handed another of chuño to Urco. He tied a third over his own shoulder. "These will get us as far as…" Naku's eyes squinted, opened and searched over Cataquil's shoulder. "…as far as Cajamarca. We will be safe there." Naku's voice was loud and clear.

"Cajamarca?" Urco repeated.

"In Cajamarca we will find safety and food," Naku said. "We will start tomorrow at daybreak."

Urco's facial muscles tightened. The young chasqui seemed to take pleasure in his new assumed leadership role. True, he knew the roads and trails better than anyone in the small group. But an uneasiness crawled up Urco's bare back. Cusimi seemed to sense the same angst he felt. Their eyes met. Without words they seemed to ask, "Weren't we going to Cochabamba?"

Cautiously, the group followed Naku back through Pachacamac to its southern edge. They made their way from the vast ocean's shoreline into a dry tropical forest. Naku dropped his bundle and quietly said, "They know we are here."

Cataquil dropped his bundle, as did Urco. Sarpay leaned against the exposed root of a large huarango tree. Topa clung to her leg. They all stared at Naku. "I do not know how close Quichamba's men might be, but his spies know we are here. He will not need to come this far. He will think we are going to Cajamarca."

Cusimi was the closest. Urco wondered if her glare might light Naku on fire.

"Did you see the spies?" Urco asked.

Naku shook his head. "I felt them, sensed them. We will not go to Cajamarca.

We were never going to go to Cajamarca, that's Atahualpa's city. We should go to Tambo Colorado. But it will be hard work. Are you ready to float?"

The group ate quietly. Naku slipped away, promising to return after sunset. Urco worried that Naku might betray them. The young chasqui had indeed saved them days earlier, but still there was not enough trust to help himself or Cusimi feel at peace. Cataquil remained silent, but very alert.

Soon the moon crept over the hills above Pachacamac, casting a silvery light on the restless waves lapping against the shore. Naku climbed into the small grove and encouraged everyone out. Six figures moved silently through the shadows. They breathed lightly, their footsteps quiet on the damp, sandy earth. Naku led them to a narrow inlet where a small, weathered canoe waited. Urco had never been on the water before. He assumed only Naku had been.

"Quickly, we must go. We have a great distance to travel before sunlight," Naku said. His eyes glinted in the moonlight. He seemed excited. One by one they climbed into the canoe, Urco steadying it as it bobbed against the water's edge. Naku handed Cataquil an oar and told him to push off. He did as Naku jumped into the canoe. With no instructions needed, Urco and Cataquil paddled in sync and drove the canoe toward the open sea.

Naku pointed behind them. In the distance, torches lit the hillside. Cataquil and Urco paddled harder. Unified in their souls, their hearts pounded a drumbeat, driving their muscles to work harder, pulling the canoe deeper into the vast ocean.

The farther they left the shore behind, the waves got rougher, the moonlight bouncing off their crests.

Sarpay gasped as a wave splashed over the side, soaking her to the bone. The water was so cold. Urco and Cataquil kept paddling. The torches became mere pinpricks of light. They kept paddling. The ocean ahead of them stretched endlessly, nothing but darkness and mystery.

"That's far enough," Naku said. "In the deeper waters, the currents are stronger and we are going the wrong way. We must stay close to the shore. They will not follow us now."

As long as the moon reflected off the shoreline, they were able to keep close enough to avoid the strong northerly currents. Occasionally a southernly wind helped quiet the waves and pushed a bit from behind. Naku and Cusimi took turns paddling. Sarpay offered, but Urco refused. By the time the moon set and faint pink light began climbing through the distant tree lines of the hills, hardly a word had been spoken.

"You said you were in Tumbes when a great craft carried by wind crossed the great sea and brought Alichu and Miquai. From which direction did they come?" Urco asked.

Naku pointed behind them. Urco knew nothing about a canoe, or a craft described by Naku but he reasoned there must be some magic that would bring them in the opposite direction of the current and wind he'd just spent the night fighting.

"Have you floated this direction before?" Cusimi asked. She too had spent enough hours paddling; she was not only sore but exhausted.

Naku shook his head.

"Do you know where we are?" Sarpay asked. Sarpay hadn't said much since she consented to make her pilgrimage to a temple possibly the furthest away from the beginnings of her trek. The weight of her failure had pressed upon her so heavily, she felt her sacrifice would be a relief to her soul. She also saw how her burden was being carried by four others who did not deserve it. They had come so close to the safety of Huascar's armies, but in fleeing Quichamba's forces, had backtracked too far.

With Urco and Cataquil manning the oars, the canoe glided silently through the cold, dark waters. The horizon was a thin, silvery line where the pink of the early morning light began to divide the sea from the sky. A chilling wind, though mild, carried the scent of salt and seaweed. As silhouettes took shape, each passenger's breath became visible in the crisp morning air.

Sarpay sat at the front of the canoe, cuddling little Topa, protecting him from the brisk night air. Her lips moved gently as she whispered quiet prayers to the gods. Though the words were not audible, the group knew she was communing with them. Urco and Cataquil paddled with rhythmic determination, their muscles fatigued, against the faint pull of the northbound currents.

Suddenly, Sarpay stiffened, her gaze focused sharply at Urco. He faltered, seeing the shift in her attention. Cusimi also noticed a tangible change in Sarpay's presence.

"Sarpay?" Cusimi said. She reached up and put her arm on Sarpay's arm as if to steady her. "What is it?"

Sarpay looked upward. Her eyes fluttered shut. She seemed to move with the waves, then in a low urgent voice she spoke, "They are coming. An innocent village, a peaceful village nestled in a bay will be slaughtered. I see them." Her voice was low and heavy with conviction.

"We must act. Or more innocent blood will soak the earth."

Sarpay's words sent a chill colder than the early morning through the group. Paddling slowed to a stop.

"Are you certain?" Cusimi asked. "We cannot risk you being caught. You know what they will do with you."

"I am certain," Sarpay said. Her voice carried an authority that silenced any further protest. "The gods sent me this vision for a reason, a reason more than just innocent lives."

This coastline was as foreign to Naku, who had taken the role as guide, as it was to anyone. They all looked to the priestess for direction. She had the vision.

"There will be a cove up ahead. If we land there, we can reach the village by foot faster," Sarpay told them. Nothing else was said.

As the light of early morning painted detail on the shoreline, a small cove became visible. Urco and Cataquil angled the canoe toward the shadowy outline of the shoreline. Waves grew choppier as they neared the coast and the crashing of the surf against the cliffs grew louder. Their paddles cut through the water. Spray from the waves added an additional level of cold to the tense and exhausted bodies.

They approached a strip of pebbled sand. Urco jumped out. The chill of the ocean clung to his legs as he waded ashore, pulling the canoe up to land.

"We must hurry," Sarpay said. She was already leading the group away from the cove through a dense grove of brush and trees. Stiff and cold muscles gave way to the urgency Sarpay projected.

As light began bathing the waves of the sea, the small village came into view. Simple huts dotted the landscape, their thatched roofs protecting innocent lives just beginning to rise and face a new peaceful day. They were oblivious to the storm of death approaching.

"Urco, you must rouse them. Now." Sarpay's strong authoritative voice left no doubt she believed she was acting for the gods. Her confidence was undeniable. "Quickly!"

Urco's voice cut through the stillness. He shouted in Quechua, his voice echoing through the village. "People of the sea! Wake! An army comes to destroy your homes!" He hoped this small village understood his words. Being on the opposite side of the empire from his Antisuyu, he was uncertain what language they might speak or even understand.

Villagers emerged from their homes, faces wide with confusion and fear. An elderly man approached the strangers. "Who are you to disturb my people?" He apparently held no fear from two jungle warriors, a young chasqui, two women, and a child. His attention remained focused on Urco, the tall, muscular leader of the group. His surprise was evident when Sarpay spoke.

"I am Sarpay, First Priestess and Princess of the Empire." Her voice was calm, steady, and firm. "I have seen in a vision that an army of your enemies marches even now. If you do not flee, your blood will stain these grounds by nightfall."

The man studied Sarpay's face. He took in her regal bearing. The deep fire in her eyes testified to him her prophesy was indeed from the gods. His slow nod affirmed his belief in her words. He turned from her and called the elders of the village to quickly gather their families and flee into the mountains.

"Do not question the gods' warning," he told them all.

The village burst into motion and became a hive of activity. The strangers worked with the villagers, packing, gathering, loading, and guiding them from the village and into the hills. By the time sunlight reached the village, only the embers of a dying fire revealed the existence of recent habitation.

"Back to the sea before the army arrives," Cusimi said.

"Where's Topa?" Sarpay asked Cusimi.

"He is safe with a new family," Cataquil said. Sarpay's firm cheeks softened. Her eyes moist and soft, she tried to thank Cataquil, but Cataquil didn't look up.

"Where's Naku?" Urco asked.

Silence.

Cusimi said again, "Back to the sea before the army arrives."

Urco put his hand on Cusimi's shoulder. "We're not going to the sea," he said. He reached up and turned her head toward the edge of the forest bordering the southern edge of the abandoned village.

The four fugitives stood still. Sarpay halted Urco's reflex to pull an arrow and ready his bow with a gentle hand on his arm.

"Those are not who I saw in my vision," she said.

# Chapter Thirty-one

## Annaberg, Saxony – Holy Roman Empire

"Martín was sitting right on top of God's silver and my indulgence. He is not going to a trial, he is going to an execution! I need you to intercede," Humphrey demanded.

"Whilst I could," Frederick said, "you would be doing nothing more than delivering Charles a second prize. You are as much an outlaw or more than the young heretic. You delivered Tyndale to safety from Thomas More's men."

Humphrey paced, stomped, sat, stood, and stomped again. He felt caged. Every part of him needed motion¬—chasing, fighting, doing. His fateful choice to protect Tyndale was tearing him apart. He needed something from Frederick, a note, a letter, an exoneration. But Frederick was right. It would take weeks. He had just yanked Tyndale from the clutches of the thugs sent by King Henry and Sir Thomas More, thugs who were led by Charles's captain of the guard, the very man sent to destroy Luther those many years ago when Humphrey chose to rescue Luther that fateful night and that captain killed Miguel.

Now, he chose Tyndale, and Miguel's son would die. He could do it. He had to do it. How many guards? If only he could overtake them on the road. Which road? They had several weeks' lead. Humphrey could not hold still.

Frederick turned slowly to face Humphrey, turning his back to his cherished collection of sacred relics he had been admiring. Every movement was slow and deliberate. Soon he would be a relic himself. "And your Gitano friend? Will he live?"

Humphrey's chest tightened to one more responsibility—Faustino. Once he knew Tyndale was safely harbored with a Belgian Romani troop, Humphrey had returned that night to the scene of the attack. Among the dead and clinging to life by less than a breath, Faustino lay unconscious but alive. Humphrey had passed a small farmhouse during his and Tyndale's flight. He returned to it and secured a wagon along with its owner, a kindly old farmer. Together in the waning light of the moon, they carried Faustino and cared for him in the man's own bed. Oh, how he wished he had some of God's silver to justly reward the man's kindness. The man's wife quickly tended to Faustino and once Faustino was stable, Humphrey returned to the Romani camp to see to Tyndale's safety.

"Your friend will be safe here," the farmer's words echoed in Humphrey's head.

Frederick waited patiently for Humphrey's answer. Finally, Humphrey said, "It is more likely Faustino lives than Nando and Martín, if they are still alive. But even now, I doubt Faustino can travel." Humphrey continued pacing. Frederick returned to his large, overstuffed chair, carefully reclining back his overstuffed body.

"Luther was the easy one. But he cost you a friend," Frederick said. "Now you must decide which you are willing to lose." Frederick took a cup from the table next to his chair, his thick neck tightening as he swallowed a bitter elixir.

Humphrey paused with his face in his hands, elbows resting on the mantle holding Frederick's collection of thorns he claimed were rescued from Christ's bloody crown woven by the Romans.

Frederick watched Humphrey in silence for several minutes. "Are you praying?" Frederick asked. Humphrey said nothing.

Frederick interrupted Humphrey's silence. "I am sure Tyndale is safe with Sir Thomas Poyntz in Antwerp. He is a man I trust deeply. Right now, you cannot do anything for Miguel's young son, but you can do something worthy for our friend Vano's son. Take him home, then return to Shropshire."

Humphrey pulled his hands free. His eyes focused on the thorns assembled into a crown. A clear mind knew they were not in any way the actual thorns that pierced Christ's head, but he also knew it was time to leave something in Christ's hands. He turned and faced Frederick. "Will you try? Please," Humphrey whispered.

"I will send a breve by my most reliable courier to a man I trust who will do as much as any man can. He can and will influence Charles to intervene, if intervention is possible." Frederick winced again as he took a swallow of his elixir.

"You will not solicit Charles directly?"

"My friend is a Dominican friar who will hold more sway with Charles than any epistle possibly can. He is a man of God respected by the king. It will be God only who will preserve young Martín. If he is to be preserved."

The same way God preserved Miguel? And Tomás? And Wycliff? And the Maid of Orléans? Humphrey's heart beat so deeply, he questioned his own faith. Did he even have faith? He just nodded, "Thank you."

After a few silent moments, Humphrey asked, "You trust a Dominican friar?"

"You trusted Martin Luther," Frederick said. Humphrey nodded, his eyebrow raised.

"We can trust Bartolomé. Your Friar Tomás trusted him." Frederick squinted at the ceiling, blinked, eyes looking at nothing particular, then tilted his head and said, "Your Tomás converted Bartolomé."

# Chapter Thirty-two

## Coastal village - Peru - Tawantinsuyu

Silence was broken by the lapping of waves on an outcropping of rock that sheltered the southern edge of the village. A small army emerged from the forest and made its way toward the foursome. Sarpay's tight lips loosened and evolved into a smile. Her head shook slowly as she looked toward the rising sun. A quiet 'thank you' flowed heavenward.

"How did my princess sister find herself in an insignificant fishing village when her powers are much more valuable to the empire if she were leading our brother Huascar's army?" Manco asked. He took her by the hands, pulled her close, and kissed her cheek.

"I might ask the same," she said.

"A young chasqui escaped, and with him an important quipu of Huascar's battle readiness. My men are commanded to find him before Quichamba does," Manco said.

The image of Naku with his eagerness to join Atahualpa's forces flashed through her mind. And now he had disappeared. She wondered if Urco and Cusimi, both listening to this reunion of brother and sister, might be thinking the same thing.

"You believe he could be down by the sea?" she asked.

"A natural way to skirt around our armies," Manco said. "It is believed Atahualpa is himself working his way toward Cajamarca, a friendly city to him and his generals. Now, more importantly, my dear sister, what are you doing so close to danger? You, my princess, are more the prize than the young chasqui."

She knew this was true. How much did Manco know? In an empire that extended thousands of miles, news can only travel as fast as a man can run. But so many months had now passed, news could have traveled, been interpreted, misinterpreted, shared, relayed, and distorted.

"Are these three all you have to protect you?" Manco asked. His tone was not meant to insult Urco and his brother-in-law. Manco certainly respected his half-brother Urco. He knew the skills of Urco's people, yet he knew an army can easily overpower a single archer. Urco stood still, yet tensely ready to prove his skills.

"I now have your army to protect me. You and yours are truly sent by the gods," she said. "Get me to Cusco. All my divine abilities will be used to end this war."

She knew Manco heard soldiers tell how the First Priestess of the Empire and her divine seership contributed to Huayna's great military conquests. It was clear to Sarpay that Manco knew if his brother Huascar, who certainly held control of Cusco, credited Manco for safely bringing the priestess to Cusco, Manco would be richly rewarded.

Manco paused, his eyes scanning the horizon, then returning to Sarpay, said, "We will get you to the safety of Cusco." He motioned for several of his men and gave them charge of Cusimi and his sister. Manco's soldiers led the two through the abandoned village toward the hills. Urco and Cataquil readied to follow.

Manco took Urco's arm. "You will help the rest of my men gather provisions and protect the rear for me," he said. Manco and the balance of his men marched off out of sight.

Cataquil and Urco joined the remaining soldiers, gathering provisions left behind by the fleeing villagers. Though he regretted looting the village, he hoped, just as Naku said, this village would have their own private qullqa with enough to sustain the village.

The soldier walking alongside Urco suddenly dropped to the ground. Blood flowed from the back of his head. Instantly, a shower of stones pounded the few remaining soldiers. Soldiers turned, shields up, pikes and clubs ready. Quickly, Urco had bow in hand and arrows ready. The noise became deafening. Like the roaring of the great waterfalls in Urco's jungles, a flood of soldiers charged into the village, seizing Manco's remaining men. Urco launched arrow after arrow, each one deadly. Bodies lay still all around him. Warriors continued into the fight. He had no more arrows. The sling hanging from his belt served no use. He had no stones, yet reaching for the many hurled at him seemed suicidal if he bared himself while searching among the dead for one. He recovered a lance and club from a fallen soldier and engaged in the brutal battle.

Cataquil's power and swiftness had never been tested like this. He did not disappoint. Urco wished he could just sit and admire the skill of the simple and quiet twin of his beloved wife. There was too much. Too many. Bodies also lay still all around Cataquil. More came and soon there was nowhere to go. A spear sank deep into Cataquil's chest. He stumbled back, tripping over the several soldiers he had just sent to an early death. Another soldier leaped onto Cataquil, knocking his club free and striking Cataquil's head. Who Urco had innocently believed could have been the God of Thunder and Lightning, from whom he took his nickname, lay still.

In hopeless anger, Urco added his cry to the crescendo and flew into a rage. Body after body fell before him. How many warriors were there? He turned to see the advancing army and saw the face of their leader, the same face he repulsed at the Pichu Citadel, Quichamba. An arrow tore into Urco's chest. Another pierced his thigh. A stone struck his shoulder so hard it spun him around. A club from behind and the morning light was out.

The tiny peaceful village lay still. The sounds of battle no longer echoed through the small harbor. The attacking warriors wasted no time with the dead and dying. There were no local citizens to punish and no benefit in destroying the village. They marched through the bloody battle scene and pursued the fleeing princess and her guards.

The sun hung in the late afternoon sky. In the stillness, the elder of the village quietly walked back through the bloody scene, stepping over and past the dozens of dead bodies. These would have been his family, his friends, his villagers. God preserved them, he knew it. He looked to the heavens and thanked Inti for his kindness sending the First Priestess to warn them.

He stopped when he got to the still body of the warrior who called the village to awaken them in the early morning hours. He placed his hand on the bloody chest and felt the faintest beat. He looked toward the sun to say thank you. His eye caught the silhouette of a canoe approaching the shore, rowed by a single person. When it reached the sandy beach, a young chasqui hopped from it and joined the village elder at Urco's side.

"He is alive," the elder said.

# Chapter Thirty-three

## The Great Pyrenees Mountains

Days turned to weeks. By the movement of the sun, it was evident to the prisoners they were on their way back to Spain for trial and certain execution. The wagon master, Martín learned, was Italian, and his horseman was from the Netherlands. Martín wanted to learn more and speak with them. Neither were willing to converse. Four soldiers accompanied them. Martín realized quickly the men had no desire to accompany two helpless heretics to their deaths. Why not execute them here and be done with it? Martín interpreted one of the discussions he overheard, where one said that only for strict and specific demands from their captain, they would have taken God's silver, disposed of two heretical bodies, and been on their way. He wondered if eventually they would. He also wondered if he might prefer it. The image of Friar Tomás consumed by flames challenged any attempt at hope.

Allowed only the one rest stop during daylight, Martín stretched, and appreciated the few moments of fresh air now that they were in the foothills of the great Pyrenees lying between France and Spain. He thought back to his journey with Marguerite. If only Nando's fantasy of a short visit to Amboise was anything but a fantasy, he pondered.

Nando was now able to climb in and out of the wagon without help. His limp generated neither sympathy or fear of escape. The soldiers relaxed enough that Martín was able to learn the Bishop of Toledo was anxious to retrieve the very indulgence that cost him not only a fortune in gold and silver, but immeasurable humiliation. There would be no penance, no mercy, and no Humphrey to ride in on Beelzebub, the devil himself.

The next few weeks were just as Martín expected. Cold and miserable. Eventually, the days and nights warmed as they left the hills and crossed the plains toward Toledo. Martín wondered if he would be burned on the same plaza where Tomás gave his life for Christ. Would he also be giving his life for Christ or just dying a painful death from delusions of his importance in God's work?

"Do you think John was right?" Nando asked as he gingerly climbed back into the wagon.

"John? John who?" Martín asked.

"John, the fellow heretic who claims we are destined by God for heaven or hell."

"Calvin? That John?" Martín's mind raced back to Henry's castle where the great debate over Nando's eternal resting place was the discussion at hand. His head tilted, eyes squinting to read something else into Nando's question. "No. You and I are only destined to burn. Where our spirits go next, I don't believe even God knows what to do with us. From the minute I agreed to help Carmelita and Faustino out of Trujillo, I have been dragged around by my nose as if I were something special. Well, I am not."

"Maybe I am the special one. God preserved you to keep me alive. Maybe I am the chosen one. God works in mysterious ways," Nando said as he laid back down on the wagon's hard floor.

"Maybe God hooked you up with me so together we could burn at the pyre for your wicked life. But trust me, tomorrow we will not be together in paradise. We will be in Toledo, roasting like pigs," Martín said.

The prison wagon creaked and groaned as it crossed the Alcántara Bridge over the Tagus River and rumbled down the cobblestone streets of Toledo. Martín and Nando made no effort to see the city through the few thin gaps in the slats that let little to no light into their mobile prison.

The horses snorted and their hooves clamored as they met the stone streets. The wagon turned into the shadow of Alcázar de Toledo. The imposing fortress loomed over the city. The wagon came to a halt. Words which Martín couldn't make out apparently satisfied the guards. The large steel prison gates creaked open. The wagon continued into the wide courtyard inside.

The wagon's doors swung open. As it had for many weeks, the sudden burst of light entering the dark, dank box forced Martín's eyes to squint and refocus with the light. Two heavily armed guards clad in chain mail and leather shouted their orders.

"Out of the wagon!"

As he climbed from the wagon, Martín's eyes focused on the guard's scarred face that bore testimony of many years of service.

Nothing more was said. The two guards simply pushed Nando and

Martín forward onto a stone walkway. Step by step, they began a descent into a stench of unwashed bodies and damp stone. The few moments of fresh air in the open courtyard might have been their last, Martín thought. Once down below ground, the hall was lined with narrow iron-barred windows on short, heavy wooden doors. A murmur of activity echoed from the depth of the prison. The thud of boots and occasional bark of a jailer rose above the groans of fellow prisoners.

Nando began a soft whispered prayer under his breath. The jailor paused, turned to Nando, and struck him across the face with his fist. "Save your prayers for the Inquisition. God won't hear you down here."

The guards led the prisoners through a heavy iron door and slammed it behind them. The ominous sound echoed through their new residence, a final punctuation mark to their fate.

The heavy iron door crept open. Faint light from lamps in the stone fortress hall silhouetted a man holding a large bucket and a bundle of what looked like rags. "You will face the bishop with respect!" he said. He set the bucket down and dropped the bundle next to it. A guard slammed the door closed when the visitor retreated.

"Water. Clean water," Nando said. "Quench your thirst before I defile it with a bath."

The two men knew their own personal stench blended perfectly with the rest of the prison's residents. But today they would be respectable. They quickly washed, the first time in months. They sorted out the bundle of fabric and even in near darkness took pride in their new attire.

Hours passed before the door creaked open again. Two guards, fresh ones, invited the two heretics out. Accompanied by two more guards, Nando and Martín followed the first two back into the courtyard. This time, Martín wanted to suck in the whole world of fresh air. He filled his lungs over and over, knowing that before nightfall his lungs would fill with smoke and ashes. They walked past a fountain. Though he only saw it in the darkness during his first time in Toledo, he knew up ahead was where he first met Humphrey. Where was Humphrey? Back home? Dragging some other orphan across four countries only to be returned for a trial and burning? They turned a corner and there stood the pyres. Looking lonely and hungry, there stood what was a cross for Friar Tomás. Yet, Friar Tomás didn't use his last words to forgive, he used them to encourage Martín to serve God by liberating the captives. How could Martín do that? He was the captive.

Nando watched Martín's concentration on the tall steel stakes, chains hanging loose with carefully bundled sticks ready to consume their next souls. He said nothing. They were ushered into a grand hall. It reminded Martín of the plaza in Bilbao where Humphrey outsmarted the bishop with the bishop's own greed. Martín knew the bishop wouldn't let that work again. At the end of the hall stood a platform, much like the one in Bilbao. Since it was inside, there was a much smaller crowd, yet a crowd nonetheless.

Mostly clergy and nobles, Martín concluded. Was this what the Diet in Worms was like for Martin Luther? The hall fell silent as Nando and Martín approached the platform. Martín recognized the bishop instantly. Rather than red with rage, his face shone with triumph. Eyes, nose, cheeks, even the ears radiated prideful joy. This was the bishop's greatest earthly design, Martín knew. Though the bishop didn't have Humphrey, he had the heretic who delivered the indulgence to the judge, and he had all he needed to erase every ounce of humiliation. Justice would be served.

Martín had nothing to fear. There was no hope, nor was there courage; there was nothing. Was this what Tomás felt? Resignation, acceptance. He hoped it would be over soon. Tomorrow. Tomorrow, I will see Tomás.

Nando nudged Martín, breaking him from the glare Martín had focused on the bishop. Martín looked to a table where the bishop laid out the evidence for the Inquisition. Martín saw the indulgence bearing the seal of this very bishop, the indulgence that freed Humphrey. Martín realized part of the success right now was that Humphrey was not on trial. Humphrey was free. It was what sat next to the indulgence. There sat the remnants of God's silver. He wanted to count it and see how much his captors had indulged during their journey from Saxony. It didn't matter anyway. But next to the silver was Martín's satchel, with enough evidence for Martín to burn for a long, long time.

The judge called the Inquisition to order and invited the bishop to speak. With pomp even greater than he showed in Bilbao, the bishop lifted the bag of gold and silver coins, most of which were destined for the bishop's own personal pockets. The bishop self-righteously began, "Here, I hold a small fraction of the sacred coins stolen from God's holy work by a demonic highwayman and his partner who now stands before you. With trickery and insult to God's church, Martín de Ziortza-Bolibar colluded to rob and plunder the Church for gain and to disrupt Christ's consecrated sacrifice. From the pockets of penitent and righteous citizens, this sinner used these hallowed funds to perpetrate heretical acts against our own holy pope, even supporting Martin Luther and England's William Tyndale."

The gathered pious crowd began to murmur as if some scandal like this was a surprise. They all knew exactly this was a show, and they performed their parts splendidly. Martín watched the bishop work his magic. There was no surprise coming. He set the bag of coins down and lifted Martín's satchel. Martín remembered what Vano said when he learned what sacred and forbidden texts Martín carried. If a young man was caught with these documents, it would certainly be his end. This was the end. He wondered if Vano knew Faustino gave his life to protect Tyndale. Faustino had given his life to protect Martín and Nando as well. He hoped Tyndale did escape.

"I hold here in my hands," the bishop began, "an illegal copy of the Latin Vulgate New Testament." A collective gasp was right on cue. "Several pages of the heretic Martin Luther's German Bible," another gasp, "and the writings of the disgraced heretic Archbishop of Granada Hernando Talavera!" Right on cue, another gasp. The bishop then held up a parchment, showing it for all to see. "Adding proof to this heretic's own personal heresy, in his own writing, he says, 'There is more that has been lost to liberty at the hands of those who should defend it than lost at the hand of tyrants.' The people didn't know how to react to this one. "This is a direct attack on our clergy and king!"

Hushed mumbles rippled through the crowd.

"And," the bishop said, "he wrote, 'Liberty is the only object worth the sacrifice of man's life.'"

This gasp was the first sincere one of the day. Martín knew there was no disputing his heresy now.

"You wrote that down?" Nando asked.

"That and enough more that we will be seeing God by night's end. I am sorry you must suffer with me."

"But it is true, isn't it?" Nando said.

"If you believe it, you deserve to burn with me," Martín said.

It was over for Martín. He knew it. From the writings of his father given him by Iñaki, these words had shaped his beliefs in the power of kings. Combined with what he learned from Marguerite, Martín concluded that if authority continued with one individual, that individual would soon destroy liberty and freedom of choice. No man, king, pope, or peasant should ever rule with unfettered authority.

"It will be an honor to die alongside you," Nando said.

Martín looked at Nando. His eyes moistened. Faustino, and now Nando? What greater love?

The bishop carried on about the foolishness of man thinking that there was access to God without communion, confession, and penance. The words were lost. Hope never made its way into Martín's soul, but he felt something he had never felt. It was a confidence, a confidence that maybe this was what he was called to do. To have his own writings read out loud as a testimony. He did not regret writing them down. He hoped those words might be repeated just as Tomás' words repeated themselves over and over in Martín's mind. "What I've declared I declare. I have only taught that Jesus Christ is my Savior and your Savior, and He alone can forgive sin. Men must appeal to Him for His mercy. Men must come to a knowledge of the Christ and choose to follow Him of their own free will."

The bishop finished his grand accusation, much of which Martín never heard over the words echoing in his mind. The crowd quieted. The hall stood still.

The judge looked into Martín's eyes for several moments, then asked, "Are these your things?" Martín nodded. "Are these your writings?" Martín thought he knew what Martin Luther felt like when he was asked to claim his works and then accept or recant. But unlike Martin Luther, Nando and Martín had no guaranteed safe passage like Emperor Charles V had offered Martin Luther to and from Worms. Nando and Martín had no protector like Frederick the Wise who could send Humphrey, Tomás and Martín's father to rescue them.

"Yes," Martín said, "they are mine. All of what the bishop said is true." He breathed in a deep breath and let it out slowly. He looked at the bishop whose bright, triumphant glow seemed dirty, foul even.

The words "Your honor" reverberated through the hall. The voice came from the back of the hall, where a tall Dominican friar stood watching the proceedings. "May I approach?"

"You may," the judge said.

The friar's steps were deliberate, slow, and confident. In his right hand, he held a scroll. The loose hood of his robe hung across his back. The tonsure haircut was perfectly groomed, yet around the front, his natural hair-loss broke the perfect circle. This was no Humphrey with an indulgence. There was no need for any more witnesses. What could this stranger want, Martín wondered. Likely, everyone else in the hall wondered the same thing. Martín looked at the bishop to see if he might understand this interruption. The glee on the bishop's face dimmed.

When he reached the platform, the friar bowed. "Your honor, may I speak?" he respectfully bowed again. A nod from the judge. When he began to speak, Martín noticed there was no introduction. This was no stranger to the judge or the bishop. "The good bishop has presented a sound and complete case in defense of our holy Catholic Church. No one could be more succinct and respectful. At any other time, there would be nothing more to add."

The hall stood completely silent. The words "at any other time" ripped through every heart and mind. The man seemed to let those words reverberate throughout the hall piercing every soul.

"I present to you the wishes of our king, our Holy Roman Emperor, Charles V, a pardon for our two young heretics."

The word pardon sucked the air from the hall. Nobody could breathe, including Martín and Nando. The bishop nearly collapsed. Then he jumped to his feet and yanked the scroll from the man's hand. He opened it and read it slowly again and again. The man waited patiently. The judge interrupted, "Bartolomé, please." The judge reached out his hand for Bartolomé to present the scroll. The friar took the scroll from the bishop and gave it to the judge, who took it and read through it twice himself.

"These two boys are yours. Please see to the instructions of our king," the judge said.

Nothing more was said. No one moved. The bishop's grand show of justice was smothered to death by mercy. The man gathered up Humphrey's indulgence and Martín's documents and satchel. He left the mostly empty bag of God's silver on the table.

"Come with me. Your liberty comes with responsibility," the friar said.

Martín's hands seemed to float, wanting to ask what had just happened. His tongue was paralyzed.

Nando's eyes were so wide, they began to hurt.

"I am Bartolomé de las Casas," the friar said. "Christ has a work for you… but not here."

They followed the friar from the great hall and into the bright sunlight where every breath was sweet. Martín's head shook slowly, trying to absorb more than free air and sunshine.

"Where?" Nando finally asked.

"In the New World," Bartolomé said. He looked into Martín's eyes, "Christ needs a disciple…" then he looked at Nando, "or two, in the New World."

# Chapter Thirty-four

## Highlands, Tawantinsuyu

Cusimi pulled Sarpay close so the soldiers couldn't hear. "This is wrong. You know it is. You are so eager to spill your own blood, you are blind to the living!" Though Cusimi's challenge was just barely a whisper, its tone landed like thunder.

Sarpay didn't react, despite the storm raging in her heart. It had now been too many months since her father, the Sapa Inca Huayna Capac charged her with the ultimate sacrifice. A sacrifice required of the gods to redeem the empire. Each effort failed and now it was clear her delay condemned the empire to decimation.

Could giving her blood on the sacred altar in the temple possibly turn the tide of a civil war massacring her people? Could the plague be stopped?

The small army escorting her and Cusimi to the Temple of the Sun in Cusco, had just skirted a village where the invisible plague left it completely desolate of life. Dead, scarred, and sick bodies lay scattered mercilessly.

Sarpay had not seen her father once he contracted the deadly disease, but she imagined his once strong powerful body had been disfigured like the bodies she had now seen across the empire. She wanted to stop and command her blood be shed right then as she had wanted for months. Will the gods forgive me and save the empire?

"We stop here," Manco said. Manco, Sarpay's half-brother, born of a lesser noble woman, took his charge from Prince Huascar very proudly. He claimed to have been hunting a young chasqui, but she felt he had actually been sent to find and bring Sarpay, the First Priestess of the Empire, immediately to Huascar in Cusco.

Sarpay needed the rest. She, like all the others, had run tirelessly for two days. Spies reported Quichamba's army was close behind. Having been foiled on the coast where Quichamba's select team tracked Sarpay's tiny group to Pachacamac, only to lose them now a second time, Quichamba now personally led a sizable force of his trained killers.

It was a race for Manco to get his half-sister to the safety of Prince Huascar's armies before Quichamba's assassins overtook them. Manco was confident his knowledge of these mountains kept him far enough ahead.

Sarpay dropped the small vicuna skin bag on the ground and plopped next to it. Now back at an altitude with crisp night air, she pulled a tightly woven blanket from her bag. It wasn't much, but if it kept the breeze at bay, it would be enough. Though Manco insisted they were only days away from safety, once her aching muscles and sore feet ceased screaming for relief, Cusimi's words echoed through her. Cusimi was right. This was wrong. Dread battled every hope for peace.

These many months on the run hardened Sarpay's body. The non-stop days and nights on the run up from the coast no longer brought raw bloody feet as they had when her caravan was destroyed by Quichamba's army those many months ago. Nevertheless, as Cusimi took her feet and gently massaged them, Sarpay finally succumbed to sleep.

The sun had yet to rise when Cusimi slipped from the camp and climbed the hills toward the small alpine river fed by distant snow-covered peaks. She left her tunic lying on a rock and plunged into the icy water. The cold water sharpened her senses. Her lungs battled each other gasping for air. It had been years since she and Sarpay found joy daring each other to take these frigid water plunges. This time, all she hoped for was a life that was more than survival of a civil war and the invisible plague, both of which were leaving an empire dismantled.

She had planned to bring Sarpay with her to the small river, but Sarpay was so deeply lost in sleep, Cusimi let her rest. She climbed from the water. A soft breeze tempted her to plunge back in to get warm. She quickly returned her tunic, which clung to her wet bare body.

Noises from the direction of the camp broke her solace. She pulled on soft llama skin slippers and dashed toward camp. She rounded a large outcropping of stone and stumbled to a stop.

She dropped to her knees and crawled closer. Sarpay stood next to Manco, while two warriors led a group of what Cusimi roughly counted to be over twenty men. The light was still too dim to be sure, but Cusimi couldn't discard the fear that the leader was none other than Quizquiz, Atahualpa's great general. The goosebumps created by the ice-cold waters paled compared to those blanketing her body now. What just happened?

There was no sign of struggle. Sarpay was challenging Manco. Cusimi needed to get closer. Yet she wasn't willing to charge in and try to rescue the priestess from an army of powerful warriors.

Why weren't Manco's men or Manco objecting? As she got closer, she realized why earlier she'd feared something was wrong. This was not a surprise. This was the plan. "Manco betrayed us," she whispered to herself.

"What have you done?" Cusimi heard Sarpay ask. Sarpay closed her hands over her face, her head shaking. "You have doomed the empire."

Cusimi knew what those words meant. They meant Quizquiz now had the priestess captured and there would be no way she would be allowed to be sacrificed. If Sarpay's claim that her blood sacrifice on the altars of the Temple of the Sun was truly what the gods demanded, there was no hope for the empire.

From the very first time Sarpay shared with her the demands of the gods, she doubted it possible the gods would demand such a perfect person spill their blood for the redemption of the people. Cusimi had always struggled with the claim that the Sapa Incas were divine. She knew men, especially those with power, were never divine. What would a man be like who was truly divine? She couldn't imagine such a man.

As the growing light brought more detail to the men surrounding Sarpay, Cusimi saw that it was indeed Quizquiz, and he had made a deal with Manco. It was evident to Cusimi that Manco planned to deliver his sister to Prince Atahualpa all along.

Days earlier when Manco's soldiers escorted Cusimi and Sarpay from the coastal village, later in the day when Manco caught up with his soldiers escorting Sarpay and Cusimi, Manco reported that since Sarpay was now safe with Manco's army, Urco, and Cataquil decided to travel on to Cochabamba. She still wondered what happened to Naku. Had he run or was he part of Manco's betrayal?

"Sister, it is better for you to side with Atahualpa than with Huascar. Huascar's armies are failing. Right now, Rumañawi is laying siege on Cusco. You would not be safe there."

Even from her vantage point, Cusimi saw Sarpay's shoulders quake. She wished she could put a warm blanket around her and hold her close.

"Dear brother, you have no idea what you have done. You are making a choice reserved for the gods," Sarpay said. She lowered her head, cupping her hands on her face.

Manco stared as if he had no idea what that meant. Cusimi recognized Manco could not understand why Sarpay did not appreciate his cunning play to save her. How could he know she was chosen to die?

The thought was fleeting, but Cusimi wondered if she could enter the discussion, offer a prayer, and plunge Quizquiz's long obsidian knife into Sarpay's heart and then pray the gods would accept the sacrifice.

She remained still.

Cusimi knew Sarpay would not go peacefully in any other circumstance, but as the only female, and surrounded by dozens of warriors, there was no chance of escape. Sarpay glanced around, evidently looking for her, Cusimi thought. Sarpay raised her hands and Quizquiz tied them together. The growing sunlight confirmed her earlier estimate. Nearly thirty men, now with Manco's few, marched Sarpay away toward the rising sun.

Cusimi remained low in the shadows. "We need Urco." But could he have stood against Quizquiz's men? No, but he wouldn't have betrayed his sister.

She wondered if Urco and Cataquil were getting close to Cochabamba, or if Naku ever returned and was right and they traveled so quickly they were already there. Had they met with Alichu and Mique, the two strangers? Were they in Paititi?

# Chapter Thirty-five

## Primatial Cathedral of St. Mary of the Assumption
## Toledo, Spain

Bartolomé laid his pen down and placed a cap on the bottle of ink. He slowly waved his hand above the drying ink. He read it slowly back to himself.

*My Esteemed Frederick, Elector of Saxony,*

*Please tell your English protector, Sir Humphrey Kynaston, his two friends are now in my custody. Your breve was thoughtful, persuasive, and timely. After considerable deliberation, our King Charles conceded and pardoned your friends into my stewardship.*

*The young Martín is proving to be gifted with words, as you claimed. He will serve as my notary, and the monk my representative for the Church. Though I have not witnessed the young monk's skill with the sword that Sir Humphrey professed, I see in him a temperament and courage uncommon to men of the cloth. I am yet to learn of his theological foundation or if there is one.*

*Be assured that your counsel to prevent Sir Humphrey from charging in to rescue his friends was prudent. The bishop would never have let him leave Spain alive. Our king would have supported his execution.*

*Our great King Charles attached certain conditions to your friends' pardon. They are not to remain within the Holy Roman Empire. I convinced him they could be of great service to the crown and the Church as my representatives on an expedition now being undertaken by Captain Francisco Pizarro to explore the great southern sea. If Sir Humphrey returns to Toledo, he would find a noose ready and his companions absent.*

*Please give my caution to Sir Humphrey as he attempts to return young Faustino to his people. Though I will never meet the young Gitano, his return to his family can be at least one triumph in a world in such commotion.*

*My friend Frederick, may the Lord continue blessing you.*


*Reverend Bartolomé de las Casas*

*Your esteemed friend in Christ*


Bartolomé signed the letter with a flourish, sealed it with his personal stamp, and slipped it into the same pouch, which carried the message to him from Frederick. He thanked the courier and wished him well on his return to Frederick in Annaburg.

# Chapter Thirty-six

## Small coastal village near Incahausi, Tawantinsuyu

Of the seven men surviving Quichamba's attack, two were Quichamba's men. Naku paid them no attention. One never regained consciousness; the other suffered only long enough for Naku to learn of Quichamba's plans. The plan was simple—capture Sarpay and kill the rest.

One of Manco's soldiers passed quietly the first night, two others clung to life two more days before dying. Though Urco and Cataquil were as badly injured as any of the survivors, and neither should have lived, both the village chief and Naku saw to their care with the utmost attention.

After a week of night-and-day care from the chief's wife, Urco was the first to regain consciousness. She had learned the magical healing arts from a nearby tribe's shaman. Though she insisted there was no reason to hope any of the four remaining men would survive, she dedicated herself out of duty to thank the gods for her village's protection.

Several weeks passed before Cataquil opened his eyes. Sumac Sisa, the chief's daughter, attended to Cataquil day and night. Small drops of boiled llama broth mixed with fermented maize kept him alive. By an act of the gods, Naku found an experienced shaman who consented to come and perform the delicate saraqay to relieve the pressure from Cataquil's severe skull injury. A large portion of his skull was carefully removed. The open skull was treated daily with a paste made from the wild molle plant.

The shaman insisted that with time and care, Cataquil's skull would grow back. Sumac Sisa was happy to provide the care. Chicha blended with coca leaves kept the pain from bringing Cataquil to consciousness too early. Besides, his other wounds—including a broken shoulder and leg—needed time to mend before he could move, anyway.

Each day, sitting at Cataquil's side, Sumac Sisa worked on weaving a fine alpaca skin skull cap for the day her patient would be ready to move. Naku and Urco both questioned, if Cataquil did live, would he ever leave Sumac Sisa's side? Or would she ever let him leave?

As Urco regained strength, he and Naku canoed up and down the coast, learning what they could from visiting chasquis about the workings of the war up in the highlands. There was never good news. The generals from the north, commanded by Atahualpa, appeared to have a general advantage in skill and experience. Huascar's armies gained the upper hand too seldom to instill hope that Cusco would not eventually be overrun.

If Cusco fell, most people thought it would be the end for Huascar's followers. There would be no survivors. It was evident that most of the Inca civilization appreciated the peace and prosperity they had enjoyed under Huayna Capac. Protection from outside forces and stability within had provided the ability to plan, plant, harvest, produce, and trade. Tawantinsuyu had been an empire of liberty.

Under the rule of Sapa Inca Huayna Capac, each village was required to provide three months of service to the empire from its able-bodied men. That service was regulated so as not to interfere with each village's crucial growing or harvest seasons. Villages prospered, and the empire prospered. They constructed the great Qhapaq Ñan Inca road system using this mandatory service. During this service, they built qullqas and filled them with provisions available to the Inca people in times of need. They built the great cities—and they protected them.

The destruction caused by war distressed everyone. Regardless of which of the emperor's sons people supported, they knew that peace and prosperity were being destroyed.

"We can sail as far as Arica. From there, hike to Lake Titicaca, then down to Cochabamba. If we beat the harvest, we can meet our friends there. By winter, we can be at Paititi," Naku said.

"Can we beat the harvest?" Urco asked.

"How fast can we travel with Cataquil? Do we bring Sumac Sisa to care for him? Do we leave him here in her care? Depending on your answers— something between two and four months. You and I can beat the harvest. All of us cannot," Naku said.

"Can you get us there through Cusco, so we may see if Manco got our priestess there safely?"

"To be sure she shed her blood in the temple?" Naku didn't maintain eye contact with that question.

Urco breathed in deeply and closed his eyes.

"Yes."

"You would rather confirm her death than reach Paititi?"

Urco nodded—tight lips and closed eyes. He breathed out.

"Let it be done. Is Sumac Sisa joining us?"

# Chapter Thirty-seven

## Atlantic Ocean - Onboard the Santa Teresa

"Reverend Father," Nando began, "one of us is confused, and maybe this time it's not me."

Fray Bartolomé de las Casas laid his quill down and folded his arms on the table. "How so?" he asked. His full attention focused on the young monk.

"You snatched us from a very painful, fiery death—one we certainly deserved as heretics. And for that, I thank you again. But you seem to play both sides of a very dangerous game."

"And what dangerous game am I playing?" Bartolomé asked.

"I call it 'the house of crumbling walls.'"

With that, Martín set the manuscript he was studying down and leaned in to hear about this new dangerous game. He wondered if Nando was still trying to conclude whether he was destined for heaven or hell.

Bartolomé raised his eyebrows. The wrinkles on his forehead begged Nando to continue.

"The roof is Jesus Christ—Christianity, let's call it. Our dear pope is one wall. The Church with all its teachings is another wall. The holy scriptures are another wall, and the bishops, cardinals, and priests make up the fourth wall."

"According to the good bishop, as heretics, Brother Martín and I were clearly in opposition to three of the four walls. I admit, though I wear this robe, I am not at any theological level to even qualify as a heretic. And for that—as John Calvin proclaimed about me—I am destined for hell."

No one tried to interpret that statement or comment on it. Both Bartolomé and Martín waited patiently.

"It seems the only sturdy wall is the holy scriptures wall," Nando said. "The other three walls do not consistently agree. And the holy scriptures wall depends on whose translation you read—if you can read."

Nando looked deeply into each man's eyes. "Because the clergy and pope do not always agree, monks like Reverend Martin Luther and Reverend William Tyndale are knocking holes in the pope's wall and the clergy wall. Forget what they and King Henry VIII are doing to the Church wall."

Martín expected that at any minute Bartolomé might revoke their pardon and send them back to the bishop. He just sat there.

"This is the game you think I am playing?" Bartolomé asked. Martín was surprised not only at Bartolomé's calm question, but at Nando's confidence in expressing such a dangerous proposition—one that hinted at Bartolomé's loyalty to the Church.

Martín finally asked, "What are you saying, Nando?"

"Right here in Matthew, Jesus says a house divided against itself shall not stand. He even says if Satan were divided, he wouldn't stand," Nando said.

"I'm just asking…" He paused as a wave struck the ship and the men held on—a move that had become instinctive over the many weeks they'd been journeying together to the New World. "Martín," Nando continued, "you and I are nothing in this. Regardless of what happens to us—life or death—we don't matter. But the good Reverend Bartolomé is somebody. He matters."

Nando turned to Bartolomé and, with as much sincerity as if asking Anne for her hand in marriage, said, "You have the ear of the king. You have influence. What you do and say can shake some of those walls. Earlier you said you disagree with the pope and the way he supports the forced conversion of the people in the New World. That seems like throwing rocks at the pope's wall. You don't believe in the Inquisition, and you believe that conversion should come through persuasion and teaching God's word. That seems like throwing stones at the clergy's wall. You rescued us from a fire we justly deserved. Are we two stones you hurled at the Church wall?"

"Maybe I rescued you too soon. I'm curious if the bishop is still there in Toledo. Do you think he would make a trade?" Martín couldn't decide whether to smile or worry. Bartolomé winked at Martín.

"The house of crumbling walls? Nando, I am impressed how confidently you can be so wrong and so brilliant at the same time," Bartolomé said.

Nando's squint took the wrinkle from his brow and deflated the pride in what he considered a gifted analogy.

"Your thinking is upside down. Flip your game. Christ is not the roof. Christ is not held up by churches, popes, clergy, or scriptures. Christ is the cornerstone—the most important stone in the foundation of faith. It is upon the foundation of Christ that the house is built. I admit, sometimes our walls seem to be built on sand rather than rock. And yes, I seem to throw a stone or two from time to time. I may disagree with Reverends Luther and Tyndale and even the pope, but the fact that we each struggle to build strong walls for our houses—we all strive to build on the same cornerstone."

Nando's mouth hung open. Martín wanted to reach over and push it shut, but he feared Nando might do the same to his.

"And Christ does not settle to just be the foundation. When we build, Christ is eager to hold our houses together." Bartolomé pulled a sheet of parchment and drew a typical stone archway. He pointed to the top wedge-shaped stone placed at the apex of the arch.

"What happens if I pull this stone free?" Bartolomé asked.

Nando seemed hesitant, as though his answer would be wrong rather than brilliant.

"The archway would crumble, along with the walls," Martín said. "That stone allows the arch to bear weight."

Bartolomé's smile joined the twinkle in his eyes. He nodded. "No other stone can replace it. This is Christ. Peter taught that Christ was the stone set at nought by the builders—which is this stone. None other will bear the weight of sin and suffering. No one else can take Christ's place in salvation. So Christ is not only the cornerstone—the foundation for faith and salvation—he is the keystone holding everything together, making salvation possible."

Martín wanted to be like this man, this Dominican friar who'd rescued him from fire and constantly taught about Christ. And he wanted to be like Martin Luther, who stood against even the emperor with his beliefs. And he wanted to be like William Tyndale, willing to give his life for Christ if he could only help the plowboy learn of Christ himself. He wanted to be fearless like Humphrey. He wanted to be knowledgeable. And he wanted to have courage.

Mostly, he wanted to get off this ship. After weeks on a rough sea, he was getting restless.

# Chapter Thirty-eight

## Panama, The New World

Little Vasco struggled to free himself from his mother's perception that he was still little Vasco. Now in his mid-teens and taller than she was, his body had become finely tuned, his muscles honed by training. He was confident with both Spanish and native weapons. Yet his protective mother insisted he stay close whenever they were in the Spanish cities.

Despite being accompanied by his young pup Ferozcito, caution never ebbed from Vasco's mother. She was the one who often told stories—like how Ferozcito's sire, Leoncito, had once captured her and brought her back to marry Vasco's father. Irony was the word Vasco had learned to describe it.

He had never known his father. And his father had never known him. His mother never made it public that her little Vasco was the mestizo son of the great explorer Vasco Núñez de Balboa. She feared it would only make his life more dangerous.

The men who treacherously betrayed Balboa were still powerful. Though many soldiers and citizens knew the charges against Balboa were false—and that all his rights and properties had been stolen—they remained silent, fearing they too would suffer injustice if they spoke up.

Vasco's mother feared that if those powerful men discovered Balboa had an heir, they would destroy him. The fact that she had been Balboa's wife did not threaten them. She was just a native woman whom Governor Dávila had dismissed as nothing more than a mistress.

The journey from their home in Careta to Panama had taken three tiring days. Ferozcito, however, was not the least bit weary. He and Vasco were ready for adventure. The young hound now stood nearly three feet tall on all fours. When excited, he could easily place his paws on Vasco's shoulders—and sometimes, the two would dance. But today, Ferozcito wanted to chase the variety of fresh smells and sounds. Like his sire, Leoncito, Vasco had trained him well. Cacica would not find a better protector.

Compared to their village of Careta and neighboring native villages, the cities fascinated them.

Friendly soldiers had whispered that Captain Pizarro was assembling another expedition to the city of gold.

Remembering the tragedies of Pizarro's first two expeditions—where more men died than survived—Vasco knew Panama had proven unfruitful for the captain. With this visit, Cacica once again hoped to find a soldier willing to reveal the fate of her beloved Alessandro, the man who after her husband Vasco Núñez de Balboa was murdered, cared for and protected her and little Vasco with a love above that of merely a concerned friend. He, along with a new Spanish friend, had never returned from the empire to the south.

Cacica had no desire to ever see Captain Pizarro again. Such an encounter would only reopen wounds she longed to heal. Forgiveness for Pizarro's execution of her husband—to steal Balboa's discovery—was beyond her. But her second loss, the disappearance of Alessandro, still cried for resolution.

What had happened to Alessandro and his Spanish companion, who had vanished and never returned to Panama?

"Pizarro has gone directly to the king in Spain," soldiers told her. Governor Ríos fumed at Pizarro's insolence.

The growing city of Panama had become a center of commerce, mostly peaceful now. The constant death and disease had taken a backseat to progress. Trade between the New World and the Old World depended on Panama and its access to the great South Sea. Explorers and conquistadors had discovered gold in abundance along the northwestern shores of the continent.

The major overland route between the Atlantic and Pacific Oceans was the Camino Real, tying the harbor city of Nombre de Dios to Panama City. Hordes of people from the Old Country, escaping poverty, persecution, and despair, now flooded into the New World.

With Alessandro gone, Cacica had become an ambassador between the local tribes and the Spanish. A devout Christian and educated native, she knew her way through both cultures. She was valuable, intelligent—

and deadly to the men who stepped out of line. But she had yet to find a single one of Pizarro's soldiers who claimed to know what had become of Alessandro and his Spanish friend Miguel.

As she scanned the new arrivals entering Panama via the Camino Real, she saw the usual mix—citizens, conquistadors, soldiers, merchants, and clergy. The weary steps of the newcomers betrayed the enthusiasm they tried to display at having finally reached their destination. Most had just walked for five or six grueling days.

A sharp, almost violent breath escaped her lips—drawing immediate attention from both Vasco and Ferozcito, who now stood alert, ready to identify and neutralize any threat to Cacica. The hound was young, but already formidable.

Vasco looked from his mother's eyes to the arriving crowd, wondering what had triggered her reaction. Nothing seemed out of the ordinary.

Cacica slowly began walking toward a monk, who was followed by another monk and a young man. Vasco was relieved to be moving again. Ferozcito sensed no danger and welcomed the chance to explore something new.

The young man accompanying the monks noticed Cacica approaching and felt her gaze. He looked around, unsure of who she was staring at. But when their eyes met, he slowed, then stopped.

The two monks stepped away from the column of weary travelers and watched Cacica approach. They exchanged glances, then looked at their companion, then at Cacica.

"Is Alessandro with you?" she asked.

The young man squinted, tilted his head and repeated, "Alessandro?"

Cacica scanned every inch of his face, assessed his stature, then shook her head. "I am sorry. I was mistaken. You must not be the man I thought you were."

A tear slipped down her cheek. Her shoulders slumped, and she turned away. The young man reached out and touched her bare shoulder. A muffled growl rumbled from Ferozcito. The young man ignored it. Vasco stepped closer.

"Was Alessandro a friend?" the young man asked.

She turned back and looked into his eyes. Her head shook. "More than a friend." She turned away again.

The older monk stepped forward. "Please," he said gently. "You believed my young friend here knew your Alessandro? Why?"

Cacica studied his face, then glanced at the younger monk, and finally back to the young man. She felt a measure of ease. The older monk's voice was gentle and rich. Her experience with church monks had taught her to discern the true disciples of Christ from the robed imposters. This one felt true.

"My Alessandro had a friend. I mistook your companion for him. I apologize if I caused any trouble," she said, trying again to leave.

"I detect the faintest accent in your elegant Spanish," the monk said. "Where are you from?"

That gave the younger monk an opening to join the conversation. Until now, he had barely taken his eyes off her soft brown skin and deep dark eyes.

"Your voice is like the nightingale's song at dusk in my country," he said. "Filled with sorrowful beauty, lingering in the soul. I imagine that when you're alone in these jungles, even the wind in the great ceiba trees hushes to listen—for such a voice must be the echo of heaven itself."

As he finished, all eyes turned to him—even Cacica's, her raised eyebrows showing surprise.

"Nando, what was that?" the young man asked.

The older monk chuckled and patted Nando's shoulder. "I still wonder if you were made for the cloth," he said.

"Thank you," Cacica said, regaining her composure.

"Is this your home?" the young man asked. She shook her head.

He continued. "Pardon me. When my companions are not spilling words meant to convert"—he nodded toward the older monk—"or seduce"—he gestured toward Nando—"they call me Martín. This, a true man of the cloth, is Reverend Bartolomé de las Casas. And the seducer is Frey Fernando—Nando to all of us."

Martín bowed, then turned to young Vasco. "And you?"

A memory flashed in Martín's mind—his own first day in Trujillo, when Señora Lopez asked his name. The young man before him was several years older than Martín had been then, but he felt something kindred.

"Vasco," the boy said.

"And your protector?" Martín asked, glancing at the dog now sitting alert on his haunches.

"Ferozcito," Vasco said.

"Is this your mother?" Martín asked.

No words. Vasco and Martín's eyes locked. It was as if Vasco were reading something deeper in Martín's question. Slowly, Vasco nodded—never breaking eye contact.

"It is a pleasure to meet such people on our first days in your country," Martín said, then turned back to Cacica.

"I am Cacica," she said. "Yes, this is my son—Vasco Anayansi Balboa."

Bartolomé's eyebrows rose at the name.

"You know of my husband?" she asked.

Bartolomé nodded. "Mixed reports rarely do justice to the lives of our explorers. I would very much like to know the truth. Would you and your son lead us to a comfortable tavern or inn?"

As Martín and Vasco watched Bartolomé and Cacica speak, Nando's eyes never left her.

# Chapter Thirty-nine

Tunari Peaks, Tiquipaya, Collasuyu,
Southeastern Tawantinsuyu.

"I think you got your strings crossed." Alessandro didn't look at Miguel as he said it.

Miguel lowered his head, pulling individual strings slowly through his fingers counting knots. "There's something I'm missing," he muttered.

"I think so," Alessandro said.

The sun hung low over the Tunari peaks, casting long shadows across the rocky ridge where Alessandro and Miguel crouched, their alpaca cloaks drawn tight against the biting wind. Below, the fields of Tiquipaya glimmered like a woven tapestry, maize and quinoa swaying in the valley's embrace. Alessandro's eyes were fixed eastward, beyond the village, where the mountains plunged into a sea of green—misty Yungas forests that whispered of secrets older than the Inca.

Alessandro's breath caught as he pointed.

"There, Miguel—do you see it?"

Miguel stopped fingering the strings. Both his eyes and mouth wide open.

A line of llamas, their burdens swaying under colorful packs, wound along a narrow trail far below. The caravan moved with purpose, guided by figures in red and black tunics, their steps silent against the distant hum of the forest. The trail snaked through a grove of alders and cedars, their branches heavy with moss, before dipping into a shadowed valley where the trees grew denser, wilder, swallowed by mist.

"Chasquis?" Miguel whispered, his hand gripping his quipu.

"No, too many llamas. And they're not heading to Cusco. Look—east, toward the jungle," Alessandro said.

Miguel's eyes narrowed, his heart quickening. He leaned forward, squinting as the caravan's last llama flickered through the trees, then vanished into the green abyss, as if the forest had claimed it.

Alessandro's voice was low, reverent. "No chasqui travels that path without purpose. Those packs… they gleamed, Miguel. What could draw them into that jungle?"

The wind howled, rustling the gnarled kewiña trees around them, their twisted branches clawing at the sky. Far below, the Yungas gave way to a darker expanse, where the Amazon's canopy stretched like an endless shroud, hiding whatever lay beyond. Could this finally be it?

"We follow them," Alessandro said, his voice firm but trembling with awe. "If that's Paititi, I'll stop questioning your quipu skills."

Miguel nodded, his eyes still fixed on the spot where the caravan had disappeared, swallowed by the forest's embrace. The mountains stood silent, guarding their secrets, as the two men began their descent, drawn toward the mystery of the golden city.

"You still want to go home?" Miguel asked.


The END

By Kent Merrell


## <u>Historical Fiction</u>

The Blade of Safavid

The Conquest of Liberty Book One
Moors, Monarchs & Monks

The Conquest of Liberty Book Two
Heritics, Something and Something


## <u>Christian Nonfiction / Religious Studies</u>

The Twelve Days of Christmas


## Motivational Nonfiction
<u>Anthology Essays</u>

Leadership & Love Unfeigned

Leaderchip Cookies


jremingtonpress.com
kentmerrellauthor.com
kentmerrell.substack.com

Kent Merrell is a historical novelist with a deep reverence for truth, liberty, and the enduring power of story. His fiction is shaped by a lifelong fascination with the forces that have formed civilization—faith, conscience, tyranny, courage, betrayal, and the relentless human longing to be free. The Conquest of Liberty: Book Two — Honor, Heretics and Highwaymen continues his commitment to telling history with both accuracy and heart, inviting readers not only to witness the past but to feel its weight and consequence.

Kent's writing is marked by meticulous research and a narrative style that blends historical realism with lyrical depth. His stories explore the collisions between power and principle, institutions and individuals, empires and conscience. He is especially drawn to moments in history when ordinary men and women were forced to choose between safety and truth—and paid dearly for their convictions.

Beyond historical fiction, Kent is also the author of leadership and devotional works, including Leaderchip Cookies, and is known for weaving insight, reflection, and moral clarity into everything he writes. His background as an entrepreneur and small business owner for more than forty-five years has given him a practical understanding of human nature, responsibility, and the cost of choices—perspectives that naturally deepen the authenticity of his characters and the realism of their struggles.

Kent lives in Utah with his wife, Marca, to whom he has been married for forty-seven years. Together they are the parents of five children and grandparents to twenty-two—a legacy that continually reminds him why liberty, faith, and truth are worth preserving and passing forward.

When he is not writing, Kent continues to study history, develop new manuscripts, and reflect on the great questions that have shaped civilizations across centuries. Through his work, he hopes readers will come to better understand the fragile gift of freedom—and feel a renewed desire to defend it.

A preview into book three:

# The Conquest of Liberty Three

## Steel, Strangers & Sacrifice

# Chapter One

### León, Nicaragua – Late Evening, 1531

"But you failed," Hernando said. "Every time."

"But I did not die," Captain Francisco Pizarro replied.

Hernando de Soto leaned forward, locking eyes with the weather-beaten captain—a man known for leading more men into death and suffering than the glory that so deftly fell from his tongue. De Soto knew why Pizarro sat across from him in León. Panama had proven barren of the riches Pizarro promised. When Pizarro first glimpsed what he claimed was an empire of gold, he sailed at once to Spain to secure royal authority before the governor—or even his own partners—could block his claim.

Though de Soto was fifteen years Pizarro's junior, he had followed enough commanders into battle to understand what drove men to swear loyalty—and how little it took to break such oaths.

He dismissed Pizarro's praise as desperation. Pizarro needed men. Horses. Ships. In Panama, despite his earlier service as alcalde of the growing settlement, his reputation had begun to sour. Too many promises. Too many graves.

"I tell you, Hernando—gold so plentiful it is woven into the walls of temples. I saw it with my own eyes."

Francisco paused, then set a golden chain upon the table. Suspended from it hung a solid medallion, nearly the breadth of his open palm. The oil lamp above them caught the metal and scattered warm light across the table.

De Soto lifted it. He tested it with his dagger tip, then turned it slowly. Symbols etched into the reverse side invited the fingers to follow their deliberate grooves—marks that spoke of meaning, authority, or devotion. He traced them absently, imagining the hands that had once worn it.

Outside, the plaza shimmered with torchlight. The last breath of sunset faded, surrendering the dusty courtyard to shadow. Soldiers, merchants, and fortune seekers murmured over wine and charred cuts of meat. Laughter burst through the steady hum of conversation. Damp leather, sweat, and woodsmoke drifted through the open window.

De Soto—young, but hardened already by campaigns in Cuba and Hispaniola—leaned back in his chair, arms folded across his chest.

"Whatever became of Alonso de Ojeda, your commander at San Sebastián?" he asked. "I heard half your men died of hunger and fever."

Pizarro flinched—only slightly. His gaze drifted toward the courtyard, where soldiers gambled beneath the rising stars.

"I had no horses then. No proper arms. No patronage. Ojeda abandoned us, and Enciso arrived nine months too late. The jungle devoured us. I do not deny it." He leaned forward again, voice sharpening. "But this time, I carry His Majesty's authority. I hold the capitulación. I am Governor of New Castile. I require only men and ships."

"And you want mine," De Soto said.

Pizarro inclined his head. "You command horses. The men respect you. They follow you willingly. With one stout brigantine, forty soldiers, and mounted lancers, we can strike like lightning."

De Soto drank slowly from his wine. "And how is the treasure divided? You wear the King's favor now. I will not bleed merely to swell your legend."

Silence settled between them.

Pizarro reached beneath the table and withdrew a leather pouch. From it, he produced a parchment sealed with the royal crest.

"I offer you the rank of Teniente de Gobernador—Lieutenant Governor—second only to me. You shall lead the vanguard. Choose your men. One-fifth of all gold seized by your company after the royal quinto is taken. And I swear this—you shall be the first Castilian to address their emperor."

De Soto lifted an eyebrow. "Their emperor? The Inca, you call him?"

"That is what they call themselves," Pizarro answered.

"How much do you truly know of them?"

"They are numerous. Wealthy. And unprepared."

De Soto leaned forward, weighing the claim. Unprepared. That word troubled him most.

The medallion in his hand made the wealth believable. But numbers? Armies? Empires were not measured in rumor.

"We brought two youths with us," Pizarro continued. "One claims his brother served as a chasqui—a royal runner. He says the emperor, the Sapa Inca, commands from a northern city of gold called Quito. The armies gather there. The runner claims their relay roads allow messages to travel from the far north to the southern reaches of the empire in twenty to thirty days."

Pizarro studied de Soto's face, watching the calculations flicker behind his eyes.

"And they have no horses," Pizarro added quietly.

"Convenient," de Soto said dryly. "Two abducted boys who speak Spanish and confirm everything you wish to believe."

He leaned forward slightly, allowing a thin smile to form. He had already decided to join the expedition. Now he negotiated only the price of danger.

Gold alone would never suffice. He needed authority. Land. Independence from another man's ambition.

His mind raced through distances. A healthy runner. Relay systems. Engineered roads. Stone bridges. The scale of such infrastructure stirred unease.

Too vast, perhaps, to govern. But conquest… conquest was another matter.

"This empire," he said slowly, "could stretch two thousand—perhaps three thousand—miles from end to end. Does your runner know its breadth from the eastern jungles to the western sea?"

Pizarro shook his head.

De Soto wondered if the captured boys understood the fate stalking their people—or if fear had already sealed their tongues with falsehoods.

"You truly believe my horses and soldiers will decide this war?"

The younger man studied Pizarro for a long moment. Torches crackled outside. Somewhere in the plaza, a flute played a low, mournful melody.

"With your cavalry, we will shatter their confidence before they comprehend the threat," Pizarro said. "Speed will be our greatest weapon."

"Your cousin Cortés made conquest sound effortless," de Soto replied. "You expect to repeat his miracle?"

Pizarro nodded, confidence steady.

"You forget," de Soto said, voice lowering, "that Cortés spent two and a half years forging alliances with enemies of the Mexica. He lost battles. He buried more than a thousand Spaniards to war and pestilence. Tens of thousands of his native allies died before he seized Tenochtitlan."

He allowed the weight of the numbers to settle.

"And you believe your handful—and my forty mounted men—can conquer an empire in weeks? Do these Inca possess rivals? Enemies who would welcome us?"

Pizarro remained silent.

What answer could he offer?

"I have seen what waits in Peru," Pizarro said finally. "If I die—and I may—it will be seated upon a throne of gold."

De Soto smiled. A soldier's smile. The kind born when death ceases to frighten, and obscurity becomes the greater enemy.

He stood and extended his hand.

"Forty men. One brigantine. Half my horses. I ride beside you. But when this is finished, I claim land—fertile land."

Pizarro gripped his hand firmly. "You shall have it."

As they sealed the pact, a wind from the Pacific swept through the plaza, stirring the torch flames. Their shadows stretched long across the courtyard stones, twisting together like conspirators.

History shifted that night—in the flickering corner of a Nicaraguan inn.

# Chapter Two

## Hacañanaka, Eastern Antisuyu Mountains

"How soon do you expect them?"

Alessandro's question hung in the thin mountain air, unanswered.

Miguel did not look up. His world had narrowed to the thin metal plate resting across his knees and the quipu draped carefully over it, as though the cords themselves might flee if he were careless. His fingers moved slowly, reverently, tracing engravings so fine they caught the afternoon light like whispered promises.

"If he secures the capitulation from your king," Alessandro pressed, "what will it take before he is here?"

Miguel did not respond.

Alessandro sighed and leaned back against the stone wall of the terrace. He had learned this patience long ago. When Miguel's mind slipped into that deep interior place—the place where languages converged and maps revealed themselves—it was useless to interrupt him. Better to wait.

Then Miguel's hand stopped.

"Alessandro," he said quietly. "Come here."

Miguel laid the quipu across the metal sheet and began arranging its cords, aligning knots with etched symbols. One string, then another. The corners of his mouth tightened with concentration. Then—slowly—his expression changed.

"This is a map," Miguel said. "Watch."

He traced a cord along the engraving. Each knot aligned precisely with a symbol etched into the metal.

Alessandro leaned forward. "You're certain?"

"I couldn't be more so." Miguel's voice trembled with something between triumph and awe. "Whoever made this has traveled far beyond the Inca roads. Farther north than Naku ever knew."

"You want to go home?" Miguel asked, still studying the plate.

Alessandro did not answer. He did not need to. Home was the one word that had sustained them through jungles, snow passes, and cities that were not what legend promised. Home—and the knowledge that Captain Pizarro would return.

Steel would return.

Alessandro unfolded the linen map they had made with Naku, the young chasqui from Cochabamba, and laid it beside the metal plate. Miguel moved his fingers between them, nodding slowly.

"The Inca roads end here," Miguel said, tapping the linen. "But the engravings continue. See how the quipu follows them? Whoever carved this has seen the Northern Sea."

Alessandro's breath caught.

"And perhaps," Miguel continued, "more than one empire."

Weeks earlier when Miguel and Alessandro entered the city they were met by a people unafraid, seemingly unprotected and at peace with themselves and with the world.

The strangers had been escorted gently through the city, always observed, never restrained. Hacañanaka was not Paititi. There were no golden walls, no temples plated in sunlight. Yet it was unmistakably ancient, deliberate, untouched. The people were not Inca. They bore no sign of conquest—no tribute scars, no imperial banners. When communication failed, they brought Miguel and Alessandro into a cool chamber lined with records and offered them access to a metal plate as though it were a gesture of trust—or a test.

Unable to read or descipher what its engravings might mean, Miguel and Alessandro were introduced to a variety of the city's residents, in hopes they thought, there might be some method to communicate.

Children followed them through the city. Elders watched with curiosity, not fear. No weapons were ever demanded. "I wonder," Miguel said once, "if this people has ever been invaded." Hacañanaka had chosen obscurity.

That name Miguel guessed was the name of the city. Or maybe it ment, "welcome to our city that has no real name."

When Miguel mentioned the name Paititi, his questions was treated as if it had no meaning to the people.

"I wonder," Miguel said once, "if this people has ever been invaded."

Over the days and eventual weeks, the strangers became friends. Again they brought Miguel and Alessandro into the cool chamber lined with records and offered them a different metal plate as though it might be easier to read.

"I've seen something like this one once," Miguel murmured. "In Africa. But I never learned it."

Miguel studied the symbols long into the night. They were unlike Quechua. Unlike Latin. Not quite hieroglyphs, yet not letters either. It was then that he recognized this was a map.

That night, as the sun dropped behind the Amazonian highlands, Miguel finally looked up and met Alessandro's eyes.

"We are going home," he said. "At least to your home."

"And my Cacica," Alessandro whispered.

"Yes," Miguel said. "Your Cacica."

They slept that night on thick woven mats in a quiet stone building, their dreams filled with roads that led away from empires already cracking.

Far beyond the mountains and forests that sheltered Hacañanaka, men were already speaking of gold again. Somewhere on a distant coast, sails would be strained against their ropes, and steel was being sharpened for a land its bearers could not name. Miguel did not know the hour, only the certainty: empires did not fall all at once. They cracked first—quietly, far from the sound of battle—while strangers traced maps, and sacrifices were already being counted.